In a Last Ru~~~
in the American West,

a Tale of Fortune, Treachery,
Love and Deceit...

WHO KILLED CHESTER PRAY?

A DEATH VALLEY MYSTERY

Nicholas Clapp

La Frontera Publishing

Front and back cover photos by C.J. Back,
courtesy of National Park Service,
Death Valley National Park

Cover design, book design and typesetting by
Yvonne Vermillion and Magic Graphix

Copy edited by Matti L. Harris

Printed and bound in the United States of America

First edition

Publisher's Cataloging-in-Publication
(Provided by Quality Books, Inc.)

Clapp, Nicholas.
    Who killed Chester Pray? : a Death Valley mystery /
Nicholas Clapp. -- 1st ed.
    p. cm.
    Includes bibliographical references and index.
    LCCN 2007933641
    ISBN-13: 978-0-9785634-2-4
    ISBN-10: 0-9785634-2-5

    1. Pray, Chester. 2. Murder--Death Valley (Calif.
and Nev.) 3. Prospecting--Death Valley (Calif. and
Nev.) 4. Death Valley (Calif. and Nev.)--History.
I. Title.

HV6533.D2C53 2007   364.152'3'0979487
                         QBI07-600208

Published by La Frontera Publishing
(307) 778-4752 • www.lafronterapublishing.com

For the lost souls
of the western deserts

Table of Contents

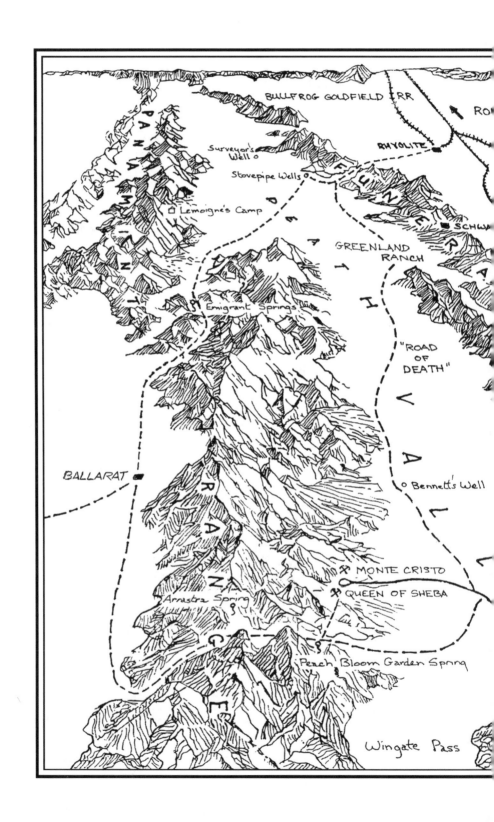

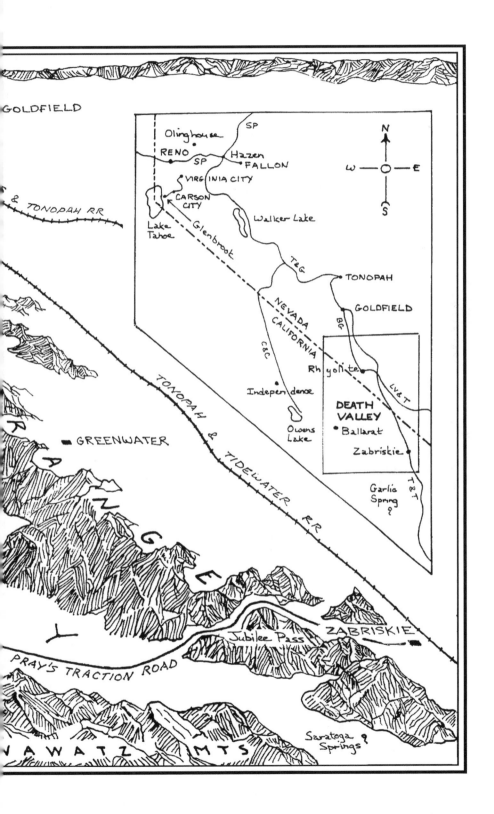

PROLOGUE

IT WAS SLOW GOING, north on Route 95. A winter storm had crested the Sierra Nevada and swept across the sagebrush desert of western Nevada. The snow swirled and eddied and buried the two-lane blacktop. From time to time I slowed to a crawl; wouldn't want to miss a curve.

For an hour it was a relief to be stuck behind a plow, until the driver pulled over for coffee in Beatty. I downshifted into four-wheel drive. I'd be lucky to make it to Goldfield by dark.

The long day, at the least, gave me time to think, to ruminate on why exactly I was out here. In part, it had to do with a widely-held view—though not by me—that the days of the Old West were over by 1880, or at the latest, by 1890. The reasoning was that a driving force of America's westward expansion was "the sordid cry of 'gold, GOLD, GOLD!'" (to quote an 1848 San Francisco newspaper). Fortune seekers rushed to California's Mother Lode in 1849, then Nevada's Comstock Lode in 1859. In years to follow, they thronged the Colorado camps of Creede, Cripple Creek, and Leadville. Further rushes populated Arizona, Oregon, and finally in 1876, the Black Hills of South Dakota. There, Deadwood rang with gunshots and curses, though not for long. A scant four years, and the gold was gone.

That was alleged to be the end of it, the finale of the Old West. Indeed, the U.S. Census of 1890 was to state: "There can hardly be said to be a frontier line."

But there was a frontier line.

It was a line circumscribing a dry, desolate region of southwestern Nevada and adjoining Death Valley. And it was there that, in 1902, word of fabulous showings of gold and silver precipitated a go-for-broke rush for riches. Granted, the West that played out there was a different West—a West with telephones, automobiles, and movie theaters. Even so, it was a West steeped in greed and innocence, as shady and virtuous and intriguing as anything before.

1

The heart and hub of this latter-day West was the boisterous camp of Goldfield, Nevada, just ahead now over a last, low pass.

A tractor-trailer that had been crowding me roared by on the descent, rooster-tailing me with snow and slush. As my Jeep's wipers stuttered to clear this, I saw ahead, a scattering of old buildings at once imposing and haunted. Some were boarded up, others hollow-eyed. As the semi highballed on to Reno or wherever, the red-yellow blur of its taillights diminished, then vanished. I slowed. I'd be spending the night.

In Goldfield's heyday, its fifty-five bustling blocks were so packed with humanity that its fortune seekers could only move at a slow shuffle. Men of all classes and backgrounds were drawn here by a literal field-of-gold, which promoters claimed would be mined for centuries, only to have the lode played out in less than a decade. The crowd moved on.

I passed the old camp's courthouse, closed for the day. I'd hoped to spend the afternoon in the Recorder's office, paging through shelf after shelf of leather-bound volumes, chronicles of birth, death, and striking it rich. I'd be by in the morning.

I continued down forsaken Crook Avenue—not a soul or dog in sight—to Goldfield's cemetery, a mile beyond the camp in a grove of snow-dusted, ghostly-white Joshua trees. Though the day's light was fast fading, there would be time, at least, to visit the grave of Chester A. Pray. Snowflakes blurred my glasses as on foot I crunched through the arched iron gate of Elk's Rest and found his cross, splintered and fallen. I did my best to set it straight. I'd brought no flowers; my presence, I hoped, was enough.

Chester Pray. Prospector, assayer, locator of one of the richest mines in Death Valley. He would, I hoped, provide a focus for the era that drew me here, a link to its free-floating souls, characters ranging from Rosemary, a harlot with a secret past, to Death Valley Scotty, the man with the secret mine. The famous, the obscure.

Nightfall and a biting wind off the Malpai Mesa to the west packed me back to Goldfield, to find the only place open—for anything—to be off Crook Avenue, on down Fifth Street: the Santa Fe Saloon, which outside or in hadn't seen a can of paint since 1905 (and doubtfully then), the year the watering hole opened. The only improvement of note had been the addition of a few rooms around back, where I could stay the night, or as many nights as I liked.

"We got Sierra Nevada on tap."

"That'll be fine. And to eat? Anything to eat?"

"Pizza," offered barkeep Elaine, "I can heat up a pizza pie."

"That's it?"

"That's it."

One by one, regulars drifted in, heartily and derisively greeting each other, welcoming the warmth of a pot-bellied stove and a drink or two or three or four.

"My kid," said the woman in the grease-stained sweatshirt, "someone remind me to pick him up after a while. You know, I have to slap the little shit up the side of the head from time to time, but I tell you, he's smart. He's smart all right."

"My dog," reflected a rheumy-eyed fellow, not exactly in the same vein, "He's so mean he'll lick you to death."

"*My dog*," rejoined another, tugging at his suspenders, "he's so good he gets a pillow on my bed." That arrangement, though, was in jeopardy, for the man's place was time-worn to the point of collapse. "Lucky to last the winter."

Suggestion: "Hey! Get a new place. But the trick is to build it so it looks like a chicken coop. You do that and you don't pay no taxes! You know, slats down the side, sawdust on the floor."

"Really? That works?"

"Your dog—he'd like that."

"I'm not so sure."

"Of course he would."

From then until closing time, all shared a single, rambling conversation. As in the old days—Chester Pray's days. An hour or two of bad jokes and good cheer, shared by a crowd of loners.

Closing time. We wished each other good night and were out the door.

The storm had moved on. Snow-covered Goldfield glittered in the light of a full moon.

Rather than turn in, I walked the near-derelict camp. I gazed up at the boarded-up, hundred-and-fifty room Goldfield Hotel. Across the way a one-story building had six front doors, doors once hung with the shingles of the likes of Little Sadie, Gertie the Desert Rose, and others of the trade. Which reminded me of the Goldfield bordello named The Louvre, the Madame believing that to be the name of the fanciest house in Paris. It was a good story, though untrue. The Louvre was an upscale eating establishment,

3

its site, like much else in Goldfield, vacant but for ice-rimed desert grasses, sage, and clumps of greasewood. Flash flood and fire had taken their toll.

All was silent, not a breath of wind. A light burned in the jail wing behind the courthouse, another in a sand-pitted Airstream out toward what was once Hop Fiend Gulch.

There was a time when garlands of electric lights—thousands upon thousands—criss-crossed Goldfield's streets. The sky was incandescent, a beacon to the far horizon. What a time it must have been, I thought, a time of expansive goodwill and bald-faced chicanery, hymns and epithets, fortune and failure. Where I now paused and looked up and down Crook and Main, a clamorous mob once surged from one to another of over fifty saloons and gambling halls.

My intent, uncertain at this point, was that a single face in that crowd could harken me back to an era a hundred years faded.

Chester Pray—at once a nobody and an everyman—might just prove to be a man to sum up life and hope and even love in a last chapter of the Old West.

—Goldfield, Nevada, January, 2004

SHOTS IN THE DESERT NIGHT

IMAGINE YOURSELF TRANSPORTED to an era a century past. Newly-elected President Woodrow Wilson had proclaimed "a new age of right and opportunity. Justice, and only justice, shall be our motto." There'd be an end to robber-baron rapaciousness; the common man would prosper. Farms would flourish; skyscrapers would pierce the clouds. Socially and economically, the nation was on the move, even as across the Atlantic there was discord and rumblings of war.

America: the land was blessed.

Imagine yourself now in a place apart from this, a place wobbly as to justice, and oblivious to affairs of state and just about everything else in the early twentieth century. In the pot-boiling prose of a reporter for the *New York World*, imagine yourself in...

> ...the loneliest, the hottest and the most deadly and dangerous spot in the United States. It is a pit of horrors—the haunt of all that is grim and ghoulish. Such animal life as infests this pest-hole is of ghastly shape, rancorous nature, and diabolically ugly.
>
> Of fresh water there is none, but a liquid having the appearance of water oozes from salt and lava beds. It is deadly poison.
>
> This is the dominion of death. It is surely the nearest to a little hell upon earth that the whole wicked world can produce.

Such was Death Valley, or as it was also known, Death's Valley.

If you were senseless enough to venture there, you moved by night. In the month of June of 1913, daytime temperatures peaked at 120° Fahrenheit, yet would drop, by four in the morning, to the low 70°s. The Milky Way, arching brilliantly overhead, would guide your footfalls across dunes, rocky plains, and salt flats.

And if your wanderings took you to the southern end of the Funeral Range, you might be startled, or at least puzzled, by a shadowy form the size of a locomotive—a monstrous iron steam traction engine. Straining your eyes, you would make out, nearby, six or seven tents pitched amidst a scattering of wagons and equipment. You might recognize a Fresno scraper, useful in grading dirt roads.

To the east, a faint smudge of indigo edged the Funerals.

A mule brayed, then another.

A soul stirred, the first player in what was to become a strange, fateful pantomime.

Crawling from his tent, a man hiked up his pants, buttoned his shirt, lit a candle, and wrote. Whatever it was, it didn't take long. The man snuffed the candle and stretched, then ambled to a tent a few yards away and chatted with a second fellow reclining on a blanket. Whatever was said prompted laughter borne on the still night air.

The man then walked away from the campsite, downhill, in the direction of the Valley's floor. He passed the hulking steam traction engine.

Then, a minute or so later, he wheeled as if to confront someone trailing him.

A white flash!

A split second later, the concussion of a gunshot, echoing off the surrounding Funerals.

There didn't appear to be anyone else close by the man, not that you could see.

He could well have been up and about hunting rabbits. For the men back in the camp, they'd be welcome fare, a change from bacon, beans, and stale biscuits. There was no shortage of jacks and cottontails this time of year.

No further shots were fired, and the man continued downhill, out-of-sight over the bank of a dry wash.

Fifteen minutes elapsed. The sky lightened.

And the coming of the dawn was shattered by two more shots, fired in quick succession, as in a shootout. Then silence.

Up at the camp, there was no visible reaction, at least for a time. Then, all of a sudden, a figure jumped to his feet and raced in the direction of the shots.

"Chester?" he called, "You alright?"

Then, "Chester! Oh Chester!" The cry was alarmed, distraught.

For a time, nothing. Silence but for the chirp of birds and, back at the camp, indiscernible muttering and faint scrapes and clinks as a motley half-dozen or so men rose, lit fires, brewed coffee, and readied themselves for another scorcher. They were oblivious to anything downwind.

The figure that had shouted "Chester!" ran back toward the camp, gesticulating wildly.

Suddenly, everyone was wide awake. A hubbub arose, with an edginess, an overtone of hostility to whatever was said or discussed. As the sun crested the Funerals, a clutch of men warily descended the slope.

If, taking care not to draw attention, you now shifted your position to gain a clearer view of what was going on, you would have seen—as did the men from the camp—a body stretched out in a shallow depression, the man's face ashen, his head oozing blood that trickled down his arm and blackened the sand, the scene all the more lurid in the early morning's orange-red light.

The men appeared to be debating what to do.

In time a team of mules was hitched to a wagon, and a fellow took off towards the east along a wide, freshly-cut track.

The rest were to erect a tent over the body and maintain a vigil all that day, that night, and the next day and night. Enduring the heat and terrible smell. Warding off coyotes.

Meanwhile, most likely on the say of the fellow who'd rode off, news of the killing spread by word of mouth and wire. Up in Goldfield, a hundred and seventy miles distant, the front page of the *Goldfield Daily Tribune* was headlined:

C.A. PRAY'S
SHOOTING IS
A MYSTERY

Young Mining Man, Well Known Here,
Meets Strange Death on
the Desert

ENGAGED TO MARRY AND
HAD MADE FORTUNE

In Goldfield's spit-on-the-floor bars and upper-class, plush parlors, speculation was rife. As most everyone in the camp knew, Chester Pray had made a major strike. It could just be the best ever in Death Valley. Indeed the paper was to report that he was soon "to marry the girl of his choice and settle down, with assurance of an ample competence for all time."

On the threshold of becoming rich beyond his dreams, Chester Pray's life had been cut short. Brutally so.

But by whom?

By Indians? Renegade Shoshones were rumored in the area. They were said to have picked off prospectors in the past. Could Chester have been the latest?

By partners? He'd recently taken on two new ones, and they would no doubt take over his operation. Though respected mining men, they were not above suspicion.

By a gun-for-hire? Diamondfield Jack, a local bad man, had a reputation for lay-in-wait desert ambushes. "Dry-gulching," it was called. And he had recently crossed paths with Chester Pray.

Could Chester's fiancée have been involved? She was a looker. A looker, it was whispered, with a shadowy past.

Three shots had been fired in the desert night.

And the question was: Whose palm had grasped the gun, whose finger had pulled the trigger that brought a sudden end to the man's short, yet eventful life?

Who killed Chester Pray?

CAPTAIN PRAY'S SON

THIRTY-SIX YEARS EARLIER, ANOTHER SHOT had been fired—to reverberate across still, serene Lake Tahoe, "the fairest picture the whole earth affords" in the words of Samuel Clemens. Boating its crystal waters was "comparable to floating high aloft in mid-nothingness, so empty and airy did the spaces seem below."

On an Indian summer afternoon in 1876, the passengers aboard the excursion yacht *Governor Blaisdel* delightedly agreed. The day had been cool but not chilly, with the views extraordinary, the eye drawn to the west and the snow-capped peaks of the Sierra Nevadas, suffused now with sunset's golden glow.

As the yacht rounded a rocky, forested point and came in sight of Glenbrook, Nevada, a portly red-bearded man—Captain Augustus W. Pray—had stepped from the wheelhouse to ram his canon "Old Betsy" with gunpowder and wadding. He had then invited the day's celebrated guest to strike a match and fire a salute. In return the citizens crowding little Glenbrook's long wharf unfurled an oversize, forty-two star flag.

In response, Ulysses S. Grant heartily waved, then turned to clap Captain Pray on the back. The General had journeyed here with reason: to express his gratitude for his host's role in the Civil War. Not that Pray had seen battle or even captained troops, but rather he had a major role in a secret society that thwarted Confederate sympathizers scheming to have Nevada bolt the Union, which would shut off the flow of the silver bullion of the silver state. This isn't to say Pray wasn't a captain. He was a sea captain reared in Maine and for years the master of trading vessels plying both the east and west coasts. In 1862 he ventured inland to Lake Tahoe and laid claim to seven hundred shoreline acres.

Captain Pray reversed the *Governor Blaisdel's* side wheel and smartly docked the yacht, so that all might proceed to his Lake Shore House, considered the finest and most luxurious hostelry on the lake. On the porch, the Captain's wife Helen awkwardly curtsied before the General and regretted that she had missed the cruise. She was in a family way, and the Captain thought it best that she remained ashore.

The Captain boasted the Lake Shore House to be a "gathering place of the fashionable of the world, a veritable 'Saratoga of Nevada.' A fine stock of cigars is kept and all kinds of tropical fruits, as well as California fruits in their season. There is an ice cream parlor for the ladies and a hand-carved cherry wood bar"—but a bar dispensing tonics and phosphates, nothing stronger. The Captain was firm in his belief that if the Devil had a nectar, it was alcohol.

The evening's fete—a banquet followed by a ball in the Captain's social hall—was long remembered. The General is said to have quite enjoyed himself, despite the lack of ardent spirits, despite his antipathy to song and dance. ("I know two pieces," he'd been quoted, "one is the 'Battle Hymn of the Republic,' the other isn't.") Camille Spooner on piano and Jack Armstrong on violin were renowned for their enthusiasm and energy (Jack once skewering Mrs. Charles Ramsey's red wig with his bow as she pirouetted gaily by).

The next morning the General awakened to a cacophony of shouts, screeches, and thudding splashes. From high above Glenbrook Bay, freshly-cut timber hurtled down a greased logway so furiously that the logs smoked and ignited, to be quenched in a shower of sparks upon plunging into the lake. There they were gathered by booms nudged by the *Governor Blaisdel* and maneuvered to Captain Pray's sawmill.

The General admired the Captain's enterprise and thanked him for his hospitality. Had he paid for his room, the tariff would have been $5.75 in currency or $4.00 in gold (then a day's wage for a highly-skilled laborer).[1]

With the General on his way, life as usual resumed in the town that Captain Pray had founded and more-or-less owned, from a general store and meat market to a livery stable and rental cottages. Though he promoted Glenbrook as a resort, he was making his mark clear-cutting both nearby mountains and the Sierra Nevadas across the lake. Virginia City, thirty miles by rail to the east, devoured all he could mill to shore up the ever-deepening mines of its renowned Comstock Lode. In the year of Grant's visit, Captain Pray's output approached twenty-three million board feet.

---

[1] See page 251 for the value – a hundred years later – of sums cited in the text.

In 1876, on Saturday, November 11th, Helen Pray was to present the Captain with an heir, christened Chester Augustus Pray, and one would be hard pressed to imagine a child with brighter prospects. Little Chester's family was rich, privileged, and respected; the sunny, serene world of his childhood would be celebrated as Lake Tahoe's gilded age.

Would it were so.

Early on, the boy was pronounced difficult to control, to be cuffed and switched. When the Captain hosted President Rutherford B. Hayes, three-year-old Chester was kept safely out of sight. By the time he was five, Chester had taken to wandering off, who knew where, to return muddied and torn. A father-son chasm yawned, with the Captain increasingly stiff-necked and bellicose in his moral superiority. As to Chester, as to anyone. A.H. Tevis, a Tahoe preacher, wrote:

> No man more positively repels the idea of giving to or countenancing the worthless and debauched than he. He is a most uncompromising temperance man. Having control of nearly all of the town of Glenbrook, there is not a drop of ardent spirits allowed to be sold.
>
> Only the other day there was a battle of some sort, or an incipient riot in the town, growing out of the conflict between thirsty citizens and Captain Pray. Some parties had erected a drinking bar at the end of the wharf, or on a boat moored to the wharf, but the veteran prohibitionist frustrated their speculation by shutting them out with a fence.

A further skirmish was reported in Virginia City's *Territorial Enterprise*:

> A man who is called 'Skippy' was fined $40 last Saturday, for selling whiskey from a boat near the wharf at Glenbrook. He claims the fine was unconstitutional. They now have a regular whiskey war up at Lake Tahoe, with Captain Pray arrayed against old King Alcohol.

Hapless 'Skippy' (fined $1,200 or more in today's dollars) and young Chester were in the same boat, with both the object of the Captain's self-righteous bluster, and both resistant to knuckling under. There's a hint of this in Chester's appearance in a group photograph (see page 122, plate 2) of a Pray social on the lawn of the Lake Shore House. For an apparently carefree event, the men are attired in dark suits, ties, and high starched collars; nearly all the women are in long-skirted white. It is likely that the stout, floppy-tied man to the left is Captain Pray, his seafarer's beard replaced by the moustache of a prosperous burgher. Two young women fawn over him, one toasting the occasion, her drink likely a fruit punch, with a pitcher on the table and another in reserve beneath. Assembled guests nibble cookies and little cakes.

It is uncertain, but the woman over the Captain's shoulder, a kerchief to her lips, may be his wife Helen. She was a troubled soul, given to spells of melancholia. As for Chester, he's away from his parents, second from the right, the youngster with the wide forehead and raw-boned features.

His life through, he would have an affinity for wide-brimmed hats and a feet-apart stance, as if bracing for and defying come what may. At the time he was eleven years old, and in his father's eyes, could do no right. Even his mother called his behavior "inappropriate." He spoke out of turn at the table; he dipped Olivine Spooner's braids in his school inkwell. He was alternately inattentive and disruptive, and given a choice, was off by himself, roaming the countryside or skipping stones across Tahoe's placid surface.

He was mischievous, a bad boy; his father assured him of that. But there was more to it. He was to recall, *"I realized I was not like other people."*

Just how, he couldn't—or wouldn't—say.

In the late 1880s, the idyll that was Glenbrook waned.

The *Governor Blaisdel* was dashed to pieces in a storm, its ribs and planks washed up on the beach by the Lake Front House, and left to rot.

The demand for the Captain's timber fell off as the deep mining of the Comstock Lode was slowed by heat so intense—120° on some levels—that miners could only work a face fifteen minutes before retreating, exhausted, to an ice room.

Little could be done for the "nervous dyspepsia" that had overtaken the Captain's wife. She had to be coaxed from her room.

Captain Pray was to fume and grouse at his reversal of fortune, and at the tremors of the palsy now upon him. He availed himself of Glenbrook's iron-rich mineral spring, "the curative properties of whose waters in certain complaints is highly lauded." But not in his case.

He was further laid low and angered by the worst winter on record, with fifteen feet of snow on level ground and drifts thirty-five to fifty feet high. The town was cut off and benighted. Coal oil lamps burned night and day. To break the monotony, the Captain grudgingly permitted dances in his social hall, only to erupt in anger as out-of-work lumberjacks raked its polished floor with their spiked boots.

Captain Augustus W. Pray, his nerves frayed and his body bloated with dropsy, died on February 29, 1892. His retainers shivered—but were free to swear and take the cork out of the bottle—as in Pray's Meadow they shoveled away snow and pickaxed the frozen earth that he might mercifully Rest in Peace.

The two souls to whom he gave little rest and peace—his wife and Chester, now fifteen—had enough of Glenbrook, and at the end of that winter fled by stage, then train to Boston and neighboring Cambridgeport, there to be taken in by Helen's sweet and considerate sister Julia, and her new husband Henry Cram.

Julia Cram quite doted on her nephew, assuming a role all but relinquished by his depressed mother. Henry Cram, on the other hand, had little interest in Chester (not that he minded the flow of funds from the disposition of Captain Pray's Glenbrook empire). As Treasurer of the fledgling Bernstein Electric Light Company, he was intent on putting his business on the map. The boy was a distraction, and at that, morose, nervous, and unruly. Henry Cram rhetorically asked, given Chester's family history, what might one expect? Captain Pray's sister was demented, and an uncle and cousin had died in an asylum in Maine. Julia Cram offered little defense, but rather felt this all the more reason to do her best by Chester—and at the time, what greater treat than an excursion to Chicago and the World's Columbian Exposition?

There, strolling the thoroughfare of the Midway Plaisance, aunt and nephew sampled a new caramel-coated popcorn called Cracker Jack, kept their distance from fierce Dahomey cannibals, and felt sorry for wilting Esquimauxs and their dogs. Whiffs of incense beckoned them to the Algerian Village, where a swarthy,

Fez-topped barker mounted a box to proclaim the delights of "An Odalisque fresh from the Seraglio! The Sultan's favorite! Renowned for her *danse du ventre*," this prompting Aunt Julia to catch up the boy up by the hand and hustle him on to join the line for a ride on Mr. Ferris' amazing thirty-six story wheel. The sun was setting and their timing fortunate. From on high, they looked down as a hundred thousand electric lights were switched on the length and breadth of the Exposition. The display was dazzling, unprecedented.

"And think, Chester, your Uncle Henry's company had a hand in creating all this. And he saw to our visit. Are we not fortunate?"

"Yes..."

"It's as they say. The white city, a dream city..."

Yet the boy was unhappy, clutching his aunt's hand and suddenly bursting into tears as their car arced down to earth.

When asked what the matter was, all Chester could blurt was, "I don't know. I don't know."

That night, he padded to the threshold of Julia's adjoining room, to awaken her with, "Auntie, I am afraid to stay here alone."

"Why? What is it?"

"Voices."

She found this peculiar. "There isn't anyone talking around here."

"I don't like to stay in there alone; can't I come in your room?"

"Of course," she said, letting him stay the night through, and ordering a single bed so that, as the boy desperately wished, he'd not be alone, day or night.[2]

There were more crying fits. Even so, Chester appears to have enjoyed himself. The Exposition offered sphinxes and mummies and Herr Krupp's "pet monster," the largest artillery piece ever machined. The Mines and Mining building featured mock-ups of shadowy, underground workings, where Chester was fascinated by a demonstration of a powerful pneumatic drill that could bore clean through a sizeable block of granite in less than a minute,

---

[2] This and considerable dialogue throughout this account appears in lengthy depositions taken when, after his death, the ownership of Chester's Death Valley mine was bitterly disputed. See End Notes for further information on sources.

against an hour with a hand-hammer and drill bit. "Got to mind yourself, though, the drill's a widow-maker," advised the man with the carbide headlamp (another innovation). Chester was taken by the idea of dull gray rocks blasted from the earth, then crushed, pulverized, and smelted to render ingots of silver and gold. Pyramids of them, on display.

Their last afternoon in Chicago, Chester and his Aunt Julia had choice seats for:

BUFFALO BILL'S
WILD WEST
– AND –
CONGRESS OF ROUGH RIDERS OF THE WORLD

---

600 MEN AND 500 HORSES TAKE PART
No Other Exhibition Has Been Received
With Such Marked Favor

The open-air, sawdust ring resounded with the hollers, hoof beats, and flying lead of a West unfamiliar—and eye-opening—to Chester, a West beyond the reach of his father's stifling hand. Where you were free to roam and free to make your mark, for good it might be hoped, but with bad having its appeal. Chester had no way of knowing that a few years hence he would cross paths with one of the show's six fancy-riding cowboys, the lean fellow in the wooly chaps. At the time of Chester's troubled Lake Tahoe childhood, the performer had been a dollar-a-day water boy for a party of government surveyors mapping the desert wastes of eastern California. A natural rider, he'd been recruited by Buffalo Bill Cody and had performed before royalty on a recent European tour; as a matter of fact, the King of Spain had offered him a cigar, and he was nearly fired when he off-handedly remarked, "I'll save the stump for Bill." The wise-cracking trick rider and roper's name was Walter Scott; he would soon enough become trickster Death Valley Scotty.

On returning to Massachusetts and Cambridgeport, Chester was to keep more and more to himself. He daydreamed of Buffalo Bill's West and couldn't wait to excuse himself from dinner and his Uncle Henry's discourses on wattage and filaments. The boy's upstairs room was cramped and stuffy, but he cared not as he lost himself in the newsprint of popular half-dime and dime novels. Dozens recounted the fearless, daring exploits of Buffalo Bill. Others invited you to ride with Sheriff Stillwater ("The Regulator of Raspberry"), be in on the rescue of little Sarah and Effie ("The Pearls of the Prairie"), and be dazzled by the riches of the Lost Phantom Mine ("The Boy Gold Hunter"). And there were hell-roaring desperados, the ilk of Hair-Trigger Tom and Bill the Blizzard, "all wool and a yard wide." The Blizzard would blow into a saloon with...

"Now hear me talk! I'm a war-horse of the hills! I run on brass wheels! I'm a full breasted roller with three tits! Holes punched for more!"
"What'll it be, Bill?" queried the man behind the bar.
"Whiskey! Whiskey chaser!"

At heart the Blizzard was good-hearted, and was to give many a frontier blackguard and bully their comeuppance. Chester liked that; he wistfully saw—hoped for—something of himself in the human tornado.

A man to be reckoned with in the West.

A man running on brass wheels.

Chester kept his dime novels under his bed. He didn't dare spirit them to school, as others did, tucked in textbooks. School was proper and strict, typified by the overbearing, hood-eye man clearing his throat to intone, "Stand now, that we might turn to 'Work, for the Night is Coming!'" Superintendent William E. Bradbury loved the hoary hymn and more often than not chose it to begin the day at the Cambridge Manual School for Boys.

Put out by Chester's distant and often sullen ways, Henry Cram had insisted on and seen to his enrollment. Indeed, he may have been the guardian who (according to a school history) informed Superintendent Bradbury, "My boy is a peculiar child and has to be treated just so," to be cut off by a lofty, "I am a peculiar man. I have to be treated just so." So much, then, for considerate treatment in a school founded with an eye to assuring Boston's upper classes with quality draftsmen, woodworkers, ironmongers, and the like.

More than once, Bradbury had Chester in tears. He had a pet analogy for even the slightest infraction. It was a pitcher of water. He'd forcibly grasp a boy by the wrist, and pour a few drops onto his palm.

"Not much you might say, but it's still water. Is it not? You agree?" He'd ask.

"Yes, sir."

Savoring the moment, he would assert, "It's the same with crime."

And Bradbury was not alone in berating Chester. There were voices, voices in his head that repeated, over and over, "I am not like other people," and, worse, "I am not fit to live. I am not fit to live." They were at his ear in class; at his heels as he walked, sometimes ran home; in his room as he pulled his pillow over his head. He sought relief with the "five nuns and the priest" (as his Irish schoolmates called it), the same as "self abuse," the term his Uncle Henry used when he caught Chester in the act and hauled him to the family's doctor, Holmes M. Jernegan, who upon examining the young man found him in good health—physically, though not mentally.

"He is suffering from melancholia, and can not seem to reason clearly on his mental condition," Jernegan thought aloud. "I can see no apparent cause." He turned to Henry Cram, lowered his voice. "There is a taint. I believe he was born defective."

Jernegan prescribed a tonic, but found Chester no better on a follow-up visit. He was to explain to the boy's uncle, "There are two major afflictions of the mind, and your boy, I regret, is subject to both. There is mania, and there is melancholia. When exaggerated, melancholia begets insanity. Delusions beset a patient; he feels that his friends and family are turning against him, talking about him, working against him."

"But you know not why?"

"I don't."

"Tell me, doctor," Henry Cram was to pose with marked distaste, "Could self abuse be a factor—a contributing cause?"

"You mean masturbation?"

"Yes."

"I don't believe—I don't think it is. If every boy that masturbated developed mental conditions, why the whole country would be crazy. I can only say that young Chester has a brain liable to storms. They may pass."

It was no more than a week or so later, in October of 1893, that Julia Cram had prepared breakfast and Henry was eating in haste, anxious to be off to work; the fortunes of Bernstein Electric were on the rise, and the Crams were considering a new and spacious home on Cambridgeport's fashionable Avon Hill.

Chester was still upstairs.

Julia called for him to come down.

No answer.

Uncle Henry rose, strode to the bottom of the stairs, summoned the boy.

Again, no response.

"Chester... Anything the matter?" Julia hastened up the stairs to first knock, then put her ear to the boy's door.

A muffled, desperate sob.

She turned the knob, swung open the door, and screamed. She struggled for the words, "Henry! Come up! You must come up!"

Chester lay stretched out on his bed, his face and hands bloody. He rolled away from his aunt and uncle, burying his face in a pillow saturated with blood. Blood spurted from a gash at the base of his neck. Henry recoiled. Julia had the presence of mind to pull a handkerchief from her sleeve and press it hard upon the wound.

"Oh dear Chester, why?"

"Chester!" demanded his uncle.

In time, the boy choked out, "Tried to get at the base of my brain. I'm not fit to live."

He would say no more.

They rushed him to the nearest hospital, where the blood was staunched and his wound cleaned and bandaged. Back home, they did their best to look after and cheer Chester, and over the next weeks and months had a measure of success. It was as if the incident, terrible as it was, had silenced or at least muted his bedeviling voices. Henry was less diffident; Julia, as ever, was there for him. "Auntie," he was to say, "if you weren't already married, I'd marry you."

At the same time, his mother Helen drifted away to live with a third sister, also of Cambridgeport. This was for the good; mother and son, both "mental," had been increasingly at odds.

Chester was by the day less morose, and the Crams were relieved, even as they were offended by his continued self-abuse.

Chester fared better at the Cambridge Manual School, where, though weak in Writing and Civics, he did well in Drawing and Bench-Making, classes where he could use his hands. He looked forward to the next term's Chemistry. At the Chicago Exposition, he had been fascinated by a working replica of an assay laboratory, and the idea of raw materials transmuted to useful purpose. He dog-eared *Huxley's Primer*; he near-memorized *Crosby's Table for the Determination of Minerals*.

But on June 5th, 1894, the voices were back, whispering at first, but then louder, even shouting. Taunting him, dragging him down.

In the mid-morning of June 9th, the school's Mr. Bradbury telephoned Bernstein Electric. "You must come at once to look after Chester Pray."

Arriving a few minutes before noon, Henry Cram found his nephew lying on a couch in the Superintendent's office, his tie and belt loosened, cold water dashed upon his face, hot water bottles applied to his feet.

"Brought here in a state of great excitement," explained Bradbury.

Two medical men had been summoned, Dr. Albert August and Dr. Walter Wesselhoeft, with the latter reporting that Chester had "descended to a state of sullenness, in which he refused to answer questions or refused to recognize any sort of directions and made, if he talked at all, idle remarks."

The doctors gleaned what they could, though more from Henry Cram than Chester. Two hours of this and Wesselhoeft counseled, "The boy is naturally a defective, a mental defective. He is not sound as a normal boy would be." He sighed and shook his head. "The only thing to do is commit him to a place of safety."

Henry Cram turned to Superintendent Bradbury, who coldly concurred, "You have little choice but to commit him to an asylum. I can not take care of him here."

"There is hope?" Henry wondered.

Dr. Wesselhoeft doubted it. "I can only say that the probability is in favor of non-recovery. Though I am not an Alienist [psychiatrist], it has been my observation that such cases usually end disastrously, one way or the other."

Guided by Doctors Wesselhoeft and August, Henry Cram drew up the necessary commitment papers to be rushed to Judge

Charles Almy, who dispatched two constables to escort Chester to nearby Somerville. A grounds man swung wide a wrought-iron gate. Across rolling green lawns rose the Grecian-pillared mansion of the McLean Asylum for the Insane. (This was in no way a bedlam; many a Brahmin were patients.)

The course of Chester Pray's lunacy and treatment was recorded in McLean case file #7960. No doubt scared out of his wits, the young man was at first reasonably tractable, "though at times he talked incoherently and was frequently profane and obscene." On his third day "he became noisy, laughing, slapping his hands and swearing and had to be put under restraint in a canvas suit with screwed buttons."

As was customary with such behavior, he was taken to a Hydriatic Suite, where he was given a "tonic bath" that rendered him docile and able to be taken off to bed, there fitfully to sleep.

His Aunt Julia was admitted for a visit.

Chester had no idea who she was.

On a walk through the Asylum's grounds, Chester broke away from other patients to seize stones and maniacally hurl them at their attendants. Escorted inside, he kicked over chairs and tables and only with great effort was manhandled down to a Hydriatic Suite where he was wrapped in cold, wet sheets, "48° to 56°," a McLean *Nurse's Manual* instructed. He then would have experienced "a sensation of chilliness... cooling of the skin... chilliness disappears... skin becomes warm... muscular relaxation occurs."

Vigilance was necessary: "If there is any unusual paleness of the face, blueness of the lips or shivering, the patient should be warmed by the application of hot water bags to his sides and feet. He should also be given a hot stimulating drink. (A teaspoonful of whiskey in hot water is considered good because whiskey dilates the blood vessels in the skin)."

His disruptiveness dampened, Chester would have been strapped into a hammock and lowered into a bathtub filled with 94° water. A canvas sheet was then drawn over the tub, provided with a hole for his head. Bandages were wrapped around his eyes and ears, with the object that heat would be his sole perceived sensation. The bath would typically last all day, with the instruction: "If a patient is very noisy, restless, or flushed or if the pulse rate is 88 or more rapid, supply an ice collar, and sponge the face with cold water. Omit during sleep."

Chester was offered nutrition, but refused to eat.

Such baths were "continuous"—for days, even weeks.

Though born to wealth, Chester Pray's life had to date been short and wretched, with the prospect now of living out his days in the confines of the McLean Asylum. Who could imagine anything to the contrary? Certainly not doctors Jernegan, August, or Wesselhoeft. Not his mother Helen, who was afflicted as well with melancholia. Doubtful his Uncle Henry.

But perhaps his Aunt Julia.

If anyone, she held out hope for the boy.

THE FIRE ASSAYER

ON HER THIRD VISIT TO THE ASYLUM, Julia Cram took heart. Chester recognized her, though "he called me terribly abusive names and wouldn't talk with me, only swear at me. He wasn't naturally profane at all. Even so: I used to go every day."

And to Chester's benefit, his further course of treatment was remarkably enlightened.

Traditionally, asylum medicine had been cruel and brutal in the alleged best interest of the patient. The theory was that, properly terrorized, inmates would "waken" from their madness. In Europe and America, all manner of medieval schemes were brought to bear. Near-drownings were popular, and one asylum routinely lowered patients into a dungeon filled with snakes. The keepers or the kept—who were the lunatics? Contrary to this, a movement pioneered in asylums run by English Quakers was to offer the helping hand of kindness. "Moral Treatment," the approach was called. In 1811, Philippe Pinel, a humane and caring French physician, set forth its tenets:

> Patients are moved from their residence to some proper asylum; and for this purpose a calm retreat in the country is to be preferred, for it is found that continuance at home aggravates the disease, as the improper association of ideas cannot be destroyed. A system of human vigilance is adopted. Coercion by blows, stripes and chains is now justly laid aside. Noisy ejaculations are tolerated; fears and resentments are soothed without unnecessary opposition.

Pinel further advised:

> In convalescence, allow limited liberty, and introduce entertaining books and exhilarating

music. Engage the patient in conversation, and admit friends under proper restriction. And so the patient will "minister to himself."

This, over time, is what the McLean Asylum offered Chester Pray. He was spared family conflicts and criticism; he was offered out-of-door exercise; doctors joined him for lunch and dinner. Calomel or cochineal was added to his food, but only if he was unduly agitated. Restraints and drugs were last resorts to prevent him from hurting himself and others. The Asylum's "tonic baths" were not as dreadful as they might first appear; posed a McLean physician, "Don't you always feel relaxed after a nice, warm bath?"

Under McLean's regimen, Chester improved to the extent that his August chart noted: "Began to be more quiet and reasonable, recognizing his relatives." He had a "violent and moody" spell in October, but by December he was better yet, and on January 6th, 1895, he was discharged "considerably improved."

The Crams hoped to re-enroll Chester in the Cambridge Manual School, only to be turned down by Superintendent Bradbury.

Chester tried working in a Boston grocery, but for cause unstated, he was let go after a few weeks.

He then either kept to his room or was down in the Cram's basement, but not in melancholic defeat. He had taken it into his head that he'd travel West, and make something of himself. He wouldn't return to genteel Lake Tahoe, but rather he'd cast his lot with common men with uncommon dreams: prospectors and miners. Quite on his own he set himself to learning all he could of the science and art of assaying. As a child he'd glimpsed the fiery, molten process up in Virginia City; he'd witnessed it again in the assay laboratory on display at the Chicago Exposition. His aunt Julia was to recall that, even when he was alienated and distraught, "He was fond of minerals."

In the summer of 1895, his Cambridgeport family was to see him off on the Boston and Albany Railroad.

Vowing to take care of himself, he kissed his mother's cheek, shook his uncle Henry's hand, and hugged and kissed his aunt Julia. He'd write; they'd be proud. He might even strike it rich. With a confidence unimaginable a year before, he swung his duffel aboard the train. The engine hissed and gathered steam. A last wave, and he was on his way to Chicago, and then, changing trains, out across prairies unbroken as far as the eye could see.

The clickety-clack of the rails, the telegraph poles flashing by gave rhythm and form to the role Chester would assume: a Westerner, the genuine, roughly-dressed article. Hardly the sarsaparilla-sipping, white-suited variety of the Lake Tahoe of his childhood. There were guides for this. Instructed one:

> In desolate country, your soft felt hat will do but instead of your stiff bosom shirt and stand-up collar you want one with a soft lay-down collar, or no collar. No cuffs but those which may be already attached to your shirt. No silk stockings. 10 cents per pair will buy you socks of fairly good weight. Yellow khaki pants are the thing. $1.50 per pair. Wear high topped lace boots with tongue all the way up to keep out sand. A coat only if it's cold. No danger of being put out of the eating houses even if you don't wear a coat.

The Great Northern's conductor swayed through Chester's car, motioning to the windows, "Slide 'em, slide 'em up!" Throughout the day, they'd sighted prairie fires, mostly distant, but some within a mile. They routed and stampeded buffalo—a few here, a dozen there, nothing like the herds that thundered through the dime novels peddled by book and candy butchers boarding at stops. No matter: the West was at hand.

"Heed! Heed! Fire ahead!" the conductor warned. Up in the cab, they poured it on, the train chuffing and shuddering as it rocketed to forty and more miles an hour.

Even with windows shut, smoke swirled through the cars, enough to bring tears to passengers' eyes. Chester wiped them away with the cuff of his blue working man's shirt. He, in fact, smiled as, to the gasps of nearly everyone else, the train plunged into a wall of fire. Smoke that couldn't be blacker blotted out the sun. Flames scorched paint, cracked windows. Two, three, five perilous minutes of this, and the train flashed through into the sunlight.

Chester clapped his hands and cheered, one of a chorus the length of the train.

The engineer throttled down; the fireman rocked back on

his shovel; brakemen spun their wheels. The train squealed to a stop. There were embers to be doused, nothing serious. And before them: the horizon rippled with the ridges and peaks of the Rockies, where not that long ago fortunes had been made mining gold, silver, and even lead.

And now, in 1895, there was word of a new promised land off to the northwest, in the hinterlands of eastern Oregon. After riding the rails of five roads, Chester Pray alighted in the frontier settlement of The Dalles to, if he could, hitch wagon rides, or if he could not, proceed by foot to where "All you had to do was shout 'gold' and ere the echo could come back from the neighboring hills, there would be before your eyes, several hundred assorted prospectors, a saloon fully equipped, and a burying preacher."

By the time he'd reached Sumpter, a fledgling camp in a piney mountain dale, Chester was thirsty, as he understood frontiersmen often were. Striding into the tent-shack Gem Saloon, he would have plunked down his nickel and drank up, hardly wincing at the taste of the tobacco plug shavings bucking up watered-down whiskey. No need to wipe your feet, wear a jacket, or take off your hat. Nobody running for doctors if you swore or carried on short of shooting someone.

Fortified, Chester toured the camp, with a tip of his hat as he passed Madame De Bilk, she and her girls raising a tent bordello. The "Golden Rule" they would call it. Across the way, Chester sought a gaunt, watery-eyed man who he believed might offer him a footing on fortune's path. The man's sign, veteran of a dozen camps, was wedged in a wagonload of cement sacks and crates stenciled "Danger!"

E.A. HICKOCK
CHEMICAL & FIRE ASSAYS
Accuracy and Honesty Guaranteed

Chester introduced himself and forthrightly offered his hand and his help. At no cost. "Just learn me how."

That being the case, "Offer accepted."

The next morning Hickock and Pray poured a ten-by-ten foot cement slab, sufficient to isolate an assayer's delicate instruments from the incessant thumps of giant powder wresting ore from Sumpter's encircling hills.

Three days and they'd erected a three-room shack with a front porch soon chockablock with sacks of ore to be sampled.

As an apprentice, Chester was relegated to a back room, windowless and dark, fitted with ironmongery to crush and screen freshly-blasted rock. With a hand-turned jaw crusher he reduced fist-sized samples to the size of kernels of corn, and then in a mortar pounded them until they were as grains of sand. These he spread on a bucking board, to be mulled with a twenty-pound iron. Rock was rendered gray, dull dust.

And could that dust yield silver and gold? The prospect intrigued Chester: hidden value in apparent worthlessness.

Emerging from his back room, he would deliver a sample to Mr. Hickock, and then tend the establishment's fire-clay, iron-banded assay furnace. He would clear it of ashes, stoke it with a keg of charcoal, and look on as his employer proceeded with the ritual of the fire assay: the measurement of a precise portion of the sample, tapping it into a crucible the size of a tapered beer glass, then adding ingredients critical to separating out evidence of precious metals. As a finicky chef might season a soup, Hickock mumbled and grumped as to the proportions right for the ore at hand—more-than-usual litharge, a pinch of argol, a nail to pull off sulfur.

Once satisfied, Hickock placed the crucible in the furnace's lower "reducing deck," there to roast at a temperature approaching 3,000°.

Patience.

The sample's trial by fire took a half hour, during which Chester would be off to prepare the next sample, though mindful of the alchemy at work in the furnace: a swirl of transmutation seeking and fluxing the sample's gold and silver, if any.

A month into his apprenticeship, and Hickock unexpectedly called for Chester. He had an appointment. Could Chester complete his assay in progress? Chester said he certainly could, and with pulse-quickening anticipation, swung open the furnace's lower deck's door, seized the crucible with a forked crutch, and poured its dazzling orange melt into a cast-iron mould. He coaxed the resulting cube, once cooled, into a shallow cupel, which he placed in the furnace's "muffle," its upper deck.

The next step was critical.

Chester cracked, then opened, then closed muffle's door to control the temperature of the cupel—formed of crushed animal bone—as it drew off and absorbed the mix's waste.

The heat was intense; the light dazzling.

The process could only be observed through a slit in a wooden paddle. Even so, tears streamed down Chester's face. At the moment there was no more time to waste—not a second before and not a second after—he snatched the sample from the furnace, to witness the *blick*—a magical, feathery flash, as the sample surrendered its latent heat.

What was left?

If nothing, the sample was worthless. But ever was there excitement if, with all else burned away, there was a glittering, golden bead. Chester would then have stepped to the office's cubby, a partitioned alcove kept as free of rock dust as possible. There, he'd open a glass-enclosed balance and precisely weigh the tiny ingot, and so determine how many ounces per ton the sampled ore might yield.

There was value in this. Gold, of course—but mastering the process meant Chester was good at something. In fact, very good. He hungered to learn more, all there was to learn.

Three months and Chester Pray was a full-fledged practical assayer, versed not only in the ways of the reducing deck and muffle, but in the "wet chemistry" that unlocked the secrets of complex ores. He was wary handling the required mercury; its vapors could set you to drooling, give you the shakes, make you feel the world was against you. And cyanide. Water laced with cyanide killed doves, but not ravens. (Was there a lesson in this?)

In his off hours, Chester took up the banjo under the tutelage of a Miss Alice Duckworth. Making himself comfortable midst sacks of ore on the assay office's porch, he played and sang, to be rewarded with kisses blown by the ladies of easy virtue working across Cracker Street at the Golden Rule and, next door, the White House Whore House (not to mince words). Further attention and favors can only be surmised; his letters to his Aunt Julia and Uncle Henry were brief and circumspect.

Sumpter boomed, its population surging from a few hundred to several thousand, with excitements under and above ground. The town boasted a railroad connection, a steam-electric plant, fancy mercantiles, two galleries (shooting and portrait), and nightly at the Gem Saloon, an "All-Lady Orchestra." And when E.A. Hickock had acquired the wherewithal to branch into dry goods and hardware, Chester Pray took over his assay office business, in a humble camp elevated to "Golden Sumpter, the Queen City."

Chester never tired of his trade, for wittingly or unwittingly, every assay *blick* was a mirror of self-wrought salvation. A lunatic straight-jacketed in an asylum now merited the smiles and nods of passerbys. The lunatic rubbed shoulders with prominent merchants, bankers, mine superintendents—and in fact was invited to join the Benevolent and Protective Order of Elks. Not in Sumpter—too rough around the edges for this most elite of American orders—but in Baker City, out on the eastern Oregon plains, a two-hour down-the-mountain train ride.

On February 16, 1904, a dozen Elks rose to greet Chester as the greeter of Lodge #338 ushered him into their comfortable, well-appointed social hall. They were ranged about a circular table, and quaffed not whiskey but Ay champagne; the salons of Paris offered none superior. Easy laughter, cigars, backslaps: he was welcome to a fraternity offering camaraderie and solace to individuals distant from family and home. "Hello, Bill!" you could shout in unfamiliar territory, and more often than not a voice would heartily answer, "Why, hello Bill, yourself!" (All Elks were "Bills.") The order dated to the "Jolly Corks," an assembly of New York theatrical vagabonds, notably members of the Ethiopian Operatic Brotherhood, that is to say, minstrels: "devotees of burnt corks, double clogs, and melodies." Indeed, Baker City's Elks carried corks as fond badges of membership.

Offering Chester a champagne cork, an Elk and his brethren produced theirs, to place them in a circle.

"Hands under the table now, and we'll see who's favored with coordination and speed. All right?"

The group nodded in assent, though not without nudges and winks. "Last one to grasp and disappear his cork pays for the bottle. On the count of three..."

Chester tensed for his move. It would have to be quick and sure against his practiced, if woozy competitors.

"One... two... three!"

Chester's hand shot up and across the table. He snatched and in a flash pocketed his cork. He *and he alone* did this; everyone else remained stock still, only to break into peals of hail-fellow laughter, for Chester was both the first – *and the last* – to claim his cork. His initiation was underway, and was largely secret, though there was no doubt as to:

What is Elkdom? 'Tis the land
Where hungry souls can grasp the fraternal hand,
Where business cares, like flitting shadows pass,
And disappear above the social glass;
Where doubts and fears, that all our pleasures mar,
Float off in clouds of smoke from your cigar.

The purple and white ribbons of his Elks rosette blowing in the icy night air, Chester walked to his hotel, his step certain and with hardly a shiver. He had established a well-paying business, he had acquired boon companions, and he had joined a Lodge ideal for those who roam, which he believed might well be his destiny. In the afterglow of his initiation, there had been talk of the Klondike, with plans for a Lodge in Dawson City. And a new name was on the lips of mining men: Goldfield, in the direction of Death Valley.

That appealed. The mystery of the desert. The desert, where the boldest of dime novel heroes tempted fate and sought fortunes.

Three blocks away, a night clerk answered his knock and saw him into the opulent Hotel Washauer, its grand clock tower a symbol that the time of the West had come. Tipping his eyeshade, the man wished him a good night. Across the Washauer's interior Palm Court, illuminated even at the late hour by its turquoise, gold, and scarlet stained glass ceiling, a dozing attendant snapped to and pulled back the accordion grid of the elevator.

Chester paused, hesitated. He heard voices, but where? The Court's tables had been cleared. No shadows flitted its tiered, wrought-iron balconies.

The truth was they'd been back—the voices—for some time. But until now indistinct, murmuring, at their worst hampering his concentration.

That night in Baker City, Oregon—when Chester truly had reason to believe in himself—they spoke with increasing urgency. The racket of the engine transporting him back to Sumpter failed to drown them out, as did the full-throated roar of his assay furnace.

"There is something wrong with your head," they repeated, over and again.

Exposure to mercury vapor, he thought. He'd go easy on wet chemistry.

The voices persisted. Their vindictive message, as back East: "You do not deserve to live."

In the fall of 1904, Chester left Sumpter. Not for the Pacific Coast, there to book passage to the Yukon, nor south to Nevada and the railroad making tracks for Goldfield, but back to his aunt and uncle in Cambridgeport, Massachusetts. He was home in time for a glum Christmas, with a commitment to the McLean Asylum in the offing.

Nevertheless, that winter through he listened for the thump of the morning paper, and was up and downstairs to glean news of the West, hoping beyond hope that he could return.

The magic name at the outset of 1905 was *Goldfield,* a strike so fabulous that a newspaper there was reported to have printed an edition in ink mixed with gold dust. A classified ad prompted Chester to mail 10¢ for a copy of *Goldfield As I Saw It,* and he poured over the booklet's profiles of the camp's mines and their "dizzying avalanche of $$$" wrested from "the poor man's land of gold... a desert of gold."

Yet he despaired, for if he were to make his way there, would there be anything left for a poor man to claim or work?

Chester's tears, tears of failure and regret, stained an accumulation of clippings and accounts. Among them, an ode to Goldfield:

> Splendid, magnificent, Queen of the Camps,
> Mistress of countless Aladdin's lamps,
> Deity worshipped by kings and tramps,
> The lure she is of the West.

THE LURE SHE IS OF THE WEST

THEY DIDN'T FLOCK TO WESTERN NEVADA for their health, or for the quality of life, or the scenery, decried in the eastern press as "a mean ash dump landscape" stretching "from nowhere to nowhere. No portion of earth is more lacquered with paltry unimportant ugliness." As for Goldfield, the camp was a "spot of mange," and "a nest of unimportant ungodliness."

What mattered—invisible to killjoy journalists—were two sunken faults that intersected to create a magical, million square foot auriferous ellipse.

Clouds of alkali dust, whipped by howling winds, had blotted out the sun on the day that Harry Stimler, part Shoshone, and his no-account partner, Billy Marsh, were prospecting the vicinity. Their outfit was pitiful: "It consisted of an old lame black horse, an old black mule, a $10 wagon, a sack of flour, a part of a sack of beans, a side of bacon, and plenty of mustard and sorry looking baking powder." Near Rabbit Springs, Harry stooped, examined a rock. Silver-bearing, he first thought. He was mistaken. The rock was shot with gold, gold stunningly free of other minerals.

Jewelry ore! High-grade! The pair's Sandstorm claim was to bring in seven million dollars in seven months and be proclaimed the:

RICHEST GOLD DISCOVERY
MADE ANYWHERE
IN THE WORLD

In print and by word of mouth, the news spread. A rush was on.

Seasoned miners flocked from played-out mines in the Rockies. Tenderfeet found their way from the East. Would that Chester Pray had the strength to join them, but sadly and regrettably, he couldn't. So it is that this account—to relate what next happens in

Goldfield—must now for a chapter turn to the story of a like young man. His name was Frank Crampton, and he and Chester had much in common. Indeed, the day would come when their paths would cross and they'd share good times and bad in the desert West.

Like Chester, Frank was born to wealth, and like Chester, he was not one for social airs and strictures. Asked to leave an Ivy League college in his freshman year, he bolted the East, falling in with a pair of footloose miners. "Hard rock stiffs," they called themselves.

Frank Crampton knew something of mining. His uncle Francis A. Palmer, president of the Broadway Savings Bank—prominent philanthropist, pious churchman, etc.—had a sideline rounding up immigrants from Baltic states and shipping them to coal mines in Pennsylvania and Utah, or to any employer who'd cut him a check for cheap labor. How mortified he'd be if he knew Frank was on his way to Goldfield, his transport a "deluxe freight car." Frank relished the idea of his uncle wringing his hands and exclaiming, "Oh! A hobo and common laborer!"

With competing railroads yet to push through a connection, the final thirty miles into Goldfield was by mud wagon, a high-off-the ground, stop-at-nothing affair. As the sun set, a pinpoint of light twinkled out on the far side of the desert plain, and increased and increased in dimension and radiance.

Goldfield.

"See how she shines!" the driver called down.

Canvas flaps were raised, heads popped out, necks craned.

Ahead now, burros strayed and tents were scattered like dice. Shrill whistles sounded, signaling a shift change, afternoon to graveyard. Gallows frames loomed, their crown wheels whirring as cage after cage of miners were hauled to the surface, with more boarding to plunge into the earth, the candles grasped in their hands flickering as fireflies. The mud wagon veered to avoid men sacking dirt from the road, rich in gold dust. A Mr. Vermillion, a lawyer who'd abandoned writ for pickaxe, guarded a bathtub-sized hole that had yielded (he said) $100,000 in high-grade ore. Around the curve into Crook Avenue and then the length of Main Street, the way was strung with strand after strand of glittering electric lights and was lined with freshly-painted emporiums offering life's every amenity, from Spanish American war surplus at Shradsky's ("Our Pants are Always Down") to the latest from

Paris at the Bon-Ton Millinery. And under construction, with carpenters hammering and masons chiseling even at night: banks and trusts with massive vaults, a French steam laundry, and a Turkish bath.

Frank Crampton joined his fellow passengers in feverishly crying out: "Goldfield! Goldfield!"

The mud wagon pulled up at the Palace Livery. Disembarking passengers harkened to the commotion down the street—night trading at the Goldfield Mining Stock Exchange. Marveled a reporter: "Outside of the exchange, the stridulous, whooping, screeching, detonating voices that kept carrying the market up could be heard half a block away." They bought and sold shares in a desert wasteland that had become:

THE MARVEL OF THE WORLD

Richest gold ore ever produced
from lodes in quantity

Comparable only to the material heaven,
that "New Jerusalem" whose gates are jasper
and whose streets are gold

That night, Frank had a considerable choice as to where to hang his hat. He might have sprung $2 to $4 for a night at the Esmeralda or Brown Palace hotels. Or he might have opted for a $2 a week boarding tent. Come morning, he donned bib overalls and a resin-impregnated "hard boil" hat, and made the rounds of the mines, where he had little trouble signing on as a "nipper," the lad who carried fresh steel to the stiffs and carted off their odoriferous thunder jugs.

The next step up the mining ladder was a "mucker," assigned to shovel freshly blasted ore into an iron rail car and trundle it to a mine's hoist.

The powder smoke hanging in the air gave Frank headaches, but he lived with it as, before long, he was making a full $4 a day wrestling the ungainly "widow maker" drills that were at the time replacing hand-held bits and sledgehammers. Three hundred, then four hundred feet down, he and his fellow miners ran drifts—tunnels—in near darkness, paraffin candles their sole illumination. A *Goldfield News* article described a typical working. In contrast to the hullabaloo above ground, an eerie, grim world.

IN THE BOWELS OF THE EARTH

The air was more than oppressive. It was sepulchral. There was the odor of decaying wood, of stagnating waters of death, of desolation. Even the solace of the miner, the twinkling of rats' eyes out of the darkness, was refused, for rats will not remain in a mine when the walls creek and groan, where darksome depths echo with the falling of rock from untimbered roofs.

The striking of a boot upon an uncertain pillar may mean quick death by a crushing blow. But there is something to relieve the tension that fixes itself upon the mine. It is to be found in the dull glitter of the walls of the cavern, where millions, maybe more, await extraction.

Sweat and hazard, indeed, had their rewards. When a candle's flicker was mirrored by a glint of gold, miners pocketed choice specimens, and could make up to $100 a day fencing the booty to shady assayers. As Frank noted, his fellow stiffs were "honest and trustworthy, excepting in the matter of gold, where nature had put it in the ground." They subscribed to the notion: "Gold belongs to him what finds it first."

From time to time, then, there were nights when, scrubbed clean of rock dust, Frank and his friends could afford to dress up and play the swells, dining at the Louvre or the Idler. Or at the high-toned Palm Grill, there to order Pacific oysters, squab on toast, and baked Alaska. They'd wash the lot down with tumblers of French wine.

After dinner, Frank and his friends would join the crowd drawn to the intersection of Main and Crook, and on opposing corners, the Northern, Palace, Mohawk, and Hermitage saloons that in drink downed and money fleeced put all others to shame, not only in Goldfield but throughout the West. On a busy night— every night—patrons were six deep at the Northern's sixty-foot bar, with twelve bartenders dispensing over three hundred gallons of whiskey a day, whiskey alone. Dice clicked and roulette balls rattled; it was but a step or a stumble to matching wits with knights of the green cloth: Billy the Wheel, Sure-Shot Dave, the Short-Bit Kid, Crap-A-Jack, or Society Red.

Around the clock, Goldfield surged with miners, drummers, clerks and cooks. Builders and wreckers. Promoters and shysters and allied "members of the leech brigade." They were united all in the avid pursuit of *the jack*, the coin surely and deservedly theirs. And to this end, a woman in her mid-twenties, new to the camp, was to thread her way through the throng. Her fashionably-frizzled hair was peach-strawberry, her features near flawless. Well-drawn, sharp even. She turned heads—that swiveled away when shot with a gypsy-hazel stare. All the same, she from time to time nervously blinked and even trembled. In her Goldfield days, she was never to admit her name, her real name.

Call her Rosemary.

Down Main Street, past Myers, she entered Goldfield's *Redlight*. There is no knowing what she thought, or what she felt. There remains, though, an impression of the district by a visiting lady journalist, Bonnie Lanagan of the *Salt Lake Herald*.

SPOILER FOLK OF GOLDFIELD

Down the street, over puddles of seething alkali mud, away from the legitimate residence district, is the home of revelry and madness, where all the good yellow stuff is blown in, answering the lure of the painted ones. Take the first dance hall— that ugly black building with every window alight sending out strains of crazy dance music far along the narrow little streets.

Step inside the door. It's getting late now. The girls wear anything from chiffon to flannelette, and only ask for diamonds and brilliant hues. As the hours grow later, the air gets heavier and heavier. Everybody is a little sleepy and a little cross, and when they are not, are either hysterical or quarrelsome.

Here an ungainly prospector makes foolish love.

The women are most of a type, the kind who flock to the rich places of the world, where men have fought and wrested with the earth, men who are willing to throw away the precious yellow stuff for a studied glare from kohl-rimmed eyes, a fervent gleam set in cheeks flushed with rouge.

Come dawn, journalist Bonnie Lanagan departed Goldfield's Redlight to file her story. No-name Rosemary stayed, prostitution her jack, if not her natural-born calling. Preferring to both keep to herself and turn as many dollars as possible, she rented a street-fronting crib, an unpainted shack with barely enough room for a bed, chair, and a battered dresser. She hung her few clothes in a back alcove; from time to time it would serve as a waiting room when mining pards (partners) came her way, and the night was cold.

She plied her trade alongside neighbors Sal, Sadie, Sylvia, and Jessie. With every girl on her own, solicitation was hardly subtle. Wanting for business, Jessie would offer a preview, thrusting her legs out her window. A few cribs away, a night-blooming harlot warbled:

As through the mines I wind my way
Bobbin' 'round and 'round
I'll tell you what I have to say,
As I go bobbin' round.

Frank Crampton was acquainted with the camp's Redlight— who wasn't? It was four city blocks and expanding, with prostitutes flocking from near and far, their reputations often preceding them. Klondike Kitty, Porcupine Nellie, Goldtooth Bess, Swivel Bottom Sue. Dozens of women from camps on the decline in Alaska, Colorado, Arizona, and California. As a mining stiff was to enthuse, "Experienced, hard, bold-faced, strident harpies. Morals looser than ashes! I love 'em!"

Not that Frank was a regular. At the end of a shift—the graveyard the worst—he was frequently up for little more than a game of cribbage, learned as a child and taught to other miners.

Yet on occasion, parlor houses had their appeal. "Welcome to the Red Top (or the Oriental or the Den), a haven of solace; working girls for the working man!" a Madame would greet a fellow. Then, as a gray-thatched "Professor" rippled the ivories, she would pour the new arrival a glass, put him at ease, make introductions, and congratulate him when he selected "My best girl." Few gents would deny there was excitement in "getting your hat nailed to the ceiling," as a Goldfield expression went. As well there was an emptiness. Passions were simulated. When one's time was up and it was off down the hall, buttoning up, there were soft but undeniable sobs seeping through pasteboard walls. A whore's life was hard.

On his part, Frank longed for a real relationship, difficult to imagine in a camp fired by men, gold, and greed. For all its stuffiness, he missed the East's sweet conversation, the heartfelt touch of young woman's fair hand to a young man's cheek.

At the same time, Frank Crampton found the excitement of life underground wearing thin. Shift after shift, he was breaking his back, even risking his life to line the pockets of mine owners and promoters, specifically George Wingfield, an ex-cardsharp who had gambled on early showings of the Mohawk Mine, now the camp's principal producer.

Frank "tramped it" —quit. He invested what money he'd made in opening an assay office, which he promoted as an above-board operation, a Goldfield anomaly. Having off and on helped himself to samples, Frank was in a position to recognize—and reject—stolen ore. Even so, he had as much business as he could handle, a good portion from desert-rat prospectors ranging from the antic, garrulous Shorty Harris to a reserved, courtly Frenchman working the far side of Death Valley—Jean or John Lemoigne, he went by both. Lemoigne's showings were first class. Silver-lead, with traces of gold.

Yet, Frank wondered, could whatever Old John found be worth it? Worth the deprivation, isolation, loneliness?

Goldfield was lonely enough.

Frank put in long hours stoking his furnace and analyzing samples, and was to lament that his life had settled into "a deadly monotonous routine," despite all that glittered in the cupels of his furnace, or in the dubious frenzy down the street. He wasn't much of a drinker, and gambling never really had its appeal. Goldfield's packed bars stank of stale breath and spilt beer.

"It was a hell of a way to waste time," he recalled.

A night came when Frank, straying into the Redlight, turned down a street he had overlooked. At the late hour, a shadowy, quiet street, with a gent here and there stopping to converse with a girl at the window or the door of her crib. Girls invited Frank in, but when he preferred to while away the time—chat for a while— he was told to make way for serious sports. It was only the near-last girl—Rosemary—who gave him the time of day, though after repeated invitations, she too asked that he move on.

Rosemary—what was it about Rosemary? Frank later wrote, "I had no intention of ending it that way."

He'd turned away, but now turned back. Rosemary looked to him, expectantly. He mouthed, "Yes." She cocked her head. He stepped inside. She drew her window shade and locked the door. Wordlessly, without hesitation, she shed what little she was wearing. Frank was part stunned, part smitten by a whore's brittle hardness tempered by a supple grace.

Rosemary was, in fact, beautiful.

Frank felt an anticipation, a warmth, surge within him.

And he asked that she put her clothes back on.

One can only imagine her astonished "What?" followed by, "What did you say your name was?"

"I didn't. My name's Frank."

"Oh Frank, I bet you're a devil with a girl."

"I'd like to talk."

"Talk? Later, yes, we can talk. If there's time."

"I'd like to just talk. How much for an hour?"

"You're sure?"

"Yes."

"Then two dollars, the same as a lay."

Frank counted out change, Rosemary rolled her eyes, and the two... just talked. Of what, Frank never said, though it's doubtful there was any of the cliché "What's a good girl like you doing..." He was beyond that. (If anything, he'd have asked the same of himself.)

The conversation, hesitant at first, more likely turned to the strange desert world into which by desire or need they'd plunged. The woolliness of it all. By the end of an hour, Rosemary's wary eyes would have softened and may even have sparkled. "You can stay a little longer, that is if you'd like."

Frank did, then took his leave, to float—a little dazed, strangely elated—off into the desert night. As he was to look back, "Strange things have happened in Goldfield, but nothing like this."

As for Rosemary, there would have been a rap or two more on her window, but come 3 or 4 AM, with the customers fewer and drunker, she would have slipped into a coat (well-tailored and quite fashionable), closed up her crib, and hurried the two blocks to the bright lights (two Edisons, dangling on twisted cords) of Emmet's Walk-in Lunchwagon. The coffee was bitter but drinkable, the bacon and eggs not bad, and the company—other girls at this hour—listless to sullen to weepy to suicidal. Hardly a week went by without a Goldfield prostitute inhaling chloroform or swallowing carbolic acid.

Desperation. Dried tears. Resigned yawns. Then, the coming of a gray desert dawn.

Mine whistles signaled the beginning of the day shift, the end of the graveyard. The girls wove back to their cribs. Some were tolerant of the grime of stiffs just off shift, for they often offered the girls high-grade as a sweetener. Others sought sleep, be it fitful or in the oblivion of "hitting the bamboo" off in the dozen and more opium dens in Goldfield's Hop Fiend's Gulch.

Frank Crampton would be drawn back, night after night, to Rosemary's crib, never spending less than an hour and often considerably more. He routinely paid more than asked—double sometimes. She'd at first refuse, but in the end accept.

He was there just to talk, he decorously maintained later in his life. And who's to care if they were lovers? The point was friendship, passionate or not, in a hard-hearted camp. One would hesitate, and the other would finish the sentence. He knew that if she bit her lower lip, she was troubled. There was a limit, though. Try as he might, Frank could not persuade her to talk about herself or the circumstances that brought her to Goldfield. Or her real name. Only of necessity and reluctantly was she "Rosemary." Recalled Frank, "she wanted to be completely without any name, even an assumed name."

He believed he loved her.

Imagine then, on an October night, his surprise and shock when, softly whistling to himself, he passed Emmet's Walk-in Lunchwagon, picked up his pace, and looked to the sign lettered "Rosemary"—only it was gone, replaced by another's. A new girl had moved into the crib, and she knew only that Rosemary had a ticket north on the morning train.

Frank was crushed.

He puzzled: "None of the other girls knew anything either, although I suspected that one or two had some idea of where she might be headed; but whatever they knew couldn't be blasted out of them, so I gave up. There was nothing I could do; the girl was gone. I did not make any more visits to the line after that."

Low and blue, he lost himself in his work, or tried to. Fall gave way to bleak winter in a rough year for Goldfielders. Gloomed newspapers:

DEATH BECKONS

JOINS HIS MAKER

THAWS POWDER & BLOWN TO ETERNITY

PIANO PLAYER SHOOTS WIFE
& OVER HER BODY BLOWS OUT BRAINS

ENGINEER TAKES "LAST SIGNAL"

"Every camp," it was said in the West, "lasts long enough to have its winter of death."

In Goldfield that year it was a plague of "black pneumonia." First came the headache, then a pain in the side, then a gurgling in the lungs, then death, with corpses blotted and bluish. An out-of-camp paper reported "...the dead were piled in the streets; dropping at every corner." An exaggeration to be sure; nevertheless coroner's records blamed the malady for four out of every five fatalities.

Frank Crampton, for one, was stricken with fever, then delirium. Companions rushed him to a hospital in Oakland, where he could be looked after by an Aunt Matilda. On his release, she prevailed on him to regain his strength in the city on the Bay, and enjoy the December holidays.

A socialite of Eastern mien, the woman "just oozed tradition and formality." The two attended a round of luncheons and teas. To Frank, fluttery and dull occasions, until: "My heart stopped beating when Aunt Matilda introduced me to an attractive and beautifully gowned newcomer—the girl from the Goldfield crib,

'Mrs. Cosgrove.' The face of the girl went the color of wet ashes."

The two exchanged pleasantries—awkward, strained—and she all but fled, only to reappear the following week on the arm of her husband at a gala New Year's dance given by Aunt Matilda at the hilltop Claremont Hotel. On sight, Frank disliked the man— slickly handsome—even as his Aunt sang his praises and snagged him for an extended conversation. This gave Frank an opening. He asked that the girl put him on her card for a waltz, struck up a few minutes before midnight, in which...

But let Frank tell it:

> I held her tighter and she rested her arm on my shoulder a little heavier. Our hands held each other's more firmly and once in a while there was pressure from one to the other. Nothing more. There was no way to say what I had wanted to say, or what I had in my mind to ask. As we danced the old year ended, and the new year came; the past was gone.
>
> As the waltz ended, her arm slipped down my back, and she held me tight a moment, as I did her, and our hands pressed each other's hard. Then she put her hand on my arm as I escorted her from the floor, thanked her formally for the dance, and left her with her husband.

Seeking his aunt, Frank inquired of the girl he had found so "light and soft and graceful," which had Matilda sputtering, "Frank, don't talk about that woman, that floozy. Do you know what she did? When her husband was accused of embezzlement and was in disgrace, and about to be arrested, she left him. Left him! And her three children as well! Then she came back the minute she found her husband's accounts were set right, and that he had not stolen the money after all."

Of course he had, Frank realized, the swindling son-of-a-bitch. And he had Rosemary to thank for selling her body to bail him out, in large part with Frank's hard-earned money. Not that Frank resented it, not at all. Better to have loved and lost, than...

Fumed his Aunt Matilda, "Don't ever, ever mention her again."

Frank Crampton was to return to Goldfield, but only for a

few weeks, for he found the camp heavy with "memories that I preferred to forget." He'd instead try his hand at prospecting, seeking his fortune over the next desert range, and the one after that, off in the direction of Arizona and New Mexico, and then back and into Death Valley.

Wherever there was word or rumor of silver and gold.

CHESTER'S TROUBLE
IN CHICAGO

OFF IN CHICAGO, MR. WILLIAM ROSE'S DAY was not as he expected.

He awoke to the sight of snow and more snow; two days and the blizzard had yet to let up. He went back to sleep, or tried to. The phone rang and he was the only one to answer it, his wife Isabel having the week before decamped to nattering relatives in warmer climes. Padding downstairs, Rose thought he might just stay home rather than bundle up and fight his way to a slow day at his real estate office.

"Mr. Rose? Is that Mr. Rose? I have a person-to-person call from Boston. A Mr. Cram." That would be Henry Cram of the Bernstein company, a supplier for the electrification of the White City; Rose was a mover in that, and the two had kept in touch.

"I don't mean to trouble you, but it's about my nephew Chester..." Henry Cram began, and had to repeat himself, fighting a bad connection. It seemed that on New Year's day of 1905, the young man in question— "the strange boy," Cram called him—had headed West to seek work as an assayer, as he'd done a few years before. But he had taken ill in Chicago. Could Rose look in on him?

"Of course, I can. Be delighted. This very day."

Rose didn't begrudge the task; quite the contrary: he was always one to help a fellow out. He had a vague memory of Chester, then a lad of twelve, attending the Exposition with his aunt, Cram's wife—Julia, he recalled.

Over a fry of static, Cram shouted the address of a rooming house on Michigan Avenue. It wasn't far, though in a working class neighborhood. Rose dressed for the frigid day and, head down, rather enjoyed the brisk walk. (He fared better than the city's outbound trains—stalled in their yards, unable to get up steam.) The day, Rose felt, would have purpose, with simple goodness its reward.

The lady who answered his ring was aware of Chester, but unsure of his room.

A floor up, someone was strumming a banjo. Rose mounted the stairs and approached a half-open door. Inside, a fellow sat on a bed singing. Rose recalled the song as "popular, if trivial." He rapped.

"Might you direct me to a Mr. Chester Pray?"

"I am Chester Pray."

Relieved to see that Chester wasn't sickly, at least to appearances, Rose introduced himself as a acquaintance of Henry Cram, at which Chester flew into a wild-eyed frenzy that had Rose backing up, bumping the door.

"I am ill," Chester anguished, "Mercury! I suffer a severe case of mercurial poisoning."

"How..."

"Laboratory work," he blurted, "Assaying..."

As Chester carried on, less and less coherently, Rose had no idea as to the truth of the matter, but had the presence of mind to seize the young man's overcoat and scarf from the peg on which they'd been hung.

"Here, then," he interrupted, "we must have you examined by a medical man." He'd take him to Dr. Arthur M. Elliot, who he knew to have an interest in diseases of the mind.

By good fortune, Dr. Elliot was at his State Street office and had the balance of the morning free. He thoroughly examined Chester.

"Hold out your hands, if you will."

Chester did, all the while excitedly pleading his condition, as if he wanted to be mercury poisoned, as if it served some purpose. But the doctor detected no tremors, or foetor of the breath, or black deposits on or about the teeth. Though it was difficult to get a word in edgewise, he asked a few questions. Anything else the matter? Had life been hard on the young man? Elliot jotted:

> Mr. Pray hysterical –
> Highly excitable –
> Morbid introspection re health –
> Difficulty concentrating & answering questions –

Chester, suddenly crestfallen, murmured, "My head isn't like anybody else's I know. My head never feels right."

Expressing his sympathy, Dr. Elliot wrote a prescription for pills he knew to be all but worthless. But perhaps not: an illusory physic for a delusory condition. He advised Chester that he immediately return to his family, "where you'll benefit from the company and comfort of dear friends."

"I had friends out West. I made friends there. I've no friends in Boston."

"But you have your aunt and uncle," William Rose gently asserted, "And you may consider me your friend. I'd be honored. Might you join me for lunch?"

"I suppose. Yes."

Thanking Dr. Elliot, Rose took Chester by the arm. The two left.

Rubbing the condensation from his window, the doctor watched as they negotiated State Street's deepening drifts. He closed out Chester Pray's file with:

> Psycho neurasthenia, with a fixed idea of imaginative mercurial poisoning.

Presented a menu at St. Hubert's Grill, Chester's eyes darted from meat to fish to fowl, with questions as to potatoes, creamed spinach, and flannel dumplings, a house specialty. He ordered generously, and Rose looked on in amazement as he downed the meal with relish and asked about seconds. At the same time he chattered about the West that Dr. Elliot would have him forsake. The camp of Goldfield was increasingly in the news, and in the desert beyond there was uncharted territory to be explored, bonanzas to be claimed. As a case in point, Chester had clipped an article about the doings of a "Mysterious Scott."

GOLDFIELD CHEERS SCOTTY

> Scotty came to town, and everyone knew it. From seven in the evening to the wee sma' hours he literally made Rome howl. He finally wound up at the Palace, followed by hundreds of people. Two or three blocks were impassable in every direction. A crowd of 1500 shouted "Hit it up, Scotty!" and

"You're wild and wooly, but you're a dandy!" In
response, he waved and grinned and flashed a roll
of $20 gold pieces.

Why the adulation for a rumpled, big-bellied man on a long-
suffering mule? The answer was that Scotty was little different
than anyone in Goldfield or, for that matter, anyone tramping
the deserts of the West—except that off in Death Valley he had a
mine, a mysterious and fabulous secret mine.

The man that but a week before hadn't the price
of a grubstake could now vie with the great financiers
of the globe. His was not a vision—not a dream—
but gold in nuggets, large and small, and in such
abundance that the knowledge overwhelmed him.
"I'm going to hire John D. Rockefeller to shine
my shoes," he boasted. "Call me 'the Croesus of
Death Valley."

"If this Scotty can strike it rich," Chester smacked his hand
palm-down on the table, "anyone can. I can. I'm up on geology. I'm
an assayer."

"Sounds like the place for you."

Taken for a moment by the young man's enthusiasm, Rose
half wished he was thirty years younger and could get in on the
excitement. A curious, strange boy, he reflected. Vigorous, seemingly
intelligent, yet caught up in frenetic dreams, good and bad. He was not
of this world, or at least Rose's world—rational, mundane, plodding
even. Rose, on occasion, lamented his life, but then he would cheer
himself with the thought that he was an honest and good man, and
considerate. Considerate of others, and there for them.

Overnight, the storm moved on, with fitful flurries in its wake.

William Rose was in his office by nine to read that the *Chicago
Tribune's* meteorologist had pronounced the day before the worst
of the new century, with the temperature down to minus 18°.

Mid-morning, and young Pray was to put in a surprise
appearance. He felt better, he said, than he had in months. He
thanked Rose for his time and trouble.

"Not trouble. 'Caring' is the better word. And you can be
grateful to Dr. Elliot. His prescription..."

"I'm not one for pills; didn't take them. Anyway, I'm here to say goodbye. I've a ticket on the noon train."

"You do? Really? West on the Santa Fe?"

"No, to Albany, then Boston. I think that's best, as the doctor said."

For an awkward minute, Rose couldn't think of anything to say that would mean anything, then settled for: "I suppose it's best for the time being, Chester. I'd agree to that. But when you come back on through—I say "when," not "if" —you know who's good for lunch! And a good talk."

Chester smiled a wistful, melancholy smile. Rose stepped forward to shake his hand, and repeated, "For the time being."

Chester hoisted his suitcase, banjo, and a fitted wooden case, its contents clinking. "My chemicals," he explained. "I checked my furnace at the station."

As Chester turned and walked away to the elevator, his composure crumbled and, unseen to Rose, tears welled from his eyes.

William Rose called after him, "Be rooting for you, Chester!"

Chester pressed the brass button lettered "DOWN."

SCOTTY'S MINE

WOULD CHESTER PRAY YET BE ABLE to seek his fortune in the West? It appeared doubtful—though not impossible, considering what he'd overcome since his time in the McLain Asylum for the Insane. And if he ever did make it to Nevada and adjoining California, he could take heart in not being the only one with "a screw lose somewhere about him" (to quote his acquaintance, the Sheriff of Wadsworth). Odd or even outrageous behavior was widely tolerated, even admired, as a fact of life in a go-for-broke time in a mind-baking desert.

Consider, for instance, a larger-than-life character—at once engagingly flamboyant and slyly conniving—who at the time colored Chester's perception of the west, and to this day remains an icon of the era.

Death Valley Scotty.

A lash-batting ingénue is said to have cozied up to Scotty in a Goldfield saloon and nudged the conversation to his fabled mine, cooing, "Not that I'd have any interest in looking for it."

"Hell you wouldn't," the man in the Texas-peaked hat sneered, "It would be like hogs going after slop."

Many were the attempts to discover the source of Scotty's gold, and he went to great lengths to throw off anyone following him into the lunar landscape of Death Valley. He'd keep an eye to his mules' ears, for they'd twitch and point if trouble was near at hand. For middle distances, he favored twelve-power Goetz binoculars, and his thirty-three power, tripod-mounted French telescope could pick up movement on the heat-hazed horizon. He often traveled by night. It was not only cooler then, but under the cover of darkness he could, if pursued, lose his tracks in the shifting sands west of Stovepipe Wells. He maintained caches of water, grub, booze, and grain for his mules the length and breadth of the Valley. He kept his mules fat.

A 30-40 Winchester was slung from his saddle, as well as a sawed-off, ten-bore shotgun fitted with a pistol grip. And there was the "throw away" pistol tucked in his shirt.

A lot went into being the Burro Man or Scooting Scotty or the Mysterious Scott, as he was variously known. If he is to be believed, he carried a jar of nitroglycerin crystals—safely suspended in heavy olive oil—to blow up a trail behind him, rendering it impassable, or to cut a new trail up or down a canyon, often by blasting a dry waterfall. He explained, "Simply pour a little of the soup into the cracks at the top of the waterfall, stick a cap-and-fuse in the cracks, and touch it off. It would blow the whole mountain down."

Still, they would track him.

He bought two heavy steel bear traps, and come dusk one day he had reason to set them a half mile south of his camp.

The screams, as he told the tale, woke him. Midnight, and he had snared an Indian, who would die if Scotty didn't screw down the heavy springs clamping his heel. The man begged to be set free, for the sake of his wife, his children. Toying with his shotgun, Scotty interrogated him, and when he wasn't forthcoming, said he'd leave him for the coyotes. This failing to loosen his tongue, Scotty gathered greasewood and "lit a fire under him and strange as it may seem the Indian told everything," confessing that he was stalking the Mysterious Scott in the employ of two white men back down the trail. Scotty had a message for them: "File them sights off your six shooters or I'll ram them down your throats. Don't let me catch you following my trail into the mountains. I'm warning you. I'll take my own back trail, and you'll never live to tell the story."

Whatever the truth of this, there were those who braved his bluster. Or they may have been cagily allowed to trail Scotty to his lair. It made for good copy:

CLAIMS TO HAVE FOUND SCOTT'S CAMP!

In a narrow, rocky chasm, surrounded on every side but one by rugged mountains, so steep that the hardiest mountain climber would not undertake to scale them, in a spot almost inaccessible to anything but an airship, is the retreat of this twentieth century adventurer, this mysterious, mystifying, mountaineer millionaire, who from all accounts holds the key to a secret for which every ambitious prospector is searching—the hidden mystery of the hills, in which gold, shining gold lies patiently awaiting the coming of man.

Scotty called the place "Camp Hold Out." No structures. Rather, a level patch under an overhang in a Funeral Range chasm had been furnished with old mattresses, a steamer chair, and a bathtub, which Scotty boasted was large and porcelain, but in reality was small and tin, stolen from the played-out Confidence Mine. The hideaway's walls were hung with curled and yellowed photos of Buffalo Bill performers, movie stars, and prominent men of industry. Towels were filched from a Los Angeles hotel, and the silverware was courtesy of dining cars of the Erie Railroad, the Burlington, the Salt Lake, the Santa Fe, and the Southern Pacific. He loved trains. They'd moved the Wild West show, and when he was fired for showing up late, he'd worked trains for profit as he'd drifted to Death Valley.

In Wells, Nevada, he and his friend Katie had peddled milk and doughnuts to carloads of emigrants. Scotty recalled, "Sometimes when our business at the train was slack, Katie would let out a couple of war-whoops to make the passengers stick their heads out the windows to see what was going on. While they was looking at her, I'd come along with a little rattan stick and knock their hats off. Then the train would pull out. They was cheap hats, but I could peddle them to people on the next train for two bits apiece."

Lolling in the shade of Camp Hold Out, Scotty regaled his "aides"—Paiute Jack Brody and Bill Key—with such stories, real or imagined. When times were good, provisions included cured hams, fancy French canned goods, caviar, after-dinner mints, and liquor. "Drunk half the time," he'd allow. "Clarifies my thoughts."

And that mine of his?

He'd tell privileged visitors, "Over yon" or "Yonder there." Yet the area showed little signs of mineralization. The closest actual mine was several miles east—the Desert Hound, an enterprise of an up-and-coming Nevada promoter named Jack Salsberry. And this, indeed, could have been a source of Scotty's gold. Rumor at the time alleged that Scotty had an arraignment to show off and peddle a quantity of Jack Salsberry's ore.

Whatever the source of his gold, Scotty boasted a haul of $80,000 in 1904 and up in Goldfield sought the spotlight, even as prominent mine owner Alva Myers publicly accused him of fencing stolen Goldfield ore, which Scotty was to brazenly allow *might well be the case*: "Of course, most people thought I had a rich mine. There was some said I was a high-grader, a feller who steals from a mine. Maybe he works in the mine; maybe he's in cahoots with somebody who works there. Some said I just enjoyed fooling the public. I've been called a liar, a genius liar, a cal-cu-lat-ing liar, a scheming liar, and a damn liar."

In search of innocents to bamboozle and fleece, Scotty was to work the California railroad towns of Dagget and Barstow, where he made a point of lugging about a carpet bag bound with dog chains and packed with ore, he confided, from his secret mine. No one bought it. So it was on to the City of Riverside to make a show of depositing the carpet bag in a bank vault and brag about how he'd presently be on his way east: "And I ain't going there on the cheap, either. I'm going ter take a special train and break all records. Say! them hoboes along the track will climb a tree when they see me coming, fur I'll make more wind than a cyclone. None of yer sixty-mile-an-hour gait fur me. I'm going to open her to the limit when I start, break off the throttle and draw fires to ease her when I see the lights of Chicago."

The dime-novel rant was not without calculation. The Scott had in mind a grandstand play that would net him the fame and fortune he believed he deserved. He'd indeed charter a train—the "Coyote Special." The snickering yokels in Dagget and Barstow could eat his dust; to hell with carping Goldfielders. What's more, at the end of what proved to be a record-breaking run,[3] he would have himself a gold-plated opportunity to cage eastern capital. It was there, spread before him, as he was ushered onto the gallery of the New York Curb Exchange. A broker looked up and called out, "Hey, you King Opulence of the blooming West!" Trading halted; all cheered.

Scotty sought and worked moneyed investors. In New York, he gained the confidence of Julian Gerard, vice president of the Knickerbocker Trust Company. In Chicago, his folksy flamboyance beguiled insurance executive Albert M. Johnson.

Cash in hand, it was back to Death Valley, to regale his sidekicks as to how the four buckles on his high-topped boots stood for his courtship of—and disdain for— "Eastern Parlor Plungers":

---

[3] Los Angeles to Chicago in 44 hours and 54 minutes. "Once we went around a curve so fast it tore a stove loose and swung it cross the diner. When you did catch a mouthful—best of everything. Champagne and caviar and patty de fooey grass."

First:	Ketch 'em.
Second:	Skin 'em.
Third:	Soak 'em all.
Fourth:	Keep out of jail.

He looked down on anyone so venal and stupid as to be suckered by him. He found them tiresome, particularly when they dogged him as to the whereabouts and viability of his mine. They'd want to see it for themselves, or worse yet, dispatch a knowledgeable expert. Scotty put them off as best he could. When "Would I lie to you?" no longer sufficed, he played up the risks of venturing into Death Valley: savage Indians, ruthless desperados, and (as he wrote the Knickerbocker Trust's Julian Gerard) "Hot, great God! Got to the lower end of the valley—liked to die."

Julian Gerard persisted—smelled a rat even—to the extent that he hired a man to trail Scotty with bloodhounds. Getting wind of this, Scotty obtained a jar of cyanide of potassium in Dagget, and headed for a waterhole, possibly Garlic Springs. Where, sure enough, setting up his French telescope, he sighted the hounds, followed at a distance by a lone figure. He dumped the cyanide in the spring and scrawled a sign:

THIS WATER IS POISON

The dogs loped up, couldn't read, and died.

Ultimately, threatened with a withdrawal of funding, Scotty had little choice but to reluctantly agree to guide a party to his mine. In February of 1906, the following assembled in Barstow:

Walter Scott.

Warner Scott, his older brother, new to Scotty's show.

Bill Key, a Scotty aide. Kept a pet rattlesnake; hailed from Stinking Water Creek, Nebraska.

Piute Jack Brody, "Scotty's Indian." Of questionable repute.

Daniel E. Owen, respected mining engineer looking after the interests of Julian Gerard and-or a New Hampshire mining promoter by the name of –

Azariah Y. Pearl. Had invented an auger that would drill square holes (he claimed). Suspected Scotty's mine was the classic "hole in the ground owned by a liar."

A "Dr. Jones." Incognito, Scotty backer Albert M. Johnson, looking after his interest in the mine.

A.W. DeLyle St. Clair, his role as suspicious as his name. Likely a spy for a further investor.

The party wended its way north. Not long and Scotty pointed out the graves of two men murdered and found dead. "It happens." On the alert, he scanned the terrain with his binoculars and at night glanced edgily into the darkness beyond the reach of their campfire. He'd been shot three times, he recounted, once on this very route: "Z-z-zip, I heard the bullet sing, and I got it in the thigh. Packed the wound with salt; regretted I wuz out of whiskey. I started for Barstow, a hundred and thirty-three miles away." The easterners were impressed by this, even a little scared, but not so much that they'd turn back.

Two days out, and mining engineer Daniel Owen didn't feel so well. Nervous and overweight, it didn't help that alkali water had somehow found its way into his canteen (though no one else's). He had to be helped from his horse and tied to the seat of the lead wagon.

It wouldn't be long before he'd be begging to turn back, or so Scotty supposed.

They camped at Lone Willow springs, close by Wingate Pass.

Come morning, Daniel Owen was weakened and miserable, but still game to ride on. This prompted Scotty to dispatch aides Bill Key and Jack Brody to "Scout ahead for danger." For all to hear, he added, "Outlaws might try to prevent the party from reaching the mine."

Once out of sight, the two hastened to an escarpment overlooking Wingate Pass, there to construct five waist-high stone redoubts (an extra three for bluff), and check their rifles. They then bided their time, comforted by a canteen Brody had filled with whiskey. It was hot, they were thirsty, and by the time Scotty's caravan was in range, Piute Jack was so drunk he'd have a hard time hitting a barn door. Who cared? The aim was to frighten the easterners off. If need be for effect, they'd drop a mule in the traces of the lead wagon.

Come late afternoon, the wagon driven by Warner Scott, the ailing Daniel Owen at his side, was first into the pass. Scotty and the rest rode close behind.

Shots rang out.

Mining engineer Owen swore it was Scotty who fired first, as a signal. Scotty insisted that that the ambushers fired first, and taking cover, he had heroically returned fire for a good ten minutes. Stagy, harmless gunplay it would seem, until a bullet hit Warner in the groin, inflicting, said Pearl, "the most painful wound a man can receive." Screaming in agony, Warner doubled over, cause for Scotty to jump to his feet and call out, "Stop firing you goddamned fool, you have hit Warner!"

That ended the shooting—and tipped Scotty's hand. He'd have a hard time talking his way out of this one.

The ambushers faded into the falling night. With thirty-seven stitches, "Dr. Jones" (incognito Albert Johnson) sewed up Warner as best as he could, and the next morning the duped and shaken party cleared out supplies to make space in a wagon for Warner and were on their way back to Barstow.

Once there, knowing no shame, Scotty telegraphed Los Angeles newspapers:

> **AMBUSHED US IN WINDY GAP STOP ONE
> SHOT FIRED AT MY HEAD STOP MISSED
> AND STRUCK WARNER IN THE HIP**

For a day or so, the press was to play up his bravery, but then, on the word of others in the Battle of Wingate Pass, abruptly changed its tune. The *Los Angeles Evening News* asked,

> What is the truth about this desert freak? He has ceased to be a joke. People are getting shot and action must be taken.
>
> Scott, his gang of desert outlaws, his fellow conspirators, his touts and boomers, after a career of unexampled audacity of fraud and bloodshed, are in need of rounding up by the law. Scott is a public nuisance and deserves to be suppressed on general principles.

Action, indeed, was taken by San Bernardino County Sheriff John C. Ralphs. Citing a damning statement by the enigmatic A.W. de Lyle St. Clair (No fury like a con man conned?), Ralphs charged

Scotty with faking an ambush in order to frighten his party into turning tail. Moreover, Scotty was alleged to have wanted mining engineer Daniel Owen shot dead, so that he might lay his hands on Owen's telegraphic code book and boost his mine with fake telegrams to Julian Gerard and God knows what other eastern investors. No matter that the last buckle on his boot told him "Stay out of jail," a warrant was sworn for his arrest and he was presently behind bars, to be decried as the DESERT VULTURE and THE DEATH VALLEY HUMBUG.

PSEUDO MINER AND ALL AROUND FAKER STANDS EXPOSED

From the Los Angeles Evening News.

The court case against Scotty was airtight, and that should have been it for the scheming, lying, even murderous Scotty.

But it wasn't.

His lawyer pointed out that, outrageous or not, the Battle of Wingate Pass had not taken place in Sheriff Ralph's San Bernardino County, but four hundred and forty yards over the line into Inyo County—where authorities, jaded as to desert chicanery, were reluctant to lay out taxpayer money for further prosecution.[4]

---

[4] Years later, Scotty confessed to, while out on bail, moving survey markers in the vicinity of Wingate Pass six miles south, creating the false impression that the ambush took place in Inyo rather than San Bernardino county.

Scotty was free. Julian Gerard, Azariah Y. Pearl, and Albert M. Johnson were out their investment. Scotty was unrepentant; he, in fact, was to complain, "These millionaires make too much trouble for you, hang onto you, and every time they see you they want to tell you about how they lost their money, and wasn't it awful, etc."

If you were new to the game, though, he'd be your man— boasting of clandestine ore shipments, flashing a fresh roll of hundred dollar bills (in reality, "upholstered" with ones). Not without cause did he proclaim, with a nod to his days with Buffalo Bill, "I'm a one man circus. The world is the audience. Death Valley is the arena, and I'm the ringmaster, performers, and men-ag-e-re."

O BE JOYFUL!

DEATH VALLEY SCOTTY'S FLAMBOYANCE was to elbow aside a number of players in life's circus in the desert in the early twentieth century. Next to nothing is known, for instance, of "Dot Leedle German Band," a seven-member troupe that walked from mining camp to mining camp in northern and central Nevada.

Its doubtful that they ever made it south to Goldfield. Now the largest settlement in the state, the camp would have been intimidating. Its population of 24,000 had a choice of popular entertainments. Satin-suited Lew Dockstader and his Minstrels played the Ross-Holley Theater; comedian Nat Goodwin laid them in the aisles at the 1,200-seat Hippodrome. And there was the draw of the five-hundred girls working the Redlight.

Goldfield was not for Dot Leedle German Band. Better that they scatter jackrabbits with a trumpet call as they approached a remote settlement, where they'd gather a knot of miners and their women appreciative of Scottishes and polkas. They'd coax a smile or two from worn faces and encourage some tentative steps and then whirls. Dust would spiral skyward, a sign: "The band's playing. We're dancing. We amount to something!"

In the flyspeck camp of Olinghouse up in the Pah-Rah Range, Dot Leedle German Band may well have cheered a black-bearded young man whose eastern aunt had taught him to dance. As well, he sang and could play the banjo.

His life, as theirs, was uncelebrated.

Chester Pray, now in his twenty-fourth year, was back out West, though no records explain the circumstances that drew him to Olinghouse. He'd disembarked a train in Wadsworth, Nevada, two stops short of Reno, and paid 75¢ for the stage to the camp's Gouge Eye saloon, where in an adjacent shack he'd set up shop as an assayer. The proximity was beneficial. Chester would get the business of prospectors drawn to drink, and barkeep Dan would benefit if a showing was good and a celebration in order.

When business was slow, Chester prospected nearby hills and ranges, and he likely staked a number of claims, but failed to record them. Exceptions were the Tohoqua #1 and #2 (from the Paiute to-ha-kum, "large white rabbit"). He filed on these in Churchill County's courthouse, only a year later to sell them for a dollar and unnamed goods in kind. One of these may have been a Colt 38 automatic, which was thereafter in ready reach of Chester's right hand, even as gunplay was falling from favor. He practiced on tin cans and became a good shot.

All considered, his life was reasonably settled, if uneventful, with his demons and their poisonous voices at bay.

An item in the *Reno Gazette*, available in Olinghouse, caught Chester's eye: The government would be giving a go-ahead to anyone interested in prospecting the Walker Lake Indian Reservation, halfway between Olinghouse and Goldfield. The territory would soon be chockablock with treasure seekers, men anxiously and in great need of having their ore assayed. Lacking only the means to haul his furnace, Chester sought out W.T. Golding, sheriff of neighboring Wadsworth, who'd been acquainted with Chester for going on two years and was to remark, "Well, I thought there was a screw lose somewhere about him."

Golding recalled his conversation with Chester:

He says, 'Ain't you got a team?'
I says, 'Yes.'
He says, 'I will go down and look at it.'
'All right.'
He went down with me and looked at it, and he says, 'What will you take for it?'
I says, 'I don't care about selling them, I need them.'
He says, 'I will give you two hundred and fifty dollars for them.'
I says, 'You can have them.'

He'd certainly say that, considering that the team consisted of five Indian-bred ponies, one an outlaw, worth maybe $15 or $20 a head, with $20 thrown in for the wagon. As Sheriff Golding was to reflect, "One thing and another, and people called him a damn fool."

"Sometimes Chester would have...a kind of erratic mood on him," Olinghouse miner Jed Thomas was to add, "He was a peculiar acting man. Defective in some way, but we couldn't tell how."

"Yes, the way he talked at times, it did not seem to me that the man was rational, in his right mind, at times," the sheriff was to conclude. "A little bit off his base. Did good work assaying, though. Very good. And he was a good rider."

Chester and an Indian friend, Willie O'Hare, readied the team and secured his assayer's furnace in the wagon. They rode south, with Chester leading the way on the best of the ponies. Sheriff Golding had to have chuckled; he had $50 in his pocket with the promise of a tidy $200 more due in thirty days.

In October of 1906, the Federal government threw open the Walker Lake reservation. The lawless camp of Dutch Creek was hammered up, with citizens reportedly ducking in and out of back doors, lest they be cut down by stray bullets. And there was a *serious* problem. Chester saw it coming in the samples he assayed. The values weren't there.

Further, there was the personal matter of a visit by a man from Reno retained by Sheriff J.T. Golding "to hunt Chester up," seeing as he had neglected to forward the balance due for the lawman's ponies and wagon. Short on funds, Chester had no recourse but to write his mother in Cambridgeport, asking that she cover the debt. She did, apologizing in a letter to Golding, "My son is very forgetful."

Or a little larcenous? And not very bright, at least in the case at hand. Not only was stealing horses or ponies a hanging offense, they were the sheriff's ponies.

Chester and the Indian Willie O'Hare rode on.

To Goldfield.

But Goldfield was not for them, Chester decided after a few days' stay. The camp's mines had been consolidated in the hands of a hard-nose, ruthless syndicate, or so the working stiffs in the bars grumbled. As for assaying, upwards of fifty offices glutted the market. And if Chester had patronized the Redlight, he would have found the girls—even if chirpy in their come-ons—terribly morose, with cyanide and iodine now edging chloroform and carbolic acid as means of taking their lives. Goldfield crowded in on him, had him thinking there were people who didn't give a damn what happened to him. Or anyone.

In any event, there was a new excitement: Rhyolite, on the brink of Death Valley.

Chester and Willie joined a rush south from Goldfield that raised "a string of dust a hundred miles long." Men on donkeys, men with wagons like Chester's and Willie's, men packed in motor car stages. "Chugs" they were called. The most popular were four-cylinder, fifty-horsepower, seven-passenger Pope Toledos. And there were rival Appersons, Columbians, Pierce Arrows, and Thomas Flyers. They were equipped with telephones. In the event of a snapped axle or one too many flats, a driver could shimmy up to the nearest pole to the Goldfield-Rhyolite line and summon help. Drivers delighted in scattering the lesser heeled—those taking "the ankle express"—with a "toot, toot, chug, chug, and a terrible horn blast like Gideon's trumpet."

At the desert cow town of Beatty, the road angled west and made for a gap between two sere gray hills. Beyond, Chester and Willie plunged into a tumult described in the first issue of the *Rhyolite Herald*:

IN THE VERY HEART
OF THE BIG MINES

Location Favorable to Make
Rhyolite the Metropolis
of Southern Nevada

One does not need an ear trumpet to hear, nor a field glass to see that he is in the heart of the mines when he is in the embryonic city of Rhyolite. The mines are here, right at our very doors, where we can see them and watch their development. They are so close that we witness a continual bombardment as round after round of giant powder explodes, throwing rock and earth into the air while the noise of the shots fill the canon with a deep roar which echoes and reechoes against the hills that rise majestically on three sides.

Past where a stone-block railroad station was rising from the sagebrush, Chester turned onto Golden Street and was struck with the feeling that this was the place for him—a camp charged with go-for-broke excitement, a camp where his odd behavior wouldn't raise an eyebrow. There were looser canons. Self-appointed bad man Diamondfield Jack Davis roared around the camp in his Reo, seeing how many jack rabbits he could pick off in ten minutes. Tiring of that, Diamondfield got drunk and, swaggering through the camp, shouted, "All you this and thats, stick your heads out and I'll shoot 'em off."

Vexed, his dinner interrupted, Deputy Sheriff J.R. McDonald rounded the corner: "Gimme your gun, Jack."

"Don't come any nearer, Mac. I'll kill you sure as hell."

Mac stopped and reached not for his gun, but Jack's, and took it away from him.

"No imagination, that MacDonald," a bystander commented, "A brave fool."

Or perhaps Mac saw Diamondfield Jack Davis for what he was. Puff and powder and no shot, at least at this point in his career.

Chester's Indian, Willie O'Hare, didn't care for cacophonous Rhyolite and within a week was on his way back home to the Pah-Rahs.

No matter, Chester had a new friend and potential partner: self-proclaimed "poet-prospector" Clarence E. Eddy, a huge, lopsided fellow with shore bird-slicked hair. His head was customarily tilted to the side, as if to clear an imaginary doorway. He wore a pocket watch pinned to his lapel, important in meeting deadlines as he dashed off poems and stories for Rhyolite's papers—the camp soon had three.

"Ten minutes and a dollar, and you'll have yourself a poem," he would promise. In the fashion of the day, his writing was overdrawn and often florid (as was he, described as "soft and bleached"). But not always. It cheered him to reside in a camp where, unabashedly...

> The saloon and the gambling table and the
> red light were far more prominent factors than the
> church, the school, and the home.

Clarence Eddy had an ear for:

> The siren voice of sin,
>   With her tilting violin.

Clarence Eddy and Chester Pray, two odd ducks, hit it off. They patronized the Redlight and applauded the debut of the eight-piece band installed as the symphony-in-residence at the Arcade Opera House. Together, they batted about the idea of prospecting to the west, and to that end Chester and "the Big Man" —as Clarence was known—struck up an acquaintance with the town's four-foot-ten "Short Man," prospector Shorty Harris.

A gabby braggart with a bushy moustache and big ears, Shorty told all who asked, and many who didn't, just who they could thank for putting Rhyolite on the map. It was, no surprise, Shorty. While chasing a burro, he'd spied an unusual blue-green rock that on closer inspection glistened with gold, this prompting him to whoop to his partner, "Hellfire Eddie, we've struck the richest jackpot this side of the Klondike!"

This was to prompt an extended bender up in Goldfield, with Shorty hazy as to the details, other than that at one point he quaffed Mumm's from a prostitute's slipper. Sobering up, he discovered he'd sold off his interest in the claim and had blown the sum treating one and all to celebratory rounds.

Chester and Clarence wished they'd been in Shorty's shoes and regretted they'd missed out on the initial big money as stocks were floated and shafts sunk. But they managed. Clarence clattered away at his typewriter and Chester picked up some assay work, supplemented by remittances from his mother or Aunt Julia.

They drank the camp's whiskey of choice, *O Be Joyful!*

And they dreamed.

The next big strike... It could be theirs.

So it was that early on a November morning they and four heavily-loaded burros plodded down Golden Street, accompanied by two additional burros in the service of C.J. Back, a local photographer looking to take and sell postcards of desert prospectors.

For the vista before them, Clarence invoked:

> O, mighty and majestic
> > Western land!
> O, mountains and plains,
> > vast and...

He trailed off. The plain they struck out across was vast... and drab. The poet-prospector took another tack:

Some from the east, and some
  Were born in the boundless west.
And some were wayward sons,
  Who left a happy home,
Seeking for gold in the wide world cold,
  They roam and roam and roam.

Where the party roamed is a matter of speculation. The obvious route was across the Rhyolite plain to the Funeral Mountains, then over Daylight Pass and down into Death Valley. Yet because the track was well traveled—with grading and a telephone line underway—the chance of a fresh discovery was near nil. It is more likely that, bearing to the northwest, the trio wended their way across the Funerals via Titus, Tule Springs, or Lost Canyon.

The day was chilly, and as afternoon shadows engulfed their route, the mercury fell, at that time of year plunging 40° or more to a low below freezing. Anxious to proceed with their adventure, they well may have stumbled on in the moonlight, their goal the crest of their chosen pass.

Come dawn, they gazed from their campsite into a yawning abyss. Clarence tried out:

In Death Valley, vast and lone...
Or should it be?
In the silent land of sage and sand...
Or what about?
In the abode of the horned toad...

The going that day was hard on knees and toes: a long, mile deep descent to the Valley to a campsite at Surveyor's Well, a four-inch pipe marked by a splintered barrel.

The next day C.J. Back managed a pretty good image of Chester with his Poca camera, its negatives ideal for contact-printing postcards. A year or so ago, film wasn't sensitive enough to freeze movement, but now it was, with shutter speeds of as much as 1/60th of a second possible. A burro-prodding switch in his right hand, Chester strides easily and purposefully along, for all the world a seasoned prospector *(see page 136, plate 22)*. His high-top boots forestall sand in the socks; a jacket warms him against the cool, even cold weather; the brim of his felt hat is jauntily rolled. The burros are tidily packed, with gear and food in readily accessible crates.

In and out of clumps of mesquite and across drifting sands, they crossed to mid-Valley Ruiz Well, then continued on to the "hyperglypics"[5] at the base of the northern Panamint Mountains. Penetrating the range, they found Leaning Rock Canyon eerily scattered with the bleached skulls of bighorn sheep. Clarence thought this could be some kind of "elephant's graveyard," except for sheep. Cottonwood Canyon was friendlier; they camped and rested in its several lush oases.

A canyon could be wide and easy going, or choked with rock falls and dry waterfalls, leaving the prospectors with no choice but to arduously climb out and drop back in. Over the next two weeks, their routine would be to work their way up one canyon, then descend the next, with deeply cut, exposed walls offering a cross-section of the range's geology. Each with his glass would examine a rock here, another there—most worthless, a few to be checked with Chester's pocket assay kit.

From time to time they encountered prospects where someone had holed a dozen feet into the country rock, found nothing, and moved on.

They spent some time in Marble Canyon and its tributaries, their presence documented by C.J. Back *(see page 130, plate 13)*. There were a number of good showings in the canyon's upper reaches, but unfortunately they had been staked and claimed with notices tucked in tobacco cans. Many were in the hand of legendary Death Valley prospector John Lemoigne. They dated to the 1890s, a few to the 1880s.

As Chester and Clarence searched and camped, it couldn't have helped but sink in that, despite their wild and rugged aspect, the northern Panamints had been thoroughly explored by prospectors past. By the light of their campfire, Clarence ruminated:

> For somehow it seems in the silent night
> When I hear the coyote's doleful cry,

---

[5] Native American petroglyphs (as they were known) were created by chipping away a whitish rock's thin coating of brown-black "desert varnish." In the northern Panamints, they depict human stick figures, god-like apparitions, and spirited bighorn sheep.

I think of the souls that have taken flight,
    The demon souls of the days gone by.

Jewelry rock was to elude the party, as was ore in any form.

But perhaps,

    In place of a substance a shadow
      Is better than nothing at all.

THE PROSPECTOR'S SECRET

U P AN UNNAMED, SERPENTINE CANYON, the old Frenchman awaited Chester, Clarence, and their photographer. He'd heard them coming—their voices, the echoing clop of their burros.

John Lemoigne was tall; his beard was bristly and graying; he wore a dust-streaked long black coat. As the sole white resident of the northern Panamints, he graciously welcomed the little party, and with a bow and sweep of his hand, ushered them a hundred yards up a draw to his eight-by-ten foot shack—sheep skull over the door, walls and roof a rusted patchwork of flattened five-gallon cans. Inside, he'd a broken-spring bed, but a decent stove. Though not one for worldly possessions, John was a good cook—he had a vegetable plot, kept chickens—and good company, a genteel godfather for all who would prospect Death Valley, as he had for going on twenty-four years.

Veteran prospector Shorty Harris often just happened to find himself up John's canyon in time for dinner, as did Frank Crampton, disheartened in Goldfield love but not in the quest for desert gold. Frank tells of whiling away a few days swapping stories and quietly reading. John had a shelf stocked with classics in French, German, and English. He would dust them daily. The works of Dumas, father and son, were favorites. *The Count of Monte Cristo* was dog-eared, particularly the part where protagonist Edmond Dantes discovers a vast treasure secreted in a wondrous cave on a desert isle.

A prospector's dream.

Chester quite liked John, and over the evening's meal was curious as to his past, how a young man schooled in Paris, London, and Heidelberg, had been drawn to this far corner of the desert. At once pleased to be asked and rueful as to what he would relate, the old prospector began, "There was a time when I wasn't John, but rather Jean Francois. And in Lamongen, a tiny village a day from Paris, the postman delivered a letter..."

The letter was penned by Isidore Daunet, a family friend

("though I was not myself of his acquaintance"), and he enclosed funds providing Jean Francois de Lamongen, if he chose, passage to San Francisco. Daunet, it appears, had discovered a surface deposit of borax, a mineral in demand as a cleanser. Its cotton-like balls were scattered across the floor of a certain Death's Valley, aptly named, for it was the "vallee la plus chaude, ce cote de l'enfer," the "hottest valley this side of hell." Harvesting the borax, Daunet explained, was easy, but refining it was not, with his best efforts degraded by impurities and all but worthless.

As a recently graduated mining engineer, could Jean Francois be of help?

So it was that Jean Francois, at the age of twenty-six, sailed to San Francisco, where his spirits rose as he took a cable car to his benefactor's second-floor Post Street rooms. He rang the bell and then knocked.

No response.

He left, to come back later—and learn from a tenant in the building that on the morning of May 28, 1884, Isidore Daunet had climbed his stair one last time. He'd wrapped a white kerchief around his head. He'd sat facing a mirror, cocked a pistol, and put a bullet through his head.

Jean Francois was stunned, though not bereft; after all, he'd not met the man. Puzzling what to do, it's likely that he sought out Daunet's recent bride and now widow, Clotilde. If so, he would have gotten an earful of their life in Death Valley.

Heat and aridity had chapped her complexion and splintered the furniture she'd had packed in. Eggs simultaneously rotted and roasted; flour bred worms in less than a week. Come summer, temperatures well over 120° prevented her husband's harvested borax from crystallizing. Men went berserk; a Chinaman who had strayed from camp was discovered by an Indian to be "performing all sorts of strange tricks, to the infinite delight of the Indian, who thought he had found a prize clown."

Misery begat misery.

Isidore Daunet had little choice but to close down his works. With Clotilde, he retreated to San Francisco, and there Clotilde announced her intent to divorce him.

"The shock to his nerves when the papers were served was too much for him." Old John paused to reflect, "A good man betrayed. In love, in life."

Whether that night or the following day, Chester Pray couldn't help but ask, "But you didn't leave, go home?"

"I'd no money. And the borax was still there..."

Accordingly, Jean Francois de Lamongen made his way by train to the railroad junction town of Mojave, then set out on a long and perilous trek to Daunet's Works, where he camped, sampled the borax, and saw no hope for the now-bankrupt enterprise.

Yet in the stark ranges to the east and west of Death Valley, he sensed a promise. Educated in the subtleties of geology, he perceived contacts between strata and colorations that could signal fissures of lead and copper, even silver and gold.

He stayed on—and came to love life in the desert as no one before, and few since. He'd return home, he vowed, only when he had made enough money to banquet the entire French army.

The aristocratic-sounding Jean Francois de Lamongen became Jean Lemoigne, then John or Old John. His early claims were christened the Robespierre and Lafayette, with his later claims the Washington, Independence, and Uncle Sam. He struck up friendships with bands of Shoshones harvesting pine-nuts in the Panamint Mountains and mesquite beans down on the Valley floor. Six miles up a narrow canyon, they showed him the black silver-lead outcropping they mined to cast bullets for their muzzle-loaders, and they didn't mind if he set up housekeeping and filed on the property.

Entertaining Chester, Clarence, and C.J. Back, Old John served up formidable pots of coffee. He confided, "It is very simple. You put in a very little water and a great deal of coffee. And then you let it boil and boil. And then boil some more. That is the secret."

Old John had another secret. It had to do with his mine up the draw, which he called his "bank." He trenched its silver-lead lode by hand, adverse to dynamite or any sort of machinery. He took only what he needed to survive, telling visitors he "didn't want to overdraw the bank."

And in this lay a secret tacitly shared by prospectors Old John, Shorty Harris, and all but the most ingenuous. The secret had to do with geology. Conventional wisdom had it that *mineral value increased with depth*, this conjuring a vision of fingers of ore reaching upward from a mother lode. Few questioned the assumption. They looked to Virginia City, with its thousand-foot shafts accessing high-grade ore. And there was Goldfield. Though it was too early to say for sure—the camp's shafts were no more than five or six hundred feet deep—Goldfield gave credence to the theory: *the deeper, the richer.*

That was all fine and good, but for prospectors in the Funerals and Panamints, high-grade surface showings, more often than not, petered out a few feet down.

Old John knew this.

He took care not to "overdraw the bank" because his bank wasn't much of a bank. The story went that he once turned down a thirty thousand buyout, ostensibly because he was offered a check, not cash. A more reasonable explanation would be that, honest soul that he was, he would as soon not sucker a speculator with a bum mine.

Shorty Harris, on the other hand, was untroubled by any such constraint, and later in his life owned up, "I have found pockets that held as much as $1,600 in gold, rich with ore with 'the eagle stamped right on it.' I typically panned out a far-sized stake, and then sold the mine while the showing was still good. When I got down to bedrock, I'd sell a claim."

As Death Valley Scotty was to sum it up, "There's many a good mine's that's been spoiled by a pick."

Was selling a shallow claim stealing?

"Why... no, not really," was the consensus. The transaction was more like inviting a fellow to twirl a few hand of dice—straight dice even. A strike could become a bonanza. Look at Virginia City, look to Goldfield and Rhyolite!

With a new (and dimmer) perspective on Death Valley, Chester, Clarence, and C.J. Back took their leave of Old John Lemoigne, described by a later visitor as "calm, polite, philosophical; with polished manners, a ruddy smile, and all the ways of a gentleman. He was a dreamy sort of fellow, quite content to live alone and let the world go by."

On this, their first foray west of Rhyolite, Chester and friend Clarence returned empty-handed. If they'd found anything at all, it hadn't been worth filing a claim. But if not richer, they were "wide awake" as to what, at best, was underfoot and what was not. A consequence was the inherent—necessary, some would say—chicanery of promoting a mine, with no dearth of takers. Clarence was to write:

Well, the public the dear old public,
    You can always depend upon.
It insists on spending its money
    until its money is gone.
Only one claim in ten thousand
    Ever produces a mine.
If it's facts that you want on investments,
    take note of this notable line:
Any mine takes a mine to develop.
    Just gaze at the thousands of holes
Where they searched for gold and for silver
    and succeeded in dropping their rolls.

They were certainly dropping rolls back in Rhyolite, mostly at the instigation of the camp's "mining men," a breed apart from prospectors and hard rock miners. They self-importantly strutted about town in their shiny high top boots, immaculate suits (corduroy in winter, tan twill in summer), and high-crowned hats. They optioned claims, floated stocks, and touted mines (not that a spade of earth had been, or would be turned). A number were cynically "hanging paper," selling shares in prospects they knew to be worthless. Yet many enthusiastically believed Rhyolite was destined to become the next Goldfield. Just two years into a glorious future, the camp had a modern telephone exchange, four banks, hotels with private baths, and three ice plants to dampen the heat of a population going on five thousand, with newcomers daily alighting from the packed passenger cars of three competing railroads.

Though not one of Rhyolite's fabulous mines was operating in the black, they were sure to. If you questioned this, look to Schwab! President and sole owner of Bethlehem Steel and the highest paid executive in the world, Charles A. Schwab—money wasn't any smarter—was a Rhyolite investor and booster, his visits cause for gala celebrations. Chester and Clarence were in town when his fleet of five Pope-Toledos whisked him down Golden Street to a welcoming luncheon at the Southern Hotel. The menu featured:

Consommé en Tass
Shrimp en Mayonnaise
Lamb Chops en Papilotte
Stuffed Tomatoes a la Richelieu
Parisian Potatoes   French Peas
Omelet au Rum

Charles Schwab rose to tell a story on himself: "As a child I'd entertained family and friends with handsprings, songs, jokes, and magic tricks. And when they applauded, I said 'Wait! I can do something else yet!' That, my friends, is why I'm here. I am an absolute enthusiast on the mining possibilities of Nevada."

The mining men of Rhyolite clapped, hoo-rahed, beat their fists on the table. The china danced. Exuberant toasts were clinked with White Seal Champagne.

"Charley, if we may call you Charley, you do us proud!"

Turkish cigarettes, Havanas all around. Though not for Chester or Clarence. Uninvited, they slouched off to a cross-street eatery for the usual: 10¢ for beans and meat of some sort, 5¢ for a shot of *Oh Be Joyful!* Clarence was moved to uncap his pen and title a poem TO HIM THAT HATH GOLD, only to cross this out and offer a lament for HIM WHO HATH NOT...

Heaven alone is the hope of the poor,
    Hoping for heaven they meekly endure,
For up in Heaven we are told,
    All is not given to him that hath gold.

Glimpses and reports of the mighty Charles Schwab humbled Clarence and Chester, as did the camp's preening, fast-talking mining men.

"Schwab. The paper says his mansion in New York takes up an entire city block. Think of it."

"And us lucky to have canvas over our head."

Clarence dug for a dime, plunked it on the counter. "Two more..."

Chester looked up from his whiskey to Clarence who was continuing to write.

"I've got a..." Chester began, only to catch himself with the thought that, for what he had in mind, Clarence, however a friend, might not be the best partner. The Big Man was readily recognizable. Not that what Chester hoped to do was against the law.

Well, maybe it was, and in that case, better that he recruit a drifter of his acquaintance, Billy Langdon. Billy wasn't the sharpest tool in the shed, but that could work to Chester's advantage. Any questions or doubts he might have would be minimal.

The scheme would benefit from Chester's skill as an assayer, and the scheme would require cash. A money order just in from his mother would help, and his wagon and team were worth something.

Billy had a good horse he could sell.

Early the following week, Chester Pray and Billy Langdon boarded a northbound train for gold-rich Goldfield, there to make certain inquiries, and when the time was ripe, initiate a transaction that would have Chester dining on Shrimp en Mayonnaise and Lamb Chops en Papilotte. Billy too.

CHESTER'S TROUBLE
IN GOLDFIELD

I N DOWN-TO-EARTH MOMENTS, CHESTER PRAY had to have realized by now that the odds of making a meaningful strike were stacked against him, or Clarence, or anyone. Consider Old John: his skill and persistence had netted him a hovel.

How, then, could Chester make a go of the mining game?

There were ways.

Like Death Valley Scotty's way: promoting a non-existent mine. Or you could sink a shaft and *salt* it by garnishing worthless rock with a dusting of gold or silver. What perked Chester's interest, though, was what could happen when *an avidly-sought precious metal was really there*—with the issue being *who got it*. Simply put, a man could hire on in a mine working a rich lode, pocket the shiniest rocks blasted free of the face, then fence them to a crooked assayer. *High-grading*, the practice was called, and Goldfield had become its glory town, with miners toting hollow picks and false-bottomed lunch pails.

Demand accommodated the supply. Fewer than one in ten of Goldfield's nearly fifty assay offices were legitimate, with assayers typically reselling high-grade for twice what they paid for it.

With the idea that he might be the right person at the right time, Chester Pray, with side-kick Billy Langdon in tow, surfaced in Goldfield in the first week of December, 1906. In his days in Olinghouse, Nevada, Chester had not only assayed ore, but as a service to local mines, had reduced quantities of it to ingots of 99.9% fine bullion. He'd do it again—with the camp's high-grade. Who'd be harmed? Goldfield's major mines were in the hands of a syndicate with little concern for the welfare of working stiffs. The syndicate could live with the loss, even deserved it.

If he knew what he was up against, Chester might have had second thoughts as to his plan. Outwardly genial U.S. Senator George Nixon was the power behind Goldfield's syndicate, with day-to-day operations in the hands of his protégé George Wingfield, an ex-professional gambler who for a song bought a controlling interest in the camp's Mohawk Mine, at the time an indifferent producer. He paid as little as 10¢ a share. He then cut costs by leasing, for set periods of time, rights to mine different areas of different levels. Lessees put up nothing. Instead, Nixon, Wingfield, and the Mohawk laid claim to half to three-quarters of anything lessees found.

In April of 1906, two miners—who'd signed onto this—broke into a literal "room of gold," and in a hundred and six frenetic days extracted $5,000,000 in ore. The Hayes-Monnette lease was the talk of the mining world. Mohawk Mine stock shot to $20 a share, a satisfying 2,000% gain for George Wingfield and Senator Nixon.

But enough was not enough. Wingfield, his personal welfare excepted, "cared for no cause; he retained to the end the narrow squint of the small-time gambler he had originally been, and that squint was unblinkingly affixed upon his accumulating stacks of silver dollars."

What galled Wingfield was not only splitting the booty of the Hayes-Monnette lease with a pair of Irish yeggs, but the continued, unabated practice of high-grading, both on and off leases. He despised the camp's working stiffs. All told, they were walking off with an estimated 40% of the Mohawk's ore.

Their high-grading dodges were nothing if not inventive. Creative haberdashery outfitted miners with socks stretched down trouser legs and two undershirts sewn together at the bottom, the combination able to conceal and make off with as much as twenty pounds of ore. A false-crowned hat was good for five pounds more. "Big Coat" men swayed as they walked downhill into Goldfield from the Mohawk, and if they tripped, required assistance to get to their feet. At the end of a single shift, a $4 dollar a day miner could be $1,800 the richer. Liberty was confounded with license, justified by the argument: "God Almighty put no more gold in the bowels of the earth for one man than he did for another."

The eighth commandment lost out to Deuteronomy's, "Muzzle not the ox that treadeth the corn."

Chester and Billy drank to that.

On December 18th, 1906, a fuming George Wingfield stepped through the oaken, etched-glass doors of the Nixon block on the corner of Main and Ramsey to address a crowd assembled for the occasion, which was eyed for troublemakers by a phalanx of bodyguards. Diamondfield Jack Davis, in from Rhyolite and now "the prize bad man of Goldfield," was in evidence, though it was unclear whether he was at the time in Wingfield's employ. Wingfield gave a nod to, but chose not to introduce an unfamiliar figure to his right: mutton-faced Clarence Sage, newly in charge of security for the Mohawk mine. He had been recruited from the hard-case Thiel Agency in Los Angeles.

The appearance was unusual for Wingfield, customarily one for behind-the-scenes, backstairs manipulation. But he felt that what he said needed to be said, and in no uncertain terms. The *Goldfield News* headlined:

WINGFIELD DECLARES WAR

Determined to Rout Out
High-graders and Crooked Assayers

In the balance of 1906, Goldfield's press reported raids on assaying dens in outlying Coon Hollow and Hop Fiend's Gulch, with a single raid netting seven tons of stolen ore. Moreover, Wingfield wanted high-grading declared a federal offence.

"High-graders," he declared, "would have to answer to Uncle Sam."

This was motivated by the fact that they were decidedly not answering to Goldfield juries. Well stocked with miners, the camp's panels were reluctant to convict accused high-graders, even those caught red-handed, for the next time around, many a gentleman of the jury could be a miscreant in the dock.

Given all this, Chester stood by his plan, with the exception that he'd not take the risk of locally refining any high-grade that might come his way. Rather, he would transport it north to the railroad junction at Hazen, where the Tonopah & Goldfield fed into the Southern Pacific's main line. He was familiar with Hazen—and its lawlessness, its disrepute—from his days in nearby Olinghouse. Once there, he'd find an abandoned, out-of-the-way building and improvise barrel chlorinators. And if Hazen wasn't the right place for this, the two and their ore would keep going, out of Nevada, across Utah, and into Colorado, where officials of the Denver Mint had a notable lack of curiosity as to what they took in, provided it was 99.9% gold.

On New Year's day of 1907, George Wingfield had cause for satisfaction. He'd terminated leasing at the Mohawk, the occasion celebrated by a grand, midnight display of "fireworks of all description" capped by the detonation of hundreds of pounds of dynamite atop Malpai Mesa to the west of the camp. No more splitting the proceeds; he'd rake in the pot, with the mine now good for a million a month—*if he could put an end to high-grading.* When it came to the Big Coat men and their God-given right to steal his ore, nothing would please him more than to "break the back of those suckers."

In the second week of January of 1907, Chester and Billy Langdon had a line on a quantity of high-grade, enough to send them scurrying to purchase a used traveling trunk and a miner's rope-handled tool box, baggage that would draw scant attention on the railroad run north to Hazen. "A stranger" (neither of the boys could quite recall his name) had approached them, and in the predawn hours of Friday the 17th, Chester examined four sacks of ore, and satisfied, counted out $2,000 in gold coin for what he estimated was $5,000 to $10,000 worth of high-grade, said to come from a lessee's share of a legitimate Mohawk contract, recently terminated. Any accompanying nods and winks went right by dim bulb Billy. He bought into the deal as "being on the open market," even if the market happened to be a shack off a back alley in the Redlight.

They packed the sacks into their containers, and with a hand cart hauled them eighteen blocks to the Tonopah & Goldfield terminal. They were first in line as a pale yellow dawn glinted the tracks, and station agent Hedden slid open his window. Suppressing his excitement, Chester purchased tickets on the 10 AM to Hazen. Chester and Billy casually weighed their baggage on the big scale by freight door: 200 pounds for the trunk, 236 pounds for the tool box.

Back down the platform at the ticket window, an individual inquired about the day's schedule, commented on the weather, and was curious as to where his friends down the platform were headed. The fellow sauntered off, and once out of sight, hot-footed it to the nearest phone to rouse his boss, Clarence Sage, who in turn alerted George Wingfield, who, appraised of the circumstances, realized that right here and right now was just the opportunity he'd been waiting for. He ordered Sage to let the pair be on their way, and then to collar them in Hazen, up in Churchill County, where there would be a far better chance of obtaining a conviction from a jury numbering few, if any, miners.

For Chester and Billy, the wait for the #23 northbound was interminable and foot-stamping cold. When the station clock finally ticked to 10 AM, the pair feigned nonchalance as they stowed their baggage and took their seats. There was a delay in the train's departure—but then, two welcome bursts from the engine's whistle and they were clattering through the Tonopah & Goldfield's yards, gathering speed, and hurtling out across the open desert. The reverberation of the whistle and the throb of the Mogul's pistons and drivers set Chester to humming. They'd pulled it off!

Chester looked to Billy. Billy giggled. They'd be, if not rich, well-heeled for the foreseeable future. As the train skirted the Monte Cristo mountains, Chester considered how he'd spend the money. They'd celebrate, of course, but then he would grubstake himself and seriously go prospecting, on the lookout for what others had overlooked. Gold would be nice, gold was always nice, but assaying had informed him of other minerals and their variant forms. Copper and cinnabar, sulphides and nitrates—with Death Valley promising in its host formations, its dips, spurs, and contacts. How he loved mining talk. Clarence did too; he'd consider teaming up again with Clarence. Not Billy, still giggling, the chucklehead. Clarence was good company, with a ready supply of stories about the ladies. Chester could do with some time with the ladies. Some "horizontal refreshment."

Two cars back, five men twitched and grumbled: Clarence Sage; Robert Grimmens, an alleged U.S. Marshal; and a trio of either Thiel Agency or Pinkerton detectives. They'd skipped breakfast, and now they either baked hunched over the car's pot-bellied stove or froze down the aisle in their seats. Their frosted breath hung in the air.

Though subject to spasms of shivers, Chester dozed. He'd been up the night through. His Aunt Julia and even his Uncle Henry would be pleased, not exactly with what he'd done, but the result: He'd never need a dime from them or from his mother; the day could come when he'd send *them* a check.

The #23 whistled along the shore of Walker Lake, the jumping off place for last year's rush for non-existent gold on Indian land.

It was well past noon and Billy was hungry—and there was no food on the train. Wait, Chester told him, they'd celebrate in Hazen. Sierra beers and blue plate specials. No, make that champagne and oysters. Then maybe a visit with the ladies.

A sallow yet burly man caught the drift of their conversation as he walked the aisle of the car to relieve himself and smoke a cigar in the Men's room. He swayed back down the aisle and through the next car to the next, with Chester and Billy none the wiser.

Nightfall.

Jackrabbits scattered into the sage as the #23 braked for an unscheduled stop. Clarence Sage ordered his men to detrain, watch both sides, and be ready for anything, with the possibility that Pray, their prey, had planned a rendezvous with a friend and a wagon. Sage sought the conductor, who said the engineer had stopped at Silver Springs to take on water, and they'd be on their way in fifteen or twenty minutes. A brakeman clambered up a trackside tower and ratcheted a spout down to the boiler.

Chester did his best to appear calm, which was difficult considering his excitable nature. With Hazen no more than an hour away, what were they doing stopped dead in the middle of nowhere?

They were not exactly in the middle of nowhere, Clarence Sage realized. Somewhere around Silver Springs they would be crossing into Churchill County. Had they already? Sage wasn't sure.

Chester thought he might have a look as to what was going on, make sure all was right up by the baggage car. He moved to rise, only to be frozen by a hand grasping his shoulder.

"Detective Clarence Sage," the man said, "and you, Chester Pray, are under arrest for grand larceny."

Panicked, Billy Langdon lurched for the aisle, to be cold-cocked by one or another of the men blocking any escape. Sage suggested that "Marshal" Grimmens hold the train and repliven the ore. Better here than in Hazen.

A few minutes after 9 PM, behind schedule but not by much, the #23 pulled into the Hazen yards. Four of Sage's men had their hands full securing a safe place for the ore. Hazen was notoriously "a rendezvous for ex-convicts, confidence men, and tough characters, and the work of keeping the peace there is anything but a soft job," appraised the *Churchill Ledger*. With the law in the sole hands of a sorry excuse of a constable, Sage chose to personally march Chester and Billy to Keller's Lodging, and without a rat's ass to due process, incarcerate them in a seedy, second-floor room.

At 9:50 PM, a mournful whistle reverberated in the desert

night. That would be Union Pacific's #3 to Salt Lake City and on to Denver, Chester and Billy's connection had they sought it.

Clarence Sage relished his dinner in the presence of his charges. He ordered his men to wake the Western Union agent and telegraph George Wingfield.

The day could hardly have gone better.

The next morning Clarence Sage and his men manhandled Chester and Billy onto the first train to Fallon, Churchill County's seat, and to an appearance before mortician-Justice of the Peace Edison W. Black. Charged with buying stolen Goldfield Mohawk Company ore, the pair was peremptorily jailed, with a hearing set for Monday, two days hence. By noon, Sage, Grimmens, and their trailing toughs were on their way back to Goldfield, where crowds would gather and there would be a call for heightened security as a history-making freight train departed for San Francisco. The *Goldfield Daily Tribune* headlined:

MOHAWK A BONANZA

Single Carload or Ore
Valued at $575,000

Richest on Record

The cards were falling as George Wingfield would have them fall. His patron Senator Nixon clarified, "We want it all; we're not here for our health."

Two hundred and fifty miles north in Fallon's squat stone lock-up, Chester Pray should have been cowed and resigned, possibly even remorseful. But he wasn't. He was indignant. There had been no warrant. He'd been jailed against his will in Hazen and Clarence Sage had prevailed on Judge Black to hold him over the weekend, even though he could come up with the $500 bail Black had set.

A box in that week's *Churchill Standard* advertised the services of:

William S. Wall
Attorney at Law
Mining and Corporation Law a
Specialty. Office in the Bank building.

The "Mining" specialty, unusual in an agricultural region, caught Chester's eye. He penciled a note. A sympathetic jailer dropped it off at the Bank building.

Attorney William Wall, as others before him, was to find Chester both feisty and flighty. And voluble. With hardly a hello, the words came in a rush. "Detained without cause! Illegally! Man claimed he was a marshal... locked up in Hazen. Took sick! My lungs, wounded! My credit too!"

He kept on: "Reason to sue! Sue them all... sue George Winfield and Senator Nixon!"

The outburst took small-town lawyer Wall aback. Sue two of the most powerful men in Nevada? The man behind the bars was crazy. But, on further thought, why not? Give the Goldfield big fellows a run for their money, jerk the chains of Sage and his goons. Wall had a place in his heart for the working stiff, though he had little doubt that, as charged, his two new clients had absconded with Mohawk ore, and that come Monday the pair would be red-handed in the docket.

For that, they would need a down-to-earth defense; Chester's defiant lawsuit could wait. What Wall settled on arguing was that *whatever crime was alleged to have been committed would have been committed in Goldfield, down in Esmeralda County, and it was there that charges should properly be brought,* not in Fallon in Churchill County. That being the case, Chester and Billy would be tried by a jury of like-minded Goldfield peers and almost certainly would walk.

The pair were subdued if not contrite when at ten in the morning on Monday they were marched over to Fallon's new, white clapboard courthouse, where William Wall approached Judge Black and was waved off. The prosecution was nowhere in evidence. Black postponed the hearing a day, gaveling Chester and Billy back to jail.

Tuesday at ten, and still no one had appeared to press charges.

Fed up with mining shenanigans pursued in his farming community, the exasperated judge ordered the pair released.

Chester couldn't believe his ears!

Billy whooped, and would have further carried on had he not been stifled by lawyer Wall.

They had no reason to know that at the time a chartered white flag Special—engine and single passenger car—was racing north from Goldfield, with the track cleared of scheduled passenger trains and freights. Clarence Sage and Robert Grimmens were on board, accompanied by renowned geologist John Wellington Finch and Reno attorney Robert Martin Price, who'd been south tending to the richest ore shipment in U.S. history. Wingfield and Nixon's ore.

Chester would now have done well to bolt Fallon and lie low. But he didn't. He instead pressed William Wall to file his suit for grievous injury inflicted by the *Goldfield Mohawk Mine, George Wingfield, Geo. S. Nixon, et. al.* Chester had Wall read aloud and revise the wording, especially the part where, without cause or authority, he had been detained—no, make that "imprisoned"—in Hazen, where he had "contacted a severe cold on his lungs, become sick and wounded, and was also injured in his credit, and was prevented from attending to his business during that time to plaintiff's damage in the sum of Five Thousand Dollars." And the same, another five thousand for Billy. They'd get back the money put down for the ore, and then some.

Leaving the matter in lawyer Wall's hands, the pair went off to celebrate, taking little or no notice of the approaching whistle of the white flag Special routed through Hazen and nearing Fallon.

Two hours later and they were back in their cell, skunked.

In a brief before Judge Black, lawyer Wall had argued that a grand larceny charge was an Esmeralda County matter. Lawyer Robert Martin Price, Wingfield's man and fast on his feet, had countered with a revised charge, actionable in Churchill County: *possession of stolen property.*

On March 1, 1907, after considerable legal wrangling, court was convened for the State of Nevada v. C.A. Pray and H.L. Langdon. Chester despondently surveyed the jury: not a miner's sympathetic pale face among them. Instead, ruddy faces and kitchen haircuts. Farmers.

Chester found it hard to pay attention, with lawyers, one then another, droning on day after day, laying out their cases, registering objections, calling witnesses. When the time came to put John Wellington Finch on the stand, Churchill County's District Attorney deferred to Reno's Robert Martin Price.

> Q.   Mr. Finch, I have entered in evidence samples of ore replivened from the accused. Would you care to examine them and, as a distinguished geologist, offer your opinion?

A.   Yes. I certainly would.

Minutes elapse as he intently considers the ore.

This appears to be... No, allow me to correct that. This is, no doubt whatsoever, ore from the Goldfield Mohawk Mine. To be specific, a crosscut on the 300 foot level of the Frances-Mohawk lease.

Q.   Can you, Mr. Finch, produce evidence of this?
A.   I can.

Trays of matching samples are produced and offered for the jury's inspection. Finch comments...

As you gentlemen can identify a crop by its seed, we geologists can identify ore by its composition. And I can say without fear of contradiction that there is only one single spot on earth that produces gold like this. Do you see? Ball-like concentrations of it, like plums in a pudding.

Q.   And ripe for the plucking. Yes, Mr. Finch?
A.   Not exactly. Goldfield Mohawk records indicate that, under the supervision of armed guards, the ore in question was properly mined and hoisted to the surface, where it was duly sacked and sampled.

Q.   Yes?
A.   And sometime in the night of October the second, 1906, there was a robbery.

Q.   Of all the ore?
A.   Not all.

Q.   How much?
A.   Four sacks.

Q. The same as would fit in a traveling trunk and tool box, heretofore introduced as evidence?

A. The same.

Q. Mr. Finch, I thank you. The court thanks you.

Judge Black turned to attorney-for-the-defense Wall, who, under the circumstances, chose not to dispute the fact that the ore in question was at some juncture stolen, but to elicit from John Wellington Finch a statement that a million-and-a-half dollar's worth of Mohawk gold had been stolen in recent months. He then argued that it stood to reason that some of that ore would have, one way or another, fallen into innocent hands, to whit, those of an eastern tenderfoot and his wet-behind-the-ears friend, "in good faith" duped by a stranger. Chester did his best to look credulous, no problem for Billy.

It was again Price's turn, and it's doubtful he enjoyed tearing apart Wall's argument. He liked the man; they'd enjoyed smokes out on the courthouse's second floor balcony.

With a heavenward thrust of his palms, Price professed amazement that anyone—anyone—could be unaware of high-grading in Goldfield, and if so, why furtively transfer the ore from four sacks to a trunk and tool box, and spirit it out of town on the next train? The jurors cocked their heads in the direction of the accused. One was a bumpkin, but the other, Price pointed out, an assayer, a trained assayer, and what assayer wouldn't question ore peddled in a Redlight alley?

Shedding his jacket and loosening his tie, William Wall now paced up, then down in front of the jury, the earnest Fallon lawyer up against the out-of-town operator (who, in truth, he'd come to like and admire).

Gentlemen,

Hypothetically, just hypothetically, say that in the case before you a crime was committed, and by the accused. That is, if you consider benefiting from the bounty of the earth a felony.

This could well have been underscored with a meaningful look out the courthouse windows, to land farmed by the jurors.

85

Well, then, is not it right and just that the crime—that is, if there was a crime—should be prosecuted where it occurred? In and of the Nevada county of Esmeralda!

Reno Lawyer Price objected, pointing out that the issue had already been dealt with, and even if the essence of the case was larceny in Esmeralda County, there was a precedent, a compelling precedent for trying it up in Churchill County. In *Grant County of State of Nevada v. Rider* it was determined that a horse stolen in one county was just as stolen when ridden to the next.

Gentlemen of the jury, I'd hazard a guess that a number of you possess horses.

Presumably, there were assenting nods at this point.

I ask you, can you argue with Grant County of State of Nevada v. Rider? I think not.

It is not hard to imagine, in lawyerly fashion, Robert Martin Price drawing out the name of this earlier case, underscoring its role in the state's jurisprudence. With a brief, well-reasoned summary, he rested his case.

On March 10th, at the conclusion of an eight-day trial, Fallon's jury found Chester Pray and Billy Langdon guilty as charged. Duly notified, George Wingfield was gratified. He'd made an example of damn Chester Pray. Lawyer Price, detective Sage, and fancy geologist Finch were worth it. George Wingfield was well on his way to the day when, concerning Goldfield, he would dictate a telegram to be dispatched to his accountant:

I HAVE TOOK OVER EVERYTHING STOP WINGFIELD

The only problem, a minor one it appeared, was that Chester wasn't all that interested in knuckling under. He and Billy would appeal! In the meantime, given a choice of 500 days in the state penitentiary or a $1,000 fine, he "under protest" paid the fine with funds provided by his distraught mother and aunt and exasperated uncle. He did this with the assurance of the courthouse clerk that if his sentence was reversed, he would be due a refund.

The case was referred to the Nevada Supreme Court, where its three Justices dismissed Chester's appeal on the grounds that by paying a $1,000 fine, he had as much as admitted his guilt. The Fallon courthouse clerk, they ruled, was in error—in fact, had acted illegally—but that made no difference.

As for Billy Langdon, he had posted bail rather than paid a fine, and was therefore entitled to a hearing, in which the Justices ruled:

Actus no facit raum, nisi mens sit rea.

That is to say: "A crime is not committed if a participant is too dull-witted to grasp what is going on." Billy... declared innocent by reason of stupidity.

Chester was nevertheless to persist in his quest for justice. He raised an issue everyone else had forgotten about, an issue six months stale: *Pray & Langdon v. George Wingfield, Geo. S. Nixon et. al.* in the matter of unlawful and debilitating imprisonment in Keller's Lodging back in Hazen. Contacting lawyer Robert Martin Price, Chester allowed that he might drop his suit—but only if Wingfield, Nixon et. al., after all was said and done, found he and Billy innocent of all charges and cleared their names.

At his Reno office, Robert Martin Price reviewed the filing:

> At the town of Hazen, C.A. Sage, by force and acting as agent of George Wingfield and Geo. S. Nixon, compelled plaintiff to go with him to an hotel, and did then and there imprisoned him, and thereafter detained him and restrained his liberty without probable cause and without right or authority so to do, whereby the plaintiff contracted a severe cold on his lungs, became sick and wounded...

Price read on, and realized there was little or no defense for this. Duly-appointed lawmen were nowhere in evidence that night in Hazen. Price had to smile; he had to give the man credit. Out of the spotlight and on George Wingfield's reluctant behalf, he acceded to Chester Pray's terms.

In an eventful year, Chester had made off with a sheriff's ponies and the gold of a U.S. Senator and his intimidating, squint-eyed partner. He'd then fought Nixon and Wingfield to a draw. His honor reinstated and his head held high, he was free to seek anew his way in the West.

But how... and where?

TROUBLE ALL OVER

THE OLINGHOUSE-HAZEN-FALLON REGION had had enough of Chester Pray, and he of it. Parting ways with Billy Langdon, he headed south. Not to Goldfield, where he'd hardly be welcome, or even Rhyolite, where he stopped to pick up his portable furnace he'd left with his friend Clarence.

For the next several months, Chester's whereabouts are unclear as he joined prospectors and opportunistic mining men roaming—stampeding, even—south from Rhyolite into the Funeral Range. A dozen camps sprang up—including Schwab, Echo, two different Lees—with their fates to be determined by the balance of an assayer's scales. Most were short-lived; there were desert asters and jackass clovers that bloomed longer.

But then there was *Greenwater*, billed as "the greatest copper camp on earth." With "huge ledges" of high-grade copper cropping to the surface over a six-hundred square mile area, "this wonderful property would carry upward of 20,000,000 tons of refined copper." At 13¢ a pound, worth over five billion dollars! That would be more copper than all the copper yet discovered in the world!

As a measure of Greenwater's promise, Mother Agnes and Lil Lang were fresh in from Rhyolite, as was flame-haired Tiger Lil. If Chester called at her bordello, he would have been greeted as "dearie" and would have been flashed a toothsome smile featuring a table cut diamond or two or three (customers disagreed). Two Tiger Lil vignettes, recalled by an acquaintance:

> Tiger Lil was a fine looking woman. She came into town wearing a beautiful dress with tiger lilies painted on it. One night down at Lil's place Red McCrimon got abusive and started tearin' hinges off the doors. Lil ordered him out but he only got worse. Lil pulled out her shooting iron, and it was shoot and jump, shoot and jump for 200 yards.

> When Billy the printer [fond of Lil's girls and cards] died, he was shaved and placed in his coffin, his right hand over his breast. Tiger Lil was going by. She stopped and said, "He just doesn't look quite natural." Lil went away for a bit then returned and asked us to leave her alone in the room. When we went back in, Billy held five aces in the hand on his breast. He did look more natural and we buried him that way.

While he lasted, Billy the printer got out issues of the *Chuck-Walla*, a monthly magazine with the persona of an oracular, talking lizard. The *Chuck-Walla* boosted Greenwater and at the same time chronicled—often wryly—its characters and foibles. As the camp swelled to a population of 3,000, it is of interest to note in its pages who was there and who wasn't. No George Wingfield or Senator Nixon; sticking to Goldfield, they sat this one out, which to the astute may have raised questions as to Greenwater's credibility. Death Valley Scotty, though, was a frequent visitor. His fabled mine wasn't far distant, or so he said. But, hissed the *Chuck-Walla*,

DEATH VALLEY SCOTTY
HAS CEASED TO BE A SENSATION

> Even in Greenwater his appearance the other day gained him no plaudits. The dogs refused to bark at him while the saloon men in town were scarcely made aware of the visit. It seems that Scotty has deteriorated in many respects. He has fallen into the unpleasant position of an ordinary piker. Bombastic words and gigantic boasts about himself have lost their efficacy. Scotty is a dead one... Next.

Next?

For one, there was mining man Jack Salsberry, who could be mistaken as a mirror edition of Scotty. They were the same age; both were rotund, jowly, and cleft-chinned. Both, defying their bulk, moved and acted with dispatch. But Jack Salsberry, he was the genuine article in the opinion of Chester Pray, who ran a number of Greenwater assays for the man and held him in high regard. Then and in the future—when Jack would profoundly impact Chester's life—Chester deferentially address him as "Mr. Salsberry," even though the two were contemporaries, with Jack but four years Chester's senior.

After attending the Van Dernalian School of Mines in San Francisco, Jack Salsberry had wielded a pick and shovel in outback Nevada. After that he had brokered stocks in Tonopah and Goldfield, and then had turned to freighting lumber to desert camps, currently Greenwater. As well, Jack Salsberry was riding high as an associate of man-of-the-hour Charles A. Schwab as he shifted the focus of his New York-based syndicate from yet-to-pay-off Rhyolite to sure-thing Greenwater. The extent and exact nature of Salsberry's relationship with Schwab was close to the vest. The *Chuck-Walla* was to puzzle Jack's renown:

TO FORTUNE AND FAME WELL KNOWN

We know who he is, what he did to gain a fortune; but why he should become famous, that is beyond us. We are told that Jack is a good fellow—heigho! Gotham knows as much about that just now as we do. It appears he is ambitious and of course New York is the place for ambitious youths who have had the good fortune on the desert to make a barrel of money. The merger of all the Schwab interests, in which Salsberry is considerably involved, needed his subtle hand to guide it into a safe anchorage. A twenty-five million dollar merger is not precisely a boy's undertaking. Charles Schwab, the guiding spirit of the deal, must have been dimly aware of this. Even though he had the experience of forming a billion dollar steel trust, when it came to organizing a copper mine with twenty-five million dollars for capital, Schwab's nerves may have failed him. It needed the assistance of nerve which was hardened under the desert suns.

The article is muddled; blame it on the machinations of American capital, or blame it on a bottle at the reporter's elbow. But there's little doubt that Jack Salsberry, with Charles Schwab's money in the offing, was on his way to becoming Greenwater's leading citizen. By turns earnest and jocular, he would backslap his way up and down bustling Salsberry Street, named in his honor. He'd hail brother Elks with "Hello, Bill!" and he had a pocketful of candy for the camp's children. If you believed Jack, this was a camp where young and old could look forward to a life of comfort and ease—Chester Pray included, though he hadn't run any first class ore for the man in weeks.

Jack didn't mind at all when he was hailed as "Nevada's Copper King," even as the copper had yet to come out of the ground. "But it would," everyone told everyone. The *Chuck-Walla* admonished:

> Boost, don't knock;
> Wake up, you've slept too long
> Get busy here—your chance will come in hell—
> Stop croaking—get the money.

> It is about this place of mystery and horror that
> great wealth is now known to be.

The New York Curb Exchange not only churned, but "positively boiled" with Greenwater issues floated to underwrite its thirty-six mines. The "Schwab crowd" —the baron's club and business friends—were lead investors. And an initial promise of vast surface outcroppings was now supplanted by the prospect of tapping a mother of all copper lodes. Over a three-month period, the *Chuck-Walla* chronicled:

> Work is going along merrily...

> There are showings to warrant the expenditure...

> The value of the mines is greater this month than it
> has ever been before...

> Sulphides are likely to be encountered any day, and
> when this occurs the permanency of the camp will be
> established...

> There is nothing like it...

The *Chuck-Walla* relocated from a tent to a substantial building. Stopping by, Jack Salsberry placed an ad soliciting subscriptions for a hotel worthy of the camp. It would boast a polished granite facade, three stories, and fifteen thousand opulent square feet.

That same week, geologist and noted mining expert Oscar A. Turner stepped from a chug ferrying passengers from the Tonopah & Tidewater's main line up to Greenwater. Sent high-grade ore samples, he had been persuaded to lend his name to the camp's promotion, and now he welcomed the opportunity to have a look around and determine what was there—or, as it transpired, *what wasn't.*

Two hours on the ground, and he realized that he and Charles Schwab *and everyone* had been duped. He fired off telegrams, the first to a Philadelphia brokerage:

**CEASE OFFERING GREENWATER
CENTRAL STOP MAKE NO MORE
PAYMENTS ON THE PROPERTY STOP DO
NOT USE MY NAME ANY FURTHER STOP
THERE IS NOTHING HERE STOP TURNER**

News of the appraisal spread. The New York Curb, heavily into Nevada mining stocks, shuddered and slid, with no offerings above suspicion. Greenwater, Rhyolite, and even Goldfield stocks were hard hit. In the months to come, the *Goldfield Daily Tribune's* newsboys would cry:

BEAR CLIQUE IN SAN FRANCISCO SELLING SHORT

WALL STREET SLUMP IS OF PRONOUNCED CHARACTER

MARKET IN THE DUMPS

A RUTHLESS SLAUGHTER OF VALUES

PLUNGER BLOWS OFF TOP OF HEAD

Jaws were set, teeth clenched, nerves frayed. Goldfield tightened its belt. Rhyolite fell on hard times and began to empty out. Greenwater was derided by pundits who all along (they said) knew the place was "the swindle of the century." $6,000,000 had been invested in dozens of mines. The return? $2,625 in copper ore, a singe carload. The once mindlessly-boosting *Chuck-Walla* ran a cynical recipe:

> To build a mining town: Take one man with money and a desire to plunge, one man with a reputation of a prospector, and about one hundred pounds of ore of good quality. Make a rich crust with plenty of nerve, a little more money, and a few damn fools. Set in the desert to bake.

When the Greenwater pie fell and crumbled, plunger Charles Schwab looked to his pockets to find they'd been emptied, thanks in part to promoter Jack Salsberry. Schwab was furious, mortified—and snubbed at his Pittsburgh and New York clubs. He, an advisor of a Kaiser and a Czar!

Less than a year earlier, he had staunchly declared, "I am an absolute enthusiast on the mining possibilities of Nevada." In October of 1907 he rued, "I may say that I have put more money into Nevada than any other man. I not only put in my own money but interested my friends. I must say that I am bitterly disappointed in Nevada. I do not think I met a man who told the truth about Nevada. Confidence of eastern people in Nevada is gone."

Schwab's deportment, the *Goldfield Chronicle* jibed, "was that of a fishwife who has lost her savings. Aside from the persiflage, Schwab has made several different kinds of ass of himself, and a few more squeals like this will make him a good candidate for the pecan ward." Besides, "it might be well to remember that Greenwater has always been regarded as sort of a fake by conservative mining men."

A like appraisal was offered by Joseph R. Weil, a promoter-swindler specializing in bogus copper stocks. He was to state: "*I don't consider anything we did as phony. It was imaginary.*"

As for Jack Salsberry, he did just fine. Representing Charles Schwab—who Jack now labeled a "distant parasite"—had its rewards, as did unloading an estimated 400,000 board feet of lumber while dropping a minimum of personal funds into Greenwater's holes in the ground. And now, with transcendent bravado, he was onto something far hotter and not to be doubted:

a copper bonanza at a sink (a depression with no drainage) in a remote reach of northern Death Valley.

As might be expected, peddling stock in Salsberry's Ubehebe Mines & Smelter Co. proved a challenge. The Greenwater debacle had burned San Francisco investors and anyone in Schwab's orbit. Yet there were prospects to be worked, with Jack now shuttling from Maryland to Massachusetts, there to court members of the Boston Yacht Club. "Come see for yourself!" he offered, whipping out a report that "Mining men who have been on the ground pronounce showings the greatest they have ever seen."

Prior investor tours to the region had produced mixed results (as in the expedition culminating in Scotty's Battle of Wingate Pass). Jack nevertheless embraced and refined the idea. A succession of chartered private railroad cars were presently on their way West to disgorge, among others, a Virginia governor, Pillsbury dough heirs, a Count Lerate of Paris, and a Mr. McAlister, a "prominent optician from Baltimore."

On October 31, 1907, the private car *Idlewild* rolled south through Nevada and was shunted onto a specially reserved siding. Aboard, a newspaper article reported, were "nineteen men of ample fortune," one of whom had brought along geologist Oscar A. Turner (whose telegrams had precipitated Greenwater's demise). Jack greeted them, and regretted that the magnificent new Goldfield Hotel hadn't yet opened its doors. Instead, he escorted the group down lower Main Street into the heart of the Redlight to *La Parisianne*, there to savor the finest food in the camp, and possibly all Nevada.

Proprietor Victor Ajax personally took their orders for a range of entrees little different than at their eastern clubs: suckling pig, lobster Newburg, braised beef tongue in piquante sauce. Jack told a story on Victor Ajax. It seems that his real name was Victor Zeus, and he was a cook for a circus that, on its way to Goldfield, went bust. Performers and roustabouts besieged the owner, who agreed to settle up alphabetically, which sent Victor Zeus rushing to the local courthouse to change his name to Victor Ajax.

"Smart, eh?," Jack tapped his temple, "for come 'M' the circus was flat out of funds. Isn't that so, Victor?"

"As you say, Mr. Salsberry."

La Parisianne was abundant in local color. The evening would make for good stories at men-only eastern clubs. The district's Madames had their tables, joined by favored girls who "generally wore a smudge of something that started a foot below their necks and finished a foot and a half above their knees."

Goldfield's resident bad man, Diamondfield Jack Davis, was a regular. Over at the bar he'd be having a row with his current inamorata Tiger Lil, "slightly wilted" after her Greenwater stand. Diamondfield would "calmly cuff her a few times," then pour himself and Lil another drink.

The nineteen took it in. As dessert was served, Jack Salsberry rose to toast "a wonderful, wonderful new country, destined to win fame in the mining world. Pure copper in great bunches! Free gold too!"

With this, thoughts of the Greenwater scam (initiated with like hyperbole) may have clouded a brow or two, but only fleetingly. As dawn banishes darkness, greed wonderfully dispels doubt. There was the bonhomie of the brandy, and there may have been a twinkle in the eye of more than one of the gentlemen who elected to stroll, rather than motor back through the Redlight.

The next morning, Jack's guests stopped by a gent's furnishings store to outfit themselves for the desert. Ankle-length dusters, print kerchiefs, and buckskin gloves were in order as they then made themselves comfortable in four new Thomas touring cars and were whisked two hours south on the road paralleling the Tonopah & Tidewater tracks. Jack held up his hand; his driver braked and stopped.

"There," Jack Salsberry gestured, "Do you see it?"

"See what?" one or more of the nineteen asked.

"A huge smelting works, right here! At the junction of the line!" The line Jack had in mind would be a sixty-two mile electric railroad snaking down Grapevine Canyon to the Valley floor, then on to the copper-rich Ubehebe sink. As they motored the route, the party spied, off on a hillside, two men working a transit and pole.

"Well, look at that," Jack shouted to the trailing Flyers, "Surveyors. Got their work cut out for them. We'll be laying the tracks up high, where they won't get washed out." He extracted and waved a yellow form, "Did I tell you? Cable came in this week from Count Lerate. Financing for the rail line is assured by French interests."

They careened down the twisted canyon to the Valley's floor and bore north in the direction of an alkali cloud.

"Pull up! Let 'em pass! Now's the time for your kerchiefs!"

Nineteen masked men of ample fortune looked on as twenty-two heavily laden burros plodded by.

"Ore! Little fellows, they tote three hundred pounds each. That makes, let's see, a thousand dollar's worth, maybe more, depending on the assay. A start. A drop in the bucket to what's to come. But a start."

The Flyers climbed a low pass flanked by grotesquely gesticulating Joshua trees.

"Like the prophet in the Bible! Pointing the way!"

They dropped down to the elongated Ubehebe sink, its center and lowest point a playa blindingly white in the noonday sun.

"To your right now, look. Salina, a platted copper camp soon to rival Montana's Butte!" —though presently four tents, a store, and a shanty saloon, with the only immediate sign of life two men sorting crates delivered by the string of burros they'd passed. "Dry goods to get Salina up and running. Ore sacks for instance. Thirty-thousand of them in this week."

A few miles on, Jack called a halt and passed around binoculars, so the nineteen might enjoy a stretch and look to the south, to the site of Ubehebe City. Not that there was anything there, but there would be once the rail line went in: an additional smelter to process at the source the sink's vast reserves. And where would the mines be?

"Wait," he said, urging his guests to the Flyers.

The route was sandy, axle-deep and slow—until they gained the rim of the sink's playa, an oval expanse smooth and slick as a macadam highway.

"A racetrack!" Jack called back from the lead Flyer, then turned to his driver and told him to pour on the gas and make for the glistening black isle at the playa's epicenter. They were there in seconds, and circled the isle, faster and faster. Jack half stood to shout to the other cars, pulling abreast.

"You ask where the mines would be?" Flinging out his arm, Jack gestured to the mountains enclosing the sink, from foot to crest two thousand vertical feet. "The answer is everywhere! Everywhere!"

Hard to believe, but they were looking at (Jack said) 50,000,000 tons of high grade copper—and that was "in sight" on or near the surface, there for the taking, locked up in 500 duly filed and certified claims.[6] Leaving the racetrack, they crossed the sink's sandy alluvium to where rising cliffs glistened green and blue.

---

[6] Inyo County ledgers record 104 Salsberry mining claims in the Ubehebe district.

The party turned to the esteemed Oscar A. Turner. "Malachite," he ventured at a first glance. "And over there, could be azurite, possibly cuprite..."

"All copper ores," assured Jack.

On their arrival back in Goldfield the next Tuesday, the nineteen men were near unanimous in their enthusiasm. Waxed a reporter on the scene, "They had seen the little ball spin, and they had seen the ace copped, and the four jacks beaten with four nines and a gin."

However the metaphor might be interpreted (ricocheting from roulette to poker) the party was "astounded at Ubehebe's showing." It should be noted, though, that the vaunted Oscar Adams Turner at this point kept his counsel, and a Mr. Thomas had his reservations.

"I am thinking, still thinking," Mr. Thomas was quoted, "It is certainly a wonderful showing, and I want more time to think it out."

Whatever his conclusions, they wouldn't have mattered, for a black cloud was fast overtaking Jack Salsberry's nineteen worthy and wonderful eastern friends.

A Wall Street crash. The Panic of '07.

The fact was that Jack Salsberry, outwardly (heigho!) a good fellow, had sweated out his potential investors' journey in the face of eastern markets slipping and sliding in the wake of the Greenwater fraud. In the week that the private car *Idlewild* set out from Baltimore, New York's Knickerbocker Trust went under, precipitating the collapse of General Electric the following day.

Roundly disparaged in recent months, Nevada shysters now fingered eastern shysters. Death Valley Scotty weighed in, finding "no material difference between a train-robber and an inside-man like the bankers who wrecked the Knickerbocker Trust—Barney Barnaday et. al. They were out for the dough and takes the best means they know to annex it."

In the course of Jack's Ubehebe inspection tour, Wall Street woe was to give way to panic and panic to ruin, with money scarce and banks failing, including two of Goldfield's three. "Big fellows" took big falls; the Knickerbocker's Barney Barnaday killed himself.

And so it was that on November 3rd, 1907, nineteen men of not-so-ample fortune reboarded the *Idlewild* and steamed on home. No one doubted Jack, at least that they'd say. He was a prince among mining men, but cajole and plead as he might, funds were not forthcoming for his grand enterprise.

Goldfield would survive the Panic of '07, the camp's cards in the practiced hands of ex-gambler George Wingfield. And it helped that there was gold in the ground. Otherwise, the slate of camps in the Death Valley region was all but wiped clean, though for a time Rhyolite would hang on, its population sliding from near 6,000 in 1907 to 611 in the 1910 census.

Even so, a few individuals held out hope. Chester Pray for one. He admired Jack Salsberry and felt the man was onto something with his Ubehebe promotion. *Did it not stand to reason that if great riches were to be found in the region, they would not be in the mountains overlooking Death Valley, but on down in its blazing, hidden, hellish heart?*

The answer was that this didn't stand to reason, but no matter; Chester, driving his burros before him, hiked to the crest of the Funeral Range, there to pitch camp with the only certainty that whatever lay ahead would try his mettle. Before its hand press was abandoned to the desert wind, Greenwater's *Chuck-Walla* had philosophized:

A LITTLE HELL IS GOOD FOR US

A little Hell is good for us. If you don't believe it try it. A little hell brings out what's in a man. This hell masquerades in many forms. It may be physical, mental, moral or spiritual or one of many other values. The man who has a little hell is a finished product. He is what he is. Either the hell has made him a man, capable of facing the hardship and stress of real life, or it has shown him up for a coward or a weakling.

Chester's burros pricked their ears, brayed. Someone was heading their way.

"The bitch..."

"Clarence?"

"The tousle-haired... snub-nosed... pop-eyed bitch. The two-timing..."

"Why hello, Clarence."

"Chester..."

A Rhyolite floozy, it developed, had forsaken the poet-prospector for a gambler who'd prospered in the Klondike.

"To hell with them both. Now it's for us to turn the cards."

In an exchange of Greenwater-Rhyolite telegrams, Chester Pray and Clarence Eddy had agreed to again be partners. The odds, they knew, were against them, embarked as they were—with a host of others—on a last and desperate quest for gold, silver, copper, anything of value.

Come dawn, the pair would descend the 6,000 feet down into the Valley, as they had the year before, but this time would be different. This time there was nowhere else to look. Certainly nowhere in the region, almost certainly nowhere in the American West.

Part 2:
OVER THE EDGE

A LITTLE HELL IS GOOD FOR US

NO MATTER THAT IN SUMMER BIRDS DIED in mid-flight and fell from the sky, a last, desperate rush was on. With fitting melodrama, Ed Busch, a Rhyolite acquaintance of Clarence and Chester, described what prospectors were in for:

> We reached the summit of the Funeral Mountains at sunrise. Death Valley, somber, silent and forbidding as a sepulchre, lay like a serpent thousands of feet below. I viewed the desolate scene in awe. As the sun rose and bathed the distant peaks it shot arrows of light down into the gloomy region. Then, as it climbed above the spiral points of the range, it spread over the valley, whose sands reflected a variety of lurid colors, giving way to a monotonous glare of white heat.
>
> In the very atmosphere there was a warning. "Thus far and no further," it seemed to say. "Test not your puny strength here to wrest from its hiding place the treasure which has so long been concealed from man! Enter now into this Valley of earth where prayers are not answered and pity is a stranger. Its restless sands deceive with the appearance of stability, but when you trust yourself upon them they shift with the winds like waves of the sea. Your feet give way under you, your tongue swells with thirst, and your cries for water are lost!

Chester and Clarence packed their burros with the essentials of their calling: hammer, pick and shovel, gold pan, piston mortar, battered cooking pots, a frying pan, and a blanket, not for warmth, but to lessen, "very materially, the chance of getting rattlers for bed-fellows" (according to a *Prospector's Manual*). For sustenance: flour, beans, rice, bacon, potatoes, onions, vegetables for as long as they'd last, coffee, tea perhaps; whiskey certainly. Water: as much as could be taken on. Knickknacks: compass, jackknife, matches, magnifying glass, and for Chester a field assay outfit. And his Colt 38. Not to be forgotten: crushed barley for the burros. The *Prospectors' Manual* advised, "A handful or two in the morning will serve to attach him to the camp and, in case he should some night break his tether it may save you many weary miles chase. Provisions for a month, on lines above indicated, will not cost to exceed $8 or $10 per person."

Four burros and two prospectors, the latter softly swearing at the former, descended the steep "shirt-tail" route (with torn cloth strips marking the way). Though stubborn and even rank, the little animals were the prospector's friend. They were sure-footed on precipitous trails, able to go two or even three days without water, and content to survive on sagebrush and bacon rinds. Down and down Chester and Clarence went, to the rhythm of crunching hooves and feet, and slaps to dispel insects alighting on noses and buzzing in ears. Loose rocks echoed down the slope.

Come noon the heat was full on. July highs typically ranged from 110° to 124°. That was in the shade. "Tingle in the air," Clarence rasped, his throat dry. "The heat. You can hear it sizzle."

"It's your brain sizzling, your poet's brain."

But they did hear something as, gaining the Valley's floor, they skirted a clump of mustard-hued hills. Crystals close to the surface heated, expanded, and shattered—loud enough to be heard yards away.

"Sounds like snapping twigs."

"Or knocks on wood... for good luck?"

Dense and whitish-blue, the air glowed and danced and baked.

Their eyes to their feet, Chester and Clarence were now on the lookout for "float," rocks with signs of mineralization.

The rocks they examined proved of value only in pelting their burros when they lagged or, for no reason, pulled up short.

Chester was now cotton-mouthed; his feet baked; his eyes burned. He believed he could feel the heat stiffening his joints. Clarence glanced his way, declaring, "Ours is the purification of the desert sun, a tonic to the smoke and sweat-laden air of saloons and dance halls."

Taken with the idea, he added, "Here we are spared the jangle of rude orchestras, the shameless come-ons of the Cyprian sisterhood. Is that not so, Chester?"

The following day.

Trending south.

Few words exchanged.

No float of consequence.

Tramping on.

The day after, night falling, they sighted a distant fire, then another close by the first. A dozen prospectors were camped at the marshy oasis of Saratoga Springs, among them the asthmatic W.A. "Whispering" Kelly and a party up from the Mexican border. The lot were working the orange-red Ibex Hills, a southern extension of the Funerals. Chester and Clarence were welcomed and queried as to any news.

"Goldfield paper ran an article on Death Valley," offered Clarence. "Called it 'the world's largest underground insane asylum.'"

"Oh yes?" One or another of the prospectors asked.

"Said the place was 'the Ultimate Thule of the neurotic.'"

"The Thule? The what?"

"The edge of the classical world," whispered Whispering. An erudite man, he had stoked himself with "facts worth knowing."

"The Latin tongue," he continued, "was obsolete about 560 A.D... Spectacles were invented by an Italian in..."

"Did the article in the paper," one or the other interrupted, "have anything to say about any strikes?"

"No, not really," said Clarence.

"And how are you fellows doing?" asked Chester.

Baleful stares into their fires. Shrugs.

No matter. Their luck could change with the crack of a hammer, and at five in the morning at the latest they rose and were off to take advantage of dawn's low light as it glinted potential float. Each had an eye out for particular minerals; each had his own and often peculiar notion of Death Valley's geology. Rust-colored hematite beckoned Clarence, for it often signaled stringers of "G-O-L-D!", as he was in the habit of spelling out with considerable gusto.

"Hammer it, Clarence!" Chester would call from wherever he was. A well-placed tap of a hand pick could determine if a sample was malleable. If not, the mineralization was iron pyrite—fool's gold.

"Seems to bend."

"Yes?"

"A little. Not much, but maybe a little."

"Spit on it!" Gold gleamed when moistened; gold look-alikes

didn't. Clarence, of course, knew all this, but he would as soon not be hampered in proclaiming "G-O-L-D!" to the surrounding peaks.

The act wearing thin, Chester would separate himself from the poet, drift away over a ridge and on his own contemplate a geological sequence that, as the ancient earth cooled, first produced feldspars and mica and then quartz, with metallic minerals still in a fluid or vaporized state. One by one—copper, lead, zinc, silver— they precipitated, with gold the very last, for gold most "desired to be pure." Gold could materialize in nuggets or stringers threading through quartz or alloyed with...

"S-I-L-V-E-R!"

It was silver now. Chester didn't answer. Exertion in the unrelenting heat got to him, no matter how much water he drank, as much as three gallons a day. He'd rest, sit on a rock, and wonder just what was he doing here. Even in this godforsaken byway, the ground was picked over.

Linking up with Clarence and then traipsing back to Saratoga Springs, Chester had reason to be discouraged by the futility of it all, but in the end, he was not. He'd committed himself to the great sink, its hardships, the lunacy of a prospector's life, and the prospector's dream of discovery, however unlikely.

Dinner at Saratoga Springs was rudimentary, the fare at once decried and wolfed down. Then the *O Be Joyful!* or the like would be passed from hand to hand, and there would be mining talk—of the Valley's distribution of Eureka sandstone, Amargosa chaos, Funeral fanglomerate, and Pognip limestone, potentially auriferous. Chester loved the words "auriferous" and "metalliferous."

Sex.

Later if not sooner the conversation would turn to sex. If Chester didn't bring it up, Clarence would, ruminating on the floozy who'd betrayed him in Rhyolite or brightening with visions of "Dark and passionate senoritas in Ti Juana, with their scanty and scarlet allure. Their eyes are as beautiful as midnight set with stars, and they are sensuous enough to seduce a saint."

Chester recalled senoritas up in Sumpter, Oregon.

"Naughty ladies..." one or the other would sigh. "Make-up's a sign; so's feathers."

Whatever anyone had to say, they were no match for Clarence and his way with words, be they lofty or coarse. "Oh to get a poke, go get a poke. Go to 'Frisco. That's the place. Don't need much, as they've put fornication and general immorality down to prices within reach of us all." He leaned forward to knowingly share, "Why, on the Barbary Coast there are blocks and blocks of wholesale establishments where you can buy the most luscious sexual diversions. At six bits per ton." Graphic and leering details ensued, enough to make a campfire's old timers uncomfortable.

In time, the subject matter would revert to mining talk, which wasn't that alien to talk of sex—with shared notions of pursuit, drilling, blasting, and conquest. Gold, women; the two intertwined deep in the psyche. In Clarence's case, the one had regrettably fetched the other: a nugget-lousy Klondiker had turned the head of his Rhyolite love.

"Thinks she can humble me, she does," he grumbled, "the bitch."

"The bitch," Whispering whispered sympathetically. Chester nodded.

"I'll find a ton of gold—no *tons* of gold," the Big Man said with resolve, "and then, you know what? I'll tell the bitch *no*! NO!" (As a poet, he would as soon not have repeated "bitch," but what else sufficed?)

Whispering poked the campfire's embers, raised a spiral of sparks. He mouthed, "The bitch."

"And will you look to the moon?" Clarence gazed skyward, a poet's fancy o'er taking a prospector's rebuff. "A wondrous crescent moon, suggesting the music and romance of forgotten worlds. Rising up and up in the eastern sky. Its very brightness..." He paused, considering where the image might take him. It proved to be back to his lost love: "The moon's very brightness menaces us, as the lure of some fair but treacherous queen."

The moon's suffused glow lit their way as, one by one, they rose to gather up their tattered sheets, immerse them in the dark waters of Saratoga Springs, and wrap themselves clammy and mummy-like in the sand, so that evaporation's cool might bring them fleeting leave of their chosen hell on earth. It was worth it, wasn't it?

Almost drifting off, but not quite, Chester cast off his near-dry sheets, walked the few paces to the spring, slipped in up to his neck, and as tiny creatures nibbled at his toes, he laid his head on a rock at the pool's edge, and slept, oblivious to the kit fox that lapped by his ear, or the lizards, gophers, and snakes that came and went the night through.

An empty-handed week, and on their way back to Saratoga Springs, Chester took note of a small, dark cloud, the first in days. It was south over the Mojave.

When an hour later the two pulled into camp, the cloud was larger, spreading, streaked with fire. It blotted out the sun. Rain fell, only to evaporate and settle to earth as a pall of humidity. Sweat trickled into their eyes; the pungent smells of creosote and sage wrinkled their noses. The air crackled and buzzed. On a northwest track, a great mass—the sky become ink—roiled overhead and across the Valley to collide with the rugged peaks of the Panamints and release a torrential downpour. In intervals between ripping thunder, Chester and Clarence believed they could hear the roar of mud cascading over cliffs and surging down canyons, gouging, then burying the range's terrain.

An intense half-hour of this, no more, and the sky brightened. The sun reasserted itself with a pinwheel of white rays, dazzling rays that pierced and abolished the gloom. Chester was awed, Clarence transfixed. "I see it," he said, a tremor in his voice, "A goddess stands with beckoning hands." There was a poem in this. Come dusk he had a stanza for his poet's pocket notebook:

> Queen of the land of sage and sand,
> > Where the golden treasures lie,
> The stars that gem her diadem
> > Are the stars of the desert sky.
> In purple mist she keeps her tryst
> > While sun and moon go by.

Asked what he thought of this, Chester complimented the rhymes. "Land and sand. Mist and tryst. But there isn't a mist and it isn't purple. It's..."

Clarence waved his hand as he'd seen poets and artists do in paintings, to continue:

> In *purple mist* she keeps her tryst
> > *Enrobed in purple* she keeps her tryst,
> She calls, "Come here, come woo me near,
> > I am the golden Queen."

Chester guessed it was a poet's right to make anything any color he pleased.

"She calls us," said Clarence dreamily. Above the darkening Panamints, the stars shone and the moon was full.

The temperature dropped to near 90° in the aftermath of the afternoon's storm. Chester made himself comfortable and was soon asleep, only to be awakened by Clarence exclaiming, "Queen of the Purple Mist!"

Chester rubbed his eyes.

"That is to be the name of my epic of Death Valley and the mighty deserts. And see!" he gestured away to the Panamints. Chester sat up.

Settled upon the range, an iridescent mist shone in the moonlight—bluish, maybe purple, if that's what suited Clarence. The poet-prospector was on his feet, rattling around, searching for the lead ropes for their burros. "We must make haste, no matter the hour."

Well before dawn Chester and Clarence were on their way, angling across the Valley toward the Panamints. As the name suggests the range had long drawn prospectors; Clarence was convinced that if Death Valley Scotty ever had a secret mine—the notion had yet to die—this would have been the place.

Sand-augers—lofty grit whirlwinds—criss-crossed their path as they skirted the northern edge of the Owlshead Mountains. By late afternoon, they'd made it to where thousands of years of alluvium had washed down from the Panamints, creating great, rubble-chocked fans. Clarence's radiant and beckoning queen or no, *there was compelling reason to prospect here and now*, for flash floods could often uncover buried ore bodies and carry their fragmented "float" miles downhill. Once discovered, this float could be traced back to its source.

They'd work the Panamint's fans—wet and muddy, spread with tons and tons of fresh debris. There were boulders the size of small houses, to be inspected for veins. There were fist-sized and smaller rocks to be examined with a glass, only to be cast over the shoulder with grumbled profanity.

Clarence, as might be expected, found G-O-L-D that wasn't, and was about to chuck an indifferent, mouse-gray rock when he thought twice about its weight. It was heavy for its size and could possibly be telluride—oxidized gold. He poked the rock with his pocketknife; it was malleable! For once and about time, Chester thought Clarence's find promising. Rummaging his assay items outfit, he uncorked a bottle labeled "NH2" below a red skull and crossbones. He placed Clarence's sample on a flat stone, uncapped the bottle, and gingerly dispensed a few drops.

Nothing happened. Clarence drew in and held his breath. Nitric acid dissolves a host of minerals—but not gold.

But then, the acid pitted the sample. They swore. Still, Chester was sufficiently intrigued to gouge out a fragment, then light an alcohol burner and heat it with the aid of a blowpipe. Several minutes of long, steady puffs, his cheeks ballooning and deflating, and he'd smelted a single, silvery-grey bead.

"Lead."

"Lead?"

"That's not so bad, Clarence. The float is a fifth lead. At the least."

"Anything else?"

"Possibly."

The Queen of the Purple Mist, for all her beckoning and talk of tryst, had led them to... lead.

Lead had its price certainly, but whatever they could get for it would almost certainly be wiped out by whatever it took to haul the ore across the Valley, and up and over the Funerals to the nearest siding of the Tonopah and Tidewater railroad.

Nevertheless, they elected to follow the float to its source, which wasn't difficult, for, where they were, the storm's debris had tumbled down a single narrow canyon. They clambered up it, stopping every so often to heft blackish stones. At first only one in a dozen was lead-laden, after a time one in three—and then not a one, which meant they'd overshot the source. They backtracked to discover a modest outcropping of what Chester believed was galena, a composite of lead, zinc, and silver.

"We'll name her the..." Clarence began, and then pondered options. He initially was for language intimating an immensity, incorporating "Empire" or "Colossus," or something with the word "Elephant" in it, which Chester pointed out was at odds with the desert setting. Clarence hit himself up the side of his head; the name was obvious: "Queen of the Purple Mist."

"Too long," Chester shook his head, "though I like the Queen part."

That afternoon they paced off and marked claims for the "Death Valley Queen #1, #2, and #3."

Clarence thought to toast the occasion. Four lines in, he sought a rhyme for "fortune-fated argosy," but gave up, his heart not in it. L-E-A-D. As in leaden, dull, lacking in spirit.

They descended their galena canyon to the valley floor, there to head north to Bennett's Well, which they found slicked with slime and buzzing with bees, though the burros didn't mind. An hour further on and they parted company, Chester to follow the remnants of an old corduroy road across the Valley's salt flats and back up to Rhyolite, there to fire assay their Death Valley Queen samples. If there was enough silver mixed in with the lead, they might well cage a grubstake and further investigate the southern Panamints. There was an appeal to the area. It was promising in its geology, grand in its isolation, and as far from anywhere as Chester could imagine.

Clarence bore north to Emigrant Pass, crossed it, and made his way up and out of the desert to the farm town of Independence, seat of Inyo County, California. The next morning he was at the cupola-topped Victorian courthouse when it opened, and the first in the door. He looked on as the Recorder opened an enormous red leather-bound volume and, with flowing penmanship, recorded the locations of the Death Valley Queen #1, #2, and #3, noting the hour and date to be 8:52 AM, September 7, 1907 (entered to the minute in the event of a race to register competing claims). The filing was in Clarence's name, but not Chester's. It wasn't that Clarence wanted to edge him out. He'd certainly jack Chester in if the claims proved up.

Walking east of town to the train station, Clarence telegraphed his brother Ralph in Salt Lake City, inviting him out for a visit. Ralph accepted, and awaiting his arrival in Independence, Clarence treated his burros to store-bought feed, and himself to indolent rambles through the shade-dappled town and down to the Owens River, there to swim and laze.

In on the Carson and Colorado Railroad, Ralph Eddy joined Clarence on a trek over to Rhyolite, with detours for desultory prospecting. Once over the Panamints, Clarence wanted his brother to experience Death Valley in its blazing glory, and so chose to make the crossing by day rather than night, to his regret.

Two-thirds of the way across the dunes, heat laid low the poet-prospector. He wasn't thirsty, just suddenly worn and terribly tired. He told Ralph to drive the burros on to water marked by two lengths of stovepipe stuck in the sand off toward the Funerals.

The Big Man would follow as soon as he had rested up. He sank to the sand. A few minutes and he'd be fine. In fact, he couldn't wait to get to Rhyolite and make noise about his discovery, not only on general principals, but for the benefit of the bitch who'd thrown him over for the Klondiker.

Catching a whiff of water, the burros took off, and with Ralph in pursuit they soon reached not only the stovepipe but a newly established plank-and-barrel bar, tent eatery, bathhouse, and, tapping into a line west from Rhyolite, Death Valley's first telephone. Surprised at an outpost of civilization in so remote a setting, Ralph had a drink, chatted with the barkeep, and was considering a second when he was stricken by a sudden thought: Clarence, what about Clarence?

He looked to the west. No Clarence.

Ralph rushed to retrace his footsteps, clear in the windless dunes.

"Clarence!" he shouted, "Clarence!"

He spied him now, and called, "It's me, Ralph!" Panic-stricken, he ran to where Clarence had keeled over. Clarence's face was terribly flushed.

He didn't appear to be breathing.

With no idea what to do, Ralph doused the big man with a canteen of water, then shook him and slapped his face.

Nothing.

Ralph rocked back on his ankles to yell, "You stupid bastard! You stupid bastard!" as much to himself as his brother. He lost control. He pummeled Clarence.

"That hurts, Ralph."

Ralph desisted, to now gently raise his brother's head so he could sip a little water. He helped him sit up, then shakily rise to his feet. Helped him stagger slowly on, to be welcomed by the fanfare of a burro's bray. A few yards short of the stovepipe, Clarence paused and gathered his strength. He looked up and down the Valley—the dunes, the salt flats, the soaring peaks, the evening star out now, with galaxies to come. Even as he'd almost breathed his last, he believed that in life's game, he was destined in this land to prosper. Or perish. The same went for his friend and sometimes partner Chester Pray.

Later. Night. Clarence was up and writing:

> The Valley where the burning air
> Is filled with burning thirst,
> The Valley famed and justly named
> As with a name accursed,
> The silent, sub-sea mystery
> Of horrors oft rehearsed.

He couldn't quite catch the conversation over at the plank bar, other than it was mining talk, and earnest.

He added:

> And golden themes and golden schemes
> And golden dreams abound...

CHESTER'S MINE

CLARENCE AND CHESTER WERE TO FORSAKE the Death Valley Queens, all three. To hold the claims, they would have had to make $450 a year in improvements. They didn't.

Be that as it may, Chester and Clarence were drawn back to the Valley, at times in tandem, more often each on his own. Clarence boasted of eight crossings in the summer of 1908, and he spun tales of his adventures in Rhyolite newspapers.

Chester kept his wanderings and whereabouts to himself. On the basis of his infrequent one-page letters, all his Aunt Julia could say was, "Well, we knew he was prospecting all the time, and we knew he took those terrible tramps through Death Valley looking for mines, and always thinking he had discovered something."

Clarence was partial to the higher elevations of the Panamints, Chester to the lower, and in early 1908 Chester found his way back to where the year before he'd taken note of two low, barren hills. He couldn't exactly say why, but he thought them promising.

Chester methodically criss-crossed the alluvium below the two hills on the lookout for float, to be rewarded with a rock that chimed as a bell when tapped with his pick. He whistled at its weight as he tossed it from hand to hand. No need for a burner or blowpipe. He was juggling high-grade lead. And, he found more float, to be roughly plotted in his head, or even on a tablet.

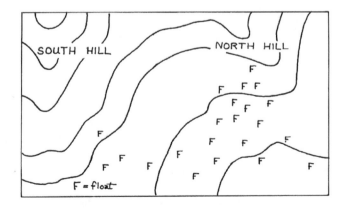

As he hoped he might, Chester saw a pattern to this: the makings of a lopsided triangle with its apparent apex—its source?—the hill to the north. But that source, Chester knew, could have long since been overlaid by a hundred feet of accumulated geological debris—or a few feet or even inches—and a potential lode would be lost to him, the case with 90% of the mineral wealth in the West. The ore would be down there, but there would be no telling where.

He worked his way up the hill's southeast flank, picking up float in a narrowing span. The bedrock was here and there exposed, which boded well, for the greater the chance of an outcrop. Better yet, the bedrock was Noonday dolomite, hospitable to lead. And patches of it were "painted" a telltale faded yellow.

Fifty feet short of the crest of the hill, Chester gasped and sank to his knees.

He wept. He cried out as he hugged a high-grade blowout. As a prospector would boast to another: "rich enough to eat." Rich enough to warrant arduously packing the ore out; rich enough to erase a lifetime of self-doubt.

"Why, Chester Pray," he could say to himself, "you might amount to something!"

He was aware that, once pursued, the outcropping could give out and disappoint, but that was doubtful, for the ore hadn't welled up from below, but rather appeared to have its source straight on into the hill. That night, by moon and candle light, he assayed a sample. Per ton (in 1908 dollars) it proved to be:

Pb	51%	[1,020 pounds of lead, worth $372]
Cu	1 1/2%	[30 pounds of copper, worth $3. A trace, but promising]
Au	$160	[A surprising amount of gold]
Ag	19 1/2 oz.	[Silver worth $11]

The ore stood to be half lead, with recoverable showings of gold and silver, even copper! The little hill would be his isle of blessed fortune. And it brought to mind another isle, in a story he'd read. A nobleman—a French Count—had been unjustly maligned and imprisoned. But then a fellow inmate, dying in the next cell, had confided the location of a Mediterranean desert isle. And hidden there, deep within a cave, was treasure beyond imagining.

Chester's mine would honor the name of that isle. He'd name it

THE MONTE CRISTO

With the first hint of light on the eastern horizon, he was up and about, scouring the terrain for prior location monuments. There were none. The Monte Cristo was his and his alone— although in years to come his friend Clarence would fancy that he was with Chester at the time and that he, Clarence, was the one who'd made the strike. Clarence back-dated the day to August 27, 1907, when a few miles to the north the two had staked the Death Valley Queens #1, #2, and #3. His life through, Clarence maintained that, magnanimously, he'd given the property to "Chester Pray so as to have company for myself in that blanching hell of desolation, solitude, thirst, heat, rattlesnakes and general dangers."

Alone, in the summer of 1908, Chester realized how truly lucky he was, for the blowout proved to be the little hill's sole outcropping. A foot or so of debris and his Monte Cristo could have forever been lost to him and the world. With a few hours' trenching, he determined the lay of the ore and tucked a claim form into a flip-top tobacco can.

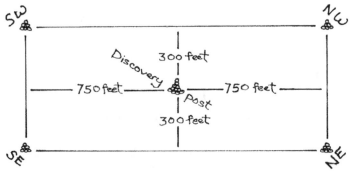

He marked the Monte Cristo's corners with cairns and just above the outcropping erected an imposing "discovery post," a six-foot rock pile wedged with the tobacco can. It would be visible a mile away. This would both discourage interlopers and guide him back to the site. (He was well aware that a low hill a prospector swore ever to remember could in a few months be the same as a hundred others, lost to vagaries of perspective and light.)

By noon he'd done all that needed be done and was on his way to Ballarat, a supply camp west over the Panamint Mountains from Death Valley. The crossing took Chester the rest of the day and all of the next. He found his way to the oasis of Peach Bloom Garden Springs, then drove his burros up over Butte Pass and down Goler Wash. At nightfall, Ballarat's few lights flickered off across the alkali flats of the Panamint Valley.

Ballarat had survived the '07 panic in part because the camp hadn't amounted to all that much in the first place. Dating to the late 1890s, it had been a jumping-off point for excitements on the western slopes of the Panamints. The population had peaked at 250, but now sagged to around 40. Hope, though, was not abandoned. Though ever infatuated with gold and silver, prospectors were actively seeking antimony, flourite, and tungsten. Radiator Bill was so-named for his belief that a vast store for uranium was there for the taking. For Chester, lead was the answer, his samples clinking in sacks slung on his burros.

Past the low, lumpy adobe buildings lining Ballarat's Main Street, Chester arranged for his stock to be looked after at Tom Biggin's "Burro Emporium." Hungry and thirsty, he headed for the Dutchman Christ Wicht's saloon, only now it was Chris Wicht, the "t" painted out. Though Chris was rarely without a vest, watch chain, string tie, and bowler hat, the place was rough-hewn in aspect and spirit. If it was grace and gentility anyone cared for, they were in the wrong bar in the wrong camp in the wrong desert.

A dozen eyes—some bloodshot, a few not—swiveled to Chester as he entered and stepped to the rail, there to have Wicht, with his signature crooked smile, pour the newcomer a shot on the house. Chester nonchalantly tossed it down, impressing no one, possibly because of the coughing fit that ensued, brought under control by a familiar hand clapping him on the back. "Chester, n'est pas?" It was the Frenchman Old John, in camp to ship high-grade from his diggings in the northern Panamints. He invited Chester to a back table, where he introduced him to J. Hollis Gorseline and the Montana Kid. The latter had made his mark in Ballarat by parting a Wicht predecessor from his beard, slicing it off with his bowie knife.

"In Ballarat," chuckled Gorseline, "we've little order and less law. I should know. I'm the judge. Seriously, it's a good camp. You'll see. Chris, how many killings we had?"

"One. Just one," called over Wicht.

"There you go. A good camp."

Chester was to drowse in the low-ceiling saloon's haze of booze and tobacco, having tramped some forty-four miles from his Monte Cristo strike. He stirred with the thought: "I believe I could use a bath."

No one disagreed.

"Don't be a stranger."

Stepping on out into the night, he walked to two-story Ma Calloway's Hotel, Ballarat's best by virtue of being only. The tariff was 50¢ a night, the same in good times and bad. According to a tongue-in-cheek article in the *Inyo Independent*, the establishment's posted rules commenced:

> #1 Guests are warned that we are not responsible for either their lives or their valuables.

> #2 Guests are requested to be careful when shooting at each other in the dining room, for reckless shooting is liable to result in the unnecessary killing of some innocent non-de-combat.

And so forth.

Though in reality short on desperados and long on stray dogs and burros, Ballarat and its citizenry were playing out a last draw of the cards in the game of the Old West. The place was remote, wooly, cheerfully godless—never was to have a church—and not without its charms, as Chester was to discover the next morning.

He was in Robinson's General Merchandise gathering supplies to prove up the Monte Cristo. Proprietor H.L.S. Robinson was a droopy, poorly-circulated fellow, come to the desert for its heat and his health. He was a relation of Robinson, the Los Angeles dry goods king. Both were Harrys; so there'd be no confusion, he went by a mildly aristocratic "H.L.S."

Ballaraters were not without airs. They appreciated a tin of oysters, a volume of Thucydides. The ladies who on occasion took up residence in the little adobes beyond the livery were "doves du prairie."

H.L.S. had just measured off a roll of fuse and was boxing a few dozen blasting caps when a screen door to the rear of the store squeaked open and sprang shut. Footsteps neared—light, soft, hardly the clump of hobnailed boots. Chester was seated at the school desk H.L.S. kept for the convenience of his customers. He didn't look up, absorbed as he was in leafing *The Practical Miner,* wondering how much dynamite he should buy. He sniffed. A flower? Lilac? A woman?

Uncertain, shy, he looked down and to the side to sight a pair of polished black boots, one at a jaunty angle with the other. He looked back to his manual, sounded a "Hmmm" and feigned intense and meaningful concentration. The boots drew him back: fashionably laced, disappearing under a flared denim skirt, with thumbs hooked self-confidently in its pockets. Higher, he encountered a starched, well-filled white shirt and jaunty red bandana. And then a most pleasing—beautiful—oval face, set with appraising blue eyes.

"I'm Clara. Clara Carlsrud."[7]

Chester dumbly blinked, at a loss for words, though not thoughts. She was short, he saw, and for it, all the more attractively rounded. She cocked her head and sweetly smiled.

"And you?"

"Chester," he managed, "Pray."

"Pray what?"

"My name is Chester Pray."

Behind his counter, H.L.S. cleared his throat, a prompt for Chester to turn and exclaim, "Dynamite! How many sticks to the case?"

"Thirty-two."

"Two cases should do."

"Miner?" Clara queried.

"Mine-owner," Chester swelled, "The Monte Cristo."

"As in the book about the Count?"

"You've read it?"

"Yes, and may his fortune be yours." She paused, then quoted the last line of Dumas' novel: "'Wait and hope.'"

---

[7] Author's note: In this account, Clara Carlsrud is the sole character whose identity has been disguised. This is in deference to her surviving daughter and grandchildren, who remain unaware of her secret life in Death Valley.

Clara Carlsrud turned to H.L.S., offering to make herself useful stocking shelves with the sacked and canned goods in on yesterday's stage. Chester rounded out and packed up his order. From smatterings of conversation as Clara came and went, he ascertained that she was visiting from Los Angeles, where she supported herself as a shopgirl at Robert L. Darrow, Ladies & Gents Furnishings, and had ventured to the desert for a few days boarding with H.L.S. and Mrs. Robinson (a change of scene possibly arranged by Los Angeles dry goods entrepreneur Harry Robinson).

"You like the desert?" Chester asked her as he counted out the $57.53 due H.L.S.

"Oh yes. I've taken walks to nowhere in particular, and though never out of sight of Ballarat, I've seen things I've never seen before."

"Like?"

"A ghostly pale flower... the red blur of a fox... and this," she said, reaching in her pocket and withdrawing a small purple stone.

"Amethyst," Chester pronounced, "Good fortune."

"Then it shall be yours."

He shook his head. "No, yours."

"Yours," she countered. "A penny's worth against the millions you'll make." She reached for his hand. The rock was cool, her caress soft and warm.

"Who'd have thought it?" she said, half-turning to H.L.S. "Out here, I've met Chester Pray."

"You'll be back?" asked Chester.

"You may count on it," Clara Carlsrud affirmed, adding "my Count of Monte Cristo" with a mischievous lilt as she retreated through the store. The thrice-weekly outbound stage would soon be rattling away to the high desert of the Mojave, and a rail connection to Los Angeles.

Chester doubted he'd ever see her again. Even so, and however fleeting, he'd meant something to somebody new—and a woman. When all that remained of the stage was a distant cloud of dust settling back upon the desert, Chester returned to his business at hand. He would need a helper, a practical miner. Versed though he was in the varieties and subtleties of ore, he was remiss as to how to free it from its dips, spurs, and angles. He was not alone in this. Prospectors didn't dig; they

PLATE 1
*Chester Pray, age 30. After a flash flood,
Emigrant Springs, Death Valley.*

PLATE 2:   *An 1883 lawn party at the Lake Shore Inn, Lake Tahoe.*
above, Captain Augustus Pray.
behind him, left: Helen Pray (?), Chester's mother.

*Behind two guests:
Chester Pray, age 7.*

PLATE 3: *A mud wagon on the road to Goldfield, Nevada.*

PLATE 4: *Main Street, Goldfield. "The Lure She Is of the West." 1906.*

PLATE 5: *Cribs in Goldfield's Redlight district.*

PLATE 6: *A hard-case Goldfield bar. One of over fifty.*

PLATE 7: *Rhyolite, Nevada, a city of desert dreams. 1907.*

PLATE 8: *Death Valley Scotty, "the fastest con in the West."*

PLATE 9: *Rhyolite's preening "mining men," scoundrels more intent on "hanging paper" (floating bogus stock) than on digging in the dirt.*

PLATE 10: *A Goldfield and Tonopah Railroad "white flag special" on the tracks to Hazen, Nevada. A similar train would have been dispatched to collar Chester Pray and Billy Langdon.*

PLATE 11: *The Fallon, Nevada, courthouse where a feisty Chester Pray stood up to George Wingfield, and George Nixon—two of the most powerful men in the state.*

PLATE 12: *A party on the crest of the Funeral Range. Here was where partners Chester Pray and Clarence Eddy began a last-ditch quest for riches in the blazing heart of Death Valley.*

PLATE 13: *Chester and his outfit prospecting Marble Canyon in the Panamint Mountains to the west of Death Valley.*

PLATE 14
*Possibly (though not certainly) Clara Carlsrud in front of the grand
Goldfield Hotel. Winter of 1911.*

PLATE 15: *Frank Crampton, about to descent a desert mine shaft, his sole illumination a paraffin candle.*

PLATE 16: *Prospector Shorty Harris. He was to proclaim, "Who the hell needs $10,000,000? It's the game, man—the game."*

PLATE 17:
Chester's friend and partner,
the poet-prospector
Clarence Eddy.
He had an ear for...

"The siren voice of sin,
With her tilting violin."

PLATE 18: *Old John Lemoigne panning for color, likely at a spring in Cottonwood Canyon in the Panamint Range.*

In a detail of the photo below: a rare image of promoter Jack Salsberry. His elbow rests on a touring car laden with prospects (suckers) to buy town lots.

PLATE 19: *The land-swindle camp of Ellendale, Nevada—hammered up in a day; faded before the month was out.*

134

PLATE 20: *Today: Remnants of a Monte Cristo-Queen of Sheba ore-loading track and bin.*

PLATE 21: *Today: The Monte Cristo's glory hole. An image of Chester Pray—the man who deserved its riches – has been added for scale.*

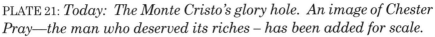

PLATE 22: *Chester Pray, 1876 – 1913.*

sought. The idea of holing underground was cause for tics and tremors. At best they'd excavate a few feet before doing their damndest to sell out.

At the time, Chester could have turned to Ballarat regulars Old John Lemoigne, the Basque Pete Agueberry, or Shorty Harris, who though generally preferring a pint to a pickaxe, was to put in some time at the Monte Cristo in subsequent years.

Chester settled on Old John. He was formally trained as a mining engineer, didn't mind isolation, and temperament-wise, had a long fuse. Old John would have helped Chester pack his supplies, suggesting additions like fast-burning primer cord to properly time blasting, and candles as opposed to carbide lamps (dimmer but cheaper). Once at the Monte Cristo, they would sort out how to best drill, load, and blast.

In the big mines of both Goldfield and Rhyolite, drilling was expedited with compressed-air "widow-makers," named for wreaking havoc on miners as well as mother nature. But with the Monte Cristo's lack of steam or electric power (or anything), there was little choice but arduous single or double jacking. To single jack, miners pulled a powder box to the rock face, upended it, and sat on it. Grasping a one-foot bit, they hammered away at it with a four-pound sledge, rotating the bit a quarter of a turn between strokes. Chester and Old John could have side-by-side single jacked, or they more likely double jacked: one man grasped the bit and the other two-handedly wielded an eight-pound sledge. The going was slow in dolomite, faster in carbonate. Trading off and using longer and longer bits, two men could sink a four-foot hole in half an hour, the first of six or eight on a shift. Then, with the vigorous application of a broom handle, they'd pack the holes with 40% gelatin dynamite.

The next step was crimping fulminate of mercury blasting caps onto lengths of fuse. This was accomplished with pliers or teeth, with the risk of blowing either a hand or head off. Cap and fuse would be poked into each shot hole's outermost charge, the result a spaghetti array of fuses dangling from the rock face. This is where fast-burning primer cord came into play. Knot it to the fuses, and it would ignite them in a predetermined order. Differing holes had differing functions.

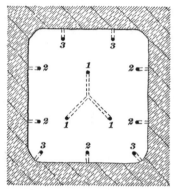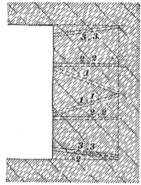

Textbook diagram of holes to be packed with dynamite:
1. hammer and toe cutters; 2. lifters; and 3. edgers. For difficult
rock, a miner might add burn holes, baby holes, breasters, relievers,
benchers, and backers.

Near the end of the Monte Cristo's first day, Chester would have taken a deep breath and with the stump of a candle "spit" (ignited) the primer cord, then watched and waited as it sparkled its round of fuses. Once satisfied that all were properly burning at a rate of a foot a minute, he and Old John would have hastened a safe distance away, to await the detonation of the cutters, followed in quick succession by the lifters, and edgers, the sequence ejecting thirty tons of rock from the hillside. Old John counted the blasts, a caution against a hung charge. With the last, Chester was on his feet, rushing into the smoke and rock dust swirling from the beginnings of an "adit," a tunnel boring horizontally into the earth. And before he could see it, he could feel it: the dense, cold slick of carbonate of lead—*everywhere he reached.* He burst back into the sunlight howling with joy. The vein had widened and could well open into a glory hole. A mountain of the stuff, that's what he'd found!

Old John wasn't so sure; he was the first to tell you that he'd shouted "Ore from grass roots to hell!" once too often, more than once too often. A few rounds more and they could be in nothing but Noonday dolomite.

Two more days, and Chester and Old John were nearly out of dynamite. But not lead.

Old John thought it time to ramble on. Knowledgeable in the ways of a canny prospector, Chester wished him well. Lemoigne would be a fool not to look for more of the stuff—and stake claims—

in the surrounding hills. This beat working for day wages, even the day wages of a friend. Chester then spent several days single jacking and sampling a hole here and a hole there, to get a better fix on the local geology. As far as he could tell, his carbonate of lead ore was associated with a fault that wended off to the south, rounded a draw, and angled across the second of the hills that had drawn him here. Indeed, it stood to be a source of a portion of the float he'd collected two weeks ago. A hundred feet up its face—where he estimated the fault to lie—he took a flyer. He set off a last few sticks of dynamite, and damned if he didn't uncover a "blind vein"! (Ore that hadn't broken the surface.)

How Chester came up with the airy and wondrous name for this, his second mine, he never said. He could have been aware of two previous claims in the southern Panamints, both with the same, magic name. Or he could have sought a rosier version of his and Clarence's Death Valley Queen #1, #2, and #3. Or he could have recalled a last paragraph of *Goldfield as I Saw It*, the 10¢ tract he'd sent away for, from Cambridgeport back in 1904:

> If the noble queen who traveled so far to see Solomon in all his reputed wealth and acknowledged glory could visit Goldfield and her sister camps, she could again truthfully say, "The half has not been told."

"The half has not been told." Could be. He hoped so. He penciled the claim form with the name of this noble queen...

THE QUEEN OF SHEBA

Happy as he'd ever been in his life, he packed up and hiked back to Ballarat.

For work to go forward at the Monte Cristo and the Queen of Sheba, he well knew there were problems to be solved. Water was one. There was a good flow at Peach Bloom Garden Springs, about four miles distant, but there was an obstacle—a steep, intervening ridge. Was a pipeline possible? If so, it would have its price.

Transporting the ore to a railhead—likely the whistle-stop of Zabriskie on the Tidewater and Tonopah line—was a daunting prospect. He would have to cut through a forty- to fifty-mile road.

He'd need capital.

Salsberry. What about mining man Jack Salsberry?

Chester was mindful that Salsberry's Greenwater enterprise (in Jack's words) had "netted him a vast fortune," and if it wasn't for the Panic of '07, he most certainly would have made a go of the copper up at Ubehebe. He would have overcome the challenges there—near identical to those at the Monte Cristo and the Queen of Sheba.

At Robinson's General Store, H.L.S. welcomed Chester to use the school desk, pen and inkwell included, to fan the flames of his discovery—and dreams. He wrote Jack Salsberry.

Weeks passed, then months, and no reply.

Chester asked around, wrote other mining men and promoters.

As the fetching Clara Carlsrud had encouraged him, there was promise and solace in the closing three words of *The Count of Monte Cristo.*

"Wait and hope."

THE BALLARAT LYING CLUB

IN THE YEARS 1908 THROUGH 1910 several thousand prospectors dared Death Valley. But a month or so of cracked lips, foul water, dismal food, and unyielding geology—and that was it.

To stay on required a mix of self-delusion and practicality, the latter geared to getting by until the cards fell right. In Chester's case, he'd hold out for financial backing to develop his Monte Cristo and Queen of Sheba. Against that day, he roofed over an abandoned Ballarat adobe and in late 1908 opened an assay office a stone's throw behind H.L.S. Robinson's General Store.

H.L.S. was in a bad way. Never in the best of health, he had been injured by the collapse of an adobe wall. His legs had been crushed, and there was no choice but to amputate his right one below the knee. It subsequently fell to Mrs. Robinson to handle the mercantile's lugging and lifting, often with Chester's help. He enjoyed the couple and was grateful for their company. He would spend hours at the school desk across from H.L.S.'s counter, tending to his ledger, writing letters, and looking up with every ring of the bell rigged to the entry, half-expecting—hoping—to see Clara Carlsrud, in from Los Angeles and pretty as a curly ribbon.

Clara did, in fact, visit the Robinsons—to Chester's chagrin, for he was off on a prospecting tour of the Slate Range to the south. He found some color, enough to record claims dubbed the Dr. Cook and the Fake, the latter not a value judgment, but a nod to advice from fellow Ballarater John A. Fake. Dr. Cook was an itinerant medical man; he may have heard Chester out when, less and less frequently, he believed himself mercury poisoned.

The phantom voices in his head were, for the time being, silenced.

On the basis of favorable assays, Chester sold his Slate Range claims and, flush with a little cash, thought he might travel to Los Angeles and put in an appearance at Clara's store.

"You needn't," said H.L.S. with a rare grin. He waved a letter. She'd be in Ballarat over the Fourth of July.

As the holiday weekend neared, Chester had washerwoman Daisy Higbee starch and iron his least-worn trousers, shirt, and kerchief. He rehearsed what he might say, how he might convey the impression of a man of substance. Worldly, with a hint of mystery.

The camp's Count of Monte Cristo.

Desert rats drifted in from far and near: Old John Lemoigne and Pete Agueberry from the northern and southern Panamints, Shorty Harris and Clarence Eddy in from Rhyolite. Frank Crampton came all the way from the Brigham Canyon, Utah, where he had been working as a surveyor. As for Death Valley Scotty, real prospectors didn't care for him, and he knew it. Conversely, he had little interest in anyone he couldn't con.

The three-times-a-week stage from Randsburg was due late in the afternoon of the third, and Chester paced the few hundred feet up and down King Avenue, greeting friends and acquaintances with a tip of the felt hat he'd washed, stretched, and picked clean of desert nits.

A little after four, Ellis York, as was his custom, set up his telescope in the middle of the street and trained it on point where the stage would cross the Argus Range, the final traverse for anyone up from Los Angeles.

Affecting nonchalance, Chester sauntered over to pass the time of day.

"By God, she's in sight!" Ellis was to cry. He pulled his watch from his vest and checked it. Collapsing his telescope, he strode to Wicht's saloon to announce that he'd sighted the stage and to solicit bets—a pool—on when, to the minute, the stage would pull in.

Not long and Chester could see it: a plume of dust switch-backing down the black basalt of the Arguses. One, then the other, he wiped his Shinola-shined boots on the back of his trouser legs. He straightened his corduroy jacket, on loan from the rack in Robinson's store. It wasn't all that comfortable in the heat, but had a good cut in Clarence's opinion. Now Chester could make out the horses and stage. Within the hour, he would suavely greet and take the hand of... who was she? He had no idea, other than what he'd gleaned from the Robinsons, who didn't know much of her either, other than that she had been born to the east of the Valley of the Moon in northern California, and presently boarded at the Florence, a downtown Los Angeles residence for single working women.

Negotiating hairpin turns, the stage driver expertly skipped his horses over their traces, at the same time hand-braking the stage's left, then right wheels. Not long and he'd gain the valley floor.

A dozen people gathered, in Ballarat a mob. Prospectors clutched little bottles of gold dust, proof of rich strikes they could be persuaded to part with; Ellis York was back with his pocket watch.

The stagecoach kicked up a cloud of alkali as it crossed the playa west of the camp, rending it invisible for five, six, eight minutes.

Chester had never felt such anticipation.

The four-horse conveyance broke free of the alkali.

Ellis counted out the time. "Six o' one... six o' two...."

The stage driver reined up.

"She's here! Six o' six!"

Over at Wicht's there'd be a happy drunk.

The horses whinnied; their shanks shuddered. The stage's side windows were streaked and grimy; nevertheless, Chester perceived a female form, adjusting a feathered hat. With rustic chivalry, he stepped forward to unlatch and swing open the door. Out stepped, and none too gracefully, "French" Marguerite, a prostitute up from Randsburg for a round of tumbles over the holiday. Two of the sisterhood followed, possibly Fay and Little Fay.

"Boys, who'll it be?"

That was it for passengers. Otherwise the compartment bore a consignment of whiskey and beer, as well as handbills and posters for the county's upcoming elections.

Crestfallen, Chester turned away, and if anyone had looked closely, they'd have seen him swallow hard and a tear escape his eye to bump down his cheek. He drooped off to his adobe, and the coming of a lonely night. He could, of course, join the crowd in Wicht's saloon, but it wasn't in him. Like as not, he ate beans out of the can, cold.

At four in the morning, the Fourth was ushered in with a bang, a window-rattling explosion. In Ballarat's heyday, there would have been further blasts and a cacophony of whistles from mines in the Panamints above town. With just about everything shut down, Chris Wicht, as a matter of civic duty, had carted a half case of dynamite out onto the playa and set it off.

Getting up and out, Chester was cheered by the shouts and laughs of Ballarat's few children rolling iron bands salvaged from splintered barrels; there would be a hoop rolling contest later in the day. Bunting fluttered here and there on King Avenue, from Wicht's saloon to the Mexican laundry and over to Biggin's Burro Emporium. It would be a hot one; by nine o'clock the thermometer in the shade of the balcony of Calloway's hotel had broken 100°. Lounging on the porch, Clarence spun a yarn that hinged on the discomfort he'd felt in Los Angeles when the temperature plummeted to an icy 80°.

Los Angeles—a faraway city and a faraway girl. As Chester was a dreamer, she was the stuff of dreams.

The parade stepped off at noon. Old John Lemoigne, long since and proudly an American citizen, was Grand Marshal, and a pick-up band featured the Montana Kid bowing a fiddle crafted from a desert gourd, Daisy Higbee on her washboard, and visiting Frank Crampton on the accordion. Thank God for Frank, for otherwise no one would have an inkling as to what they were playing. Shorty Harris did his best to keep an American flag from dragging in the dust. Chester had thought to add his banjo to the band, but instead he bore a purple and white B.P.O. Elks flag provided by H.L.S., who would have carried it if he could. Everyone joined in, to the point that the sole onlookers were a couple of kids up a windmill and H.L.S., swaying on his crutches. As it took no more than five minutes to march from one end of Ballarat to the other, the grand company processed back and forth several times, with each time H.L.S. almost losing his balance as he clapped and pointing to an individual, then another, and gave them a thumb's up.

Chester gave him a thumb's up back. The truth was that— even with an absent Clara Carlsrud—there was no place he would rather be.

The Fourth of July picnic was gala and first class: a side of beef, Basque bread baked by Pete Agueberry, and roasted Indian corn. The only thing missing was self-aggrandizing politicians. With few locals on the voting rolls, Inyo County electoral hay was better made off toward the Sierra Nevadas in the prosperous ranching and farming towns of Independence and Bishop. Ballarat would have to content itself with handbills and posters, languishing where they'd been unloaded from yesterday's stage.

Judge Gorseline offered a few words, and Clarence made a little speech that commenced with: "When I first hove in sight of Ballarat I thought, 'what a hell of a place this is. Nothing doing here and nobody to hum.'" He was wrong, he said, though not altogether. He admonished "one and all to become merry and forget all the old grudges, if any, as to conflicting claims. We should care for one and another, and our animal friends too, offering them bacon rind, brown sugar, and Three Ex Borax soap, which things all prospectors know are a delight to the appetite of every burro."

A baseball game was organized, then a single and double jack contests as to how deep a hole an individual or a pair could sink in a block of granite in fifteen minutes. Chester washed out early on, strong enough but lacking in rhythm. Frank Crampton was the day's champ.

There were contests for children: the hoop race, the spoon and potato relay, and the three-legged race. For the ladies, Daisy Higbee excelled in nail driving, and a fifty-yard dash was scheduled, but was later cancelled as three of the more eligible participants were at the time otherwise occupied. Four men's races rounded out the afternoon: the sack race, the fat man's race, and the fifty and hundred yard dashes, the last the object of serious betting brokered by Ellis York.

Chester put money on Chester. Back and forth to his Monte Cristo and Queen of Sheba claims, he'd trained on the flats of Butte Valley. He worked out how much he could push himself and not be knocked out by the heat. A hundred yards looked to be optimum.

A shot from a gun fired by H.L.S, and Chester was off the mark and flying down the street, until, with a second or two to go, his legs seized up, but not so he couldn't hurl himself across the finish line. To come in first! He gasped, stumbled, and fell to the ground, to be in an instant delighted and revived.

"Chester Pray," she exclaimed, " I knew you'd win!" Her elbow rested on the open passenger door of a Reo touring car. Chester had glimpsed it motoring to the finish line as the race was forming up.

"Why, Clara!"

"And Chester, I'd like you to meet my friend Antoine. Antoine Barber. He has a place in Los Angeles. On Coronado Street, up the hill from mine. He's in the automobile business. What is it you do, Antoine?"

"Insurance adjuster, and sometimes I specially outfit cars. This one has big tires and an extra radiator. Ideal for the desert." Barber extended his hand. "Clara told me about you, and I jumped at an excuse to come here. You know, she thinks the world of you."

Chester wasn't sure about this Antoine Barber, but took heart when Clara advanced to kiss him, smack on the mouth. At the same time, Clarence, providing distraction, complimented Barber on his motor car and presently had him on the sideline and all ears as to "catching the immensity," Clarence's expression for finding and extracting Death Valley's gold.

"This immensity," queried Barber, "It's a great lode?"

"Maybe yes, maybe no. I'm not yet at liberty to say." It pained Clarence, but he felt it best that for a time he keep his counsel as to "the immensity."

"I'm thirsty. You too?" Clara asked Chester. She linked her arm with his, so that the two might stroll in the direction of Chris Wicht's, adorned for the holiday with a new sign: HEADQUARTERS SALOON. Their entrance was cause for admiring glances and nudges. Who would have thought it? —peculiar Chester scoring more than a footrace. The two knocked back whiskeys and chased them with the fresh, if warm beer Chris had unpacked from crates in on the Randsburg stage.

The place buzzed and whooped with conversation particular to a desert watering hole—gossip on a clear track to legend. Recently, Clara learned, there had been a showdown between washerwoman Daisy Higbee and her deadbeat husband Billy. One had beaten the hell out of the other, but with a twist. Citizens within earshot of their shack were alarmed to hear Daisy shout, "Don't kill me Billy! Oh, oh please don't kill me!" But then a look through the window revealed Daisy wailing her husband with one, then the other of his hobnailed boots.

Barkeep Chris grimaced. He was at the time recovering from a fancy taken to a spoken-for Randsburg woman; she'd stabbed him with sheep-shears, an inch from his heart. And the woman's boyfriend had shot him "plumb square in the ass."

Clara stifled a laugh, giggled. She loved Wicht's place, the crowd, the night, Ballarat. As for Chester, she pressed her knee to his and stroked the back of his neck.

"You'll never guess!" cried poet-prospector Clarence, entering the saloon in the company of his new friend Antoine.

"Who cares?"

"Pour me another."

"Me too."

"You'll never guess!" Clarence, not to be deterred, shouted.

"We've no idea."

"That's a fact," chimed Clara.

Chester rose to the bait. "And just what exactly is it, Clarence, that we'll never guess?"

"The burros!" They abounded in Ballarat over the Fourth. "They've got at the politicians' posters in on the stage! Come see!"

A contingent took him up on this. They could use the air. They were curious.

They were disappointed.

A poster had been unrolled, and it appeared to have been licked or bitten here and there. A lid was off a crate, revealing a stack of handbills, a box of tacks, and a jar of paste. Two or three burros looked on at a distance.

"The posters! They need to go up!" incited Clarence (exactly why he kept to himself).

After an initial uncertainty, the cry of "Plaster Ballarat!" echoed in the night. "Slap 'em up!" Crates of rival politicians were pried open, and their earnest faces and bogus promises were soon everywhere. The sheet most in demand was:

"ROUGH HOUSE" KELLY
IF ELECTED, WILL RESIDE HERE!

What better candidate for the camp's every privy?

An hour of this, and they were all back in Wicht's saloon, with more stories of life a few feet from hell: talk of petrified monkey eyes, electrical rattlesnakes, and the magnetic ledge that wouldn't let go of Jim Farley's mule, inopportunely shod with iron shoes. The ledge seized up Jim as well, or rather his hobnailed boots; it was a long walk to camp in his stocking feet. The incident explained—somehow—why Farley had crazy spells between the full and new moon.

A little before eleven, Clarence quietly stole away, to return, all excited, with the news: "The burros! 'They've gone and done it! They're at it now! Hundreds of them! Eating all those posters—all those candidates, all those politicians—with gusto and delight! And do you know what that means?"

"What, Clarence, does that mean?" Clara humored him.

"An hour and you'll see. We'll all see! AND HEAR!"

Come midnight and Clarence exited, to re-enter, elbow through the crowd, and bust up a game as he clambered up onto the sole pool table between Rhyolite, Nevada and Independence, California.

"WHAT A NIGHT! LIKE NONE OTHER!" he proclaimed with a theatrical shudder. "A storm-wracked night lit by great flashes of sheet lightning!"

This was news to Chester and Clara, in fact to everyone, but if that's what the poet would have, that was fine.

"And this celestial drama, for all its wonder, is but a backdrop for the GREAT DRAMA of this eve! For what, I ask you all, does it mean for the many burros of Ballarat to have dined on POLITICIANS, their paper and paste to their liking?"

All present shook their heads, baffled.

"For hours now, the innumerable burros of Ballarat have ingested great quantities of GAS!" He spelt it out: "G-A-S!" Upon which he cupped his hand to his ear. "And you can hear it now! A STUPENDOUS PASSING OF COLIC WIND!"

"A fart? He means farts?"

"A continuous sound as of ripping silk," the poet-prospector elaborated, "or the tearing of heavy canvas, with a tremendous chorus and orchestra of burros emitting a sound of a hundred jazz bands all playing at once in a vast fanfare and frolic! Future generations will recall, upon this momentous night a mighty and protracted report reaching out from the small and unimportant town of Ballarat! A vast tidal wave crashing all over Nevada, California, Arizona, and New Mexico!"

The many stupefied and the few sober were in awe.

"A report shaking the mighty, snow-capped Sierra Nevadas, Idaho's Sawtooth Mountains, and for all we know, echoing against the far Appalachians!"

And let it be said, from that hour of that night of the Fourth of July, 1908, every Ballarater felt a little better about himself. In Clarence's words at least, they mattered; their motley burros mattered. They cheered and clapped. The Big Man bowed, leapt from the pool table, and his back slapped many times over, made his way to the bar.

"Clarence, your pleasure," offered Chris, "a glass on the house! And that goes for all of you, all of us!"

Whiskey was poured all around, but not drunk. Not yet. A toast was in order, and Clarence was pressed. Could he top the drama of the STUPENDOUS PASSING OF COLIC WIND? He raised his glass, hesitated, then rhymed:

There is a destiny that makes us brothers,
None goes his way alone.
All that we send in to the lives of others
Comes back into our own.

Each looked to his neighbor, reflected on this, and knocked back the last of the night's liquid joy.

"Two in the morning," Chris called. "Time to put the cork in the bottle."

"Walk me to H.L.S.'s?" Clara asked Chester.

"You bet."

On the way they passed Barber's touring car, with a somnolent Antoine draped over the wheel. Clara patted his arm, "Sleep well, Antoine." She turned to Chester. "I would like to visit your mine. Could I?"

"You could. Only there's no motoring there. You'd have to ride a burro. Or walk."

"Fine by me."

She kissed him, and he kissed her back.

"I believe in you, Chester Pray," she whispered in his ear, "you and your mine. It wouldn't be much, but I could send money to help you out."

Chester held her, and he could not believe his fortune. They kissed again, and parted. She let herself into the store, and he walked the few feet to his adobe out back.

Over at Wicht's HEADQUARTERS SALOON a single oil lamp burned low. All was quiet but for the strains of the Montana Kid's gourd violin, accented by rings of the little bell he'd fixed to the instrument's neck. Desert rats lolled in their chairs and were scattered across the beer-sloshed floor. Sighing, twitching, stirring, lapsing back to sleep.

Chris closed out his brass register and wiped his bar clean. He sat back, lit his pipe.

A long, plaintive draw of the bow ended the Kid's piece.

"'Night, Kid. The pool table's yours, if you like."

The Montana Kid took him up on it, rolled the balls out of the way, and stretched out on the green felt, cradling his curious gourd violin.

The next morning, Chester saw Clara Carlsrud to where Antoine Barber emerged from under his Reo, having cleared brush from axles and given them a shot of grease. Clara donned goggles and a duster. Antoine fired up the Reo with a first turn of the crank. He slid behind the wheel.

"Soon?" Chester asked Clara.

"Not soon enough."

"And nice meeting you, Antoine. Take care."

"I will."

They drove off, shifting from first to second, then second to third. Antoine and Clara talked. Then Clara thought to turn and wave to Chester.

He waved back.

Out across the playa, the Reo's oversized tires raised a cloud of alkali dust, and the vehicle was barely visible, then vanished from sight.

PROSPECTORS IN LOVE

CHESTER WAS SMITTEN.

As were others in the desert.

Whether transient or abiding, love had its place. Sipping his *Oh Be Joyful!*, Shorty Harris would recall proposing to Bessie Hart, an Amazonian lady prospector of the Panamints. Rejection, regrettably, was swift.

"You're a good friend and a fine man, Shorty. But as a husband? You're just too small for a damn big job."

Old John Lemoigne, on the other hand, was believed to have found solace in the arms of a Shoshone squaw, and when she died, another. Their graves were up the hill from his shack and mine.

To court Clara Carlsrud, Chester was to trim, and then cut off his beard. It had made him look old, Mrs. Robinson felt. "And looney," added H.L.S. from across the store, "loonier than he already is."

Chester then anteed $8 for the stage to Randsburg, where $3.25 bought him a coach seat into Los Angeles' grand Santa Fe Station. Trading the desert's solitude for the city's clamor was jarring, but only at first. Every day there'd be time with Clara. He'd be at Darrow's store when she got off, and they'd enjoy dinner and a movie show, or take the streetcar to Westlake Park's Victorian gardens. The nine o'clock curfew at the Florence Residence put a damper on anything further. If Clara could take more than a half hour off for lunch, they'd meet at Cole's Pacific Electric Buffet, with its specialty "the dip sandwich" (later to gain immortality as the "French dip"). A hangout of cops, bankers, politicians, and when in town, Death Valley Scotty, the cafe was on the ground floor of the largest and tallest building in Los Angeles, headquarters for Henry Huntington's Pacific Electric "Red Car" line.

"Chester," Clara said as they finished their desserts, "there's a man I'd like you to meet, a lawyer friend." He was seated at a corner table across the sawdust-strewn white tile floor. They sauntered over and chatted, and when it was back to work for her, Frank

McNamee invited Chester up for a drink in his office. The building, with its soaring Greek columns crested with the intertwined initials P.E., was a high-toned address for not only Henry Huntington and his associates, but also the city's business elite.

McNamee's paneled suite, with its heavy oak furniture and wall of law books, at first agitated Chester; it reminded him of the courthouse where he'd been convicted of attempting to fence Goldfield gold. But then, with a cigar and Scotch in hand, he took his surroundings to be elegant, what might be expected if a fellow struck it, floated stock, and became a respected mining man. McNamee allowed that he was versed in mining law, with considerable experience in Nevada, both in private practice and, earlier on, as District Attorney for Lincoln County. Framed diplomas, licenses, and photographs attested this. An image of a black man with the look of a pugilist caught Chester's eye.

"A brave, fine man, worth fighting for. His name was Ellis, George Ellis. He was a road grader up in Fay, Nevada. He took issue with being shortchanged on his wages, which prompted his boss and his boss' lowlife friends to break into his cabin, catching him asleep. They ordered him to dress, at the same time emptying his billfold of $22.25, his every cent."

"The bastards," murmured Chester. Reminded him of the Mohawk Mine detectives who'd waylaid him up in Hazen.

"And they didn't let it go at that. They tied his hands, dragged him to a nearby canyon and threw a noose around his neck. They hoisted him up and had a mighty good laugh before lowering him a heartbeat short of strangulation. They then demanded that Ellis tell them what he knew of a series of Fay break-ins, and when he professed to know nothing of the crimes, they raised and lowered him a second time. Still he denied his guilt, so up he went a third time, with a particular son-of-a-bitch grabbing his legs and pulling down to hasten his death. But, merciful God, the branch broke. Desperate, poor Ellis confessed to the burglaries. For this he was clubbed on the head with the butt end of a pistol and ordered to make tracks for the Utah line. 'And don't come back,' they called after him, firing over his head."

Chester shook his head. He'd nothing against black men, or Indians, or anyone really.

"Ah, but George Ellis did come back," lawyer McNamee continued. "A brave man, he told Sheriff Jake Johnson what had happened, and for his trouble was arrested."

"No surprise, I suppose."

"But there was a surprise." McNamee rose from his chair, paced an imagined courtroom. "It fell to me to prosecute Ellis for burglary, but, you know, I didn't. I went after his accusers, turned the table on them. I nailed them, every one, for assault with intent to kill. It was my honor to wish the good man 'Godspeed.'"

Chester was impressed. If anything came of his workings, he'd call upon him. Frank McNamee was sharp and a straight shooter.

Chester took his leave, and he walked to where Antoine Barber had offered him a couch in his Coronado Street apartment. Antoine had left his job as an insurance adjuster, and was working as an electrician. He'd immensely enjoyed the desert, he said, and had been reading up on geology.

"I believe I might have it. The aptitude."

"To be?"

"A mining engineer. I've some training as an engineer."

"Could be, Antoine."

"You get your mines going, and I'll be there. Do what I can."

While down in Los Angeles, Chester wished he could see more of Clara. She was behind the counter ten hours a day, six days a week. The next Sunday, they took the Red Car to Santa Monica, where they strolled along the pier, rode the Ferris wheel, and got sticky with cotton candy. They unlaced their shoes and waded in the ocean. From time to time, a winter wave would break close to shore and send them scampering past sandcastles, flooding and collapsing.

"A castle. Do you ever dream of a castle?"

"I have."

"We could have one if..." She trailed off.

Chester shared her sentiment. The fantasy was common to Death Valley prospectors: a hovel one day and the next, a castle in the sand. There had been talk in Goldfield of raising funds to erect a grand edifice shared by all who sought their fortunes in the desert. Its white granite turrets would be visible for miles; the soaring entry hall would glow with stained glass by day and electric chandeliers by night; there would be halls for concerts, banquets, and billiards. Construction costs would exceed $1,000,000. It was a dream destroyed—washed away—by the Panic of '07.

"Needn't be a castle," Clara squeezed his hand, "a bungalow would do. A cozy fireplace, a piano..."

"You play?"

"I'd like to learn... So when can I come visit your mines?"

Chester swelled as she said "mines," not the singular "mine." It made him feel a man of means; his toes curled with the thought of it.

"I can get off, plead a deceased uncle up in the Valley of the Moon. Or better yet, a sick mother. I've no shortage of complaints up there."

They agreed on dates for a week's journey to the mines and back.

"Won't be fancy. Camping out, bacon and beans. But the weather will be good, warm but not hot."

"Can't wait. I can't, Chester. Really."

Back in Ballarat, he reserved a night's room at Ma Calloway's, the one with the plush, though threadbare, settee. Over at Biggen's Burro Emporium, he negotiated an extra burro and schooled the animal. On the morning of the appointed day he picked a bouquet of desert flowers—yellow asters, Indian paintbrush, and blossoms he knew not—and decorated the burro's bridle.

The stage was late, but no matter, she was on it and flew into his arms. He insisted she ride the burro, even though it was but a few buildings through the twilight to Ma Calloway's, there to dine on creamed hash and spuds. "You should have been her last night," Ma was fond of saying, "Glazed pheasant supreme, White Star on ice."

Amused by the *Inyo Independent*'s recently-printed satirical rules of her hostelry, Ma had written them out and posted them by the coat hook in Clara's room.

> #7 Guests wishing a light in their rooms can take
>   a feather from their pillow; that is light enough
>   for anyone.

> #8 Guests requiring a drink of water in the night,
>   raise the mattress and you will find a spring.

In the morning, Chester and Clara stopped by Robinson's store, visited with H.L.S. and his wife Lucy, and were on their way. Their route took them down the Panamint Valley. An hour south, Chester pointed out the gallows frame and tailings of the Cecil B. mine. Scotty at one point had something to do with the operation, and when it had gone under, Chester had hauled its machinery to Ballarat and sold it for scrap. He got $50 for it.

Noon, and the wind stirred, kicked sand in their eyes, and was to whistle the day through. As her burro plodded on and on, mile after mile, Clara's spirits flagged. The landscape was dull and dreary. She ached. She got off and walked. Chester did his best to cheer her, but got a sinking feeling.

They pitched a dry camp. Clara wasn't sullen; she just didn't have much to say, just wanted to roll up in a blanket, her back to Chester and the wind. Normally, it died away at dusk. It didn't, blowing the night through and into the next morning.

They angled east toward the seemingly impenetrable gray-black Panamints. As they neared the range, Clara spied a deep, shadowy slot where two wagons would be hard-pressed to pass. As they now entered Goler Wash, her frame of mind improved. They were out of the wind, and there was an air of mystery to the twisting, turning, wildly convoluted chasm. At intervals it widened, to be penetrated by sunlight, with spring flowers sprouting amid the abandoned workings of "demon souls of the days gone by," to quote a Clarence poem. Chester pointed out the Belmont mine, a good producer in its day, and nearby an earlier Queen of Sheba, filed on in 1892.

And somewhere in or near the chasm was the Lost Guller mine, its heat-crazed locater unable to retrace his steps.

"The fellow had told his partner, 'I want water; gold will do me no good.'"

"He must have been thirsty. *Very thirsty*," Clara laughed. She'd eased up. The word "gold" had a salutary effect. She'd no complaints as the canyon ascended to a pass cresting the Panamints, a gain of over 3,000 feet.

"And it's downhill from here. You like the view?"

She did: before them, the sweep of Butte Valley. Rolling white and purple fields of flowers. In their midst, blue and yellow Curious Butte was a geological confection, a layer cake.

They lengthened their strides, even skipped and ran across Butte Valley and down a canyon orange with poppies and red with monkey flowers. An hour before sunset they reached Peach Bloom Garden Springs.[8] A zephyr rustled the surrounding oasis'

---

[8] This was Chester's name for today's Warm Springs. And what a 1920s mineral survey identified as Curious Butte is now Striped Butte.

cottonwoods and palms. Wild grapes were ripe for the picking, and in his comings and goings, Chester had planted and tended a little orchard and garden. They'd have peaches and strawberries tonight. And figs, if Clara liked figs.

"Listen," said Chester.

A bird sang and, taking wing, flashed in the golden light.

"A mocking-bird. Strange he would wind up here."

"We have," whispered Clara.

They laid out their camp and turned loose the burros; they'd not wander far. Chester thought to entertain Clara with his banjo; he'd been working on a rag—"Pickles and Peppers." She'd like it. But, with his banjo back in Ballarat, he instead asked for her hand and gently led her to where he had diverted the outflow of the hot spring that watered the oasis to create a rocky pool a couple of feet deep and large enough for two people to splash about— and make love. They did, both in the misty warm water and on a blanket spread on the soft sand at its edge. "Oh Clara! Oh Clara!" he exclaimed, and doubted it could ever be better than this.

Later, they danced, Clara singing "Glow Worm" and "Only Me." And the mocking-bird serenading the moon.

Sunrise, and Clara was awakened by a clattering of rocks— Chester erecting corner monuments and officially staking his claim to this Death Valley Eden. "A place for a castle, maybe, when the mines pay off."

At the springs, they left the established trail and bore north to cross a precipitous ridge and behold the shimmering void of Death Valley, to Clara the end of the world as she knew or could imagine it.

They reached the mines, or rather, where the mines would be. And where Chester saw glory close at hand, Clara wasn't so sure, surveying a crude dugout and half a dozen shallow, rubble-choked tunnels. He explained that they were "exploratory, blocking out ore, ore that's worth near a hundred thousand."

He could have fooled Clara. "It's there," he assured her.

He demonstrated his ability to single-jack shot holes.

"Good, you're good at that," she half-heartedly encouraged him, or meant to. She looked distractedly away, off into lifeless, lonely space. But then Chester was to get her attention when, he fished in his pocket and offered her a box of matches. He'd packed the holes with dynamite. "Go ahead, light the primer cord."

"Me?"

"Sure." And she did.

"We have to wait now. Make sure all the fuses are burning properly." Twenty, thirty seconds ticked by. "Looks all right. Now we can leave. But walk, don't run. Trip up and that could be final."

Two minutes, and a staccato series of explosions rocked the earth. The tunnel ejected debris and belched smoke. Their shift over, the two descended the Monte Cristo's hill to boil up and take tea on Chester's dugout's little porch, its timbers scavenged from an abandoned mill across the valley. Chester sat on a powder box, Clara on an actual chair. The sun set on the Funerals.

"Old, drab, bum rock, now all rosy and glowing. Why Chester, it's beautiful." She appeared to mean it.

"Mountain's majesty," he agreed, "and with no trees cluttering things up." He was at peace here. At home. And just look who was joining him for dinner.

And the night.

For two days she was by his side, in bed and in one or the other of his workings. Chester taught her to double-jack, she holding and turning the drill and he pounding away. She was at first skittish handling the dynamite and ramming it into the drill holes with a broom handle, but got over it.

Back out in the sunlight, they'd hug and kiss as fuses burned, the dynamite detonated, and the hill shook and rumbled.

Examining a rock blown loose, Clara believed she detected specks of gold. Chester agreed, "Sure enough is, you bet!" Which was what he'd say no matter what she found.

On their third day at the mines, they had company. Clarence Eddy came their way and, in Clara's presence, was all flowery talk and tail feathers. He was one for the ladies, the fact recently testified in print. A column in the *Inyo Independent* had imagined "the breathless adventures and the God-like aims of this modern conqueror creating awful havoc in the Young Ladies Seminaries of the country. Eddy is a brave fellow, but he had better beware. He surely trifles with fate."

Chester, though, needn't have feared a move on Clara. Clarence was well stocked in the female department. Pulling up an extra powder box on Chester's porch, he extolled Mabel's cooking; reveled in Juanita's sauciness. But then, what of the delights of exotic Asia, the dancer? Thus rhapsodizing, he appeared to confuse one with the other. After an amorous turn with Mabel, it was Asia who pinned up her long tresses. He'd had a row with Juanita, then reconciled with Mabel.

"How could that be?" Clara puzzled.

"How could *what* be?"

"You'd fought with Juanita, then you'd made up with Mabel."

He leapt from his box, flung his arms wide to address not only Chester and Clara, but also the desert beyond and all America.

"Mabel! Juanita! Asia! They are facets—sparkling and radiant—of a single, glorious woman! I've found her, Chester, and oh, will that Rhyolite bitch regret, lament, and rue the day she left me for that Klondiker. She'll be consumed, consumed with jealousy! For your friend Clarence has courted and shall wed T-U-D-D-L-E!" He spelled out the letters, as when prospecting, he shouted "S-I-L-V-E-R!" and "G-O-L-D!"

"Her name," Chester puzzled, "is Tuddle?"

"No! It is 'T-U-D-D-L-E!'"

"And that," asked Clara, "stands for something?"

"It does, my dear, and it will forever be... our secret." The pause, his inflection, his arching of his eyebrows, supposed a naughty secret.

The next morning Clarence made himself useful, not hammering away at the Panamints, but composing a letter on Chester's behalf to promoter Jack Salsberry. He set the scene: "far from the madding crowd's ignoble strife." He described the ore: "splendid and of very permanent character, already worth some millions."

He then waxed, "It is the claim of some that even our best and greatest dreams will become realities if we persist in the right line," which in this case was coming up with "a little ready money to prime the pump." Clarence then did his best to flatter Salsberry, knowingly complimenting his successful ventures, skipping over Greenwater and blaming his Ubehebe debacle on the timidity of effete, eastern investors. As he rambled on, the opportunity for profit escalated: "some real permanent money" became, a paragraph later, "a vast fortune," and finally "a mint only to be expected from a boom that will electrify the mining world."

Jack Salsberry, Clarence wrote, was "the lone prospector's true friend," and that's why Chester was writing him, "not the

Guggenheims or the W.A. Clark interests," or further unnamed "spectacled, cold, and calculating financiers."

"You are my man, Mr. Salsberry!" the letter signed off, "My choice to step up to the plate, be in on the ground floor!"

Chester wished he could write like that.

The next morning the poet-prospector was on his way, where exactly he wouldn't say, other than he was on a "mission of mystery."

"The immensity, the immensity," he confided, "It beckons me, calls me, awaits me." He wished Chester—and the little lady, too—luck with the mines, even though whatever they might find would be a drop in the bucket of world finance when "the immensity" proved out, which it assuredly would.

Fifty yards down the slope in the direction of Death Valley's alkali flats he called back, "Nice to meet you, C-L-A-R-A!"

"You too, Clarence."

"Toodle-lo, Chester!"

A day or so later, Chester and Clara were on their way back to Ballarat, where assays confirmed they were in ore, and it was good, with the quantity of lead up from 51% to 66%. Not as much silver as at first; gold per ton holding steady.

The two parted, to write often. When she could afford it, Clara enclosed a modest postal order, so he might block out more and more ore.

Chester considered Clara his fiancée; her feelings about this are less certain.

He missed her, terribly at times.

She was there in Ballarat on the Fourth of July, 1909, driven up by Antoine Barber. They'd bought a hundred feet of hose and Antoine had cobbled a gasoline-powered air pump, small enough to pack to the mines, so Chester could burrow deeper into his hills, and deeper yet.

"Why thank you, Antoine. You've a true friend."

"It's nothing, really. Clara and I believe in you, Chester."

The Fourth this year featured a performance of John Lambert and his "One Man Rodeo."

But the holiday couldn't match last year. Not without Clarence around. He was off in San Francisco with Mable-Juanita-Asia, who a few months earlier had become "wifey." And when Clarence next returned to Ballarat, he spoke not of "T-U-D-D-L-E!", but with a knowing wink, "T-I-W-U-D-D-L-E!"

What that meant no one was the wiser.

"As do I, she writes," Clarence boasted, "poetically if not poetry." On a Saturday night in Chris Wicht's saloon, he unfolded a page and read aloud:

LIFE

by Juanita Eddy

What is life?

Darkness and formless vacancy for a beginning, then a dim lotus of human consciousness, finding itself afloat upon the bosom of waters without a shore.

Then: a few sunny smiles and many tears, a little love and infinite strife. Fierce mockeries from the anarchy of chaos and whisperings from Paradise.

Dust and ashes and once more darkness circling around, and in this way rounding or making an island of our fantastic existence.

Life?

Laughter and tears, seeming realities and absolute negations.

Shadowy pomp and pompous shadows. Love, hate, dread, hope! So it has been, so it is, and so it will be forever and ever.

The camp's gathered rats gazed into their drinks, then looked to each other, then back down to their drinks.

"Some truth to that, I guess," one mumbled.

"Bejesus."

"You say her name's Juanita? Doesn't sound like a Juanita to me."

"Sad."

"Isn't life?"

"Though she said it was fantastic."

"You never know what's on a woman's mind."

"That's a certainty."

"Drink to that!"

Tending bar, Chris Wicht poured out the last of a bottle of *Oh Be Joyful!* and opened the next.

WILD MEN & RICHES FOR ALL

AS CHESTER PRAY AND HIS FRIENDS came and went, prospected and mined, they from time to time encountered Death Valley's native Americans.

Once, Tomesha—"land afire"—had been theirs. Shoshones inhabited the Valley's east, and Paiutes the west. By the early 1900s they were dispossessed, with many now laborers on the edge of the white man's world. They worked on track crews for the railroads, broke rock in Rhyolite mines, and did anything for a dime in Ballarat.

Yet there were holdouts, bands living as they always had, or trying to. High in the Panamints, a scattering of Shoshones gathered pine nuts, tended small gardens, and laid in wait at waterholes frequented by bighorn sheep. Their war-chief was Panamint Tom, abetted by his hulking brother, six-foot, four-inch Hungry Bill.

They were cause for white-man wariness. In a journalist's eyes,

> They were warriors of the old school and seemed to have made a business of killing off stray prospectors to get their burros and supplies. Quite a number of men have gone into Death Valley and never been seen again, especially when they stopped at Bennett's Well, where the band of Hungry Bill camped.

The man reflected on what he'd written.

> Fact was, most of those men needed killing. The Shoshones are to be excused if they killed a few white men in those harum-scarum days. [9]

---

[9] Carl Wheat in *Death Valley Tailings: Rarely Told Tales of Death Valley*, p. 36.

Uncertainty and suspicion persisted as Ballarat and other Death Valley camps sprang up, and for one very good reason—or rather, question: Just how would a prospector feel if he had been run off a claim rightfully his? He would certainly be angry. And chances were he'd be bent on vengeance. Similar emotions were imagined for the Shoshones and Paiutes, their tribal lands encroached and exploited.

A 1906 article in the *Goldfield Chronicle* believed:

> There is something uncanny about the way men continue to disappear in Death Valley. There is the specter of foul play of some kind, likely by the renegade Indians who inhabit the Panamints. They are a sullen, malicious, conniving rattlesnake species.

In this context, a brouhaha was to erupt and be picked up by newspapers across the country. The major players were Death Valley Scotty, Clarence Eddy, and a clutch of unidentified "wild men" —maybe Hungry Bill's, maybe not.

Or were the "wild men" phantoms of feverish imagining?

It all began, at least in Clarence's mind, when in Rhyolite he managed to wheedle information as to the location of Scotty's ever-elusive mine. Scotty, in fact, had taken Clarence to the summit of a nearby mountain and with his telescope zeroed in on a locale high above Bennett's Well in the Panamints (a dozen miles northwest of Chester's claims). Why he would have shared this is puzzling. Be that as it may, Clarence, as quickly as he could, was packed up and on his way in the company of E.G. Gould, an acquaintance down from Reno.

A week later, in a state of great excitement, Clarence burst through the door of the *Rhyolite Herald* crying, "Clemens! Where's Clemens?"

"Over here, Clarence. I'm right here," said editor Earle Clemens, looking up from his next issue's layout. A coronet was at his elbow. He practiced on off days.

"Stop the presses! Toot your horn! Get out your forty-point type!"

Clemens sighed, a heard-it-all, world-weary sigh.

"Stupendous pannings of gold! *Ten thousand* ounces of silver to the ton! Would you believe it? T-E-N..."

Clemens cocked his eyeshade. "The 'immensity,' Clarence?"

"Well, not *the* immensity. But surely *an* immensity. The L-O-S-T..."

"Clarence..."

"I-N-C-A!"

"Clarence we've work to do," said Clemens, easing the poet-prospector on his way. "But congratulation. I'm sure you'll be rich—"

"—beyond my dreams! Or yours!" Clarence completed the thought.

Down went Clemens' eyeshade. He was back to his front page, its lead story welcoming a delegation of money men due in from Los Angeles.[10]

Clarence strode down Golden Street in the direction of the rival *Miner*. What was it about Rhyolite? His fiancée had taken up with a no-good Klondiker; his old friend Clemens had shown him the door. Well, at least he'd shown the bitch a thing or two, marrying Tiwuddle. If only Tiwuddle didn't drink and think so much, and get morose and weepy.

Clarence could use a drink.

He shared his news of the Lost Inca with a sparse late afternoon crowd at the Combination Saloon. They could have cared less, which Clarence interpreted as receptive. By the time he resumed his journey to the *Miner*, his tale had taken on a whole new dimension. Entering the paper's Golden Street office, he strode to a sunset-facing window. His brow furrowed—troubled—he gazed off in the direction of the Panamints.

"Can I help you, Clarence?" inquired editor Frank Mannix. Mannix owed him a hearing, considering the small change he'd paid for the Big Man's poems and stories.

Seizing the editor by a shoulder and lapel, Clarence, began, "It was getting dark up there. I was monumenting the claim." Sweat beaded his brow; the words came in a rush: "Croppings fabulously rich. Then, upon me, Mexican half-breeds or Indians... broken English... evil intent. They said I should 'vamoose.' Ordered me to 'hit the grit!' Then they left. It was getting dark, so no choice but

---

[10] The article promised potential investors that "touring the treasure vaults of the district will give the lie to your *Los Angeles Times*, which is constantly maligning us as a lot of cutthroats and assassins."

to pitch my tent. Done with that, I had a look into the little valley below where I'd camped. Saw fifteen... twenty or more! Redskins wildly gesticulating!"

The *Miner's* few employees paused in whatever they were doing and listened up.

"Did I sleep that night? Oh, no. Couldn't. From off in the shadows, a rifle shot! I rose to business... discharged my revolver! Frightened them away!"

Clarence turned to linotyper Guy Keene. "Punch that in hot lead!"

"Clarence," Mannix asked, "is this some sort of dream you had?"

"Oh, no, no, no. If you want my opinion: conspiracy! I was set upon by renegades in league... in league with... SCOTTY!"

Even for Death Valley tales, this was on the tall side, yet Frank Mannix went along with it. Just could have happened, he supposed. Hungry Bill had a camp in the vicinity and was a ready villain. The *Miner* had previously reported, "He claims the whole country, lives in a low, savage state, it is claimed, having taken his own daughters to wife." The following day the *Miner* ran:

WILD MEN ATTACK
POET PROSPECTOR

Attacked by wild Indians and driven from the fastness of the Panamint range of mountains is the story told by Clarence E. Eddy, the poet-prospector as he returned to Rhyolite last night fatigued and disappointed.

In Mr. Eddy and party's narrow escape it is possible that the mystery of the Death Valley tragedies have all been cleared up. If his version is correct, a small band of bloodthirsty redmen are hidden away in the wilds of these mountain fastnesses, who have never been conquered by the white man. They are armed and equipped and have for years preyed upon the immigrants and prospectors who have braved that region.

They have probably killed for all of these years, and their victims have been charged to the heat and privations of the desert.

While examining a promising ledge, Mr. Eddy was met face to face by a warrior fully armed and equipped for battle. The man, who bore the face of a brute rather than that of a human, was able to speak broken English: "This is the Indians' country. The white man has taken all the rest; this is ours. We give you warning!"

The savage then turned away and joined a party of half-clad, but armed warriors further up the mountain. As Mr. Eddy and his party were leaving the place they saw that they were being watched by the dusky fellows.

Mr. Eddy thinks it possible these men are in league with "Death Valley" Walter Scott and are guardians of his mysterious mine.

Mr. Eddy has no inclination to return except under the protection of United States soldiers.

In a follow-up article a week later, Clarence declared he'd no need for an armed military escort. He'd take matters into his own hands.

POET PROSPECTOR
LEADS PARTY TO
ATTACT REDSKINS
[sic]

Clarence E. Eddy, the poet-prospector, accompanied his brother Ralph Eddy, of Chicago, and his partner E.G. Gould, of Rhyolite, superbly mounted on swift horses and armed to the teeth left under cover of darkness Monday night for the Panamints to locate "Death Valley Scotty's" mine and oust the warlike band of redskins whom he encountered on his recent visit, and whom he believes to be the henchmen of the mysterious Scott.

A seasoned Indian fighter, the brother Ralph appeared eager for the fray, as, brandishing repeating rifles and automatic revolvers, the trio cut sand for the Panamints.

Eddy had discovered rich ledges, so he states, and says that he is going to monument them according to the laws of the United States, or die in the attempt.

Whatever did or didn't befall the brave trio failed to make it into subsequent editions of either the *Miner* or the *Herald*. What the *Miner* did report was that SCOTTY OF DEATH VALLEY IS HOT. And what steamed him was not that Clarence was after his mine—that was good publicity—but that Clarence had claimed his attackers were "redmen in league with Scotty," and were "bad" and "savages." "Most redskins are friendly," he refuted.

In its next issue, Frank Mannix and the *Miner* had enough of both men and invoked a poker term for a bluffer with a card short of a flush.

SAYS "SCOTTY" AND POET-PROSPECTOR ARE FOUR FLUSHERS

No Bloodthirsty Redskin in the Country—Only a Few Harmless
Bands of Natives

The old prospectors in camp laugh at the Scotty-Eddy imbroglio and state it as their firm conviction that the whole matter is only a medium grade of hot air from start to Finish. "Warlike Indians!" said a grizzled old timer, "Bosh!" About all the Indians in that part of the country are a few superannuate squaws who make a living from picking pine nuts, and the alleged ferocious braves subsist from this income.

It is my opinion, however, that the poet-prospector and Scott have concocted a scheme to gain notoriety. Both, if I am able to judge correctly, court the limelight.

Across town, the *Herald* concurred, admonishing, "I do not know whether Eddy knew any better, but he certainly should have known what he was talking about before spreading his wild stories." As for his Lost Inca mine, it was "a fake, pure and simple."

In a final article, the *Miner* was to give Clarence dubious credit—for out-bamboozling Scotty: "Eddy has Scotty, the Death Valley wonder, faded for a few notches. In other words, this most estimable newspaper thinks that the poet-prospector has a greater range of fancy, a more picturesque imagination, and therefore has scored against Scotty on this account."

Derision. Ridicule. What of it? The write-ups gave the two grandstanders the attention they craved. And, hardly missing a beat, Clarence went on to promote his imminent discovery of the "real immensity" in a new partnership with E.G. Gould (along on his Panamint wild man adventures).

Scotty fared less well. Not only was he one-upped by Clarence in Rhyolite, he was in for big city comeuppance. The *Los Angeles Times* called him "a penny Dare-Devil Dick of the Desert, woefully lacking in ingenuity of the high-class kind, clutching a whiskey bottle by the neck and posing like a five-cent hero in a five-cent drama."

If that's the way they felt down there, Scotty chose to be off to San Francisco—where he was arrested for attempting to unload stolen ore, likely from Goldfield.[11] According to the city's *Call*, he double-talked his release, and "Chief Biggy, finding the man tiresome, advised Scotty to get out of the city and not annoy people with his cheap advertising methods. The best thing he could do was go back to his mine and stay there."

This wasn't the first, and hardly the last, time Scotty was to have a run-in with the law. He boasted, "If I am a thief, I am a smart one—to beat 38 arrests."

Then came #39, which had him hauled down to Los Angeles.

Years ago, in his staged "Battle of Wingate Pass," his brother Warner had been shot in the groin, prompting Scotty to promise a Dr. C.W. Lawton $1,000 if he could save Warner's life. Lawton came through; Scotty didn't, and he was now jailed pending payment of the bill. Surely this would be no problem, considering that he'd recently boasted of taking $600,000 out of his mine.

---

[11] Earlier in the year, Scotty had asked Frank Crampton to refine several sacks of ore at an assay office he'd opened in Goodsprings, Nevada. Frank was to recall, "It looked a lot like Mohawk high-grade from Goldfield. The answer was 'no,' as Scotty knew it would be, but hoped otherwise."

But he hadn't, and the Death Valley wonder was on the ropes. The judge brought him down with:

Q. Just how much money have you taken from mining ventures in the last three years?

A. None. I have no secret mine.

Q. Did you ever have a mine?

A. No. Between chasing my jackass and rustling grub and water, I didn't have much time for prospecting. I didn't keep books, didn't find any gold, so what the hell is the fuss about anyway? I ain't got nuthin' and I never had nuthin'.

He hung his head, and in open court, cried. Spectators felt sorry for him—humiliated, undone. And that suited him, for if bluster didn't work, there was failure—the more abject, the better—as a ploy. As he was once heard to coach his dog, "Walk lame, Windy, and you'll get a bigger bone." Which Windy did, her faltering gate mimicking her master's until they reached his car. Man and dog then hopped nimbly in and were on their way.

A bone—a very big bone—was presently to come Scotty's way in the form of the largesse of Albert I. Johnson, founder and president of Chicago's National Life Insurance Company, and a millionaire many times over. Among those "ambushed" at the Battle of Wingate Pass, he saw through Scotty the confidence man, but nevertheless found him amusing, and even was to have a hand in his antics. While previously cutting swaths through Los Angeles, Scotty had paid a newsboy a dollar for 3¢ paper, and tipped a bellhop $100 for carrying his grip. In a widely reported incident, he took pity on an unshaven, disreputable hobo and gave him a thousand dollar bill.

Johnson is believed to have footed Scotty's extravagance—all but the handout to the bum. He didn't have to.

The bum was a grubbily-disguised Albert I. Johnson.

Why?

It is difficult to say. Johnson was a retiring, enigmatic man, as close-mouthed as Scotty was brash and noisy. An 1899 train wreck in Colorado was a factor. The accident killed Johnson's father and broke twenty-seven-year-old Albert's back, leaving him incontinent and in chronic pain. Drawn to the desert, he found it palliative. And he'd not be bored there. Scotty was quick-witted and ever up to some new and entertaining nonsense. Johnson enjoyed saying, "Sure I know Death Valley Scotty, that's him sitting right over there. He's my partner."

Johnson and Scotty talked of building a spacious and shady hacienda at Grapevine Springs at the northern end of the Valley, with Johnson's acquaintance Frank Lloyd Wright as the architect. Not long, and the project assumed the dimensions of... a castle.

Scotty was all for the idea; it would validate the existence of his much-maligned mine. How else could a prospector afford a castle?

Scotty's castle.

In the end, Scotty had his mine. He'd struck gold in the deep pockets of Albert I. Johnson.

Over in Ballarat, Clarence Eddy was more confident than ever that *his* day was at hand. The Lost Inca could stay lost; the time had at last come for "the real immensity." For two critical years, he'd been mum as to its location, but now he and his partner E.G. Gould laid claim to thousands of acres, and believed it was only a matter of time before the mining world would gasp in awe.

At issue was a novel geological theory that had struck Clarence over by Furnace Creek. A boulder had caught his eye, cracked open by the cool rain of a summer cloudburst pelting its superheated surface. Clarence wiped clean his glass and had a look: the interior of the boulder glistened with "flour," tiny particles of free gold. Not enough to reclaim, but significant in the genesis of Clarence's theory that "For centuries, ages, eons, such wealth-laden rocks had rolled down from the mountains and been crumbled and *dissolved in the bed of the valley.*"

"It's there," he regaled the desert rats in Wicht's saloon, "Tons of rich deposits out there beneath the crust in the solutions and slimes we've trudged over time and time again! And not just lying there, but enhanced—concentrated—by the fact that Death Valley is the world's largest volcanic crater! For years we've found gold, only to have it peter out. Now we know where it's gone. It's simple, elemental!"

Any who knew to the contrary kept it to themselves. (Pulverized gold does not concentrate; rather it diffuses to the point of vanishing.)

"Think of it! And this prompts a gift." He turned to Chester.

"My friend, you've been good company in the development of the Monte Cristo and the Queen of Sheba. Let all here gathered be my witness as I give you my share in these properties!"

(Not that he had a share to give. He was never more than a casual visitor as Chester doggedly developed the claims.)

"Why thank you Clarence," said Chester anyway.

"No need to thank me Chester. Your workings, I regret, will be a hard go when *it* comes in. *It* being the IMMENSITY."

Clarence had raised Salt Lake City money. Preliminary assays, he allowed, had isolated both gold and silver flour.

"How much?" a rat asked.

"Two dollars to the cubic yard." A dazzling concentration!

"To the cubic yard, Clarence?"

"Well, no, actually. To the ton."

"That's all?"

"A beginning, my friends. A beginning. Why right now, my associate Mr. Gould is arranging for a gold dredge soon to be freighted to Ballarat, and then to be hauled to the Valley floor."

Having worn out his welcome with the editors of Rhyolite's papers, Clarence took his case to Goldfield, where a staffer from the *Tribune* heard him out. Needful of upbeat mining news and with few qualms as to exaggeration, the paper proclaimed:

DEATH VALLEY THE TREASURE BASIN OF THE WORLD

Death Valley proper contains about 500 square miles, and within this area there is sufficient wealth to make every poor man in the world richer than Croesus; to make King Solomon's mines and Monte Cristo's treasure look like penny savings banks. It is literally composed of gold, silver, copper and lead. It only requires the ingenuity of man to secure it. He will do it. The time is not far distant.

For ages the rains and snows have been beating these mountains down into Death Valley. They are filled with precious metals. Down, down, down they have rolled for centuries! The ore may be 100, 1,000, 10,000 feet below, but it is there, and when the process is discovered by which it may be reclaimed, all the world will be rich, and gaunt poverty will cease its weary journey in the land!

At his Monte Cristo and Queen of Sheba workings—soon to be near worthless if his friend's theory held up—Chester Pray had a balcony view of Clarence's immensity, with Eddy and Gould fly-speck dots out on the Valley floor. Every few days they'd up and move their drilling equipment to a new location, sampling more and more acreage.

They bored test holes, a dozen in the first month.

They fell out one with another, worked separately, and then were back together.

They estimated the extent of the deposit to be a full 30,000 acres.

They sunk hundreds of holes.

To absolutely no avail.

The best assay was $2.30 in gold and 30¢ in silver a ton. What they *did* establish was that beneath its crust, the Valley's muck was, at the most, fifty feet deep, a bit short of ten thousand. The heralded gold dredge never made it to Ballarat or the Valley. In its stead, the U.S. Geological Survey showed up to drill four of its own wells.

Their finding: "no gold or even potash, the principal dissolved constituent being sodium chloride."

Clarence packed it in and retreated to Rhyolite, there to knock about, shrugging, "Chicken one day, feathers the next." He reworked his epic, "Queen of the Purple Mist," dropping a stanza here, adding a new one there.

> Some win by luck, some win by pluck
> And some win not at all,
> Some lie forlorn by sage and thorn
> With the purple mist for pall;
> While life endures, the spirit lures
> And gold allures us all.

So what if he and Gould had come up empty-handed? There'd be other strikes. The gold was out there. Somewhere. In the meantime, he busied himself. The *Miner's* "Doings About Camp" column reported:

Clarence E. Eddy, the poet-prospector, says that his output of verse for the month ending Friday, March 13 at 12 o'clock midnight, is 33 feet 9 3/4 inches by actual measurement, and that every stanza is a gem more precious than diamonds, no mention being made of rubies, quartz, or telluride.

SUNSTROKE

FREE-SPIRITED AND GABBY, death valley's prospectors were good press.

Flip open a notebook or uncap a lens, and as if by magic, Shorty Harris and one or more of his burros would appear, pose, and let a reporter in on his latest strike. This in the utmost confidence, of course, to be sealed with shots of *Oh Be Joyful!* If Shorty was scarce, quotable desert rats were fixtures in the bars of Rhyolite and Ballarat.

Clarence the poet-prospector was ephemeral. He would generate a flurry of copy, and then drop out of sight for months or even years, his whereabouts known only to Tiwuddle, if even she.

Chester was scarcer yet. Much of his life remains a mystery, and was at the time, even to his mother and aunt. There was mention that sometime between 1906 and 1912 he was off to Mexico, and he may as well have been a Klondiker; Clarence Eddy, in a letter to his brother Ralph, refers to him as "my friend from Alaska." This may have been no more than campfire talk, where fancy seasoned many a tin plate of beans.

As far as can be determined, Chester now enjoyed a relatively calm few years: running assays in Ballarat, prospecting with various partners (a dozen names accompany his filings at the Inyo County courthouse) and as his income allowed, working the Monte Cristo and, to a lesser extent, the Queen of Sheba. He appears to have sacked considerable ore, yet was shy the financing—and road—to freight it to the Tonopah & Tidewater Railroad, forty miles distant. Antoine Barber remained his friend, helping him rustle and install the machinery required for a transition from prospecting to serious mining. At the Valley's failed or played-out workings, old generators, compressors, and hoists were theirs for the scavenging.

For Chester, there had to have been intervals of great, even awful loneliness. On prospecting trips, he would often be the only soul in several hundred square miles, his only company his burros

and characters in books lent by H.L.S. Robinson or Old John
Lemoigne. A slip on a rock or a mishap with a charge, and there
would be no one to tend to him, mourn his passing, or bury him. It
was no wonder that prospectors were so antic when the press was
at hand; it was an antidote to their solitary lives, however those
lives may have been egged on by hope. Illusory hope. As Clarence
Eddy was to sign off a letter, "The tonic for bitterness is illusion."

For Chester, working his claims was little different than off
prospecting. Alone. Lonely. Tossing and turning in the night would
be the worst, with the option of jumping to his feet, and climbing the
hill to seize a sledge and bit and single-jack until dawn. He'd then be
"down the hill talking to himself" (as the miner's expression went).
Sitting on his porch and gazing into Death Valley's void, he'd imagine
his mines come to something... imagine life on "the outside."

A bungalow, a piano.

Life with Clara. Marrying Clara.

He looked forward to supply treks to Ballarat, where he did
his best to cheer H.L.S. Robinson, who in 1910 had his right leg
re-amputated, this time between the knee and the hip. Chester
shared any letters in from Clara, postmarked from Los Angeles
and from her home town up by the Valley of the Moon. There were
parts better kept to himself.

"Go ahead, Chester, go on..."

"I can't, H.L.S.," he'd blush and grin.

In the winter of 1910 Chester spent some time in Goldfield
trying to persuade promoter Jack Salsberry—or anyone—to have
a serious look at the Monte Cristo. Clara joined him, in from Los
Angeles on the Tonopah & Tidewater. A photograph survives. *(see
page 131, plate 14)* A foot of snow has fallen; she stands at the edge
of the wide sidewalk fronting the Goldfield Hotel, billed as the
finest hostelry between St. Louis and San Francisco. Its spacious
lobby boasted gilded columns, carpeting woven to order, capacious
copper and brass cuspidors, and a conspicuous safe. At its opening
gala in June of 1908, a stream of champagne ran down the front
steps and pooled where Clara now stood.

Clara is bundled in a fashionable high-necked dark coat and
a jaunty wool and fur hat. She neither smiles nor frowns; her gaze
is clear-eyed and calm, receptive to what her time with Chester
in the wintry desert might offer or promise. Not now, but when
the Monte Cristo paid off, they could play the swells: pull up in

a Thomas Flyer, whisk through the lobby, ascend the elevator blazoned with the brass G, and luxuriate in a $20 suite with velvet curtains, a marble bathtub, and a balcony view of a landscape that, depending on where and how you had staked a claim, offered oblivion or fawned-upon fame. You won or you lost. Rarely was there a draw.

Whatever headway in Goldfield Chester may have made with Jack Salsberry, he was to suffer a terrible setback when the following spring the snow line receded to the crest of the Panamints, the desert's flowers bloomed and withered, and the land was desolate and parched. In the letters and recollections of Chester's friends as to that summer, there's mention of sunstroke. Though details are sketchy, there is little question that he had a dreadful time of it and that he suffered serious and lasting damage.

Progressing from mild disorientation to death, sunstroke or "thermic fever" (as it was known) is a malady of degrees, and if properly recognized, can be countered with sips of water, shade, and rest. Chester experienced the full gamut and agony of the condition, as had many prospectors, notoriously on the Valley's twenty-two mile "stretch of death" from Furnace Creek across the salt flats to Bennett's Well. The risk of the route was exacerbated by crossing in the summer, by not having the sense to travel by night, and by the liability of "new boots." This last plagued Rhyolite cook Alfred Nard, whose feet so "sweated and unbearably swelled" that he unlaced and discarded his new footwear. "With his feet bleeding, his lungs raw, and his throat coated with chalky dust, it didn't take long for the elements to finish Alfred Nard." [12]

Though Chester Pray often came this way—it was the shortest from Rhyolite to the Monte Cristo—his friend Antoine recalled that it wasn't the "stretch of death" that laid him low, but a trail across the Panamints and down into Ballarat. It was a different route than the Goler Wash route Chester had taken with Clara. It was a full seventeen miles shorter, but at a price: an additional and arduous 2,700-foot climb. He'd taken this shortcut a number of times and was familiar with its landmarks and springs. Even so, a lesson of the desert—often ignored—is that even a minor lapse in common sense can precipitate disaster. And death.

---

[12] Daniel Cronkite in *Death Valley's Victims*, p. 10.

A summer storm could have left the desert fleetingly damp and cool, prompting Chester to set out in the morning rather than wait until later afternoon and the night. Resting at Peach Bloom Garden Springs, he could have neglected to top off his canteen. Why should he, when in a few hours he would be at Arrastra Spring in Butte Valley?

The long, dry uphill climb to Arrastra Spring may have dulled or addled his mind, prompting him to keep going, and reach Ballarat all the sooner.

Or Arrastra Spring may have run dry, or been choked with mesquite, or had its flow fouled by animals dead or alive. Prudent judgment could have said *light a fire and boil the water*. Or simply, *cut over to another Butte Valley spring* (and take the easier Goler Wash route). But Chester could have looked up to the pass (now Rogers Pass), and could have been beckoned by shady stands of pinyon pine. Not far, just a few miles. From there, the trek would be easy, downhill.

Sunstroke is insidious. It affects the mind well before the body. It makes a man careless, even reckless.

Thirsty? Not really, not particularly.

As the sun arced higher in the sky, the day would have been increasingly hot and crackling dry, with the effect of both exaggerated by a stiff wind across the Panamints, evaporating perspiration before it could soften and cool the skin. A newspaperman friend of Clarence's wrote:

> One would turn his back upon the unwelcome gusts only to find that it played upon the back of the head and neck with more damaging results. The head began to ache and the brain was dizzy. The burning wind has baked many a poor wretch's brains and sent them reeling to the ground with a canteen about their necks well filled with water, never to rise again. [13]

This may have been the case—almost—with Chester, or he may have simply drained his canteen and not had the wits

---

[13] Paul DeLaney in "A Trip Across Death Valley," *Bullfrog Miner*, August 3,1907. See End Notes for sources of further quotes from Chester's day.

about him to do what his friend Pete Agueberry had done in the Panamints north of Ballarat. Pete had returned to his camp with an empty canteen, there to discover that his burros had ripped apart his water cans and hightailed off. It was hot; the closest spring was forty miles distant. Calmly gathering up his gun, gold pan, and a bag of salt, he searched for the animals the night through and half the next day. Near dead of thirst when he found them, Pete had the presence of mind to shoot one, cut its jugular vein, and catch the blood in his gold pan. He was able to slake his thirst, and adding salt to prevent the remainder from curdling, poured it into his canteen. He lived to tell the tale many times over in Chris Wicht's saloon.

If only Chester had been so resourceful, but he wasn't, and what may have gone through his mind is recounted in abundant Death Valley lore.

A roaring in the head is said to presage the insanity that makes them run wild...

When reason departs out there, death soon follows...

Of these thirst-driven-mad men, after they get to a certain stage, the first thing they do is to strip stark naked and commence to run. Afterwards they drop down on the sand and vigorously paw into it, like a dog.

Some indeed found water... in the welling of their delirium. Bill Corcoran lived to ask himself:

How long without water? From Friday to Monday. I'll never forget it. Three days wanderin' outa my head with angels flyin' alongside o' me pourin' water out of a silver pitcher into a silver bowl. I could hear the rustle of their wings and the splashin' of water. I could see more water than I ever knew was on earth before. Water was runnin' in all directions, and I could hear it rainin' plainer than it ever rained when I was myself. I'll never come closer to dyin' and not go.

177

Men were found flailing about to escape drowning. Or:

> Joseph Valles was brought in imagining he was on fire. He is a raving maniac.

Delusion escalating to delirium would explain Chester's failure to drink when in the last few miles of the canyon down to Ballarat, flowing springs gave rise to a creek, marshy with desert willows and cattails. He could have sloshed through water, and not thought to take a drink. Neither had D.H. Boye:

> He kept aimlessly plodding on, and his condition was something too fearful to be described. His tongue had swollen until it was so thick that he could hardly breathe. He took his shoes off and swung them around his neck by a string. The alkali dust filled his nostrils and left him bleeding. His feet were literally parboiled by the hot ooze of the marsh.

In another's first hand account:

> I felt dreadfully sleepy, vomited violently several times. Then everything around me commenced to whirl and the sunlight turned black.

In less than an hour, a man would die—in burning, choking, racking convulsions—exacerbated, not dulled, by delirium.

> When found he begged to be shot.

Chester Pray's gums, nostrils, and eyelids would have blackened. His face would have drained to a ghastly, ashen purple. His hearing would have been muffled, his pulse slowed.

Minutes now, and he would be consumed by his body heat.

California's *Mining Review* reported that in a previous Ballarat summer "eight prospectors and miners had been brought in dead, perished of heat in the desert."

His eyes afire with grit, Chester would have sighted Ballarat, tilting at crazy angles as he jerked onward. Tom Biggin might have been out working in his corral, watering stock; Ma Calloway might have been walloping a blanket slung over her hotel's balcony. If only Chester could shout. His tongue was so bloated he could barely breathe. His teeth—he believed they were melting.

Whatever may have propelled him on—the hope of the Monte Cristo, the love of Clara—he staggered into Ballarat and collapsed in the dust.

Someone saw him, called for others. In the blessed darkness of Wicht's saloon or Robinson's general store, he would have been dosed with bromide and had mustard of turpentine applied to the nape of his neck. He'd have been given water a sip at a time. Gulping down a glass of water could kill you, as it did a Russian over in Rhyolite.

In sunstroke's split-lipped, blistered aftermath, few were ever the same again in body or soul.

His carelessness in an unforgiving land would leave Chester with recurrent aches and fevers, and raise questions as to his state-of-mind.

In his Death Valley adventure and enterprise, Chester Pray had managed to outrun the demons of his youth, had lived with loneliness, and had stood up to a hellish environment.

Could he still?

CLARA'S SECRET

CHESTER STUCK CLOSE BY BALLARAT, and if he wasn't doing all that well, neither was the camp. Back in 1908, when he'd first stopped in for supplies, the population hovered at forty; two years later it was half that. H.L.S., a camp fixture, now had his left as well as his right leg amputated, and was confined to a wheelchair. He had cancer. Chester accompanied the Robinsons to Los Angeles and did his best to help out in the course of H.L.S.'s treatment. It was the least he could do: Robinson had lent him a desk in his store, let him purchase on credit, and when he couldn't pay up, considered the money due a grubstake.

Over the next two years, Chester was frequently in Los Angeles, spending time with Clara, visiting his friend Antoine Barber, and at Clara's suggestion, consulting with lawyer Frank McNamee. Talk of war in Europe had triggered speculation that the price of lead could rise, even soar, with the promise that a handsome profit could be made freighting ore from the Monte Cristo and the Queen of Sheba. McNamee was astounded when Chester admitted he had "monumented" his mines, but never had gotten around to recording them at the Inyo County courthouse.

Chester took his advice and did just that, filing on four adjacent claims.[14]

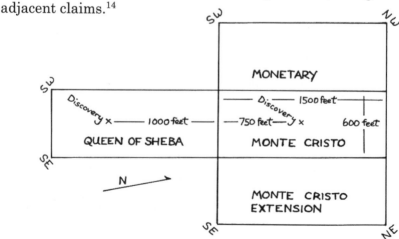

180

The filing would give Chester and grubstaker H.L.S. Robinson a lock on "lime and quartz croppings in which is contained valuable deposits of gold, silver, lead, and other minerals in place."

It was a timely move, for soon thereafter promoter Jack Salsberry, with an eye to the future of the metals market, found his way to the Monte Cristo to discover that the mine was everything Chester said it was, even if the man himself wasn't all there. The truth was that Jack could stand a new and profitable enterprise. Since his failed Ubehebe promotion, nothing had quite clicked, despite his best and increasingly slippery efforts.

One such scheme sprang from a marginally workable ranch that Jack owned northeast of Goldfield. He sniffed profit when, off on its rangeland, a pair of mom and pop prospectors happened on a modest showing of gold—which had Jack pacing off and platting a camp destined (he said) to be "a new Goldfield." Ellendale! Jack beat the drum for the place, with R.H. Quackenbush, a free-floating mining tout, sounding the trumpet.

Nevada newspapers, including the *Goldfield News*, fell for it. The site was "a little mint." No, make that "the greatest mining discovery of the age!"

But, alas, there appears to have been a dynamite problem—it blew Ellendale's fragile leaf gold into tiny fragments, scattering them far and wide and hopelessly across the desert. There was a further problem: there was precious little of the stuff, leaf gold or otherwise.

Amid protests of "the misdirected efforts of booster" or, more to the point, "a swindle to sell lots," Ellendale fizzled and died away, though not before imparting a unique memento, a rare (possibly the only) photograph of Jack Salsberry *(see page 134, plate 19)*. Center stage in a crowd fronting the Montana Cafe, he's the self-assured pudgy fellow in a vest and big-knotted tie. Nearing forty, he appears far younger. As suited his needs, he could be blandly poker faced or hail-fellow effusive, whatever was needed to mask his wiliness, his calculation.

Ellendale was to leave Jack Salsberry a little richer, but not by much. As Nevada swindles went, his land sale was small time, and by 1912, despite appearances—a suite at the St. Francis in San Francisco and offices in the nearby Hearst Building—Jack

---

[14] The Monetary and the Monte Cristo Extension filings were protection if, underground, Monte Cristo veins crossed the claim's boundaries.

was down on his luck and short on capital.

To remedy the situation, he now partnered with Ed Chafey, an easy-come, easy-go mining man who liked nothing better than to don his scuffed boots and tattered corduroys and hold court in the lobby of Reno's Golden Hotel. Reminiscing, buying the occasional little lady a drink. What counted was that Ed had funds. Not a lot, but some.

Ed accompanied Jack on his inspection of Chester's Monte Cristo workings. "Kinda like my mines," Ed commented, "the Black Hole and Little Hope."

"Mines he got going up by Winnemucca," Jack filled in.

Chester looked to Ed. "I've heard rosier names."

"I suppose. And it was true, nothing much came of the Little Hope. On the other hand, the Black Hole was in the money, with rock half gold. Yessir, enough so that with a clear conscience I could promise investors a twelve-hundred per cent return. And by God, they got it, or some of it. Town sprang up, just like that."

"Named after him," Jack said.

"Chafey?"

"Chafey. That's right. We had an Opera House, or meant to. We broke ground on it, laid a cornerstone, but then the cost of milling the Black Hole's ore caught up with us..."

He trailed off. Chester knew it could well be the same with the Monte Cristo. No problem with the ore; the problem was getting it to where its could be shipped to a smelter. Though Jack and Ed were aware of this, they were nevertheless impressed with what Chester had blocked out and would see what they could do, between them, to bankroll the property's development.

"The Monte Cristo, yessir, we'll put her on the map."

"You can count on it."

At last!

Chester wrote Clara with the news, and he could hardly contain himself when next he was in Los Angeles. She'd no longer need to send him postal orders. They'd be rich; they'd get married.

"If we can find us a preacher, how about in Ballarat?"

Clara gazed away, put her hand to her cheek. Chester looked to his shoes, then back up, and thought to soft-pedal his enthusiasm. "Doesn't have to be right away, Clara. How about next year, on the Fourth? There'll be money in from the Monte Cristo..."

"Chester..."

"Clarence can write us a poem. Old John can..."

"Chester, I'm married."

"But if you'd prefer, we could tie the knot in Los Angeles," he blurted before realizing what she'd said. "Married? You're married?"

Tears welled. Her voice choked as she got out, "Chester, dear Chester, all along I didn't want to hurt you. Only help you."

And it came out: she was Mrs. Arne Carlsrud.

Arne Carslrud... Burly and a charmer, he had labored as a northern California lumberjack. But then he figured there was better money to be made in a landscape where back-breaking exertion, loneliness, and thirst had men heading for the nearest saloon. Accordingly, Arne opened the Union Bar and Cafe just east of the Valley of the Moon. He then met and courted Clara. The two married, and for a time all was well. But as Sonoma County land became logged out for miles around, the Union fell on hard times. With the place empty for hours at a stretch, Arne drank, cursed his fate, and beat diminutive Clara.

"Badly?"

"Yes. Hit me, knocked me down, kicked me. One time he was on me and..."

"And?"

"Choked me. Choked me until I passed out."

She had fled, first to Sacramento, then to Los Angeles.

Arne had written, pleading forgiveness. Three times she had fallen for it, the explanation of her "family problems" up north after she'd met Chester.

Chester didn't know what to think or feel. He was once angry at Clara's mistreatment, but at the same time upset that she'd run back to the man. Two-timing, he supposed, was the expression. (Fleetingly, the thought may have come to him: And what about Antoine Barber, ever "a friend"?)

"Is there more? Anything else you want to tell me?"

"No," she said with a shudder, "that's it, that's enough." Defensively, she hugged herself. "Chester... I'm divorcing him. McNamee said he'd have the papers served, and handle things." She sighed and quietly wept.

"And then..."

She looked up. "I'll marry you."

"You'll not regret it. Clara... dear Clara." He took her in his arms. He would never let harm come to her.

Only happiness. And fortune.

IN SIGHT:
"THE EVERLASTING JACK"

RETURNING TO BALLARAT on Saturday, September 12, 1912, Chester hastened to Robinson's store. H.L.S.'s wife Lucy was restocking shelves with desert staples: oatmeal, cornstarch, and Spam, new from Hormel.

Missing legs and cancer notwithstanding, H.L.S. was back at his desk.

Chester ventured, "You're looking..."

"...like hell. But that's all right."

Cheered Lucy, "If he can't pick himself up and keep on going..."

"... no one can. That's a fact," Chester finished Lucy's thought. He then asked of H.L.S., "I've got something I need to write up. All right?"

"Always."

Seating himself at the store's school desk, Chester wrote a page, tore it up, wrote up another, and handed it to his friend. "This is my Will. I want you to take care of it for me. You may read it."

Will
Sept. 21, 1912

1/3 of all property to Mrs. H.A. Pray 17 Chesham Road, Brookline Mass. In case she does not out live me—Mrs. H.B. Cram of same address to receive 1/3.

1/3 of all property to Miss Clara Carlsrud, Los Angeles, Calif.

1/3 of all property to H.L.S. Robinson, Ballarat, Calif. H.L.S. Robinson to be administrator.

In case of my death please notify B.P.O.E. Baker City, Oregon and Mr. H.B. Cram 17 Chesham Road and burn my letters.

Chester A. Pray

"Why, thank you Chester," H.L.S. looked up, "I'm honored, though Lord knows there's little use leaving me anything. I'll die before you. Doctors give me a year."

As implied in the Will, Chester's mother Helen was also in failing health, nearing the end of a three-year siege of cancer.

Drawing up his Will at the age of thirty-four, did Chester have cause to believe his days were numbered?

It's doubtful. Rather, there was proven, valuable property at stake. He had a lot to live for, and someone to love. In the Will, Clara is "Miss" not "Mrs." Chester wasn't about to reveal her secret—or for that matter, anything of their romance, which might explain his terse "burn my letters."

H.L.S. poked the page in a pigeon-hole in his roll-top, there to gather dust, or so he thought. In the meantime, Chester had written up a second page:

> I own 2/3 of the Monte Cristo and Monetary claims, 2/3 of the Warm Springs [same as Peach Bloom Garden Springs] water rights and all the equipment except a light A [frame] tent and bolt of new canvas.
>
> I own 1/2 of the Queen of Sheba and Monte Cristo Extension joining the Monte Cristo.
>
> C.A. Pray

However down-on-himself Chester had been over the years, he was now possessed by a restless, manic energy. He gathered up:

2 cases dynamite	$9.00
200 ft. fuse	$1.30
200 caps	95¢
2 doz. candles	$2.40
Grape Nuts	20¢
2 cans hash	$1.00
3 lbs. onions	20¢
Corn tamales	25¢
25 lbs. barley	$1.50

That fall and winter, Chester was frequently back and forth to Ballarat for more of the same. He skipped Christmas in the camp. He had work to do at the Monte Cristo, and increasingly, the Queen of Sheba, now dispensing riches with every foot he drilled and blasted. He thought to go to Ballarat for New Year's—and the cheer of Chris Wicht's Headquarters Saloon—but he couldn't.

All across Death Valley, it snowed.

Chester's friend Pete Agueberry claimed that you could hear it snow. "The snowflakes, as large as half-dollars, were wet and heavy and when they struck the ground the sound they made was plop, plop, plop."

A three-day storm blanketed the Valley from the crest of the Panamints all the way down to the salt flats, well below sea level. At Chester's mines, the temperature dropped to 15° Fahrenheit, the coldest ever in the Valley. He took refuge in his workings, where year round, the mercury reliably hovered in the high 60°s.

It snowed in San Francisco, even Los Angeles. Not once but again, in the week of January 20th.

In early February, a stagecoach slipped and slid into Ballarat, to deliver overdue mail, including a Special Delivery letter to Chester, carried across the Panamints by the next to travel his way. It was from his Aunt Julia. His mother had died in an operation to excise her cancer, and she had been buried in Boston.

The news saddened and agitated him. Helen Pray's time on this earth had not been a happy one. She'd never escaped the pall cast by her husband the Captain, righteous and demeaning. Shuttling between sisters in the Boston area, she was a fragile, lost soul, her life kindled by little more than flickers of hope for her son, that he might lead a better life, somewhere out West.

Chester considered taking the train back to Boston, to lay flowers on her grave and to disperse her few belongings. But Aunt Julia, in her letter, had reported Chester's Uncle Henry willing to handle this, and on February 14th Chester wrote him:

> I most sincerely appreciate your kindness to my mother and myself. Nothing would please me more than to have you administer the estate.

What Chester could do was make up for his mother's unfulfilled life by proving himself, by breaking free of all that had tormented mother and son. Looking back on the years he'd roamed the West, he now believed his adventures—even his misadventures—could be interpreted as leading to a culminating year: the year at hand.

If he'd gotten away with his stolen Mohawk ore, he could well have sunken to a life criminal and dissolute. Instead, shunned in Goldfield, he'd committed himself—do or die—to Death Valley, where he'd staked his claims and held out for the wealth he was convinced was in the ground, not run off in pursuit of "the next big thing."

And so: he had in his sights "the everlasting jack" —ore and a deal that would pay off for years to come. Jack Salsberry and Ed Chafey had looked the Monte Cristo over and, before a single sack of ore was shipped, valued the operation at $45,000 (at least $1,300,000 in current dollars).

1913. It would be his year, a year with pretty Clara on his arm. Clara Carlsrud would become Clara Pray.

In the next weeks, Chester went up to Goldfield to negotiate with Salsberry, then down to Los Angeles to see Clara and consult with lawyer McNamee. On his return, he plotted the route of a wagon road from his mines to the railroad and then, barely catching his breath, took off prospecting. He had, he believed, the touch. With Antoine Barber he located the Copper Dome #1 in the Argus Mountains west of Ballarat. With Ed Chafey he staked the Apex #1 and #2, the Lead Pipe, and the Cinch, all in the southern Panamints. When the price of lead rose, as it surely would, the region for miles around could pay off.

It could be a last great excitement!

Chester was in on organizing a "South Park Mining District" and having its boundaries duly recorded in Independence. The district ranged over five hundred square miles: "...from Wingate Pass to Chuckwalla Canyon & crest of Panamints to middle of Death Valley. Salsberry, chairman, C.A. Pray recorder and secretary."

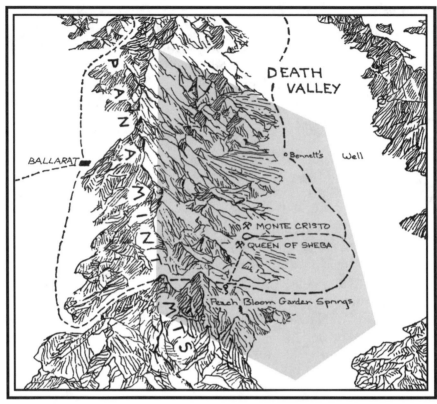

South Park Mining District

A mining engineer looking over the new district reported that hardly a day went by without Chester staking a claim. Independence's Index to Mining Claims attests to twenty-one entered in a single day, from the Isolation to the Iron Pant to the Sure Thing. With the Tohoqua #1, #2, and #3, he revived a name he'd used a dozen years earlier. He wrote H.L.S. Robinson (in Los Angeles for a renewed course of treatment) that the only thing slowing him down was:

> My tooth started aching and now it is raging. I guess it is ulcerated, as my face is all swelled up. I might stick it out.
>
> Yours in pain, C.A.P.

The next day, March 23rd, he thought better of sticking it out.

> Going to Goldfields tonight.

He was to add:

The old man raised his price, didn't he?

The "old man" was Jack Salsberry, and this is a first allusion to a bond that would insure Chester's diligent development of his workings, a bond that would protect investor-partners in the event that he misspent or absconded with the funds they advanced. Typically, it fell to the operator of a mine—in this case, Chester— to agree to and make timely payments. There was nothing that unusual about this (yet). Chester wasn't all that concerned. Once the mine was shipping ore, there would be no problem; if it wasn't, he could, if he had to, sell off a share of his interest in either the Monte Cristo or the Queen of Sheba.

Chester signed off his letter with...

I believe it is going to snow.

It did, and slowed Chester as his toothache painfully worsened. It took him four days to cross the Valley and the Funerals. His jaw swelled, then his neck. It helped a little when he packed his mouth with snow, to spit it out smeared with blood and pus. He was on the verge of collapse when a light shone and brightened in the swirl and gloom of the storm—the headlamp of a northbound Tonopah & Tidewater locomotive. Chester pulled off his coat and waved it over his head. The conductor helped him aboard.

He thawed out by a passenger car stove, and late that afternoon in Goldfield he sought a dentist. Five years ago, the camp had over a dozen; now it was Dr. Forshee or Dr. Ducey, and by good fortune the latter was still in his office. He was startled by the haggard man at his door, his neck so swollen that he was barely able to talk.

Dr. Ducey guided Chester to his chair and took his temperature—104°, with a fluttery pulse. He then examined and probed Chester's mouth, and on a bakelite tray, assembled screw-operated forceps, elevators, clamps, little knives.

Whatever apprehension Chester might have felt was dispelled as, with the snap of an elastic band, Ducey clapped an inhaler to his face and spun the valve on a nitrous oxide gasometer. Only once did Chester feel the pain, and then he really felt it, as with a curved tool Ducey dug out a broken root.

189

Dr. Ducey cleaned out the suppuration and packed Chester's gums with gauze and mercuric chloride. He then kindly walked him the two blocks to the Goldfield Hotel, there to order up Syrup of Licorice and an opiate painkiller in the basement pharmacy. He saw Chester to a $1.00 third floor room.

"Bed rest... a week of it," advised Ducey. "You take care, Mr. Pray."

Chester took his advice, wobbling little further than downstairs to sip bowls of soup, and then pick at a 40¢ Merchant's Lunch. Settling in the lobby, he passed the time reading the *Goldfield Daily Tribune*. The glory days of the camp had come and gone, even as the paper's editor favored the adverb "still," as in GOLDFIELD STILL A PEERLESS CAMP and GOLDFIELD STILL ON THE MAP. A state law had ended round-the-clock gambling; once rowdy dance halls had been torn down for their lumber; only a few of the fifty brothels were still in business.

"The only women left," a visitor noted, "were a scattering of slatterns without money enough to leave." Uptown, "Sand and tumbleweeds blew inside the broken windows of once fine houses and birds nested in living rooms not so long ago the glittering scenes of social triumphs. The moguls were gone."

A second March snowstorm buried the camp. The *Tribune* blamed it on sunspots.

The newspaper, in a wan attempt at humor, ran the first of several articles about a local hen laying a golden egg. On the opposite page an article reported Thomas F. Dunn's return from a mortician's convention in Reno, where "he'd had a gay time at a banquet described as nothing less than sumptuous." Chester noted that undertaker Dunn stood to be short a client, the region's resident bad man.

DIAMONDFIELD JACK
DAVIS MAY BE DEAD

FORMER GOLDFIELD CHARACTER

News has been received of the recent execution of Diamondfield Jack Davis, who is said to have been killed by a firing squad in Lower California for having joined a party of insurrectos and taken up arms against the Mexican government.

Davis was in Goldfield during the boom times and was one of the most conspicuous men of the camp, usually going about heavily armed, and during the labor troubles of this district he was in the habit of carrying two or three revolvers, a bowie knife and a sawed off shotgun, the last named weapon swung by a harness under his long fur coat.

On Chester's third day in Goldfield, sunlight pierced an oppressive overcast and the temperature was in the 70°s, where it ought to have been. Snow became slush, and slush mud. He ventured out and found himself sufficiently recovered to hop puddles, and sufficiently bored to depart on the Tonopah & Tidewater southbound the following day. He believed himself very much improved as the car's wheels clickety-clacked, and a name came to him, a name for the camp that would flourish down the hill from his Monte Cristo and Queen of Sheba. As "Goldfield" was a field of gold and "Rhyolite" was reddish country rock rich in gold, Chester would name his camp for its ore: carbonate of lead, or simply:

Carbonate.

With Goldfield sliding into obscurity and Rhyolite a bust, the time was ripe for a third great treasure camp.

Carbonate.

———◆———

Off the train at the whistle stop of Zabriskie, Chester rendezvoused with Ed Chafey and the two went on over to Carbonate—Ed liked the name—for a week's development work that included discussions and plans as to where the mine and assay offices would go, then the mill, then the boarding house and dining hall. And there would be the town itself, platted with streets and lots.

On April 3rd, they were on their way back to Goldfield, and the deal that would clear the way for the full-scale development of the Monte Cristo. (Chester and H.L.S. Robinson would retain rights to the adjoining Queen of Sheba.) Jack Salsberry

191

had drawn up a three-way partnership and had forwarded the relevant documents to lawyer McNamee for review on Chester's behalf. McNamee would have joined them in Goldfield except that he was tied up representing senator and entrepreneur W.A. Clark in a scheme for a railroad that would exploit Nevada's agricultural potential.

As often happens in the desert, winter skipped to summer, with hardly a thought for spring. It was hot in Goldfield, and humid. And buggy, with swarms of flies breeding in stagnant pools left by March's melting snow. Checking into the Goldfield Hotel, both Ed and Chester listed "Carbonate" as their home town. While they would have been content with $1.00 rooms, manager Earle Hewitt gave them side-by-side $2.00 rooms. "Accommodations on Jack Salsberry," he smiled.

Ed excused himself to run a quick errand. Dropping by the *Tribune*, he saw to a notice in the **Personal Mention** column.

> E.S. CHAFEY, veteran of the Chafey district, Goldfield and other camps, has retuned to Goldfield with Chester A. Pray from a trip to Carbonate, California.

That night, the pair parted with 80¢ each in the Goldfield Hotel's glum, near-empty, dining room. They then might have taken in the show at the Exchange Theater: a Mutt and Jeff cartoon, a two-reel Lubin comedy, and from Essaney, *Bronco Billy's Last Deed*. Chester would have had enjoyed a good night's sleep but for the flies, lighting on his nose, neck, and ears. He buried his head in his pillow, as he had as a child. The drone was punctuated by snores and moans down the hall, a whiskey bottle dashed on a wall a block away, the bell signals and whine of hoists hauling and dumping rock in the ripped-up landscape to the east—mostly waste, but still some ore.

The next day, Sunday, April 6th, a bleary Chester, Ed too, arranged for a car and driver, and motored to the Tonopah & Goldfield depot to collect Jack, due in on the 12:40 from Reno. Ed looked down the track, checked his pocket watch. Chester paced.

"It'll be fine," said Ed, "you wait and see."

They caught sight of the locomotive—or rather its sooty, rhythmic chuffs—when it was twenty miles out on the sage flats to the north. An eternity came and went and the train wasn't any closer.

Then, suddenly, it was steaming through the Goldfield yards. Three freight cars, a flat car, and a single passenger-freight car.

The deal—the money—was imminent.

With a squeal of steel-on-steel and a cacophony of clanks, the train slowed and stopped. A dozen passengers emerged, stretched, shouldered their duffels, and headed for town. There were sallow-faced miners, a mine superintendent's wife back from a family visit, Augustus Cox looking to buy a horse, and a Mr. Fred W. Shroeder, a San Francisco speculator. The engine vented steam; there'd next be supplies to offload at a round of mine sidings.

A figure stepped through the evaporating cloud.

Jack Salsberry, waving his valise.

"Papers! All drawn up, boys! All in order!" He strode up, greeted them effusively, and was all avuncular cheer as they motored to the hotel. Jack pointed out operations—a stock brokerage, a lumber yard, mines to the east—once his. Waving a fly swatter, an urchin ran alongside.

"What you got there, son?" Jack would soon enough find out. The epidemic had prompted the *Tribune* to hand fly swatters out to boys and girls over seven who promised to make good use of them. As was his custom, Jack tossed the kid a handful of candy.

Mining men with a future, not a past, the three mounted the steps of the Goldfield Hotel, and Jack had his grip sent up to his $3.00 suite. "How about it, what say we sit down right now and tend to business. It'll be cooler here in the lobby."

"Suits me," said Ed, depositing himself a big black, desert-cracked leather chair and scoring a bull's-eye in the nearest spittoon, as did Jack. Flies took wing, to be drawn back to the stink.

Chester was dry-mouthed, and he felt a little feverish. Two weeks since he'd had the toothache, and his jaw still ached.

"Lots of lawyer stuff," said Jack, unlatching his valise, "but straightforward if you look it over paragraph by paragraph." He withdrew five documents, shuffled them, rolled one for a swat at a fly, then unrolled it and handed it to Chester.

"Clerk?" Jack's voice echoed across the lobby, "what about these damn flies?"

"We're doing our best, Mr. Salsberry," the man answered, "Manager Hewitt has ordered a shipment of traps."

"And when does manager Hewitt expect these traps?"

"They should be in next week. Catalogue said the traps were 'guaranteed sure death to the insect.'"

"Sure death in a dying camp." Jack mulled the notion, adding, "Present company excepted. Right, boys?"

Ed nodded, Chester too as he unrolled and read, "This Agreement, Made and entered into the 7th day of April, 1913, by and between C.A. Pray and Ed Chafey, parties of the first part, and John Salsberry, party of the second part, Witnesseth..." The wording was stilted and dense. A mining claim became a "property located, appropriated, preempted, used and acquired." Rights to water and timber were specified where neither existed. A dollar was attested to be "lawful money in the United States."

Essentially, the document gave Jack Salsberry a one-third cut of the Monte Cristo and Monetary claims. This would be in exchange for his anteing up unspecified grubstaking and development costs and a token (but binding) $1.00, which he peeled from a sizeable wad.

"You'll have more of this, lots more," he assured Chester, "all you'll need." He twitched the bill, folded and unfolded it. "What you've got there is pretty much what your McNamee approved." He waved off a buzz of flies.

"Pretty much," Chester agreed, though he wasn't all that sure. At the same time his head couldn't have helped but swell... Chester Pray, a "party of the first part" courted by renowned mining men. What had Greenwater's *Chuck-Walla* said of Jack? TO FORTUNE AND FAME WELL KNOWN.

Jack glanced to Ed, who said, "If you can't trust Mr. Salsberry, Chester, I don't know who you can."

Jack uncapped and offered his fountain pen.

"All right," Chester said. And signed. As did Ed.

"Hang onto that pen," said Jack with a rub to his jowls, "there's more."

A second agreement called for Salsberry's participation in the most promising of the claims Chester and Ed had staked in the last few months: the Apex #1 and #2, the Lead Pipe, and the Cinch.

Signed.

A third agreement called for a three-way split of the water rights to Peach Bloom Garden Springs, valuable if it was feasible to run a pipeline over to Carbonate.

Signed.

The fourth agreement gave Jack and Ed the option of, for $2,000, buying a two-thirds interest in Chester's undeveloped Tohoqua #1, #2, and #3.

"Who knows?" Jack smiled, "There doesn't have to be just one Monte Cristo!"

Signed.

The documents were repetitive, changing little but the names of the properties. Chester could skip through the legalese. He relaxed, letting down his guard.

"Cigars? Chester? Ed?" Jack offered Cuba Flora panatelas. "Shoo the flies."

The day's fifth and last agreement revisited the ownership of the Monte Cristo and the Monetary. It entitled Ed Chafey to buy out a one-third share owned by ailing H.L.S. Robinson. The specified price was $7,500.

"Shouldn't that be more?" Chester ventured. "Shouldn't a one-third cut be $15,000?" In February, he remembered, Jack and Ed had said the Monte Cristo to be worth $45,000. At a minimum.

"No, son," said Salsberry with a patronizing air, then turned to Chafey. "Ed, you said you checked with H.L.S. down in Los Angeles?"

"I did."

Chester was not aware of this.

"And?" asked Jack, savoring his panatela.

"H.L.S. said fine."

"Could use the money I suspect," Jack reflected.

"He could," Ed agreed.

Chester shrugged, not seeing how the payment affected him. But it did: the worth of the Monte Cristo and adjoining Monetary had been devalued by half.

The document then hazily alluded to a transfer of funds from Chafey to Salsberry, something to do with a "certain interest" Chafey would have in Chester's share.

"There they go again, the lawyers," Jack explained the matter away, at the same time reaching into his valise to produce a $2,000 cashier's check drawn on the Los Angeles Day-and-Night Bank, and payable to Chester A. Pray.

"As called for, this will get you going, son, carry you through April and May. Then there'll be more, another $5,500. After that you'll be shipping ore, with no need to look back."

"What's the price of lead now, Jack?" Ed asked stiffly, as if on cue.

"Nudging $90 a ton at close yesterday. Gold's steady and silver—silver is taking off. Chester, how much silver you got to the ton."

"A little over twenty dollars worth."

"Well son, I'd say that the way the market's going we can count on doubling, even tripling that." His cigar clenched in his teeth, Jack leaned forward to give him a fatherly squeeze to the shoulders.

Chester beamed.

Jack checked his pocket watch. "Gents, we best wrap this up if we're to record these by close of business over at the courthouse." He pressed Chester with his pen.

"Give me a minute, just a minute," Chester asked, so that he at least might skim the balance of the document. In getting lawyer McNamee's advice, he didn't recall anything saying that the $7,500 Jack had committed to lay out would entitle him to *a first lien on the property.*

Jack shook his head, chuckled. "My lawyer. The man just doesn't understand a sure thing."

Chester signed.

He handed the pen to Ed, who signed as well, as did Jack. The three were then driven the five blocks to the camp's castle-like, turreted courthouse, where they caught Carroll Henderson, notary public in and for the country of Esmeralda, just as he was tidying up for the day. Henderson affixed the five agreements with his seal and attested that Jack, Ed, and Chester had "acknowledged to me that they executed the same freely and voluntarily and for uses and purposes therein mentioned."

"Best of luck, men," he said with a noticeable lack of conviction.

"Whaddaya say boys, dinner at eight?" asked Jack Salsberry, adding, "On me."

As they motored back to the Goldfield Hotel, Chester saw a light burning in the window of the basement barber shop. As the others went to their rooms and then down to the bar, he stopped in for a haircut and, why not, a steam facial. He could afford it. At the conclusion of an attentive half hour, the barber positioned a hand mirror behind Chester's head, reflecting the image on the shop's beveled mirror, edged in frosted scrolls.

The barber had done well.

Chester saw his collar to be frayed. He'd buy a new shirt. Maybe several. And boots, new trousers, and a hat.

He gave the barber a generous tip.

"Why thank you, Mr. Pray. And God bless you!"

THE MONTEZUMA CLUB

CHESTER SLEPT IN. FLIES OR NO, he appreciated a feather pillow and starched, clean sheets.

Jack needed the time to have a last document—*the big one* that would pull everything together—typed up by hotel manager Hewitt's secretary. He'd refined it on the train down from Reno.

Chester looked up to the electric ceiling fan, a luxury afforded to a $2.00 room. Fate had given him a nod, and about time. Last night they'd dined at the Palm; he could get used to champagne and oysters, to the strains of a string quartet. There'd been little mining talk, other than Jack's assurance that the document they'd be reviewing today wasn't about dividing things up, but the opposite: uniting to form a corporation and issuing stock. Chester could see it: certificates with elegant script, sunbursts, spread-winged eagles, embossed seals—*for his mine.*

At ten in the morning, the latticework of the Goldfield Hotel's elevator parted, and Chester stepped into the lobby. Jack and Ed were getting their boots shined over by the hotel's safe.

"Mornin', son," Jack greeted him. "Ed and I were just talking. I believe we could use something less in the way of flies. That so, Ed?"

Ed smiled, nodded.

Flipping the bootblack a silver dollar, Jack led the way a block down Crook Avenue to an oaken double door and a plaque engraved "The Montezuma Club." Jack pressed a buzzer, and through a speaking tube bellowed "It's Mr. Salsberry!"

The Montezuma was once a sanctum, private and exclusive, of Western mining men. Members included Senator Nixon, Governor Sparks, and mogul George Wingfield. But in 1913 the plaque was tarnished, and trash eddied by the wind had collected in the entryway. With the Panic of '07, the club had dissolved, though not entirely. Diehards gathered in its old quarters, passing the hat to retain a steward and a part-time attendant or two. An out-of-town guest found the Montezuma "transformed from a roaring place of joy unconfined to a gloomy retreat where one might contemplate suicide and find it attractive."

The lock clicked. Jack turned the knob, and the three men mounted hobnail-worn stairs to a second floor above the Palace Saloon. He ushered Chester and Ed through a once-red velvet curtain into a club room outfitted with Mission furniture, tear drop chandeliers, and a pressed-tin ceiling, all considerably the worse for wear. Sunlight streaming through an arched window highlighted a haze of cigar smoke rising from a corner table.

Salsberry waved in the table's direction, wished a "Mornin' Jack."

"Mornin' yourself, Jack," replied the man in the sateen shirt and broadcloth swallow-tail, both black. With the heat he'd forsaken his trademark fur coat.

Chester was startled, for, there among the living sat gunslinger Jackson Lee "Diamondfield" Davis. He'd clearly not been executed by a Mexican firing squad, as the *Goldfield Tribune* had reported and Chester had read. The truth was he had been shot, but up in Butte, and not fatally. Of late, Diamondfield hadn't fared well. After a stint as bodyguard and labor-intimidator for George Wingfield, he'd promoted an outcropping and camp—Diamondfield—five miles off to the north. With that fizzling, he had turned to *fraction jacking*, in which, with the aid of a surveyor, he sought Goldfield mining properties that had been roughly paced off by prospectors and were recorded a few feet short of what they should have been. He then was off to the courthouse to file on the resulting wedges, some as little as six inches wide. Armed with a legal right to deny access, he'd then squeeze mine-owners to pay up if they wished to continue their operations. This, literally, was a chiseler's game, and he was roundly despised for stooping to it. Presently out of heads to knock and fractions to jack, he was sullenly available. For anything, including "cutting it in smoke."

His deep-set gray eyes took note of Chester.

Jack Salsberry distributed carbons of a document calling for the organization of a Nevada corporation that would issue 10,000 shares of stock, par value $10, to purchase the Monte Cristo and Monetary claims, with the proceeds to be shared as specified in yesterday's first agreement. Paragraph upon paragraph of "Whereas" and "Therefore" subsequently set forth an array of stipulations.

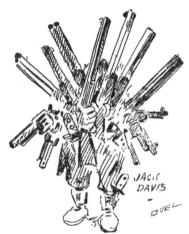

Period cartoons of two Jacks—Salsberry and Diamondfield.

There would be Treasury stock and Promotional stock. There would be a fund in which each participant would "have the equal option and refusal to purchase the same or on as favorable terms as the party offering to sell has offered the same to any other person, and this condition shall be expressly set forth in such receipt."

Chester read and reread the agreement and still didn't quite understand it, but at the same time didn't want to appear ignorant, not in the mining man's haven, the Montezuma Club. He had little choice, he felt, than to trust Jack, take his word that the document was heavy with routine boilerplate. It is doubtful if Chester noticed that, buried in the verbiage, Jack Salsberry was assured that if anything went seriously awry, he, as first lien holder, would assume undisputed ownership and control of the corporation.

If only Chester's lawyer McNamee was present. But he wasn't.

With hail-fellow gusto, Jack signed first, then Chester, then Ed.

"And, of course, one last thing," Jack said off-handedly, "The bond on the Monte Cristo. Got it right here."

Now, although the other documents executed by the three men on this April 7th and 8th have survived as a matter of public record, this private bond has not. All that is known (in a letter from

Chester to H.L.S. Robinson) is that it called for, on Chester's part, an initial cash payment of $5,500, due sixty days after signing.

That would be on June 8th, 1913.

"Time enough," Jack assured, "to cut a road—nothing fancy— and get some wagons in and some ore out. God knows you've enough of it sacked. True?"

"True…"

"Then no problem."

"I don't know, Mr. Salsberry." Chester thought aloud: "It's forty miles across the Valley and over the Funerals. I need to think on this."

"Do that, son. Nobody's rushing you. Take your time."

Jack kneaded the back of his neck, stretched, called across the room, "Say Diamondfield, we're just about wrapped up. Whaddaya say, come join us for a round?"

Diamondfield, a reporter had noted, often had some trouble rising from his chair, such was the weight of his armaments. Accomplishing this, he ambled over with the studied gait of a desperado. Ed's "Hiya, Jack," was accompanied by Chester's "Nice to meet you, Mr. Davis."

Whatever pleasantry he might have had in mind, Jack couldn't get it out. It was tough being a bad man when you had stammered since childhood. This, though, was worse. "God! God… damn plate!" he cursed.

"Make yourself comfortable, Jack."

"Plate in my… goddamn… mouth. Stuck there. By a goddamn… Salt Lake… City dentist."

The bullet he'd taken up in Idaho had made a mess of his jaw. As he pondered this, Diamondfield's already ruddy face further reddened. He unsheathed his Bowie. "Gave the bastard… a… taste of this." He whacked the blade to the table, cutting a plug of tobacco, which he popped in there with the plate, effectively rending him non-verbal.

"I just don't know, Mr. Salsberry, I just don't know," Chester waffled.

"I had a big bond on my Black Hole mine, now that I think of it," Ed said in his offhand manor. "More-or-less the same terms. And you know, I got the operation up and running, and paid it off with time and money to spare. Nothin' to it. A cakewalk."

Chester reached for the pen. Hesitated, pulled back.

The two Jacks exchanged looks. Diamondfield extracted a revolver from the interior of his swallowtail and laid it on the table. Unknown to Chester, he was given to doing this, mostly for show, though not always.

"Chester, it'll work out," Ed assured. "Always does."

Chester's head spun. Seven documents. Stipulations. Whereases. Wherefores. What was he in for? Could be ruin...

Could be a fortune beyond his imagining...

Diamondfield chewed noisily—both his plug of tobacco and a handlebar of his moustache. For those who knew him, a sign to tread lightly. No sudden moves or verbal ejaculations.

"Chester?" Jack Salsberry arched his eyebrows.

Diamondfield's hand crept to his gun. His face was near scarlet. To appearances, his fuse was spit.

"Have confidence," said Jack Salsberry, patting Chester's arm. "No time and you'll be in the velvet."

Wordlessly, Chester picked up the pen and signed.

"Drinks all around!" Salsberry hailed the attendant on duty. "What'll it be, gents?"

As this time of day, a beer was fine for Chester and Ed, a scotch for Jack Salsberry.

"Po... win..." Diamondfield struggled.

"Sir?" queried the attendant.

"The man will have his usual. Port wine," Jack Salsberry clarified, then rocked back, content with two good day's work. He'd set the deal, slick and sure. The bond was key for it was doubtful Chester would be shipping any ore by early June, and certainly not in time to get a check issued and deposited from the lead smelter in Salt Lake.

When the bond payment came due, the bounty of the Monte Cristo would count for naught.

There was more to Jack's calculation. Call it a hard-headed business tactic, call it swindle. Come the critical June 8th deadline, Chester, on the plus side, would have in hand $7,500 in development funds to be advanced by Jack—*but he'd be precluded from drawing on this for the bond payment.* This was implicit in yesterday's fifth and last agreement. Not only that, Jack's advances would be doubly protected by his grant of *a first lien on the property,* which, under the circumstances, he'd delight to exercise.

The key to the arrangement was its complexity, near-impenetrable at the outset, binding when the time came for its execution.

The stage was set for a takeover.

Chester would default; the mine would be Jack's.

The identity of the bond holder is unknown. Los Angeles' Day-and-Night Bank wasn't overly inquisitive about such matters and was favored by mining men in eastern California and Nevada. Or the bond could have been issued in Goldfield by H.B. Lind & Co. over on Ramsey Avenue. It is possible even that Salsberry himself underwrote the bond.

Jack, all charm when it suited him, looked to Ed and Chester, and reached to vigorously pump their hands. "I'd say you boys better be on your way to the Monte Cristo. I look forward to it paying off. And soon. Of that I'm confident."

As Ed and Chester took their leave of the Montezuma's upstairs quarters, Jack half-smiled to Diamondfield, who meant to smile back, but winced. It hurt to smile.

"Tell you what..." Salsberry began, his voice hushed.

In the writing room off the Goldfield Hotel's lobby, pausing only to wave off flies, Chester dashed off letters to lawyer Frank McNamee and H.L.S. Robinson. He believed he'd done the right thing.

"Mr. Salsberry is one of the best and wealthiest mining men in the state. Forwarding contract."

Even so, he wished that one or the other—with their business sense—could have been present. Or even Clarence. For all his wild imaginings and schemes, the poet-prospector had insights. He knew a thing or two about the intersection of the human heart and mineral bounty.

Clarence Eddy had written:

> All too well I have learned that the finder of fortunes has a really fearful fate. Avarice and cupidity lie in wait for him, and the worst passions of the world are turned loose upon him to pursue and persecute him until he shall perish.

THE ROAD TO
THE MONTE CRISTO

AT FIRST LIGHT, TEAMSTER JOHN NEIS cajoled, then cursed. His mules strained in their traces; his Fresno grader shuddered, then scraped northwest from the railroad siding at Zabriskie.

"A road to riches!" exclaimed Chester. "Right, Ed?"

Ed Chafey gave him a thumbs up.

In less than a week, Ed and Chester had recruited ten men and rounded up the necessary equipment, mules, and supplies. They had first thought to cut the road west-to-east, in which case they'd beat it out of Death Valley ahead of the summer's debilitating heat. But this was impractical in that Jack Salsberry had promised the use of a giant and awkward steam traction engine, and there would be no way to maneuver it across the Valley for a start at the Monte Cristo.

Instead, they would cross the Funerals east-to-west, up over Bradbury, then Jubilee Pass. From there, Chester's forty-mile route would descend to the Valley floor, there to skirt the salt flats and cross over to the Monte Cristo.

That first day, they knocked off mid-afternoon, six miles behind them. The going was easy; they were on an old Zabriskie to Greenwater road, a straight-shot with little more than bumps to be leveled and hollows filled.

The next day, they bore west, up an alluvial fan into the Funerals. Cutting a fresh track slowed them, though not seriously. Here and there a half-stick of dynamite took care of the larger boulders. By the first of May, they had surmounted Bradbury Pass, and Chester was sufficiently pleased with his crew's progress to let them continue on their own while he put in some time over at the Queen of Sheba, blocking ore. The principal vein had swelled like a snake that had swallowed a rat, and now did it again. This was a stroke of luck, for that week a party headed by Oakland mining engineer Frank M. Manson showed up and expressed their serious interest in buying into—or even buying out! —the Queen of Sheba. Here, Chester saw, was a way out in the event of a crunch on the Monte Cristo bond payment due June 8th. (Jack Salsberry and Ed Chafey as yet had no stake in the Queen of Sheba; Chester's interest, a 50-50 share with H.L.S. Robinson, was free of encumbrances.)

Mining engineer Manson had reservations. He recalled:

> I went down with a view of taking the property over, but once there, doubted its worth. The mining business thrives on hot air. It is the breath of its nostrils.
> Still, we were willing to take the chance.

Manson sat down with Chester, at the time busy mending his trousers: "I just got to put a patch on right now, or my knee will be clear through." Chester was like that, his behavior odd or inappropriate in the face of serious business. Manson recalled:

> I talked to him relative to prices and the conditions of the mine. And his ideas seemed so wild that I didn't go any further with the conversation. I was led to believe the man was affected by the heat. In other words he was unbalanced. His mind was unbalanced. He was very excitable; extremely so. He'd fly off if things would be said that didn't suit him, when the value of the property was doubted.
> He was mad. Also, he was sullen.

Reporting that Chester "whistled gaily" one minute and fumed the next, Frank Manson wouldn't be recommending the Queen of

Sheba to Bay Area investors. Just as well, Chester thought, for down in Los Angeles, lawyer McNamee had sparked the interest of a prominent industrialist, a Mr. W.C. Price, President of the Wellman Oil Company. If Manson was out, Price wanted in. A Los Angeles meeting was scheduled for late Saturday, May 31st.

In the meantime, Chester headed across the Valley to rejoin his crew. In the past few days, he'd sighted a cottonball of smoke, then another and another, puffing up from the Funerals—detonations advancing the road. He and Ed had rounded the crew with experienced miners, men with the ability to move a lot of rock. Even so, the going had seriously slowed, to a mile a day on the climb from Rhodes Wash up to Jubilee Pass.

Chester could see the newly-arrived behemoth long before he got there: a fire-breathing Roberts-Doan steam traction engine. Jack Salsberry had used it in his Nevada lumber operations. Jack, in fact, was there and greeted him. "Good to see you, son. Off prospecting?" The inquiry had an edge to it.

Chester shrugged; he couldn't exactly say he was trying to sell off a property that in good faith he could have offered Jack and Ed.

"That's all right, Chester," Jack continued. "So what do you think?" He gestured to the iron contraption, a three-wheeled affair with a vertical boiler mounted between massive rear wheels. "Just the ticket to flatten the roadbed, then haul us some ore."

Chester wasn't so sure. The hulking engine required enormous amounts of wood and water; it was cumbersome, over twice the width of a freight wagon. Top-heavy, it could teeter and fall on its side.

"I'd like you to meet Mr. Shaffer, a road man and good friend. He knows what it'll take to get the Roberts-Doan through. From now on, he'll be specifying the road, calling the shots."

Chester looked to his boots, then up again. "As you say, Mr. Salsberry."

Just then, a hundred yards to the west, crew foreman Jack Gallagher shouted, "Fire in the hole!" and a minute later an explosion shattered a boulder the size of an outhouse. Hardly waiting for the smoke to disperse, Roger Kennedy and J.P. Madison were in there, hand-clearing the rubble. Jack Neis urged on his grader mules. Gallagher chalked the next obstacle with white "X"s, guides for double jacking and ramming home charges.

"Good crew," observed Jack. "Stepping lively."

"But..." Chester began, but stalled.

"Yes, Chester?"

"But..." he tried again, and got out: "...the road. Accommodating the traction engine can't help but take longer." (If it was up to him, Chester would have settled for a rough route through, the minimum for mule-drawn freight wagons. A better road or even a railroad could follow.)

"Whatever it takes, son."

"What about the bond payment?"

"Not my problem, son. Yours."

For a time neither spoke, their eyes to the road crew. The men sledged and shouted; the animals strained and brayed. Then of a sudden, Jack turned jocular. "Hell, Chester, you're a mining man, and mining men find ways to get through near anything." A pause, then: "Oh, and by the way, regards from Diamondfield."

"Diamondfield Jack Davis?"

"Piece of work, isn't he? A walking arsenal. And tightly wound, a hair-trigger on him. Can no more be controlled than shafts of lightning from high heaven. But Diamondfield's all right when you get to know him... as I have. One thing and for certain, he knows his way around mining. Matter of fact, he expressed his interest in having a look at our Monte Cristo and your Queen of Sheba."

"That would be nice, I think. But maybe not yet."

"Of course, Chester. But as the occasion warrants."

Chester couldn't have helped but wonder if this was a threat. Had Salsberry been tipped that the Queen of Sheba was up for sale? Without a doubt, he was upping the pressure, at the same time making it difficult for Chester to keep on track by saddling him with the traction engine and its attendant Mr. Shaffer. Jack ambled over to the thing, told Chester how effective it had been hauling lumber thirty miles from his sawmill in the Sierra Nevadas to his planing mill at the edge of the desert.

"It so scared the hell out of people and their horses that we had to send a mounted man ahead, warning 'em." He repeated and chuckled, "*warning 'em.*"

A desultory discussion of other matters—payroll, supplies, morale—and Jack Salsberry was on his way, up over Bradbury Pass and on down to the railroad. Boarding at Zabriskie, he'd be back in San Francisco in twenty-two hours, there to enjoy the comforts of his suite at the St. Francis Hotel, where, "Son, we'll be pulling for you."

In the next weeks, Chester may or may not have updated Salsberry on his progress. He did, though, scrawl several letters, the first to H.L.S. Robinson on May 7th. H.L.S was ill, but determined to stay on in Ballarat.

> Cheer up.

> Please send over a wheelbarrow, umbrella & hat.

It was heating up; on that day 102° in Death Valley. On May 15th, Chester wrote Antoine Barber:

> Road coming along fine.

> Have been making assays. Have 12 feet of $50.00 ore and 4 in. of $106.00.

> Garden is doing fine. Grapes will be up about the middle of July.

> Hastily, C.A. Pray

The garden he mentions would have been at Peach Bloom Garden Springs, and the assayed ore was almost certainly from the Queen of Sheba. Chester was apparently back to the vicinity of his mines, strayed again from his road crew.

Construction lagged, in part because the daytime temperature rose to as much as 120°, and he had cautioned his men not to overexert. He knew from experience that "Heat can do terrible things to a man." Also, as the crew had moved its camp closer to Jubilee Pass, the gears of Salsberry's Roberts-Doan monster had jammed on the steep grade, and couldn't be pried loose for love nor money, the attempt wasting the better part of a day.

The June 8th deadline for the bond payment loomed.

Chester, as he had planned, was now off to Los Angeles for a deal that could net him the necessary $5,500, with thousands to spare. Late on Saturday afternoon, May 31st, he rendezvoused with lawyer McNamee in his fourth floor Pacific Electric building office. He thanked him for paving the way for W. C. Price to buy out his share in the Queen of Sheba. They were to meet him at the Wellman Oil Company office at six o'clock.

"You'll find his terms generous, most generous."

"Shouldn't we be on our way?" Chester didn't want to be late.

"Why, yes," McNamee said, as he led Chester across the hall from suite 404 to suite 405, the lettering on its door simply "William C. Price, Investments," with no mention of a Wellman Oil Company. Their knock was answered by "W. Clay Price. Mr. Pray, I presume?"

Chester must have wondered: What was going on here? A questionable oil company, its president "William C.," then "W. Clay." Whoever he was, he had a cozy relationship with lawyer McNamee.

What happened next puzzled, then assured Chester.

Quite unexpectedly, Frank McNamee excused himself and left for the day. Price confided to Pray, "I would have invited him to join us, but you see, one can entertain the same guest only once every so often."

Closing his office door behind him—Chester never got a look inside—he led Chester to the floor's bank of elevators. He pressed "UP."

"Mr. Price, good evening," the operator greeted him. "The club?"

"The club," Price nodded, and they ascended to the building's ninth floor, where they stepped into a marble rotunda capped with a stained glass dome, aglow with flower petals and stars. Greek statuary vied with oriental vases as tall as a man. The club—the Jonathan Club—was a Kubla Khan palace.

"Before we take drinks and have dinner, come admire the view."

The two ambled out onto a rooftop garden, past trellises woven with bougainvillea and star jasmine. The city sprawled to the west.

"A city, in large part, born of the desert," Price observed. "Up there, on Bunker Hill, you see mansions built with the silver of the Mojave's Cerro Gordo mines. And over there, on Adams Boulevard, that's where Randsburg money settled in. And Chester, my friend, where you might you build a fine house *with your $25,000 from the Queen of Sheba?*"

Chester was dumbstruck. At the very most, he'd hoped for half that. He was in a daze as Price took his elbow and escorted him to the Jonathan's dining room—and familiar faces.

"Goldfielders," smiled Price, "We boast a number as members."

This, Chester realized, was where the money came, and stayed. If his friend Clarence's illusory Queen of the Purple Mist had pointed with one hand to the southern Panamints, the other directed a treasure-seeker to the opulence of the Jonathan Club that night. Price flattered him with "I could propose you as a member, one of a roll strictly limited to a thousand."

A thousand, and a single word described them: *Elite*. For Chester, what a far cry this was—from low-lifers hocking hit-or-miss dusty goobers across rude saloons to gentlemen covering the mouths with one hand and holding back their neatly-trimmed beards with the other as they discretely expectorated into the Jonathan's spittoons, one to a table. Lest they stink, they were frequently emptied by one or another of the club's Chinese stewards.

"Now as to the terms..."

Post dinner, they repaired to the Moorish room. Gentlemen only, a choice of cigars. Heavy oriental tapestries, ivory inlaid chairs.

Price began: "For a dollar..."

What he was interested in, he now explained, was an *option* to buy out Chester's share of the mine.

"Not to worry," he said. It would be a short term option to be consummated on or before June 12th, when he'd convey a down payment of $2,500, the rest to follow in time, as the Queen of Sheba became a producer.

Chester was stunned, but managed to tamp his disappointment. "The payment," he blurted before thinking through the offer, "Could you make it by June 8th?"

"Perhaps. It depends. Deals like this take a little doing."

Chester did his best to put on a good face, masking a dismal, sinking feeling. Even if Price came through with the $2,500, he'd still be $3,000 short of the $5,500 called for by the Monte Cristo's bond.

"Mr. Price, I'd be forever in your debt if..."

"Chester, I'll try."

Hands in his pocket, head down, Chester walked through the night, across downtown Los Angeles to Antoine's apartment, where he'd be spending the night, before seeing Clara and then returning to Death Valley.

He wasn't in trouble, he told himself, in that he had a last way to raise the bond's $5,500 (or $3,000 if Price came through). Two weeks ago, he'd written his Aunt Julia and Uncle Henry explaining his fix. He'd made, he believed, a reasonable request that his Uncle Henry, as executor of his mother's estate, advance him the $7,000 that would come his way at the conclusion of her Will's probate. Uncle Henry could even consider this a commercial loan; Chester would pay interest, whatever Uncle Henry thought appropriate.

At the same time, Chester had dashed off a note. All it said was:

Dear Clara, I want to see you.

What he failed to realize was that he had switched envelopes, and it was his aunt and uncle who were to receive his note to Clara and be perplexed as to who she might be—with no knowledge or heed as to the deadline on his bond.

What, then, about Clara? Chester assumed she'd gotten his message, yet the next day, Sunday, she wasn't to be found at the Florence Residence, and the lady at the reception desk wouldn't say whether she was in Los Angeles or not.

Chester stayed over an extra day, to be at Robert E. Darrow, Ladies & Gents Furnishings when it opened.

No Clara, and no one with any idea where she might be, at least that they'd say.

With uncertainty heaped on uncertainty, Chester would have been frantic beyond measure had not Antoine Barber volunteered to accompany him back to Death Valley, in part to calm him down, but also because, fascinated with anything automotive, he believed he might revive the Roberts-Doan traction engine. Antoine packed up his tools and gathered gears and fittings that could improvise as parts. If they could get the albatross up and over Jubilee Pass, they'd have a case—look what they'd done! —for forestalling the bond payment until the funds from W.C. Price came through, or a money order arrived from Chester's Aunt Julia and Uncle Henry.

A few days at the most, and Chester would meet his obligation.

Wednesday, June 4th

The Tonopah & Tidewater station agent at Zabriskie handed Chester a half-dozen telegrams.

From Jack Salsberry.

Jack was disappointed. Why hadn't he heard from Chester?

Busy as he was in San Francisco, Jack was of a mind to return to Death Valley. Set things straight. Personally collect the payment due on the bond.

Chester and Antoine reached the road camp late that afternoon. Despite the rugged terrain, the crew had made considerable progress and were within a mile of Jubilee Pass.

Sunset.

Chester settled onto a blanket in front of the tent that he'd be sharing with Antoine, who offered him a cup of freshly-boiled coffee. Chester shook his head and cradled his forehead with his hands.

"I dread it, I dread it," he told Antoine: "What Salsberry will say, what he'll do."

"He's bullying you. But stand up to him—show some sand—and he'll back down. I guarantee it."

"And Diamondfield. What about him?"

Antoine smiled, for with mention of the name, Chester had instinctively reached for his holstered 38 caliber Colt.

"If it came to it," said Antoine, "my money'd be on you."

Day in and day out, Chester had worn the gun since for as long as anyone could remember.

He was a good shot.

"Seriously, Chester, Diamondfield's bluster," assured Antoine. "One part head and ten parts mouth, and nowhere in sight if there's real strife. Though I grant you he might have the courage to shoot a man from behind. Or asleep."

Chester wasn't so sure.

"Good night, Chester. Things will look better in the morning."

"'Night, Antoine. *My only true friend.* You know that, don't you?"

Antoine hesitated, thinking in particular of Clara, who he'd recently spent some time with, even as Chester hadn't.

"I do," he said. "And you know, of course," Antoine added, "that the men like you. They're glad to have you back, peculiar though you might be."

Chester smiled, though wanly.

WAIT & HOPE

NUMBING GOOD SENSE, the desert's burning sun can incite the irrational, the paranoid, even the delusional in thought and deed. The long hours of the next three days would have their effect on Chester Pray. With a fortune at stake, he would ruminate on who might take advantage of—even betray—him? Who could he trust? His new partners Jack and Ed? Alleged oilman W.C. Price? Lawyer McNamee?

Clara?

(He missed Clarence. There wasn't a mean bone in his shambling body.)

And events now to unfold would be incomplete without a final, if phantom player: Edmond Dantes, the Count of Monte Cristo.

Serialized in a French newspaper in 1844-45 and printed in English in 1846, Alexander Dumas' novel rivaled the Bible as a well-thumbed staple of the American West, recounting as it did the story of Dantes' escape from the dungeon of the dank Chateau d'If, his one possession the knowledge of a vast treasure, its location rasped by a dying Abbé in an adjoining cell. Dantes sails to the desert isle of Monte Cristo, there to explore a mysterious cavern. Deep underground, he discovers an enormous chest.

> Dantes inserted the sharp end of the pickaxe between the coffer and the lid, and burst open the fastenings. A vertigo seized Edmond. He closed his eyes as children do in order to perceive in the shining night of their own imagination more stars than are visible in the firmament; then he reopened them, and stood motionless in amazement. Three compartments divided the coffer. In the first, blazed piles of golden coin. In the second, bars of unpolished gold were ranged. In the third, Edmond grasped handfuls of diamonds, pearls, and rubies, which as they fell on one another, sounded like hail against glass.

Having touched, felt, and examined these treasures, Edmond rushed through the cavern like a man seized with frenzy; he leapt on a rock from whence he could behold the sea. He was alone, alone with these countless, these unheard-of treasures. Was he awake, or was it but a dream?

It was no dream.

And it was a dream, the dream of the lone prospector of the American West. *Monte Cristo*. The name was everywhere. North of Goldfield, Chester had many times skirted a white-bluffed, isle-like range risen from the Nevada sands—the Monte Cristos. East of Goldfield, a Monte Cristo camp had flourished and faded.

South from Goldfield, Chester made his Monte Cristo strike.

Chester could well identify with the novel's Edmond Dantes. Both men, through no fault of their own, had been incarcerated: Edmond in the Chateau d'If and Chester in the McLean Asylum for the Insane. Both had contended with loneliness and alienation. Both sought to rid themselves of personal demons that might find a measure of equilibrium and peace. Even poisoning had its role: Edmond contending with "brucine," a distillate of the deadly seed of an Asian tree, and Chester fearing the effects of mercury, an agent in assaying and amalgamating ore.

Both men felt life, "however painful it may be, is yet always so dear."

Seeking to avoid financial disaster and shame, Chester—as the Count—came to realize that "In business, sir, one had no friends, only correspondents," and that a sad fact of life could be "the treachery of those we thought to be friends."

Thursday, June 5th

"Think of what you have to live for!" Antoine encouraged him. "One way or another, the money will come through, at least from your aunt and uncle. Have they ever failed you?"

"No... they haven't."

"Or hell, Jack Salsberry could ride up the road, see what all you've done, and let you off the hook on the bond payment. Don't think he can't afford to."

Chester took heart.

A singular point in *The Count of Monte Cristo* was that "All human wisdom can be summed in two words: wait and hope." With that in mind, Chester threw himself into overcoming "the washboard," a rocky, corrugated uphill stretch that defied their Fresno grader and had the entire crew hefting pickaxes and sledgehammers. Chester set a furious pace, as if every rock was a demon to be broken to bits and kicked or chucked to the side of the road, life's road.

On a water break, Antoine feared that Chester was overdoing it, and cautioning him, Antoine popped open the umbrella H.L.S had sent over. Chester would have none of it.

Despite the day's exertion, neither slept that night. There was too much on Chester's mind, with Antoine doing his best to put him at ease. There was no getting around how much was at stake, with a $5,500 bond payment due in two days.

"It'll work out."

"I don't know what I'll do if it doesn't..."

Up by Jubilee Pass, coyotes yipped and howled, first one, then a pack of them, a crescendo of frenzy. Newly-born cottontails were out foraging, and the worse for it.

Friday, June 6th

At dawn, rock wrens sang, but soon took wing for higher elevations. Cicadas buzzed for a time, then fell silent. The camp stirred. Coffee was boiled and bacon fried, the grease dripped to soften week-old biscuits, dry and stale.

Though terribly tired, Chester stretched, ate the eggs Antoine had scrambled, and was back to the washboard.

Intent on reviving the Roberts-Doan traction engine, Antoine, along with its driver, the Indian Bob Lee, walked down to where it had jammed a gear and slid off the road.

Sometime that day, Chester had a dispute with L.M. Shaffer, the issue being whether or not to cut switchbacks on the steep grade up to Jubilee Pass, over 10%. Shaffer was in favor of the idea; Chester vociferously objected. Shaffer acceded. As the two then flagged the route with strips of shirting, Chester gazed off, from time to time, in the direction of the railroad. If a telegram or letter made it to Zabriskie, he had arranged for his friend Joe Duro to rush it to the camp. His hopes rose as he sighted a figure, but faded as the man stopped for a talk with Barber and Lee. It was an Indian looking for Lee.

Mid-afternoon and approaching wheezes signaled that Barber and Lee had fixed the gearing of the Roberts-Doan. About time, the contraption was good for something: crunching and compressing the washboard.

Laying down their picks, leaning on their shovels, the road crew cheered.

Sunset.

"Tomorrow this time, Chester, you'll be up and over..." Antoine paused, asked, "Chester?"

Chester didn't answer, just stared off into the darkness. He had put on a good face by day, but that night, despite Antoine's best efforts, he was increasingly glum and, by the early morning hours, all but inconsolable. Antoine was to write "of the worry and the heat incident thereto" and that—

> He became so discouraged and melancholy that he could not sleep and he expresst [sic] to me his intention of doing away with himself. He was thoroly [sic] imbued with the idea that he was incapable of handling his business.

For a second night, neither slept.

Saturday, June 7th

At first light, Chester spit a fuse up by Jubilee Pass, shouting the customary "Fire in the hole!" As he hastened back down to his men, he smiled and cracked a joke. It was as if he'd come to terms with what he might face. In quick succession, three blasts echoed through the Funerals. The pick and shovel brigade attacked the rubble. Jack Neis and his mules and Fresno scraper followed. Behind them, the Roberts-Doan rolled up and back, compressing the road. Bob Lee was at the wheel; Antoine Barber pointed the way with a long-spouted oil can.

Every half hour or so there would be further blasts, up to four at a time. Chester's mood markedly improved; he joshed with the men, regaled them with an off-color story or two. They picked up the pace. By noon, against expectation, the ragged procession—men, mules, and the hulking Roberts-Doan—was up to and over Jubilee Pass.

"A cheer!" Antoine proposed, "for our Chester Pray and his Monte Cristo! For our roll on down to the floor of Death Valley!" From a letter we know that H.L.S. had sent Chester a camera, used now to "Kodak" the crew. Had the image survived, it might well have captured a beaming Chester, with worry and care apparently behind him. It just could be that he'd sunk so low that there was nowhere to go but up.

"Hit bottom hard enough, and you'll bounce," the saying went.

Jack Gallagher recalled him being "jolly as ever and cutting up." Concurred Bob Lee, "he was jolly and happy all throughout the day."

As the crew knocked off early to move the road camp—equipment, supplies, and tents—over the pass, Bob Lee asked for a few words with Chester. His little daughter was sick and had been taken to the hospital in Las Vegas. Could he take a few days off to go see her? Antoine Barber, Lee felt, could look after the Roberts-Doan.

Chester told him to take as long as he needed and promised to issue an advance on his pay the first thing the next morning.

Sunset.

Antoine was to write Chester's Aunt Julia:

> I argued and joked with him continuously for three days and nights & tho't I had talked him out of the notion [of doing anything rash]. I told him to forget all about it and take it easy and that I would stay by him and see the whole deal thru for him & then as soon as we could he should come back to Los Angeles and stop at my house for a few weeks until he had recovered his equilibrium. He said I was the only friend he had left in the world (aside from his uncle & aunt), and that I would never know how much he appreciated my offer.
>
> He seemed greatly cheered.
>
> The conversation took place on Saturday night while we were on our bed spread on the sand. I was so worn out, and his apparent change in mental condition, caused me to relax my vigilance.

Antoine—awake in the desert for sixty or more hours—drowsed and fell fast asleep.

Chester, too, may have drifted off, his last thoughts being to hell with Mr. Jack Salsberry and his tricks and tactics.

Or, in a darker vein...

He might have dwelled on a chapter in *The Count of Monte Cristo* that recounted the ratcheting despair of a merchant and shipowner, M. Pierre Morrel. To meet the obligations of a 300,000 franc debt, Morel had counted on the timely arrival and docking of his ship the *Pharoun*, only to be dealt a terrible blow. A report reached Marseilles that the *Pharoun* had foundered and sunk in a storm.

M. Morrel faced ruin and contemplated suicide, with a deaf ear to his daughter Julie and son Maximilian.

> "My father! My father!" cried the young man, "why should you not live?"
>
> "If I live, all would be changed; if I live, pity would become hostility; if I live, I am only a man who has broken his word and failed in his engagements—in fact, only a bankrupt. If, on the contrary, I die, my corpse will be that of an honest but unfortunate man. Living, my best friends would avoid my house; dead, all Marseilles will follow me in tears to my last home.

The passage's harsh, but well-argued point: suicide in certain circumstances is honorable. Faced with shame or death, death was preferable. This grim sentiment was widely held in the late 1880s and early 1900s, and in the instance of *The Count of Monte Cristo*, M. Morrel and Chester Pray shared an eerily similar plight. To outward appearances, both men were the envy of all who would covet riches. And in common, they faced an inexorable deadline—coincidentally, ninety days—from the point of making a seemingly routine commitment. In the end, both could be saved only by a miracle.

Both were honorable, M. Morrel resolutely, and Chester when it mattered.

The hour of his deadline approaching:

> Morrel fell back in his chair, his brow bathed in perspiration. Yet he was resigned. His eyes were moistened with tears, and yet raised to heaven.

The clock hand moved on; the pistols were cocked; he stretched forth his hand, took one up. He no longer counted by minutes, but by seconds. An agony stronger than death clutched at his heart-strings.

The clock gave its warning to strike.

He placed the muzzle of the pistol between his teeth. Suddenly he heard a cry—it was his daughter's voice. He turned and saw Julie; the pistol fell from his hands.

"My father!" cried the young girl. "Saved! —you are saved!"

She held out a receipt. A mysterious stranger[15] had paid off M. Morrel's looming debt! And as M. Morrel puzzled this turn of events, a servant burst into the room.

"The Pharoun!" he cried; "the Pharoun is entering the harbor!"

Morrel fell back in his chair; his understanding, weakened by such events, refused to comprehend such incredible, unheard-of, fabulous facts.

Chester Pray would have read and reread this, a breathless moment in a favorite novel.

Midnight approached. Antoine, by his side, slept soundly.

Chester looked to the east, where in a few hours the sun would rise on Sunday, June 8th, 1913. As Morrel's debt had been relieved and the *Pharoun* had rounded Marseilles' breakwater, there was still a chance—dwindling, remote now—that a redeeming figure would crest Jubilee Pass.

---

[15] As revealed in the novel's next chapter, none other than a disguised Count of Monte Cristo.

A DEATH IN DEATH VALLEY

SUNDAY, *JUNE 8th, 1913*

Awakening sometime before dawn, Antoine Barber lay on his back, rubbing the desert grit from his eyes. He turned to Chester, and Chester wasn't there. Alarmed, he scrambled to the tent's front flap and was relieved to catch sight of a figure standing twenty feet away: Chester, quietly chatting with the Indian Bob Lee.

Propped on an elbow, reclining on a blanket spread before his tent, Lee was cleaning his pipe.

Chester handed Lee the check he'd promised the afternoon before. Barber caught a word here and a phrase there of Chester wishing Lee's little daughter well, then joking with him, cheering the Indian.

"Too early in the morning to wake the boys," Chester told Lee.

Normally, the crew would be up and about at five, or today, Sunday, a little later. Even so, some of the men had stirred. Crew foreman Jack Gallagher pulled on his dust and grime-caked overalls, and he struck a match to boil up coffee. He checked the time.

Angled to reflect the light now lining the horizon, his watch read 4:15.

Chester got a laugh out of Bob Lee. Lee thanked him for his consideration.

Then, according to Lee, "Mr. Pray walked down the road and that was the last I saw of him."

Concurred Roger Kennedy, "I heard the men walking down the road toward the valley." (Chester and who else? Or had Kennedy meant to say "the man.")

Antoine Barber later wrote that he "thought nothing of it" as he watched Chester walk past where the traction engine was parked.

> He headed on down a gully to a distance where
> he was lost to sight and about a hundred and fifty

yards from camp. I was only half awake and dozed off to sleep for perhaps five minutes when I was awakened by a shot which I heard whistle right over our camp.

Jack Gallagher looked to his watch. It was "half past four to the second."

Bob Lee scratched a match and lit his pipe.

It wasn't that unusual for Chester—or anyone—to be up and about for a little target practice, or to pick off a rabbit for dinner.

Some five minutes ticked past, and Jack Gallagher—though no one else—heard a second shot. (Possibly, he imagined it. Or the others who'd stirred had dozed off. Roger Kennedy was to testify that he "heard one shot and went to sleep.")

Some five to ten minutes later, two more shots were fired in quick succession, fifteen or less seconds apart.

Abruptly, Bob Lee sat up, prompting Antoine to call over, "Who's doing all the shooting around here?"

"I think it's Pray," replied Lee.

With no great urgency, Antoine checked his boots for scorpions, shaking one then the other.

Lee took a draw on his pipe, exhaled, watched the smoke curl in the pale sunlight stealing across the camp. "Barber," he called, pointing west with his pipe, "Pray went down there to try his nerve."

Antoine was suddenly on his feet. "Try his nerve"? He wrote:

> I dresst [sic] hastily but said nothing and went to look for Chester. Two or three hundred yards away I saw him lying in a depression in the sand & hoping against hope that he had just laid down to rest or think, I called to him twice. Receiving no answer I ran down to within 20 ft. of him and stopt [sic]. I saw by his color and by the wounds on his head that he was beyond help—that he was absolutely dead—and I ran back to camp.

Jack Gallagher was the first to see Antoine—Antoine gesticulating wildly.

"What's the matter?"

"Dead" was all he could say.

"Who's dead?"

Antoine stopped and for a time couldn't speak. Then choked, "Pray dead."

The Indian Bob Lee rose and approached Jack and Antoine. Antoine said, "Pray dead down the road."

Wrote Antoine:

> The men had begun to get up then and when I told them, they immediately askt, [sic] "What were you doing down there with him so early?" and I saw I was suspected of having shot him. None of the men knew me.

To protest his innocence, Antoine insisted that the men follow his tracks. They did: Gallagher, Kennedy, Madison, Shaffer, Neis, Bob Lee, and two or three unaccounted for.

"Stop! Look!" Antoine pointed out where he'd turned back, a good twenty feet short of Chester's body lying in a hollow in the sand. Antoine wrote:

> They saw I had gone alone but still they suspected me.
>
> The Indian [Bob Lee] said nothing.

The stunned men advanced. As Jack Gallagher described, "Pray lay right flat on his back one left hand over his breast and the other down his side." Blood from a wound to his head ran down his right arm to where his hand rested beside his 38 Colt. An empty shell casing gleamed in the sand; a second shell, empty as well, was fouled in the weapon. On firing, it had failed to eject.

With the exception of Antoine Barber, the men doubted Chester had taken his life, and a first reaction was to scan the area for evidence of "dry-gulching," desert slang for a cowardly ambush. Death Valley had its share of such incidents, most notoriously "the Battle of Wingate Pass," the handiwork of a scheming Scotty.

And Diamondfield Jack Davis, as the occasion demanded, was rumored to be a dry-gulcher. It assured him of a first shot and then cover if he missed.

The road crew checked the area for additional shell casings or tracks beyond their own. They found neither.

With no evidence of a lurking stranger, and dismissing the idea of suicide, the men next believed the shooting to be accidental. The fouled shell in the Colt was taken as evidence of a malfunction that Chester was attempting to clear, only to slip or fumble in the dark and trigger a fatal shot. The more the men considered this, the more this made sense, considering that no more than half an hour before, Chester was in apparently good spirits, idly bantering with Bob Lee.

Teamster Jack Neis headed back to camp to hitch up a team to transport the body. The others spent half an hour debating if this was the right thing to do, in the end determining that in the interest of justice, Chester should not be moved, but left as he'd fallen, pending the arrival of a coroner.

It was at this juncture that a man—his identity undisclosed and a mystery in subsequent testimony—stepped forward to take the reins of Jack Neis' team, swing up into the driver's seat of the wagon, and be on his way to Zabriskie to alert the law and see to a coroner. He was also to alert the press; the very next day, the story made the front page of the *Goldfield Chronicle*. Written on short notice and a hundred and seventy miles from the scene, the article was remarkably well informed concerning Chester Pray and what had happened.

C.A. PRAY'S SHOOTING IS A MYSTERY

Young Mining Man, Well Known Here, Meets Strange Death on the Desert

---

ENGAGED TO MARRY AND HAD MADE FORTUNE

Companions in Road Camp Heard Shots and Found Bullet Hole in Head

---

News was received here yesterday of the death of Chester A Pray, a young mining man who is well known in Goldfield and other mining camps of Nevada. According to the report received here Pray was killed by a shot from a revolver, which is supposed to have been accidentally discharged by himself. The fatal shooting occurred at a road construction camp between Zabriskie station, on the T. & T. railroad, and Carbonate, Inyo county, Ca., where the victim of the shooting had important mining interests.

A coroner's inquest is being held today to determine the cause of death, the justice of the peace at Zabriskie having gone to the scene to hold an inquiry.

In the absence of any detailed information regarding the circumstances of the death of Pray, it is believed that he accidentally shot himself while examining or handling the automatic gun as the point where he fell was only a short distance from and nearly in sight of the camp.

Chester Pray was 36 years of age and had been prospecting and mining in southern Nevada for several years, having been in Goldfield at various times during the boom times and again about two months ago, when he stayed here for a fortnight or more. His father, mother and sister are dead and the only relative he is known to have had is an aunt, a Mrs. Cram, who lives at Brookline, Mass. He was associated with E.S. Chafey and John Salsberry in the ownership of the property at Carbonate, which is regarded as being of great value.

It is said that the dead man was engaged to be married to a young woman in Los Angeles and that he was only awaiting the completion of negotiations for the sale of his mining property to marry the girl of his choice and settle down, with assurance of an ample competence for all time. Mr. Chafey has been in Goldfield, where he heard the news of the fatality, and left by the next train for Zabriske. Salsberry is in San Francisco and was notified at once of the death of his partner.

Surprisingly detailed and accurate as to Chester's age, family, and business affairs, the article had to be based on more than a telegram or telephone call up the line from Zabriskie. It is likely that Ed Chafey, registered at the Goldfield Hotel Sunday and Monday, June 8th and 9th, put some time in at the paper (and placed his name before Salsberry's). Antoine Barber might have been the source for the article if he was the man who rode to Zabriskie—but he was not. He was at the road camp, and he wrote of the two days and nights following the killing:

> We covered Chester with a tent and sent a man
> & a team back to the R.R. to get coroner. Sunday
> night we had to stay up and fight the coyotes away
> from him. Monday night the coroner arrived...

Barber spares details of the deterioration of the body as the temperature in the tent climbed to 130° or more. For the demoralized crew, minutes would have been hours and hours an eternity. There was little to do but puzzle what had happened, and, human nature what it is, suspicions were raised and theories put forth.

The notion of an accident was abandoned. It was hard to imagine a man as handy with a gun as Chester clearing a jam with the barrel aimed at his head. Was it murder after all, dry-gulching by a stranger in the shadows?

Or by a stranger in their midst? Antoine Barber. He'd shown up in camp and for three nights he and Chester had talked and argued. He'd discovered the body, and even though his footsteps stopped twenty feet away, who's to say the two men hadn't had it out, trading oaths and shots? Several of the men, miners at the Monte Cristo, were aware of Clara Carlsrud, courted by Chester and friendly with Antoine. Did she figure in this? If she hadn't, she would. Chester's Will gave her a major stake in both the Monte Cristo and the Queen of Sheba.

Antoine and Clara. Conspirators?

Why, Antoine wondered, wouldn't the Indian Bob Lee admit that Antoine had gone looking for Chester, not before, but after the shots were fired? And why, when Chester headed into the night "to try his nerve," hadn't Lee moved to discourage or stop him? Apparently, Lee didn't give a damn whether Chester lived or died.

Shoshones roamed Death Valley. Had Chester had a run in with Lee's people?

Speculations were tabled when, late Monday afternoon, John Neis' wagon crossed Jubilee Pass to deliver Zabriskie Justice of the Peace J.P. Gates. He would be "acting coroner," standing in for Inyo County's elected coroner over in Independence.

Contending with the heat, flies, and a terrible stench, he hazarded only that Chester had been shot, twice it appeared.

But he wasn't sure; Chester's blood-soaked hair was tangled and matted. Gates asked that Chester and his effects be secured in the wagon, and come dawn of Tuesday, June 10th, the Monte Cristo's road crew cleared the camp. They rode and walked the road they had cut over the past two months, and in the early afternoon, rounding Sheephead mountain, they were in sight of Zabriske, two hours distant. A faint, distant whistle signaled the afternoon Tonopah & Tidewater train, southbound from Goldfield.

A supply town with not much to supply following the 1907 Greenwater debacle, Zabriskie was little more than a saloon, Hugh Fraser's general store, a few railroad buildings, and a boarding house with "MY WIFE IS BOSS" painted over its porch. Other than that, a few tents and a scattering of shacks.

As the weary road crew approached, they were hailed by a figure in black, sitting on a pine coffin in the shade of a T & T warehouse: Frank T. Dunn, the twenty-five-year-old son of Goldfield undertaker Thomas F. Dunn.

"Salsberry contacted us. Said to come down, embalm Pray." He gestured to five gallons of formaldehyde and a wooden box packed with the tools of his trade: syringes, hoses, oil of cedar to temper the formaldehyde. "Funeral's been set for the Elk's Lodge, Thursday afternoon."

The Dunns, father and son, had no use for feigned bereavement—"a refreshing contrast," Dunn senior had jibed, "to men of the cloth entitled to a certain kind of reverence for the splendid character of their lying." From time to time the *Goldfield Chronicle* noted that the Dunns were rarely at a loss for customers; at a morticians' conclave in Reno, they were "the object of much interest and some professional jealousy among the fellows of the craft."

Surrendering Chester to Dunn, the road crew straggled to Zabriskie's saloon for a late lunch and a stiff drink. A little after four o'clock, they were summoned to a coroner's inquest convened at Fraser's store, Justice of the Peace Gates presiding. T & T railroad agent P.V. Fuentes would take down their testimony, and six locals, hastily recruited as jurors, would determine the cause of death, and who might or might not be guilty, or at least suspect.

One then another, the road crew testified, with Gates handling the questioning as to name, age, occupation, and what exactly happened just before dawn two days past. At the outset, their recollections were at odds, particularly as to how many shots were fired—with the number ranging from none to four—and at what intervals. The discrepancies, though, were reconciled when allowances were made for men asleep or groggily half-awake, with a dim perception of time.

Suspicions raised by the road crew in the shadow of Jubilee Pass were revisited by the Zabriskie jury. The likelihood of an accident was considered—and, for the moment, dismissed as unlikely, especially if there'd been two shots to the head.

Chester Pray's death, it would appear, was willful.

The specter of Indians on the warpath was raised, and there was a reasonable argument for this. Chester's mines would require water to be piped in either from Bennett's Well or Peach Bloom

Garden Springs. Both were Shoshone winter campsites. Bob Lee, on the road crew, was an Indian. Was he complicit?

The consensus was "no." He'd no quarrel with Chester, though he was often sullen. A lot of people were sullen; it went with scraping by in the heat and dust. Suspicions of dry-gulching by Indians—or anyone—were allayed by an absence of evidence of anyone in the area. Jack Gallagher vouched for this.

> Q. Jack, did you notice any strangers around the camp in the last day or two?
> A. None whatever.

This being the case, what of the man who, to most of the crew, was all but a stranger: Antoine Barber? There was only his word that he'd been up at the camp, not down the road, when the shots were fired. But then, in the course of his testimony, Bob Lee broke his silence on the matter.

> Q. Where were you when the shots were fired?
> A. Was laying in bed awake smoking my pipe.
>
> Q. Did you notice any other man awake at that time?
> A. Yes. One Barber.
>
> Q. Did Mr. Barber get up just then.
> A. No. A little while afterwards.

Antoine was relieved to be cleared, and he could never understand why Bob Lee remained silent as others on the crew accused him of shooting Chester. The two had struggled with the Roberts-Doan traction engine and had gotten on well enough.

J.P. Gates swore in and questioned Antoine Barber:

> Q. I judge that you were an old acquaintance of Mr. Pray's?
> A. Yes Sir.
>
> Q. What was the condition of Mr. Pray's mind on June 7th?
> A. He was melancholy and absent minded.

Q. Did he make any statement to you that he contemplated self destruction?

A. Yes sir, Friday night while we were camped at what they call the washboard.

Q. Did he tell you at that time why he was depressed in mind?

A. Road failure was one he held himself responsible for. Failure of road and humiliation of Mr. Salsberry. Particularly in my estimation he claimed he was financially broke. He feared that he would loose his interest in the mines.

Q. Did he in so many words estimate to you he contemplated self-destruction.

A. Not definitely. He said, "I have a notion."

Still, the jury found it difficult to believe that Chester would have taken his life. The day before he was found dead he was "jolly as ever and cutting up" (according to Jack Gallagher), as he well should be on the threshold of a dream come true.

Less than an hour ago it had been the jury's consensus that two shots to the head ruled out an accidental death. Wouldn't it be the same with suicide?

Could anyone shoot himself in the head—twice?

It was then that a figure passed the dusty front windows of Fraser's store and with his elbow, nudged open the door. Silhouetted against the glare of the late afternoon sun, he held a sack in one hand and a pistol in the other. For a time, young Frankie Dunn stood there, blinking, his eyes adapting to the store's dark interior. He then stepped forward and laid the pistol—Chester's—on the nearest counter.

"His effects. Who's to see to his effects?" Dunn asked.

Antoine Barber said he would and took possession of the Colt automatic, a gold Waltham watch and fob, and two dollars and thirty cents.

"And now, you best all come with me..."

With Gates and his six jurors leading the way, the crowd at the inquest exited Fraser's store and walked the hundred yards to the Tonopah & Tidewater warehouse, there to view Chester laid out in the coffin Dunn had brought from Goldfield.

"Couldn't embalm him. Too far gone for that. I cleaned him up as best I could."

"And?"

"You'd like me to explain?"

"As expeditiously as you can, Mr. Dunn," Gates prompted. "Do you swear to tell the truth, nothing but the whole truth, so help you God?"

"I do."

Clerk P.V. Fuentes hand wrote:

> Q. Please state to the jury your age and occupation.
> A. Age 25, occupation Embalmer. Residence Goldfield Nevada. I was called to attent [sic] to the body of Chester A. Pray at Zabriskie, June 9th, 1913. I found the body in advance state of discomposition. Under right side of the head abut [sic] quarter of an inch to the back and above the right ear, I found a bullet wound about a 38 caliber. The wound ranges up towards the top of the head where the skull is fractured in three places but no outlet for the bullet. On the top of the head starting about an inch from the right side of the crown of head and about two inches long ranging towards the left side of crown I find a scalp wound about 2 inches & half long made by 38 caliber bullet. No other marks on body excepting where discomposition had set in the wound made on the right side of head above right ear. Pierced the brain and fractured the skull in three places.

That appeared to clarify matters. Chester had initially fired one or two shots—at rabbits or more likely, in the air, judging from the whistle over the camp. Then for several minutes he'd "gotten up his nerve" (as Bob Lee said) before turning the Colt on himself and firing two shots in quick succession, the first grazing his scalp and surely dazing him, but not so much that he couldn't lodge the barrel in back of and just above his right ear and pull the trigger.

The upward trajectory of the bullet—to all appearances—would rule out the hand of another.

"And there's this..." said Frankie. A crumpled note:

I am sick as well as in trouble. C.A. Pray.

Dunn tucked it back where he'd found it, in the pocket of Chester's vest.

As the sun slipped away over the Funerals, the jurors walked from the warehouse back to Fraser's store and acting coroner Gates didn't mind if a bottle, then another, was uncorked and drinks poured. He swore in and briefly questioned—no more than a page or two each—the remainder of the road crew. There were no contradictions, nothing at odds. Two jurors had minor questions, nothing of consequence. A finding was agreed upon and readied.

In the matter of the inquisition on the body of Chester A. Pray.

We the Jurors summoned to appear before J.P. Gates Acting Coroner of Inyo Co. California of Zabriskie Inyo Co. on the 10th day of June 1913 to inquire into the death of Chester A. Pray, found dead at about 25 miles west of Zabriskie. Having been duly sworn according to law and having made inquisition, after inspecting the body, and hearing the testimony, adduced upon our oaths find the deceased was named Chester A. Pray. Native of California. 35 years of age. That the cause of his death on the 8th day of May 1913 was from gunshot wound inflicted by himself.

> A.Y. Roman - <u>Foreman</u>
> W.B. Current
> John Herson
> Martin Peicco
> Frank Harnish
> Herbert Rosen

To which J.P. Gates appended:

Suicide without a doubt.

"Good work, boys."

———◦◆◦———

The Justice of the Peace thanked and dismissed his Coroner's Jury. The men drifted out into the night, some to the saloon, others to the boarding house or shack or tent they called home. The affair had been unsettling and sad, with the thought "Could've been me." Chester wouldn't have been alone in staring down a barrel or eyeing a razor.

Gates had a few words with Fuentes as to filing the proceedings in Inyo County's courthouse over in Independence, with neither realizing that the transcript of the inquest glossed over—in fact, *completely omitted*—a major factor in the road crew's testimony and the jury's deliberations: the intimidating presence of two, possibly three men in the shadows of Hugh Fraser's general store.

Ed Chafey

Jack Salsberry

Though not certainly: *Diamondfield Jack Davis*

There was no question that Chafey was there. The *Goldfield Chronicle* said he was on his way. But Jack Salsberry? Not if you believed the previous day's article.

> ...Mr. Chafey has been in Goldfield, where he heard the news of the fatality, and left by the next train for Zabriske. Salsberry is in San Francisco and was notified at once of the death of his partner.

The truth of the matter was that Jack Salsberry had been out at the Monte Cristo's road camp for going on five days. His alibi in the *Chronicle*—almost certainly the handiwork of Ed Chafey—was a lie, and would have served its purpose had it not been for two items, one after the other in the *Goldfield Tribune's* **Personal Mention** column on Thursday, June 5th, the day Chester and Antoine, up from Los Angeles, joined the road crew as they neared Jubilee Pass. The items were likely placed by Ed Chafey. He liked to see his name in print.

> JOHN SALSBERRY came down from Reno this morning on his way to a mineral property in

which he is interested over the
line in California.[16]

E.S. CHAFEY arrived from
the north this morning and is at
the Goldfield. He is en route to
his mine at Carbonate, Cal.

The two of them, then, were on a collision course with Chester
Pray. Jack would have caught the afternoon train to Zabriskie,
and he would have been on his way to the road camp the first thing
the next morning, there to take over the operation upon Chester's
imminent default of the bond payment due on the Monte Cristo.

Chafey would overnight at the Goldfield Hotel, to follow a
day later.

It was a convergence worthy of *The Count of Monte Cristo*—
or a dime novel. The villainous creditor. The writ—the bond—
spelling ruin.

But hadn't Jack Gallagher testified that there'd been no
strangers in or around the camp at the time? He had and *he was
correct in this*. The crew was well acquainted with Salsberry and
Chafey, the two the source of their paychecks. This in mind, they'd
be loathe to connect the partners with the death of Chester Pray.
Further, their two days guarding his body gave them ample time
to reach a consensus on this. It should be noted that, testifying at
Zabriskie, only Antoine Barber (not on the payroll) mentioned one
or the other of Chester's new partners. Chester, he had said, was
depressed by the "humiliation of Mr. Salsberry."

As to that humiliation, Jack would have arrived at the
camp a day or so after Chester, there to play on his fears and
insecurities. One can only imagine the sneers, digs, and threats,
with an occasional "son" thrown in to assert his role as a father
figure, the equal or better of Chester's real father when it came to
demeaning the boy and now man. And canny Jack wouldn't have
left it at that. He would have paled around with the crew during
the day, and at night might well have invited them, a few at a

---

[16] A search of mining records confirms the Monte Cristo to be the sole Salsberry
property at the time "over the line in California." His prior relevant filing had
been in the Ubehebe district in January of 1908.

time, over to his and Ed's campfire to share a snort, swap stories, and have a good laugh.

The camaraderie across the camp couldn't help but deepen Chester's despair, letting him know how alone he was. He'd only Antoine to talk to. All night for three nights, and ultimately to no avail.

Though it can't be proved, Jack Salsberry may have had company. Diamondfield Jack Davis, the record would show, would soon have an interest in the Monte Cristo mine. This could have been how he earned it. Intimidation was his sport. The man was feral—darkly glowering, fondling his weaponry, foul-mouthed.

The strain on Chester would have been unbearable. Enough to drive him to kill himself, with his final testament: "I am sick and in trouble." He had given his all to make a go of life, work, and love—and failed.

Ed Chafey's whereabouts in this critical period are uncertain. Heading south from Goldfield on the Friday the 6th, he would have made it to the camp on June 7th. He'd either stayed on for a time or had returned to Zabriskie to be Jack's man in easing the takeover of the Monte Cristo. He was definitely back in Goldfield by the evening of the 8th, the day of Chester's death (signed into room 216 of the Goldfield Hotel). This enabled him to feed the story to the paper and see to arrangements with undertakers Thomas and Frankie Dunn. Handling this, he would have acted in concert with the unnamed man who had left the road camp for Zabriskie a half hour after Chester's death—almost certainly, Jack Salsberry. Jack had little or no reason to linger at the scene, and every reason to recruit J.P. Gates as acting coroner, and pack him on his way to the road camp. In Zabriskie, Salsberry could then assemble a Coroner's Jury. And pay them. The quicker Chester was in the ground, the better.

To wrap the matter up, Ed Chafey returned to Zabriskie on June 10th, the day of the inquest (on the same train as embalmer Frankie Dunn). The inquest concluded, the record has Chafey stepping forward to take possession of the body. This kept Jack Salsberry—ostensibly on his way from San Francisco—clear of the matter.

<hr />

The morning after the inquest, the northbound Tonopah & Tidewater #9 braked for a red flag, to hiss and throb as Chester's coffin was borne from the railroad's warehouse to a baggage car. Three, possibly four passengers boarded. Frankie Dunn would have had a hard-backed seat in second class. Monte Cristo partners Salsberry and Chafey—and Diamondfield Jack?—would have their pick of the empty seats in a first class Pullman. (No one was flocking to Goldfield in 1913.)

Jack Salsberry was pleased. Too bad about Chester, of course, but had he lived, the chances were that, excitable and feisty, he'd have tied up the development and exploitation of the Monte Cristo with injunctions and lawsuits. Jack didn't need lawyer McNamee papering his backside. The entanglement could forestall printing up and touting Monte Cristo stock, a lesser though viable road to riches if the mine fell short of expectations. Now, at the most, Jack would have Chester's executor H.L.S. Robinson to deal with, and with no legs and near everything under the sun wrong with him, H.L.S. was as near dead as Chester.

Across the aisle, Ed Chafey reclined his seat and drew his window shade. The bleached scenery crawling by was all too familiar. Did he have misgivings? Possibly, but not for long. In the desert, fortune rarely, if ever, was free of taint.

Too bad about Chester, of course.

Ed dozed.

Jack and Ed would have agreed: when you pulled up your chair in the mining game, the odds were stacked against you. When it came down to it, there was an abundance of worthless country rock, and precious little ore. Yet, with guile and deceit, the odds could be evened, and in the end, the scale tipped. Often at a price. People were hurt, even killed. It happened all the time, an occupational hazard. Men went crazy in the sun, got slabbed underground. They knifed and shot each other. They died for all kinds of reasons. Often for gold, but if the price was right, even for lead.

Lead. A fortune of it in sight! And there was silver, a good showing. And gold, gold as well.

So what if Jack had driven Chester Pray to kill himself?

If Diamondfield Jack had been along, he'd have customarily sat to the rear of the parlor car, his back to the wall of the men's room. He was a bad man, but not the worst. On the #9 northbound on June 11th, that would be Jack Salsberry, his affability masking a cold edge of cruelty, his crime the betrayal of Chester's innocent trust.

At three in the afternoon of the next day, Thursday, June 12th, a contingent of Elks gathered at their Goldfield Lodge. Exalted Ruler Charley Sprague went along with the Dunns' suggestion that the casket be closed. The carnage of two 38 slugs and four days in the heat were beyond his or anyone's repair. Besides, only a handful in attendance really knew Chester. There'd be little if any call for lingering looks and tearful farewells.

Of Chester's friends, Antoine was there, as was Clarence, in from Rhyolite. Over in Ballarat it's doubtful that H.L.S., Chris, Shorty, and Old John knew that he was dead. Even if they did, they wouldn't have had time to cross Death Valley and make it up to Goldfield.

No doting Aunt Julia; no diffident Uncle Henry.

There's no knowing if Clara Carlsrud came up from Los Angeles. If Antoine had sent her a telegram, she'd have had time for the journey. Though recently stand-offish with Chester, she had encouraged him and shared in his dreams. She may have loved him.

Jack Salsberry was there of course, as was Ed Chafey. A generous Elk, Jack had stepped forward to purchase Chester's Burial Robe and cover the costs of the funeral, for the Dunns typically $65.

With Tom Dunn signaling the Elk's Brother Organist to pedal and play, all sang "When They Ring the Golden Bells for You and Me" ("...in that far off sweet forever"). An interval of solemn Elk ritual followed, with the Lodge's Chaplain, young Frankie Dunn, leading the Brothers in prayer. When the time came for a eulogy, Charley Sprague gladly deferred to Elk Clarence Eddy. The Big Man toted himself to the Lodge's lectern, cleared his throat, and, fingering the watch pinned to his lapel, began with something about time and its passing, and how his friend Chester, well before his time, had been "called to the Great Beyond." He then couldn't help himself in modestly allowing that it was *he*, Clarence Eddy, who had discovered the Monte Cristo and had cut Chester in "so as to have company for myself." After five years "of ceaseless toil, I parted with this big ledge. He stayed there and worked on it until driven insane by the heat and solitude."

Clarence thought poetry in order. And what more appropriate than his "Queen of the Purple Mist." He recited:

> A purple sheen enwraps the scene
> Beneath the desert sky,
> And some behold a mist of gold
> That lures them 'till they die.

His hand upon Chester's coffin, Clarence voice rose and fell, with a poet's touch of tremolo.

> With dry canteens, in dry ravines
> They sleep, no more to wake,
> And in your sleep, so strange and deep
> Great heaven's dawn shall break.

This choked him up, and many in the parlor as well, even Elks who weren't quite sure who Chester was. For a time Clarence said nothing, simply patted, then actively thumped the coffin, and, his voice booming, proclaimed:

> Some win by luck, some win by pluck
> And some win not at all,
> Some lie forlorn by sage and thorn
> With the purple mist for pall:
>
> Oh, the golden queen of the purple sheen
> In the land of golden schemes.
> She waves her hand across the land
> To where heaven's glory gleams.

He laid his manuscript on the coffin, and overcome with apparent emotion, stumbled as he stepped back, to be guided to his chair by Frankie Dunn.

Exalted Ruler Sprague rapped his gavel four times, the signal for the assembly to rise as one and file around the coffin, each offering a sprig of the Lodge's flower, "Hope's gentle gem, the sweet Forget-me-not."

The coffin was then borne to the Dunns' motorized hearse, to be escorted by a phalanx of Brothers the mile west to Goldfield's graveyard at the foot of Malpai Mesa. The cemetery mirrored the camp's fortunes with its handful of grand monuments and its multitude of wooden white crosses, many nameless. The Dunn's hearse drew up and pallbearers bore the coffin through the gate of "Elk's Rest," there to lower it into freshly-dug grave #4, row 2. From the pocket of his coat, Charley Sprague withdrew a single white glove, cast in on the coffin, and wished Chester well "On your way to God's acre, far across the ferry yonder. All please join me in crossing our arms and joining our hands that we may sing 'Auld Lang Syne.'"

That night, Goldfield's Elks gathered in their Lodge. At eleven sharp, elbows and drinks were hoisted, and, an Elk's tradition, all in unison recited:

> There is no flock, however watched and tended
> But one dead lamb is there.
> There is no fireside how-so-e'er defended,
> But has one vacant chair.

Lowering his drink, Charley Sprague looked to Jack Salsberry, as did Frankie Dunn, and soon, all of the Elks present. Jack's eyes darted from one to the other, his expression one of uncertainty, even fear. But he quickly regained his composure, realizing that as a prominent mining man, as a respected Elk, and as the partner of the "one dead lamb," he'd be expected to say something. He cleared his throat.

"Chester A. Pray," Jack Salsberry intoned, "May your strifes and fears and sorrows deep vanish in the Lodge of joy at last."

—◆◆◆—

Though laid away in Goldfield's arid garden of death, Chester Pray was not forgotten, at least for a time. A hundred and seventy miles to the south, Death Valley's Jubilee Pass would for some years be known as "Suicide Pass." Edna Brush Perkins, a Death Valley adventuress and author of *The White Heart of the Mojave*, attributed the name to "a miner who'd taken his life when swindled." She added, "Yon yellow mountain had a scarlet spot that looked like a wound that bled."

Eventually, the name "Jubilee" would be reinstated—and the pass to the east (between Jubilee and Zabriskie) would no longer be known as Bradbury Pass.

The highest pass on the road to the Monte Cristo would be, and remains to this day, "Salsberry Pass."

JACK'S MINE &
OLD JOHN'S CASTLE

W ITH CHESTER PRAY MOURNED and buried, Jack
Salsberry had the road crew back on the job, though
they were slowed by the summer's escalating heat. As well, he hired
a superintendent, a Mr. Bruce, to initiate the full-scale development
of the Monte Cristo lode, which he now called the Queen of Sheba
(even though he had yet to cut himself in on the actual Queen of
Sheba).

Monte Cristo evoked Chester Pray and a bad end.

Uncertainty about Chester's death lingered, with rumors
circulating from Rhyolite to Ballarat to Independence, where
the *Inyo Register* expressed "doubt whether Pray shot himself
or someone else did the deed." Chester's new partners had to be
suspect, though no one dared say as much, thinking twice about
crossing Jack Salsberry or short-fused Diamondfield Jack. In a
further article, the *Register* reported that Chester "was supposed
to have committed suicide, though some hold to the belief that he
was murdered, likely by Indians."

Better—and safer—to blame it on the Shoshones.

Whatever suspicions were raised, they dwindled and were
forsaken as the region's weather took an apocalyptic turn in
early July of 1913. There had been a premonition of this when
a Goldfield ad for electric fans had proclaimed A HOT TIME IS
COMING! But how could this be, considering that the region had
just experienced the coldest winter on record? No matter, it got
so hot that Salsberry had no choice but to suspend work on the
road and put the crew to work underground. In the words of a
correspondent for the *Goldfield Daily Tribune*,

> I saw enough to convince me that Hades would be
> considered a summer resort when compared with this
> climate. At the mine, Mr. Bruce, the superintendent,

informed me that he put the thermometer out in the sun one day, but it ran up so fast that he was afraid to leave it out long, fearing that the mercury would break the glass in its haste to reach the top. It had reached 164 degrees [in the sun, not the shade] before he took it into the tunnel.

For this reason, the men employed at the mine live and sleep in tunnels, and the kitchen and boarding house is also in one of the tunnels.

The article was headlined: JOYS OF MINING IN NEAR-HADES. And for an unrelenting week, highs in the shade exceeded 127° at a newly-established recording station on the floor of Death Valley; it was no more than a degree or two cooler at the Queen of Sheba.

On the afternoon of July 10th, the mercury rose to and hovered at 134° in the shade—the hottest sustained temperature ever recorded on earth, before or since.[17] Indeed, the temperature may have exceeded that, for the thermometer in question shattered on reaching its maximum of 135°. Said a man on the scene, "I thought the world was going to come to an end."

By any measure, 1913 was a terrible year. And strange.

By night, phantom lights flickered out on the Valley floor, as if in eerie memorial to Chester Pray. From the vantage of the Queen of Sheba, "It looked like a spook procession."

On closer inspection, the source proved a "sizzling, whitish substance not unlike a Chinese 'spitter.' The fire fairly shot forth as if blown out of the gooseneck of a plumber's furnace." The phenomenon was attributed to saltpeter and spontaneous combustion.

A few weeks later, a correspondent for the *Goldfield News* was to look up and see "the night sky full of strange lights, like the flashing of fireflies, the phosphoric phenomena of a weird spooky waste."

And in September, capping the year's stigmata and wrath, flash floods laid waste to the land. In Goldfield "a foaming wall many feet high came down to South Main street, sweeping before it cabins and tearing through the redlight district."

And Jack Salsberry? All the while his focus was on taking over

---

[17] The highest transient temperature ever recorded – 136° F – occurred in a freak "heat flash" in Libya in 1922.

Chester's workings and prevailing in Death Valley. Come October, the Queen of Sheba boasted a payroll of a hundred-and-thirty-five, and the road successfully cut through from Zabriskie. Mules and wagons freighted ore up and over Suicide Pass; the Roberts-Doan steam traction engine (too thirsty for the desert floor) then hauled the ore on to the railroad. The *Inyo Register* reported:

Inyo's Latest Camp

> The new mining town and camp of Carbonate, in Death Valley, Ca., is now looming as the latest sensation of the western mining world. A typical desert boom is trending that way.
>
> It was only a few months ago that Ed Chafey and Jack Salsberry, the well known mining men, became interested in a strike developed by the late Chester Pray. A Los Angeles woman to whom Pray was engaged has now helped, it is said, to finance the mine quite heavily.
>
> Developments have now progressed to a depth of 300 feet, largely in lead-silver values. The town which is growing there is said to be a typical desert metropolis, constructed with tents, rocks, tin cans, dry goods boxes, whiskey bottles and anything that comes handy. It is a mecca of the adventurous followers of new fields, and "Diamondfield" Jack Davis is one of the latest to take the trail.

The goings-on at the Queen of Sheba were to perplex the reporter, to the extent that he wrote a follow-up article questioning whether this "new Eldorado" was reality or illusion. Whatever it was, Diamondfield Jack Davis was cited as more than a casual visitor: "It is not difficult to trace his fine hand in the invention which has so much foundation as the beautiful mirages that are found in that section of the Universe." The somewhat puzzling quote would indicate that Diamondfield Jack had not only been cut in on the deal, but was complicit in a mirage-like misrepresentation.

And what is to be made of the renewed role of Clara Carlsrud?

In that: "A Los Angeles woman to whom Pray was engaged

has now helped, it is said, to finance the mine quite heavily." If Clara indeed had money, wouldn't she have helped Chester with his bond payment, rather than benefit Jack Salsberry?

More likely, her "financing" was a cover for Jack's buyout of her share of Chester's estate. Be that as it may, whether paid off or penniless, she was presently to quit her job in Los Angeles and, up by the Valley of the Moon, reconcile with her husband Arne. Did she tell him of her Death Valley adventure and her affair with Chester?

The answer is probably *yes*, for early on a September morning, Arne was to load a rusted pistol and in their backyard try it out, the shot awakening and startling several neighbors. He then re-entered the house and shot himself in the head. Clara slept through both shots, at least that's what she said. At six in the morning, she discovered her husband, age 50, dead on the kitchen floor. *A chilling repeat of the death of Chester Pray*, with a Coroner's Jury verdict: "Deceased died from a self-inflicted gunshot wound with suicidal intent during a temporary aberration of the mind."

At the same time, over in Death Valley, Jack Salsberry was to secure his hold on the Queen of Sheba by elbowing Ed Chafey and H.L.S. Robinson aside and out of the picture, this accomplished by selling "said premises and every part therof" *to himself*, a legal maneuver that defied understanding (unless, of course, you were a swindler). That done, Jack's mine—his and his alone—was to pay off handsomely as ordinance for World War I required lead and more lead. The price per pound nearly tripled, from 3 1/2 to 8 1/2 cents. Jack replaced animals and steam traction with a fleet of sixteen trucks to haul forty to a hundred tons of high-grade ore a week to the railroad. The shipments brought in anywhere from $175,000 to as much as $1,000,000 a year. The range is due, on one hand, to undervaluing the mine to keep ex-partners and heirs off Jack's back; on the other, an inflated output would draw investors as the occasion rose for a round of "stock jobbery."[18]

Flushed with success, Jack was to write out a Queen of Sheba check for $10,000 and post it to Woodrow Wilson as measure of his support for the war effort. The President responded with a personal note, praising Mr. Salsberry's patriotism.

---

[18] This was a Salsberry specialty. In future manipulations, the value of Queen of Sheba stock would be fraudulently driven up anywhere from 400% to 1,000%, with Jack and his associates then cashing out.

As chicanery and fortune favored Jack Salsberry, prospects for others in Death Valley faded, with 1918 to prove a fateful, farewell year. Of a galaxy of hard rock mines, nearly all were abandoned. Only a single star shone, and that tarnished: the Queen of Sheba.

And of all the Valley's boom camps, only one held on, now to fold: Ballarat.

Chris Wicht, who swore he'd never leave, shuttered his saloon and moved on. H.L.S. Robinson, remarkably still alive, closed out his general store and gave away a remaining few of Chester's possessions: "one burro, one pack saddle, one assay outfit."

Clarence Eddy, Ballarat's bard, was to drift north to Idaho, there to promote a Cash Box Mine ("$10,000,000 easy," he assured a potential investor), a venture that, no surprise, came to nothing. Ever the poet, he was to write one, then two state anthems: "Hail to Thee, Idaho" and "Nevada Our Home."

Of all the Ballarat regulars, only Shorty Harris remained, holed up in the camp's abandoned schoolhouse. Old John Lemoigne cleared out his shack in the northern Panamints and might have resettled in Ballarat, where he'd long traded high-grade silver for beans and flour. But he didn't. He kept on going, rattling south on the old Wingate pass road, his buckboard packed with his mining tools and worldly possessions.

The source for what next became of Old John is Frank Crampton, remembered for his 1906 bittersweet romance with an Oakland socialite who'd been, for a time, a Goldfield prostitute. Frank was thereafter to work as an assayer, surveyor, and mining engineer throughout the West, yet he was time and again drawn back to Death Valley, where he made a point of seeking out Old John. In 1917 Frank tracked him to Garlic Springs, a palm and mesquite oasis south of the Valley yet comfortably shy of civilization. Old John's closest neighbors, over a hill and down by Bicycle dry lake, were Ma and Pa Gilson. Ma fed wayfarers in a "Desert Eating House." Out back, Pa distilled a potent red corn.

With scavenged lumber Old John had built himself a one-room shack, and he made do selling canned goods to old timers and tenderfeet bound for Platena, a platinum strike a day's journey northeast in the Mojave. These were to include his acquaintances Jay Ginn and Steve Larsen, who, bereft of funds, asked if Old John might grubstake them for a look at the hills beyond Platena. He gave them what could spare, well aware of the odds against a return.

"Good luck, boys. Tap her light." (Don't blow yourselves up.)

A month passed, and the boys were back down the road. They weren't looking for a further handout, but instead had a paper for Old John to sign. They'd tapped a lode of platinum, and a major company had jumped at the opportunity to develop the property, with three partners—Jay, Steve, and Old John—due a handsome share of the proceeds.

Old John couldn't complain. Though late in life and back-handedly, fortune had favored him.

Checks—sizeable checks—rolled in, care of nearby Ma Gilson. Old John was at once pleased and troubled, having a longstanding distrust of banks and their accounts. That being the case, he signed his royalties over to Ma Gilson, who, traveling to San Bernardino, exchanged checks for gold coins to be stashed at her Desert Eating House.

More checks came in. Sacks of gold coins piled up.

A small fortune.

Ma feared theft. She became increasingly nervous. She went over the hill to Garlic Springs and delivered an ultimatum: Old John would either have to assume responsibility for the gold, or spend it.

"On what?" He was content with what he had.

"You've enough, more than enough, for a fine home," countered Ma, hands on ample hips. "Build yourself a castle... Old John's castle!"

Luxuriating on the wide front porch of a magnificent edifice had long been the dream of rag-tag prospectors. But Old John demurred.

Ma wouldn't have it. She threatened to go load up the gold, cart it over, and dump it on the floor of his shack.

Old John balked. Ma turned on her heels and strode to her rig.

"No, no," Old John called.

A castle it would be.

Presently, Garlic Springs was abuzz with workmen in from San Bernardino, with Ma and a desert layabout by the name of Link Shaw as architects. As Frank Crampton wryly recounted:

> It was a large square building, with round turrets at each corner, and a church-like spire. The porch, surrounding the house was fifteen feet wide,

with an ornate railing and rococo filigree under its overhanging roof.

Ma Gilson and Link had put in a long shift designing the interior. The first floor had a music room, dining room, kitchen, parlor, and library. Rooms on the second floor were worked into the complexity of a gabled roof with multitudinous dormer windows. Chimneys came up in a dozen places, like quills on a porcupine.

For the house's furnishings, Ma Gilson had carefully planned an interior design of her own inspiration, which provided the one great, glorious spree of her bleak existence. Like many others, she had longed to buy everything pictured in mail-order catalogs. This was her golden opportunity to use a free, unrestrained, and flowing hand. No catalog or mail-order house was slighted; all received a share of Ma Gilson's bounty.

The grand, garish edifice completed, Old John Lemoigne settled in, or tried to. What need did he have for gilt French furniture, plush carpets, exotic-flowered wallpaper, crystal chandeliers? Or hot and cold running water.

"Never had a use for hot water," he told Frank, "and too late for such foolishness now."

In the course of the next few months, Frank had occasion to be back and forth on the road to Platena, and he found Old John increasingly fidgety and cranky, a hostage of opulence. He noticed that with scrap lumber and bailing wire, the old prospector had spent some time repairing his buckboard. When queried he muttered, "May want to go somewhere, soon, Frank."

The next visit, Frank took his leave with, "I'll see you in a week."

His castle looming behind him, Old John said nothing.

With Frank out of sight and mind, he returned to his business at hand. According to Ma Gilson, he had recently taken delivery on twenty cases of dynamite, forty sticks each. He would have been in a cheerier mood now, humming his favorite, "I'm going to make like a hoop and roll away, roll away..." He tucked sticks in the pillows of a French divan, he teetered on piled boxes to wedge sticks in chandeliers. The grand piano had room for a case.

He took a break to load his buckboard with his pick, jacking gear, muck stick, ore bucket, and a rope-wound windlass, the lot worth more to him than a world of gilt furniture. His burros Johnny and Jennie were fat and rested.

Though full, the moon was a candle to the brilliance that flared in the night sky when Old John spit fuse after fuse—and eight hundred sticks of dynamite blew his castle to smithereens.

The blast rattled the Desert Eating House, three miles away, and Ma and Pa Gilson rushed to the site. They poked and probed burning embers, afraid that Old John, along with his castle, was no more. Come dawn, they were relieved to discover the ruts of his buckboard, heading north, back to Death Valley.

Nearing Stovepipe Wells, he appears to have slipped a burro collar over his head and across his shoulder in an effort to pull his buckboard through deep sand, trying work for a man in his late seventies. He then stopped to rest, tying Jennie to a wheel and Johnny to a scraggle of mesquite. In the searing mid-day heat, he sought what shade he could. He hung his watch on a thorny branch.

And so it was: Old John's time in the desert was up.

His faithful burros mourned his passing, with no attempt to break lose. They died as well.

Old John's death, more than anything, marked the end of an era. Prospecting since the early 1880s, he was there when the curtain rose on the desert's excitements, and his 1918 departure rang the curtain down.

The significance of this—grasped at the time—had rival parties taking credit for discovering his body, wrapping him in a blanket, and laying him to rest in a shallow grave. Wrote Frank Crampton, "Shorty and I buried Old John where we found him, in the heart of Death Valley."

Recalled Scotty, "Sure, I knew him. Nice old feller, come from Paris. Spoke with an accent, tall with white hair and beard. I found him stretched out dead. I dug a hole and buried him right there by a clump of mesquite."

The old prospector's estate was valued at ten dollars, a testament to the fact that it was the journey, not the reward, that mattered to Old John Lemoigne and a crowd that, from Goldfield to Ballarat, knocked back *O Be Joyful!* and dreamt of the big strike. And God willing that they found anything, anything at all, they would rid themselves of it as expeditiously as possible. As Shorty Harris had once declared, "Who the hell wants $10,000,000? It's the game, man—the game."

They'd be back on the trail, fortified with grub, the tools of their trade, and one of life's few assurances: be it by sweat or guile, whatever you find, you leave behind. In the words of a prospector's adage, "Ain't no pockets in a board overcoat."

So would that have been Chester Pray's story, had he not died? Would he have blown the mining fortune rightfully his, that he might seek anew a glory hole in the desert that gave him a measure of peace—a desert he loved? Or, settling down with Clara, would he have tended his fortune, built himself a fancy Los Angeles mansion, joined the opulent Jonathan Club, and become a city swell?

We'll never know of course, since his time in the West was cut short in his thirty-sixth year. We'll also never know the precise circumstances of his death. There's a suspicion that there well might be something missing—something critical. If Chester's first bullet grazed his head, would he really have had the determination to fire a second round? Could someone at the scene have egged him on? Could Diamondfield Jack, anxious to cut himself in on the Monte Cristo, gotten out of hand, dry-gulched Chester, and then terrified and intimidated the road crew? Either before or after Chester's death, had Clara taken up with Jack Salsberry? Many are the possibilities for a piece of the puzzle fallen to the floor.

In a gulley down the road from Chester's last camp, mystery yet lingers in the desert air.

Go there. Walk the dry land. Gaze away into Death Valley. You'll feel it.

EPILOGUE

A S THE QUEEN OF THE PURPLE MIST beckoned Chester and Clarence to draw nigh, I would forever have reason to explore Death Valley.

At dawn on a recent May morning I set out in search of John Lemoigne's last, lost rest. Two hours and I'd just about given up when, by the ruts of an old wagon road, I came upon a weathered cross and, protruding from the sand, bones. Ribs. Someone had dragged the remains of Old John's burros over to his grave.

I imagined Old John trailing his Johnny and Jennie through heaven's green pastures, which brought to mind a tale, oft told in Ballarat. Though the harp music was cloying, the prospectors up there enjoyed the gold—streets of it—until word came of a new strike, which had them packing up and on their way.

"And guess where that strike was?" Old John or Shorty or Clarence would ask.

As one, the crowd at Chris Wicht's saloon would exclaim, "IN HELL!"

That afternoon, an hour north in the Valley, I visited a second grave, Scotty's, on a knoll overlooking his castle in Grapevine Canyon. Five years after Old John detonated his Garlic Springs castle, Scotty broke ground on his, bankrolled by insurance magnate Albert I. Johnson. And what an affair it was. Waterfalls splashed in the living room, and upstairs in the music room, with no one able to play worth a damn, Scotty and Johnson had ordered a 1,000 pipe Welte roller-driven organ. It could rattle a tambourine, ripple a harp, twitter bird calls.

Was Scotty any happier? Not really, he'd say. He slept in his elegant quarters only when he had to; when Johnson was gone, he bunked in the castle's kitchen. He was to shake his head, "Me living in the kitchen, cats playing in the organ, and dogs bathing in the sitting room fountains. This place is just a lot of hooey—just plain hooey."

Scotty outlived all his contemporaries; he died in January of 1954 on the way to a Las Vegas hospital, on the floor of a saloon at Slim's Corners, Nevada.

I drove on. To Goldfield.

Close by desert route 95, wild horses barely gave me a glance as they grazed the outskirts of the camp. I checked into a room at the Santa Fe Saloon, got a good night's sleep, and the next morning tramped through a jumble of rocks in an abandoned quarry south of the camp. In the course of my researches, I'd enjoyed the company of a variety of Goldfielders, and today joined Bryan Smalley, Goldfield Deputy Sheriff, and Dominic Pappalardo, president of the local historical society.

Bryan, a stout fellow in his early forties, wasn't feeling all that well. He was recovering from a broken jaw, and it hurt. Nonetheless, he hoisted and turned over stone after stone, until he found one the right size and shape. He heaved it into the bed of his desert-dented pickup; it weighed a good hundred pounds.

The sky darkened as we bumped back to the camp. Flowers, red and yellow and surprisingly robust, were blooming. It had been a wet winter. Even now, in May, it began to drizzle.

"Normally, I'd do this outside, 'cause of the dust," Bryan explained as he and Dominic lugged the stone into a ramshackle workshop to the rear of his house, where he hooked up an air chisel and, with a bandit-like kerchief over his mouth and nose, evened the slab's face. He then laid out lettering with the aid of a Victorian-style stencil of his devising. **CHESTER A.** Then a next line, **P R A Y.** Then a third, **1876 - 1913.**

"It gets to me, it does," he said as he worked, "That cemetery out there gets to me, with its crosses falling to pieces, names faded to nothing. All those lost, forgotten souls out there. Drives me nuts. It truly does."

He'd done something about this. In his off hours, he had sought names and dates and lives to match unmarked graves, not only in Goldfield, but throughout his Esmeralda County beat.

There wasn't the slightest hesitation when I asked if he might carve a tombstone for Chester Pray.

He composed the inscription as he went along, line by line, ending with a "D.V." for Death Valley. With alacrity, he routed the letters, then reached for a pickle jar of black paint. "Makes the inscription stand out, not in just the right light, but anytime, day or night."

He admitted that commemorating lost souls had become an obsession. "He'd get off a graveyard shift as Deputy Sheriff," his friend Dominic filled in, "and skip sleeping. In a frenzy, he'd carve... how many at a time?"

"Fifty, maybe sixty."

"And how many so far?" I asked.

"Four hundred, maybe five, maybe more. I've lost track."

Drizzle had turned to cold rain, but this was no deterrent as Bryan and Dominic carried the finished headstone through the iron portal of Elk's Rest and set it in place as I took pictures. We three honored...

I silently thanked Chester for harkening me back to an era I was aware of, but at the outset couldn't quite grasp. He became a kindred soul, a guide to the tumultuous, scoundrel-fraught, *Oh Be Joyful!*-drinking times that bid the Old West farewell.

That night, rain became snow, blanketing the camp's cemetery... and the rest of a lost soul, remembered.

NOTES, SOURCES, & ACKNOWLEDGEMENTS

PART I: TO THE BRINK

Captain Pray's Son

The author's acquaintance with Chester Pray dates to a technical bulletin: *Geology of the Queen of Sheba Lead Mine*, compiled by Paul K. Morton and issued in 1965 by California's Division of Mines and Geology.

A major strike was credited to the pick and perseverance of "a Nevada drifter." Who was he? What became of him? (Initially, I'd no idea Chester had been shot.) Curiosity initiated a prolonged rummaging of archives and tramping of desert trails. Along the way, I greatly benefited from the advice of keepers of California and Nevada lore. The first was Beverly Harry, Clerk of Inyo County, who explained the complex ins and outs of mining records and disputes, and who directed me to nearly four hundred pages of Pray-related contracts, correspondence, receipts, and recollections, these last with an abundance of quotable "He said" / "Then I told him" dialogue.

As to Chester's childhood, his family's role in Lake Tahoe's gilded age is documented in period Carson City and Virginia City newspapers and in Myron Angel's *History of Nevada* (Oakland: Thompson & West, 1881).

As to the value of a dollar a hundred years ago: a blue plate lunch in the West, coffee and desert included, was 50¢. Today, the tab at a comparable cafe would be $15 or more. Underground, a skilled miner earned $4.00 a shift. In contemporary Nevada, a miner's decent day's wage is upwards of $250.00. By these and other measures, figures cited in *Who Killed Chester Pray? A Death Valley Mystery* should be multiplied by a factor of thirty to as much as sixty times to approximate their value in today's dollars.

The Fire Assayer

Records of Boston's McLean Asylum were eye-opening. I'd expected a bedlam-like, 1800s warehouse. Instead, I read of treatments with success rates the envy of twenty-first century psychiatry.

With a send-off in the jovial bar of Elks Lodge #338 in Baker City, Oregon, I retraced, as best I could, Chester's western odyssey. Two weeks later in Mina, Nevada, traditional assayer Jim Meyers ran a sample I'd prospected, and expounded on a furnace little different from Chester's. Two hours of roasting and reduction and, "You've got 50-50 gold and silver." The bad news was that, per ton of ore, this was "seven dollar rock—not really commercial, but enough to go back, keep looking. Who knows?"

The Lure She Is of the West

Goldfield's rise and decline is engagingly chronicled in Sally Zanjani's *Goldfield: The Last Gold Rush on the Western Frontier* (Athens, Ohio: Swallow/Ohio University Press, 1992), and in her *The Glory Days of Goldfield, Nevada* (Reno: University of Nevada Press, 2002), as well in as Hugh A. Shamberger's *Historic Mining Camps of Nevada: Goldfield* (Carson City: Nevada Historical Press, 1982). Lively first hand accounts include Emmett L. Arnold's *Gold Camp Drifter, 1906-1910* (Reno: University of Nevada Press, 1973) and Frank Crampton's *Deep Enough* (Denver: Sage Books, 1956). I enjoyed an afternoon's visit with Frank's widow Esther at her home in Bisbee, Arizona.

Goldfield's five major newspapers are preserved in microfilm at Nevada's State Archives in Carson City; a number of fragile originals are at the Huntington Library in San Marino, California (with special thanks to Alan Jutzi, Curator of Rare Books). The papers were rich in color and hyperbole as they promoted:

ACTION SURE
and
PROFITS LARGE
and
FORTUNES HOT IN THE MAKING
Will you get your share?

And an abundance of Goldfield lore is to be found in the archives of Tonopah's Central Nevada Museum, ably and enthusiastically curated by Eva LaRue.

Chester's Trouble in Chicago

Two turning-point days in Chester's life were described in remarkable detail by William Rose and Arthur M. Elliot, M.D. (their depositions on file in Inyo County's courthouse).

Scotty's Mine

Journalist Dane Coolidge, in his *Death Valley Prospectors* (New York: E.P. Dutton, 1937), serves up a Scotty as Scotty would have himself portrayed—folksy, charming, a bit of a rogue. Yet Coolidge's hand-written field notes, preserved at Berkeley's Bancroft Library, paint a darker picture—of an opportunistic schemer. And mean. If anyone had designs on his wad of bills, they'd discover the pockets of his Ulster coat lined with fish hooks. When Goldfield's newsboys set out to deliver their papers, he would scattered nickels and dimes in the street, and delight in stamping the little kid's fingers as they dove to retrieve them.

Scotty was to lead writer Hank Johnson a merry chase, the result his commendable *Death Valley Scotty: the Fastest Con in the West* (Corona del Mar, California: Trans-Anglo Books, 1974).

Oh Be Joyful!

The mining camps that sprang up on the brink of Death Valley are documented in Stanley W. Paher's classic *Nevada Ghost Towns and Mining Camps* (Berkeley: Howell-North, 1970) and in Alan H. Patera's *Rhyolite: the Boom Years* and *Funeral Mountains: Mining Camps and Mines* (Lake Grove, Oregon: Western Places, 2002), as well as in Harold and Lucille Wright's *Greenwater* and their *Rhyolite: Death Valley's Ghost City of Golden Dreams* (both published by: Twentynine Palms, California: Calico Press, 1953). Time and again, I consulted David Myrick's encyclopedic *Railroads of Nevada and Eastern California* (Berkeley: Howell-North, 1962). Published in Rhyolite in the years 1907-08, *Death Valley Magazine* offered profiles of Scotty, Shorty Harris, and Clarence Eddy. Rare copies of Eddy's verse are in the Harris Poetry Collection of Brown University's John Hay Library.

The Prospector's Secret

In exploring Death Valley, I was guided by Roger Mitchell's *Death Valley SUV Trails* (Oakhurst, California: Track & Trail Publications, 2001). Mitchell's droll trail ratings escalate from (1) "only slightly worse than a graded road" to (4) "the body of your vehicle may suffer a little" to (6) "insane, for the foolhardy only." I would typically drive as far as I could, then continue on foot, relying on Michel Digonnet's excellent *Hiking Death Valley* (Palo Alto: Quality Books, 1999).

Chester's Trouble in Goldfield

In a deposition, Nevada Sheriff W.T. Golding recalled that Chester "got into trouble in Goldfield; arrested in Hazen, I believe." A lawyer's objection precluded him from saying more, the incident deemed irrelevant. I suspected Pray had stolen a horse or two, but for the longest time found nothing of this—or any miscreance—until, after prowling what was left of tough-town Hazen, I stopped by Churchill County's museum and archive in Fallon. It was five minutes until closing, but not to worry, curator Bunny Corkill assured me, I could take my time in scanning old issues of the *Churchill County Eagle*. An hour into this and Bunny interrupted, not to ask me to leave, but to offer a battered ledger: REGISTER OF ACTIONS, DISTRICT COURT. Entry No. 84 began:

> Chester A. Pray, Plaintiff, against
> Goldfield Mohawk Mining Company,
> Geo. S. Nixon et. al.

"They'd thrown this out of the courthouse," Bunny explained. "I picked it out of the dump." The entry led me to three newspaper articles and eighty pages of court proceedings.

Trouble All Over

The *Death Valley Chuck-Walla*, printed to recruit eastern investors, was a font of mining mendacity. When the paper's office burned down, the contemporary *Las Vegas Age* considered it poetic justice: "The *Chuck-Walla* was roasted alive by the Angel of Fire because of the many unholy things it has printed." For years, the magazine's press remained canted in the sand, cenotaph to a colossal scam. It's now at Death Valley's Furnace Creek Ranch.

A remarkable link to the past, Mojave resident John O'Donnell shared his childhood memories of a candy-dispensing, outwardly genial Jack Salsberry. Concerning Jack's Ubehebe promotion, Death Valley mining expert Mel Essington was of the opinion that, despite some superficial staining, "the geology didn't support any significant copper deposits."

PART 2: OVER THE EDGE

A Little Hell Is Good for Us

Death Valley literature dwells on illusion. In this vein, the author's choice volumes are:

1892   John R. Spears, *Illustrated Sketches of Death Valley and Other Borax Deserts of the Pacific Coast* (Chicago: Rand, McNally). Picturesque in its portrayal of a land of heat and dread.

1906   Orin S. Merril, *"Mysterious Scott" the Monte Cristo of Death Valley and Tracks of a Tenderfoot through the New Gold Fields of Nevada* (Chicago: Orin S. Merril). Captures the flavor and flim-flam of Chester's era.

1922   Edna Brush Perkins, *The White Heart of the Mojave* (New York: Boni & Liveright). In extravagant prose, Edna pioneers the desert as other-worldly, yet romantic: "a palace of dreams... a place of strange, terrible happiness... anything could happen in that terrible bright place."

1937   Dane Coolidge, *Death Valley Prospectors* (New York: E.P. Dutton). The desert rat as desert archetype.

1986   Richard E. Lingenfelter, *Death Valley and the Amargosa: A Land of Illusion* (Berkeley: University of California Press). A sprawling, staggeringly well-researched survey of the Valley's history.

Chester's Mine

A History of Mining in Death Valley National Monument, a typescript manuscript by ranger Linda Greene, was an invaluable resource, as was the guidance of Park librarian Blair Davenport.

For an introduction to life underground, I thank my grandfather Daniel McRae, a Nova Scotia coal miner. And in recent years I have enjoyed the company of Billy Varga, Jr., a free-spirited hard rock miner roaming California, Nevada, and Idaho. He loved exploring abandoned mines, blasted miles of his own tunnels, and was a practical joker. Taking a lunch break at the bottom of a shaft, I was alarmed when Billy, high above on a rickety ladder, shouted down through the darkness, "Shit, oh shit! The shaft! The whole goddamn shaft's coming in!" I dived for the cover of an ore car. A thundering freefall ensued—of a dozen empty cardboard boxes.

My grandfather Daniel was killed in the mines. Billy was felled by hard living above and below ground; he rests in Virginia City, Nevada's history-haunted cemetery.

The Ballarat Lying Club

The chapter's portrait of a Fourth of July in Ballarat sprang from an unpublished, untitled Clarence Eddy manuscript in the collection of the Marriott Library at the University of Utah. I thank Death Valley ranger Kari Coughlin for initially bringing the poet-prospector to my attention.

Articles and books by amateur historian George Pipkin brought ruined Ballarat to life. See *Ballarat 1907-1917: Facts and Folklore*, co-written with Paul B. Hubbard and Doris Bray (Lancaster, California: privately printed, 1965). Pipkin's daughter, Margaret Brush, graciously granted me access to his Death Valley files.

Prospectors in Love

For any who might venture to the Monte Cristo and Queen of Sheba mines, be aware that the way is strewn with rocks and boulders with a penchant for leaping from the ground and battering whatever you might be driving. At the site, structures and scattered artifacts for the most part date to reworkings in the 1930s and 1940s. The crude stone foundations of shanty-town Carbonate are apparent down the hill from the Queen of Sheba, and there you can imagine Chester and Clara in their best of the times, smitten and dreaming.

Clarence's infatuation with Mabel-Juanita-Asia-TUDDLE-TIWUDDLE simmers in letters archived at the University of Utah.

Sunstroke

A 1913 geological survey map and a 2002 Landsat 5 space image were key to tracing Chester's near-fatal shortcut from his Monte Cristo mine over to Ballarat. The final, agonizing stages of sunstroke (pp. 176-178) are graphically recounted in Paul DeLaney's "Lost in Death Valley," *Death Valley Magazine* (August, 1908); in two articles in the *Goldfield News and Weekly Tribune* (June 13 and July 28, 1906); and in Bourke Lee's classic, *Death Valley* (1930).

In Sight: "the Everlasting Jack"

A telltale resource for the comings and goings of Chester and his partners proved to be the register of the Goldfield Hotel, preserved at the Central Nevada Museum in Tonopah. In decrepit glory, the hotel still stands, and I thank Sandy Johnson of the Esmeralda Commissioner's office for tracking down the key and accompanying me on a tour from the basement ("Let's get that over with first. Gives me the willies") to Chester's room (#334) on the eve of partnering with Jack Salsberry and Ed Chafey.

The Montezuma Club

Blustery, gun-crazed, a coward, Diamondfield Jack Davis was fictionalized in "The Embarrassing Conduct of Benjamin Ellis, Millionaire," an October, 1908 article in the *Saturday Evening Post*. And as "Mart O'Toole" he stalks the pages of Sewell Thomas' memoir of his senator father, *Silhouettes of Charles S. Thomas* (Caldwell, Idaho: Caxton Printers, 1959).

Gunslingers died young, but not our Diamondfield. He died in Las Vegas, with his boots on. It wasn't that he was old and slow on the draw. Rather, in 1943 he was flattened by a taxi, a Glitter Gulch cabbie neglecting to check his rear view mirror before backing up.

The Road to the Monte Cristo

Jack Salsberry left his mark on the Zabriskie-Monte Cristo route: east-to-west there's Salsberry Spring, Salsberry Pass, Salsberry Peak, and Salsberry Well (back now to Bennett's Well). The fate of his Roberts-Doan steam traction engine is unknown; a similar behemoth, "Old Dinah," rusts at the entrance to Furnace Creek Ranch.

A Death in Death Valley

Chester Pray's hastily convened inquest may have been an instance of verdict-by-sundown frontier justice, but it was nevertheless recorded in detail by railroad agent P.V. Fuentes, his hand-written pages preserved in file 488 of Inyo County's courthouse. The file includes a twelve-page letter from Antoine Barber to Julia Cram; in remorseful detail he recounts Chester's escalating desperation and death.

I was for a time perplexed by Chester's sidearm, variously referred to as a "revolver" and a "Colt's automatic." They're different: one relies on a cylinder to chamber bullets, the other utilizes a clip inserted in the handgrip. The answer was: the Colt automatic, first available in 1900. At the time revolvers were ubiquitous—so much so that the term was applied to any handgun, whether its mechanism revolved or not.

Little but broken glass remains of Zabriskie, excepting that Hugh Fraser's General Store, the scene of the inquest, was hauled five miles north to Shoshone. It presently houses a museum of local history.

As to the verdict rendered that long-ago day in Zabriskie, I believed a present-day opinion might shed some light, and consequently sought out Esmeralda County's current coroner, only to learn that there isn't one (so sparse is the population). Rather, suspicious deaths are autopsied up in Reno, by Washoe County Medical Examiner Vern McCarty. Sporting a flowing, frontier moustache, McCarty was an affable Nevadan raised on a ranch and a student of the past. My impression was that years of dealing with desert mayhem hadn't gotten him down. Nonetheless, his eyes narrowed as I handed him a copy of undertaker Frankie Dunn's statement at Chester's inquest. With considerable deliberation, he read it aloud, twice. He shook his head. "I have to say, this fellow Dunn, his examination was, at best, cursory, but what can you expect? Hot as hell warehouse, badly decomposed body, and he wouldn't have known what to look for. Like powder deposition, which can give you a good idea, a really good idea, at what range a shot was fired." He rocked back in his chair. "You want me to ramble?"

I nodded.

For well over an hour, he did—raising an issue, mulling it, then either laying it to rest or leaving it an open question. He covered:

> *Two shots to the head*: "Doesn't mean murder. Your Chester could have done it, particularly if the first shot was a graze, which would have left him stunned, but all the more wanting to do away with himself.

> *The fatal shot's up-angle trajectory*: "Inconclusive as to suicide. The man could have been standing on a rise or tilting his head when someone took a shot at him."

> *Entry wound and compound skull fracture, but no exit wound*: "Not that unusual, even when a weapon is fired point-blank."

"Going on the physical, forensic evidence—what there is of it, and that not terribly reliable—I'd have to rule the cause of death 'Undetermined.' But there are other ways to look at what happened. What you might call human nature considerations. In this case, there's a medical examiner's commandment."

"And that is?"

"Follow the money." He repeated, *"Follow the money."*

We discussed this, for not only did the money lead to Jack Salsberry, but he actively saw to it that it went no further as, one by one, he shed everyone with an interest in Chester's workings: Clara Carlsrud, Ed Chafey, H.L.S. Robinson, and Julia Cram.

"You think it could be murder after all?"

"I don't. The coroner in me says no. The coroner in me says suicide. Clumsy and desperate, and sad. And from Jack Salsberry's point of view, why kill a man when he could be driven to do it for you?"

Jack's Mine & Old John's Castle

Given Death Valley as a land of illusion, there's the question of the veracity of Frank Crampton's account of the construction and explosive demise of Lemoigne's castle. Was this a fanciful *au revoir* to a dear friend? At the site, now within the boundaries of the U.S. Army's Fort Irwin, there is a recognizable footprint of a 25 by 35 foot dwelling, certainly a step up from Old John's previous 8 by 10 foot shack. Archaeologists attached to the base have surface-collected and catalogued some 240 shards of blue-and-white china in shapes suggesting platters, tureens, and fine dinnerware.

Epilogue

In addition to individuals previously cited, the author thanks Judy Kessler, Jon Silberg, Tom Fuchs, Marilyn Engle, and Bonnie Loizos for their encouragement and sharp-eyed review of the manuscript. Period photographs were restored by David Meltzer and Judy Kessler. And it has been a pleasure to work with Mike Harris, founder and editor-in-chief of La Frontera Publishing; Matti Harris, the project's skillful and insightful editor; and Yvonne Vermillion, who created the book's cover and graphic design.

Photo and Illustration Credits

PLATE	PAGE	
1	121	Photo by C.J. Back, courtesy of National Park Service, Death Valley National Park, California
2	122	Nevada Historical Society
3	124	The Huntington Library, San Marino, California
4	124	Photo by E.W. Smith, courtesy of Nevada Historical Society
5	125	Estate of Sewell Thomas
6	125	Photo by A. Allen, courtesy of Nevada Historical Society
7	126	Photo by A.E. Holt, courtesy of Nevada Historical Society
8	126	Photo by Dane Coolidge, courtesy of Arizona Historical Foundation Photo by E.W. Smith, courtesy of Huntington Library,
9	127	The Huntington Library, San Marino, California
10	128	Photo by Clarence M. Oddie
11	128	Churchill County Museum & Archives
12	129	Photo by P.E. Larson, courtesy of Nevada State Musuem
13	130	Photo by C.J. Back, courtesy of National Park Service, Death Valley National Park
14	131	Nevada Historical Society
15	132	Estate of Frank Crampton
16	132	Photo by Dane Coolidge, courtesy of Bancroft Library, University of California, Berkeley
17	133	Nevada Historical Society
18	133	Photo by Dane Coolidge, courtesy of Arizona Historical Foundation
19	134	Central Nevada Historical Society
20-21	135	Photos by Nicholas Clapp
22	136	Photo by C.J. Back, courtesy of National Park Service, Death Valley National Park

Index

About the Author

"Stricken by curiosity," is how Nicholas Clapp describes himself. He adds: "Hopelessly."

After graduating from Brown University, he was to follow a life of adventure and discovery as a documentary film maker. A hundred projects have taken him underwater, through jungles, across deserts, and into Arctic whiteouts.

In the early 1980s Clapp became intrigued by Ubar, a lost Arabian city thought only to exist in myth. His curiosity and tenacity lead to an expedition that (to everyone's surprise!) discovered and excavated the site, once a prosperous caravansary of the frankincense trade. The find was rated by *TIME* as one of the top scientific achievements of the year. The story of the search for Ubar is recounted in *The Road to Ubar* (a *Los Angeles Times* #2 Best Seller). He then wrote *Sheba: Through the Desert in Search of the Legendary Queen* (a *Los Angeles Times* #1 Best Seller).

In recent years, Clapp has roamed a desert closer to home—and his heart—to research and write *Who Killed Chester Pray? A Death Valley Mystery*. The tale is at once non-fiction whodunit – and a portrait of the last, go-for-broke rush for riches in the American West.

Ordering Information

For information on how to purchase copies of Nicholas Clapp's, *Who Killed Chester Pray*, or for our bulk-purchase discount schedule, call (307) 778-4752 or send an email to: company@lafronterapublishing.com

About La Frontera Publishing

La frontera is Spanish for "the frontier." Here at La Frontera Publishing, our mission is to be a frontier for new stories and new ideas about the American West.

La Frontera Publishing believes:
- There are more histories to discover
- There are more tales to tell
- There are more stories to write

Visit our Web site for news about upcoming historic fiction or nonfiction books about the American West. We hope you'll join us here — on *la frontera*.

La Frontera Publishing
Bringing You The West In Books
2710 Thomes Ave, Suite 181
Cheyenne, WY 82001
(307) 778-4752
www.lafronterapublishing.com